LAVIS

The No

FEATUR
KAREN PELLETIER

"Dobson moves easily between impassioned evocations of forgotten women writers and catty contemporary shafts at familiar ivory-tower targets."
—*Kirkus Reviews*

"Few are better than Dobson at recording the minutiae of academic committee-speak, power plays in body language and jargon, and what ignites a classroom."
—*Booklist*

"An intriguing mystery with excellent secondary characters."
—*Rendezvous*

AND JOANNE DOBSON'S AGATHA AWARD–NOMINATED DEBUT MYSTERY

Quieter Than Sleep

"A white-knuckle ride through the hallowed halls of higher learning and through the dangerous rapids of personal conflicts with a delightfully funny heroine who gives as good as she gets."
—*Rendezvous*

"A genuinely good read."
—*Time Out New York*

JOANNE DOBSON

The Northbury Papers

BANTAM BOOKS

New York Toronto London Sydney Auckland

All of the characters in this book are fictitious, and any resemblance to actual persons, living or dead, or locales is purely coincidental.

This edition contains the complete text of the original hardcover edition.
NOT ONE WORD HAS BEEN OMITTED.

THE NORTHBURY PAPERS

PUBLISHING HISTORY

PUBLISHED IN ASSOCIATION WITH DOUBLEDAY,
A DIVISION OF RANDOM HOUSE, INC.
DOUBLEDAY HARDCOVER EDITION PUBLISHED NOVEMBER 1998
BANTAM MASS MARKET EDITION / AUGUST 1999

EXCERPT FROM POEM #640 REPRINTED BY THE PERMISSION OF THE PUBLISHERS AND THE TRUSTEES OF AMHERST COLLEGE FROM *The Poems of Emily Dickinson*, Thomas H. Johnson, ed. Cambridge, Mass.: The Belknap Press of Harvard University Press. Copyright © 1951, 1955, 1979, 1983 by the President and Fellows of Harvard College.

Song lyrics from "Cover Me" by Bruce Springsteen copyright © 1984 by Bruce Springsteen. Reprinted by permission.

ISBN: 0-553-57661-5

Published simultaneously in the United States and Canada

Bantam Books are published by Bantam Books, a division of Random House, Inc. Its trademark, consisting of the words "Bantam Books" and the portrayal of a rooster, is Registered in U.S. Patent and Trademark Office and in other countries. Marca Registrada. Bantam Books, 1540 Broadway, New York, New York 10036.

PRINTED IN THE UNITED STATES OF AMERICA

WCD 10 9 8 7 6 5 4 3 2 1

For Dave

Acknowledgments

This novel has been inspired by the many talented and courageous women writers of the American nineteenth century. Assigned to oblivion by modern literary critics, the female authors for whom Mrs. Serena Northbury serves as a fictional counterpart are finally benefiting from the scholarly attention that will assure them a foothold in American literary history. Also deserving of mention are the scholars and editors who have devoted themselves to the recovery of these "lost" writers, particularly Elizabeth Ammons, Nina Baym, Paula Bennett, Judith Fetterley, Frances Smith Foster, Mary Kelley, Susan K. Harris, Leslie Mitchner, Jane Tompkins, Jean Yellin, and Sandra A. Zagarell.

I wish to thank Fordham University for leave time, Eve Keller for insight into curriculum revision matters, Arthur Kinney for a visit to the newly opened Renaissance Center in Amherst, Massachusetts, Jeanne Christman for medical advice, Deborah Schneider for her savvy and support, and Kate Miciak and Amanda Powers for their kindness to a new author.

Sandy Zagarell, Phyllis Spiegel, and other friends have proven steadfast throughout the writing of *The Northbury Papers*, and I have benefited from the knowledgeable advice of members of my crime writers workshop, Gordon Cotler, Eleanor Hyde, Diane Ouding, Jonathan Harrington, Leah Ruth Robinson, and Bernice Seldon.

Lisa Dobson Kohomban, David McKinley Dobson, and Rebecca Dobson are the best children in the world, providing support, understanding, good ideas, cookies, and grandchildren. Myriam Denoncourt Dobson's enthusiasm and flowers are much appreciated, as is Jeremy Kohomban's generosity with his computer expertise. Dave Dobson has lent me his imagination, enhancing the world of Enfield College—and my life—with character, color, and incident. Thank you all.

"She makes a good living out of such stories, they say;" and he pointed to the name of Mrs. S.L.A.N.G. Northbury under the title of the tale.

"Do you know her?" asked Jo, with sudden interest.

—From *Little Women* by Louisa May Alcott

One

The bookplate was ornate in the nineteenth-century manner, a rich cream-colored rectangle with a wide border of morning glories and tangled vines. In Gothic lettering it read *Ex Libris Mrs. Serena Northbury*. I closed the book and turned it over to look at the title. Mrs. Northbury's bookplate was affixed to the inside front cover of a well-preserved, half-morocco-bound copy of Charlotte Brontë's *Jane Eyre*.

"Wow," I said to Jill, "where'd you get this?"

Jill Greenberg slid her tray across the Faculty Dining Commons table, pushed the unruly red hair back from her forehead, and sat down next to me. "You know that antiquarian bookstore in Pittsfield, the one on North Street?"

I nodded, fanning lightly through the pages in search of any possible Northbury artifacts; you never know what you'll find preserved between the pages of an old book.

"Well, I was browsing there with . . . well, I was browsing, and the cover caught my eye. Then I saw Serena Northbury's bookplate and knew you'd be interested. It's beautiful, isn't it?"

"Yeah, they really knew how to make books in those days." The title was stamped in gold on the leather-bound spine of this one, and the dark blue covers were spackled in green. "A lot of the time it didn't much matter what was inside, but the book itself had to be a work of art." Finding no treasures between the ragged-edged pages, I handed the volume to Jill.

She pushed it back toward me with both hands. "Keep it, Karen." She picked up her ham and Swiss on rye and nibbled. "You're probably the only person left in the entire universe who cares about Northbury."

"Jill, I can't take this." I wanted the book. It had been owned—been touched, been *read*—by a nineteenth-century American novelist with whom I was becoming increasingly fascinated. But I couldn't afford to indulge myself in luxuries. On the scale of professional salaries, English professors rank just slightly above church mice, and the average church mouse isn't paying tuition for a daughter studying premed at Georgetown. "This must have cost a fortune."

"Nah." Money was never an object with Jill. It had never had to be; she was the daughter of a Park Avenue psychiatrist. A psychopharmacologist, yet. The streets of the Upper East Side are paved almost entirely in Prozac, and Papa had a great deal of money in his pocket. At the age of twenty-five, Jill had no education debts, and no one but herself to lavish her salary on. "It wasn't that much. The book dealer said the book wasn't a first edition or a particularly valuable one, so basically he was just charging for the binding."

"Well," I said. "If you're sure . . ." I turned the handsome volume around and ran my forefinger over the gilt lettering of the title. "I'm a little surprised to find that Northbury read *Jane Eyre*. Her own novels are nothing like it. They're really quite—well—sentimental. But they're so *interesting*. . . ."

" 'Interesting,' my foot. Why don't you just admit you like trash?"

"It's not trash." I felt defensive; the grip Serena Northbury had on my imagination wasn't easily explained by any of the usual literary or feminist rationales. Northbury wasn't a great prose stylist, and she certainly wasn't a flamboyant feminist rebel. Her forty best-selling novels were conventional tales of young girls who face hardship and moral danger, but through unassailable virtue and mind-boggling diligence win out in the end.

I could relate to that; it sounded like my own life. Well . . . maybe not *unassailable* virtue.

"I know she's no Brontë," I admitted, "but there's something quirky in her stories. I don't know how to describe it, but I think I'm addicted."

Jill laughed and took a second bite of her sandwich. "A Ph.D. in lit, huh? A professor at Enfield, one of New England's most respected colleges? Karen Pelletier, you ought to be ashamed of yourself!"

"Come on, Jill. You of all people should know popular literature is a perfectly legitimate field of study." Jill is a sociologist, and literary studies are becoming more like a branch of the social sciences every day. "I'm simply reconstructing cultural conditions of literary reception." Yeah. Right. I had read every one of Serena Northbury's books I could get my hands on. Her popular novels enthralled me in the same way they must have captivated her multitudes of nineteenth-century readers.

"Lighten up, Karen. Face it; you're reading garbage!" Jill was joking; with a tattoo just above her left ankle and a gold ring where she didn't talk about it, Jill was a pop culture nut.

I lightened up. "Yeah, Jill, you're right. I'm a lowbrow." I stroked the copy of *Jane Eyre* as if it were still warm from Mrs. Northbury's hand, and set it down next to my plate. "Thanks for this. I owe you."

Jill made a dismissive motion with a hand that wore

a half dozen silver rings and took another nibble of the sandwich. I picked up my mug of black coffee—I needed a jump start before I went into the classroom—and glanced at Jill over the rim.

My young colleague wasn't looking her best. I was used to the untamable red hair and the funky clothes— today a short, sleeveless cotton shift in a turquoise-and-lime flying-toasters print worn with black Converse basketball sneakers and one dangling garnet earring—but the mouselike appetite and the listless expression were something new. Jill Greenberg usually had the appetite—and the brute energy—of an adolescent hockey player.

"You okay, Jill?" I buttered my crusty whole-wheat roll and took a bite.

"I'm fine." Her tone was abrupt. "I'm just a little tired is all." She put the nibbled half sandwich back on her plate, aligned it with its untouched mate, and pushed the plate away. "And the food here gets worse every day."

The food in the Enfield College faculty dining room is okay. It's *more* than okay. It's downright *good*. And most days Jill proved that by putting away a full dinner entree at noon and then topping it off with a sundae from the self-service ice-cream bar. For a college professor—even for the child prodigy she was—Jill usually ate, well, prodigiously. I narrowed my eyes at her. Something was definitely wrong. Could Jill be having boyfriend trouble? As far as I knew, she hadn't been seeing anyone lately. Come to think of it, though, with Jill, that in itself was worth notice.

"Jill?" I ventured.

But she was gazing past me. "Karen, don't look now, but something weird is going on over at the Round Table."

I immediately swiveled around and stared.

The large round table in the far corner of the Faculty Commons is reserved for group luncheon meetings. On

Thursdays, for instance, it's the women's studies table; once or twice a month, black studies has dibs on it. Today it was crowded with college administrators and department heads. From where I sat I couldn't see everyone, but it would have been impossible to miss Miles Jewell, English Department chair. Miles was holding forth in a voice that had begun to rise beyond a decorous decibel level. He was ignoring President Avery Mitchell's attempts to quiet him. His round face was even more flushed than usual, and a cowlick of thick white hair had flopped down boyishly over the ragged white eyebrows. Halfway across the large dining room I could hear the outraged tones of Miles's protest—something about insupportable assault on traditional standards.

"Karen, don't gape."

Jill was right; I was gawking with prurient curiosity as my department head made a public spectacle of himself. I turned back to my tablemate. "That's a pretty high-powered bunch there, and they don't look like happy campers."

"Sure don't. I wonder what's going on. Look—I mean, don't *you* look, for God's sake; you're too obvious. I'll *tell* you what's happening. Now Avery's got the floor. The voice of sweet reason, as usual. God, he's a beautiful man. Those hands—like a concert pianist. Oh, baby—he can play *me* anytime. Now Miles is sulking. You know how pink his face is? Well, now it looks like a humongous *strawberry*. Jeez, I hope he doesn't have a coronary. Sally Chenille is jabbering on now, probably 'interrogating the erotic subtext' of something or other." Jill laughed. "You should see Sally's hair—no, Karen, don't turn around. I'll *tell* you. Today, Professor Chenille's hair is a lovely Day-Glo orange, a very, *very* nice visual contrast to Miles's strawberry—no—*raspberry* complexion. Okay, now your pal Greg Samoorian is talking—why do only bearded men seem to have that deep authoritative voice? I can't hear exactly what he's saying, but it looks like he's on Avery's side. At least Avery's nodding, and—"

"Okay, okay, I don't need a blow by blow. If Greg's involved, I know what it's about. He told me Avery was getting together an exploratory committee to investigate collegewide curriculum reform. As the new chair of Anthropology, Greg's part of that. This is probably the planning group."

Jill whistled softly between her teeth. "Whew, no wonder Miles is so upset. The college might actually stop requiring his course in the Literature of the Dark Ages."

"Yeah." I laughed, but it wasn't funny. In the current culture wars, the English Department faculty was factionalized between the old-guard professors who taught Literature (with a capital L) as high art, and the avant-garde who taught almost anything that had ever appeared in print—and had completely discredited the very idea of art. And now it looked as if the contest for the hearts and minds of Enfield students was about to draw blood. Miles Jewell was representative of the older contingent, utterly conventional in his approach to literature: Chaucer, Shakespeare, and Milton were his gods. Henry James deserved serious consideration—maybe. Jane Austen—well, okay, she wrote nice little stories. But beyond that, no woman had produced anything worth consideration. And *minority* literature? A contradiction in terms.

Since I'm in the opposing camp—I'd been hired to teach American women's literature—I was at frequent odds with my department chair. As an untenured professor, I could be made pretty uncomfortable at times. Miles, and the other old boys, seemed to think that the department got more than it bargained for when they hired me. My work on Emily Dickinson was acceptable, of course; after all, the woman had somehow wormed her way into the canon of American literature, that body of texts professors had taught since time immemorial.

But now, two years into my position at Enfield College, I—young upstart that I was—was exposing my students to all sorts of *noncanonical* stuff: slave narratives, sentimental novels, working-class literature—the books people actually *read* in the nineteenth century. *Garbage*. And now, God help me, I was also thinking about writing the biography of an obscure woman novelist named Serena Northbury. I hadn't told the department yet, but Miles would freak out when—and if—I mentioned it in my annual faculty activity report.

I sighed and nudged my empty plate away. Time to get back to work. There were papers to grade, classes to teach. And I needed to make time to write a good long letter to my daughter. Even though Amanda had been away at college for two years, I missed her. We talked on the phone all the time, but letters were better: You got to slit the envelope, pull the missive out, smooth it open—and read it over and over again.

Jill picked up her sandwich, examined it with a curl of her lip, dropped it back on the plate. "I guess I'm not hungry. Are you finished?"

I slid the canvas strap of my book bag over my shoulder and picked up the copy of *Jane Eyre*. "Yeah," I said. "But I actually ate something. Are you *sure* you're okay?" Jill had the milk white skin of the authentic redhead, but today she was paler than usual, and her mouth had an uncharacteristic pinched look. She drained her water glass, then rose from the chair.

"I'm fine. It's just that—Karen, watch out!"

But it was too late. As I moved from the table, intent on Jill's response, Miles Jewell stormed away from the curriculum meeting and barreled into me. He hit me broadside and, in a blind fury, kept on going. I staggered, fell back, and caught my balance by grabbing hold of the table. My book bag slipped from my shoulder, my arm jerked painfully, and the old book in my hand plummeted to the floor.

Miles continued his retreat. As he exited the wide

French doors of the Commons, I stared after him in astonishment. Miles may be conservative, even retrograde, but he was *never* rude. What could possibly have been said at the Round Table to cause this gentleman of the old school to forget his manners so shockingly?

"Karen." Avery Mitchell, Enfield's president, was at my side, his hand on my elbow. His tone was solicitous. "Are you all right?"

I wasn't sure. I didn't know whether Miles had knocked the bejesus out of me, or if my current inability to breathe was due to the close presence of Avery Mitchell. Our distinguished president tends to have that effect on me. Tall, lean, and elegant, Avery is the consummate American aristocrat, the type of man my working-class origins had taught me to think of as effete and dangerous. A member of the power elite. A parasite on society. I get palpitations of the heart every time he comes within six feet of me, but I doubt it has anything to do with my politics.

"I want to apologize for Miles," Avery continued. "He's extremely upset."

"I could tell." I had worn my long hair loose today, for a change, and now, pushing strands away from my face, I struggled to control my ragged breathing. That was particularly difficult because Avery still had hold of my arm.

"Yes, well . . . You know he would never behave like that if, ah, well . . . under normal circumstances. Please don't take offense." Avery reached for the copy of *Jane Eyre* sprawled open on the parquet floor. "You dropped this." As he handed me the volume, something fell from between the pages. He stooped again, retrieved a photograph, gave it a cursory glance, and held it out to me. I took the picture by its corner without really looking at it.

"I've got to get back." Avery waved his hand in the general direction of the Round Table, smiled at me ruefully, then strolled over to reconvene the disrupted meeting.

"Always the old smoothie, isn't he?" Jill was at my elbow. "God, that man has *all* the moves." Without responding, I took the book bag she held out to me. I had no intention of being sucked into any gossip about our exalted president.

"What's that?" Jill asked, motioning toward the sepia photograph in my hand. I glanced at it, suddenly curious. A picture of a baby, the old photo must have been pushed deep into the center of the book, or I would have come across it earlier when I'd rifled through the pages. The infant was about six months old, propped against a plump pillow with intricate lace edging, and dressed in smothering layers of white mid-Victorian ruffles.

"Poor thing. She looks uncomfortable." I assumed the child was a girl—a waterspout curl on the top of her head was tied with a white bow, and on a chain around her neck she wore a heart-shaped locket of what looked like gold filigree.

"Who do you think it is?" Jill asked. "One of Mrs. Northbury's kids?"

I turned the stiff photo over. On the back was written *Carrie, August 1861.*

"No," I said. "Serena Northbury had her children in the 1840's, when she was in her early twenties. They were named Lavinia, Josephine, and Hortense. There was no Carrie."

"A grandchild?"

"Too early. Her daughters weren't married yet. Must be the child of a friend. Or maybe she just liked the picture, used it as a bookmark."

Jill took the photo from me. "This looks like a studio shot."

"Yeah," I said. "The table with the paisley cloth, the ornate book, the vase of flowers: they're all photographic conventions. Cameras weren't easily portable, then. This isn't a casual snapshot. Somebody really wanted a picture of this baby."

"I don't blame them; she's a beautiful child," Jill said. "Those dark eyes, the curls."

I retrieved the photo and looked at it more closely. "Huh. *That's* interesting."

"What?" Jill seemed enthralled with this long-vanished baby.

"Look." I took the picture over to the window, where the light was better. "Yes," I said, "Jill, I think this is a black child. What do you think?"

She gazed intently at the sepia print. "It's hard to tell, the image is so dim. She's light-skinned, but her features do have an African-American look. I wouldn't be surprised; there were a great many biracial children coming off those plantations."

"Yeah. Right." I shook my head sadly. The rape of slave women by their masters was well documented by nineteenth-century slave narratives. "I wonder what Serena Northbury was doing with a photograph of an African-American baby?"

"Was she an abolitionist?"

"Well, yes—she seems to have been. But she was never outspoken in the way that women like Harriet Beecher Stowe and Lydia Maria Child were. She was—genteel, you might say."

"Sounds deadly. I'm surprised you're interested in her."

"Yeah, well . . . There's something there. . . ."

I shrugged, tucked the photograph back into the pages of *Jane Eyre,* where it had reposed for at least a century, and slipped the book into my big canvas bag for safekeeping.

Crossing the quad on my way back to the office, I sipped carefully at a second cup of coffee and recalled the farcical scene with Miles Jewell. Then I thought about the chaos certain to descend on the English Department when we began to reassess our course offerings and curriculum requirements. If Miles and I hadn't been at loggerheads before, we certainly would be now.

It wasn't until I slipped my key into the lock of my office door that I realized Jill had never told me what was bothering her.

Two

Fifteen minutes into a seventy-five minute session on Ralph Waldo Emerson my brain had shut down. Three cups of black coffee will do that. And it didn't help that I'd spent the hour between lunch and my American Literature Survey class leafing through Mrs. Northbury's copy of *Jane Eyre* instead of reviewing my notes on "Self-Reliance."

I was tired of Emerson, anyhow. Tired of talking about abstract ideas. I wanted to be teaching stories. I felt like whipping out *Jane Eyre* then and there and reading aloud, *"There was no possibility of taking a walk that day. . . ."*

Today was a *perfect* day for taking a walk, and the class in front of me was somewhat decimated from its usual twenty-two students. After a seemingly endless winter, a day of unseasonable warmth had resulted in an unusual number of absences. And no wonder. The classroom in Edwards Chapel was grim—large and boxy, with scuffed hardwood floors and dreary green wainscoting. Fluorescent strip lights competed feebly with the mid-March sunshine, and several students dutiful enough to have come to class gazed dreamily out the tall multipaned classroom windows. Sunshine slanted across my desk, splashing over the purple-and-green flowered print of my long challis skirt. I toyed with the idea of dismissing the class early.

Instead, I opened the American Lit anthology and began reading from "Self-Reliance": " *The nonchalance of boys who are sure of a dinner, and would disdain as much as a lord to do or say aught to conciliate one, is the healthy attitude of human nature.'* " This is typical Emerson, and always sets my teeth on edge. "So . . ." I said to the blank faces in front of me. "What d'ya think?"

Sometimes when you're totally at a loss in the classroom that question actually works. Today didn't seem to be one of those times. The boys—excuse me, young men—in the back of the room had stopped paying attention as soon as I'd finished discussing what they would be responsible for on the midterm exam. Thibault Brewster II, commonly known as Tibby Two, was drawing something on a page of his notebook. His neighbor, Howie Reynolds, looked over at the sketch and sniggered.

Tibby's father was a powerful man at Enfield College, Chairman of the Board of Trustees. This made handling Tibby difficult. Without his father's influence, my disruptive student would certainly have been suspended this year. From an unremarkable but amiable freshman and sophomore, Tibby had become a renegade junior. When I had gone to Earlene Johnson, the Dean of Students, about his behavior in the classroom, she told me Tibby had been a problem for several months: drinking, missing classes, brawling in the dorm. When she'd suggested counseling, Tibby had given an odd little laugh. "My *mother's* a shrink," he said. "Are you telling me I should go talk to *her?*"

I glanced around at other faces—Charlie Batistick,

Emily Hannon, Amy Franks—but none of my old reliables seemed willing to get engaged in this discussion. They could probably sense my own ennui.

"Well, Professor Pelletier, I'll tell you what I think. I think there's something wrong." Shamega Gilfoyle was a very vocal student, and her contributions to class discussion were often provocative.

"Wrong?" My neurons were swimming in pure caffeine.

"I mean something's wrong with Emerson's reasoning. Don't you think?"

Oh. Emerson. Of course. "Why don't you tell us what you mean, Shamega?"

I sat on the edge of my desk and looked at the one minority student in this class of mostly white-bread, upper-middle-class kids. I hoped my expression was one of benevolent intellectual engagement rather than the spaced-out lack of interest I actually felt. Shamega leaned back in her seat and stretched her feet in their thick-soled black boots out so far they almost touched the platform on which my desk sat. Lug boots. Those heavy crenelated soles are lug soles. I don't know how I knew that.

Shamega was thoroughly middle-class, her mother a high-school teacher, her father a social worker, but for the past few weeks she'd been styling herself by the street. Today she wore an oversize T-shirt, baggy jeans, and, of course, the lug boots. She was small and dark, and delicate facial bones gave her a deceptively fragile air but, in her sloppy rap-star clothes, she radiated Attitude.

"*Well,*" she said, "just look at his metaphor. I mean, *think* about it. Emerson says the 'healthy' state of mankind is that of a nonchalant boy certain of his dinner. I mean, *jeez!*"

"So what's wrong with that?" The challenge from the back row was male. Tibby Brewster was putting in his twenty-five thousand dollars' worth. At six feet, with broad shoulders and big hands, Tibby made a striking contrast to the petite Shamega. He had a square pale face with a prominent nose and a surprisingly girlish mouth. His curly brown hair was cut ruthlessly short and he wore a navy blue cable knit sweater over carefully pressed khaki pants.

"You got something against boys, Shammy?" Tibby's neighbor sniggered again. Shamega had just gotten a buzz cut.

Shamega's lips tightened, and she addressed her response, not to Tibby, but to me. "What I mean," she said, "is that the sexist and classist figuration of Emerson's metaphor implies a kind of irresponsible privilege predicated upon someone else's labor." Never in his life could Tibby have come up with that kind of sophisticated analysis, and Shamega knew it.

"Yeah? So that's a problem?"

I opened my mouth to intervene, but Shamega swiveled around in her seat to confront him. "Apparently not for you, Tibby Two." Tibby had been baiting her all semester, but this was the first time I'd seen Shamega lose her cool. "Daddy inherited all the money *you'll* ever need, and Mumsy doesn't have to lift her little white hand to chop an onion. They'll hire someone who looks like me to make certain *you* get your dinner."

"Well . . ." eyebrows raised as if he personally had invented the word "supercilious," "isn't that what capitalism's supposed to be all about?"

"Well, yeah, of course, capitalism in a stinking racist patriarchy . . ."

"Okay. Okay." I slid from my vantage point on the teacher's desk and walked down the aisle next to Shamega's seat. If I didn't get into the fray, I was going to have full-scale war raging in the sedate corridors of Edwards Chapel. I made a mental note to speak to Shamega after class, find out what was going on.

I began to talk about unexamined assumptions, the way in which "Self-Reliance," for instance, seems to be based on Emerson's assumption that all people have the type of freedom in society that he had, as a white, educated male with plenty of money. I made my way down the aisle as I spoke. As I approached the back row, Tibby ripped a page from his notebook and crumpled it noisily into a ball. Howie snickered. I ignored them.

" '*I shun father and mother, and wife and brother, when my genius calls me.*' " I quoted Emerson. I was getting into it now. "Of course, radical individualism—Emerson's notion of unfettered personal freedom—is all well and good, but what does it mean to a black slave driven by an overseer, or to an impoverished Irishwoman with thirteen children?" Shamega nodded vigorously.

And what had it meant to me, I wondered, when I was a pregnant eighteen-year-old in Lowell, Massachusetts? When *my* genius called me to accept a full scholarship to Smith College nineteen years ago, I was three months gone. I got married instead, gave birth to Amanda, and slumped around a dreary apartment in North Adams for a couple of long years until I wised up. When I left my hotheaded trucker husband Fred, I put my daughter in day care, went to work, went to college, then grad school. There was no way I was going to *shun* Amanda, and that made everything so hard. But I did it. And now here I was, an assistant professor of English at Enfield College. And Amanda was a sophomore at Georgetown. Self-reliance? Well, I guess. But it's easier for some than for others; Emerson never had to sling hash in a truck stop.

"And what did it mean to someone like Harriet Jacobs, the fugitive slave?" Shamega's sharp query brought me back to the present moment. "*She* spent seven years hiding in a cramped garret so she could be near her children, rather than escape to New York alone."

"Has anyone else in the class read ahead to Jacob's slave narrative?" I asked. No hands in the air. "Well, it's scheduled for next week, and it would be useful to think about Emerson's individualist philosophy when you read it, since Jacobs's story embodies an almost exactly oppositional ethos, one centered around the people she loved."

"And," Shamega continued, "what about someone like the black abolitionist, Joseph Monroe Johnson? What did Emerson's philosophy mean to him? He actually met Emerson in Boston, and thought the great man was a space cadet."

"Johnson?" Tibby responded, dismissively. "Never heard of him."

"Really?" I wasn't about to let this pipsqueak taint the discussion with his patronizing attitude. "That's too bad, Tibby; you should read more." The comment hit home; Tibby's eyes narrowed. I ignored him. "Shamega, why don't you tell the class about Johnson?"

"Joseph Monroe Johnson was a fugitive slave from Virginia who lived for a while in Boston in the 1850's," she said, running a hand over what remained of her hair. "He joined the abolitionist community there under the name Brent Josephs and helped whisk other fugitives out of the reach of the U.S. marshals, who were charged with returning escaped slaves to their *owners*." She spit out the word as if it lay rotten on her tongue. Her dark eyes were alight with fervor. "What struck me, Professor, when I read this Emerson thing was that Johnson didn't think like Emerson did. Johnson didn't put himself first, and he certainly didn't shun his family. As a matter of fact, he made really dangerous trips back south to rescue them. Each time he reentered the slave states he risked being captured and sent back into slavery. He was killed in Louisiana in 1860. Shot dead by his young sister's 'master.' I think he probably preferred death to being reenslaved." The class was paying rapt attention.

I took up the discussion. "Johnson's first foray was a trip back to Norfolk, Virginia, to free his mother. After

that, things got so hot for him in this country that he fled
to Montreal and left Canada only for trips back to slave
country to liberate other members of his family.
Shamega's point is that not everyone would choose to
put their own genius before the needs of other people, as
Emerson seems to advise. Emerson's radical individualism is an ideology responsible Americans have to ex-
amine very closely."

In the end, it wasn't necessary to let class out early;
the ensuing discussion was lively, even contentious, and
continued well beyond the bell.

I intercepted Shamega on her way out the door.
"What's with you and Tibby? You two have a feud going on?"

Her expression shut down. "Nothing I can't handle.
Don't worry about it."

"You sure?"

"I'm sure." The set of her delicate jaw told me that
if I asked even one more question, I would be entering a
mine field.

I was silent just long enough to let her know I'd
gotten the message. "Well," I said, "you know where I
am."

"Yeah, I do." She smiled. "And I appreciate it."
Then she changed the subject. "Good class."

"Thanks to you. With Emerson you've always got to
be aware of just exactly who's talking. And he *is* white,
male, well-to-do. That is *not* universal experience he's
touting there."

Shamega seemed in no hurry to leave. Mrs.
Northbury's copy of *Jane Eyre* was sitting on the desk.
She picked it up. "I love this novel," she said. She leafed
through the pages, and the photograph of the baby fell
out. She glanced at it, then looked more closely. Then
she looked up at me.

"Who's this little sister?" She pronounced it *sistuh*,
perhaps as part of her new in-your-face racial attitude,
parading her blackness in deliberate contrast to the priv-

ileged upper-crust whiteness of her fellow students. Enfield did that to me, too—made me want to throw my
French-Canadian, mill-town origins in the face of its
WASP smugness, wear jeans and cowboy boots to class,
play Emmylou Harris during office hours.

Shamega continued to study the photo. "She *is*
black, isn't she?"

"I think so. And I don't know who she is. That picture was in the book."

"Cute kid," she said. "I hope she darkened up a bit
when she got older."

After Shamega left, I packed up my books, took the last
sip of cold coffee, and surveyed the room, checking, as
usual, to see if anyone had left anything behind. A crumpled sheet of paper on the floor in the back caught my
eye. I picked it up, intending to toss it in the wastebasket. On an impulse, I smoothed the paper out. It contained a vicious penciled caricature of Shamega Gilfoyle
portrayed as a stereotypical pickaninny, in a ragged
dress, with braids poking out all over her head, and
heavy lug boots on her enormous feet. I went cold with
anger. Tibby Brewster had drawn this ugly thing; I knew
that, but I had no proof.

I had my hand on the knob of the Dean of Students'
office door, thinking to show the offensive cartoon to
Earlene, when Shamega's words came back to me, warning me off. "It's nothing I can't handle," she'd said. In
other words, "Buzz off, Professor." This vicious cartoon
was surely a different matter than mere heated repartee
in class, but I didn't think it came under the category of
hate speech: It hadn't been posted or mailed. Shamega
didn't know about it, and I didn't particularly want to
show it to her. If I brought the Dean of Students in at
this stage, would she feel duty-bound to pursue the issue? If she did, Shamega would hate me. I turned back
and headed for my office.

.   .   .

The coffee shop has fake mullioned windows and white stucco walls with pseudo half-timbering. In the good old days, when Enfield students were all male, and eighteen-year-olds were legally permitted to pickle their brains in alcohol, it had been a beer cellar. When I stopped by on my way to the parking lot, it was crowded with late-afternoon snackers. Tibby Brewster was seated in a booth near the door with a middle-aged woman whose blond hair looked as if it had been ironed permanently into its shoulder-length blunt-cut pageboy. He sipped at a can of Dr Pepper, while she ignored the coffee in front of her. As I passed their table the woman's low, heartfelt tone became almost inaudible. Tibby's mother—I assumed that's who it was—leaned as far toward him as he slouched away from her; like all parallels, the lines of their bodies never came to a meeting point. Mrs. Brewster's expensive hairdo swung stiffly across her face, but I could see the family resemblance nonetheless in the soft mouth, the bow-shaped lips. On her, it would have been attractive had she not been so very fashionably skinny.

I hefted the coffee pot and tried to eavesdrop. Shamelessly. Maybe this conversation would help me understand what was going on with my troublesome student.

Mrs. Brewster had ceased speaking, but the urgency in her gaze was compelling. The enormous dark eyes, hollow cheeks, and pale skin were arresting. As if drawn by a magnetic force, Tibby's eyes met his mother's. For a few seconds he appeared vulnerable, his girlish mouth quivered. Then the heavy coffee-shop doors flew open, and Shamega entered, laughing up at the attractive male student who followed her. Her friend was tall, dark, and lithe, and I thought I recognized him from the basketball court. Instantly, Tibby's expression shut down. He dropped his gaze from his mother's face, his lips twisted, and the line of his jaw hardened. I'd poured a full cup of coffee and paid for it before I remembered I'd come into the shop in search of a Coke.

I had wanted to talk to Tibby about the drawing that was burning a hole in my pocket, but this didn't seem to be quite the right moment.

Three

"Mr. Smallwood?" I peered over stacks of books on the battered oak table that served as a desk in this cluttered secondhand bookstore. The arc of ornate gold lettering on the plate-glass window said Smallwood's Antiquarian Books, but this musty, miscellaneous gathering of nineteenth- and twentieth-century volumes spoke more of the old-and-unwanted than of the antiquarian.

"Ayah?" The down-east voice emerged from behind a display case that held a small collection of leatherbound books in decent condition. I peered over the case. An elderly man with a fringe of gray hair surrounding a shiny pate sat cross-legged on the hardwood floor with a dust cloth in one hand and a large, ornate, blue-covered book in the other. He made no attempt to rise, just sat there regarding me quizzically. I stared at the book in his hand. Surely that couldn't be a copy of Rufus Griswold's midnineteenth-century *Female Poets of America*? It looked exactly like the one in the Rare Books collection of the Enfield College Library. A wave of book-lust engulfed me. I resisted it; I was here on an altogether different quest, trying to find out where the *Jane Eyre* with the Northbury bookplate had come from. I was hoping that the previous owner might have more of Serena Northbury's books. It was an extremely remote possibility, but if I *did* go ahead and write her biography, it would be useful to know what else Northbury had read.

"Mr. Smallwood, my name is Karen Pelletier." Rather than continue to loom over this gnomelike figure, I hunkered down beside him and pulled *Jane Eyre* out of my jacket pocket. "Last week you sold this to a friend of mine."

The man made a show of pulling rimless spectacles out of his shirt pocket, donning them, giving the book a thorough perusal. Then he glanced up at me.

"Pretty girl? Red hair?"

"Sounds like her. Well, I—"

"Purple jeans? Weird boyfriend? Tall, skinny fella?"

"The jeans sound right. I don't know anything about the boyfriend."

"Yep. Sold her this. Gave her a good price on it, too. Pretty girl. Lotsa life. Don't know what she was doing with a sourpuss like that." He passed the dust cloth over his shiny head, then applied it to the book in his hand. "A real sourpuss." He handed me back the newly dusted Brontë.

"Mr. Smallwood, do you remember where this book came from?"

"Ayah."

Nothing more was forthcoming. He picked up the large gold-embossed tome again, finished dusting it, and replaced it in the showcase. I waited. Then he took a small red-covered book, applied his cloth, concentrated on dusting.

"Could you tell me?" I ventured. "Please?"

"Tell you what?"

"Where the Brontë came from?"

"Oh, ayah." Mr. Smallwood replaced the red book

in the case and sat back on his heels. "It was one of that there Dr. Hart's books."

"Dr. Hart?" Was I supposed to recognize the name?

"Yep. Nice lady. Lives over Eastbrook way. Brought me in a buncha books a year or so ago. Musta been in February; there'd been one a them big storms, and . . ." At length, he went on about the storm, the perilous sidewalks, the cost of heating his store.

I waited him out. Then I asked, "Do you have any more of Dr. Hart's books?"

"Probably." He waved a hand at the cluttered shelves.

I blanched. "You don't keep records?"

"Only for first editions and other rare books. The rest just go on the shelves. Coupla dollars each. I kept the *Jane Eyre* up here . . ." he pointed at the case, " 'cause it was so nice. Don't remember 'bout the rest."

"Eastbrook, huh?"

"I *think* it was Eastbrook. *Somewhere* over there."

I thought about the myriad small towns sprinkled across the mountains of western Massachusetts like salt on popcorn. Should I even bother? What could this Dr. Hart, nice lady though she might be, possibly tell me about a hundred-and-fifty-year-old book that somehow had fallen into her possession?

I rose when Mr. Smallwood did, but with considerably less groaning. Dr. Hart *might* know where the book had originally come from, but it was a long shot. Certainly not worth the time it would take to comb the New England wilds; there were probably dozens of Harts scattered through those hills. This was a wild-goose chase, and I wasn't going to waste any more time on it.

"Thanks for your help, Mr. Smallwood." I walked past the sagging shelves to the door. It closed behind me with a jangle of bells and I turned back down North Street toward the center of town. The unseasonable warmth lingered through this sunny Saturday, and the shoppers on the wide sidewalks moved just a little less briskly than the usual New England late-winter double-time. As I passed the bookstore window with its dilapidated arc of gilded letters, I glanced in at the volumes on display. Not an impressive selection: A copy of the original *Joy of Cooking;* an array of *Reader's Digest Condensed Books* from the 1950's; a shabby set of Hardy Boys mystery novels. In the back of the shop, Mr. Smallwood's diminutive shape was visible. He was fumbling through a small metal file box. *Hmm,* I thought, and pivoted, setting the bells to ringing again as I reentered the bookstore.

"*There* you are," he said. "Thought you might want the address."

"The address?"

"Yep. That nice Dr. Hart, good-looking lady. Said she had boxes of old books in her attic, if I ever wanted to take a look. Said someone should have the use of them."

"Really?"

"Yep. Said something about her grandmother wouldn't want them to go to waste."

"Her grandmother?"

"Grandmother. Great-grandmother. Something. Was a writer or something. Lady said no one in her family was interested in the books. I just never found the time to go all the way over there. Good-looking lady, though. Nice, too."

Her *grandmother!* My hand shook as I scribbled down the address from his index card: Dr. Edith Hart, Meadowbrook, Eastbrook, Massachusetts.

Serena Northbury's *granddaughter?* Could it possibly be? I did some quick mental arithmetic. Maybe great-granddaughter? Great-great-granddaughter?

"*Thank* you, Mr. Smallwood. Thank you *very* much. By the way, is that a copy of Griswold's *Female Poets* you've got there?"

Well, it was tax-deductible.

Walking back down North Street with the cumbersome volume of poems under my arm, I caught sight of myself in the plate-glass window of the old England Brothers' Department Store. Big dark eyes, at the moment appearing slightly bemused. Straight dark hair pulled back in a barrette. Pale face with long, thin French-Canadian nose. No makeup. Denim jacket with big patch pockets. Jeans. Amanda's cast-off cowboy boots. I wondered how Mr. Smallwood would describe me to his next customer. *Tall lady. Kinda nervous. Doesn't know how to dress.*

I always keep my car radio tuned to WENF, Enfield Public Radio, for its mix of alternative music, NPR programming, and local-interest interviews. But when I reached my reliable old VW Jetta and turned the ignition key, the last thing I expected to hear over the airways was the familiar voice of Lieutenant Piotrowski of the Massachusetts State Police Bureau of Criminal Investigation. "Well," Piotrowski was saying, "homicide investigation isn't as dramatic in real life as it is on TV. Basically what ya gotta do is just slog along, one foot in front of the other. And ya gotta pay attention to every little thing. Ya can't ignore *nothing.*" He laughed. "Believe it or not, one case was solved by a letter from Emily Dickinson. The poet, ya know? From the 1800's?" But, in spite of the interviewer's titillated questions, the lieutenant didn't go on to elaborate. When I got home, I sat down and wrote Piotrowski a note thanking him for not dwelling any further on the Enfield College murders of the previous year, and *especially* for avoiding any mention of my part in helping to resolve them.

I *missed* Lieutenant Piotrowski. I realized that as I signed my name to the note. Last year's incidents at the college—in the real world they would have been called *murders,* but within the ivy-covered redbrick walls of Enfield College, they were referred to, if at all, as "unfortunate incidents"—had brought a deluge of police officers to campus. When it became apparent to the lieutenant in charge of the case that the deaths had something to do with the nineteenth-century research of one of the victims, he had retained me as a consultant to look into that research—to re-research the research. Working with Piotrowski had been comfortable; the big cop was smart, sensible, and down-to-earth. I liked him. Besides, I was used to cops; Tony, my longtime lover, was a cop. Him, I *really* missed. I peeled a self-adhesive stamp from the packet in my desk and affixed it to Piotrowski's letter. A Valentine's Day leftover, the stamp featured a chubby Cupid and a lace-edged heart.

Tony and I had broken up when he protested my decision to take the job at Enfield and move a hundred and fifty miles away from our Manhattan home. And now, Amanda told me, Tony was getting married. My daughter *loves* Tony, the only father she remembers, and she keeps in regular touch with him. Up until Tony set the date for the wedding, Amanda had been hoping he and I would get back together again. She'd informed me of Tony's marriage gently, as if she were afraid the news would break my heart. But—no problem, I'm not that fragile. I'm fine.

The phone rang. *Tony!* I dropped the note to Piotrowski and knocked my American lit anthology off the desk in my haste to grab the receiver.

"Karen? This is Miles Jewell."

My brain registered it: *Not Tony.* And then, Heaven help me—Miles. My department chair. Again. Miles had been hassling me all semester about the syllabus for my survey course; he thought I was giving Emerson and Melville short shrift in favor of "lady writers" and slave narratives. What now? Was he calling to apologize for almost knocking me down in the Faculty Commons?

"Yes, Miles?"

"Karen, I've been reviewing the Department course offerings for the upcoming fall semester, and I'm a little concerned about the American lit coverage."

"Yes?"

"Well, it's just that—this seminar you've got scheduled? The one on Emily Dickinson?"

"Yes?" I wasn't going to make this easy for him.

"Well, it seems to me a tad—well, *limited*—for a senior seminar. You know, focused on women's issues."

"Oh?"

"How would you feel about offering a course on Walt Whitman, instead?"

Oh, God. "But, Miles, wouldn't you be concerned about Whitman's focus on *men's* issues?"

"Oh, that wouldn't be a problem. Whitman's concerns are universal."

"Oh? And Dickinson's aren't? Let's see, last time I looked she wrote about God, love, death, art—"

"Yes, but from a *female* perspective—"

"And Whitman wrote from an *ungendered* perspective? Is that what you're saying?"

"Well, no. But he—"

"No, Miles, I *won't* teach a seminar on Whitman. Maybe sometime, but not now. Just leave the Dickinson course on the schedule. And thanks *so* much for your concern."

"But—"

"Good-bye, Miles." I hung up gently. Then I groaned. Unless Miles retired before I came up for tenure, I was in deep trouble. He was going to battle me every step of the way.

I retrieved my American literature anthology and the note to Piotrowski. While the heavy book was in my hand, I leafed through it casually, looking for the Dickinson section. Ah, here it was. I turned to a favorite poem.

I cannot live with You—
It would be Life—
And Life is over there—
Behind the Shelf

The Sexton keeps the Key to—

Was Tony really getting married? Really? I closed the book with a sigh.

I'd met Tony Gorman when I was a Ph.D. student at Boston University. He was a New York State Police drug investigator who'd come to BU undercover, pursuing an interstate, intercampus drug trafficking ring. He'd enrolled as an M.A. student in the English Department, where a hotshot young American literature professor visiting from NYU was peddling more transcendence than Ralph Waldo Emerson, even at his spaciest, ever dreamed of.

I'd noticed Tony immediately. Who wouldn't? He was so quiet and serious, and those smoky blue eyes looked straight at you, unlike the self-involved, uncertain gazes of the men around me. But I hadn't paid much attention. I was too busy for men: studying, taking care of Amanda, teaching my freshman composition courses.

Then, in the middle of a class on the American Renaissance, when Professor Speedball was waxing incoherent about the "exalted, antimaterialist, infinitude of the human spirit," and I was doodling eyeballs all over my otherwise empty sheet of notepaper, Tony turned his blue Irish gaze on me across the wide seminar table, shot me a surreptitious lopsided smile, and winked. I blinked, blushed, and spent the next six years of my life with him. Two years ago, the Enfield job came up, tenure-track and prestigious, and I couldn't turn it down. Not after I'd worked so damn hard at my career. So I left New York, my teaching job at a big impersonal city college with no guarantee of a future, and Tony. And I'd spent most of my adult life on my own; I don't need a man to make my life complete. It was just that hearing Piotrowski's voice reminded me of Tony. Too many things do.

Maybe I should give Tony a call. Just to wish him well. I picked up the phone, held it for a moment, then put it down. Maybe I shouldn't.

I slipped the Am lit textbook into my canvas bookbag. Maybe I should concentrate on a new scholarly project instead. Writing the biography of a long-forgotten woman writer could be just the ticket to distract me from any nonsensical regrets about the course of my love life. I pulled my copy of the *Encyclopedia of American Women Authors* from the shelf and turned to the entry for Serena Northbury. A photograph of a striking fair-haired woman with a straight nose, square chin, and delicate mouth topped the short paragraph the *EAWA* had seen fit to devote to Northbury. Dark eyes gazed directly at the camera, and straight into my imagination. Picking up the receiver again, I dialed the number I had copied from the precise, printlike handwriting on Mr. Smallwood's index card. Dr. Edith Hart, great-granddaughter of the American author Serena Northbury, answered the phone on the third ring.

Four

It didn't take me long to find the town of Eastbrook itself, but locating Meadowbrook was something else again. If Dr. Hart hadn't given such precise and detailed directions, I might have found myself, Rip-Van-Winkle-like, lost in the mountains for twenty years, the roads were so circuitous. But Meadowbrook's stone pillars were right where she'd said they'd be, five miles up the mountain road, two miles beyond the Summit Inn, just after an abandoned one-room schoolhouse, a quarter of a mile down a winding, unpaved lane, and past a couple of horses grazing in a stony field.

It was an early-April Tuesday, and I had somehow miraculously cleared an entire afternoon to visit Serena Northbury's great-granddaughter at Meadowbrook, the Northbury ancestral home in the Massachusetts hills. As I topped a ridge and caught my first glimpse of the house, I gasped; the car slowed, as if of its own volition, and I brought it to a stop. Meadowbrook was a gem. A small estate complete with a tenant house, and barns, set in a hillside clearing. The main house was a rambling three-story nineteenth-century rustic "cottage," shingled in brown-stained cedar splints, and wide fieldstone steps led to a white-pillared wraparound veranda overlooking a vista of wooded mountainsides, reddish now in the early spring sun. Cleared pastures, demarcated by low stone walls, extended as far as I could see.

When I pulled the Jetta up under a porte cochere, next to a shiny black Chevy Suburban and a dusty maroon Lincoln with New York M.D. plates, a bulky gray-haired man came down the porch steps. He introduced himself as Willis Thorpe, Dr. Hart's longtime medical partner and current houseguest, and led me through a wide hallway into a large double parlor furnished in late Victorian style.

Edith Hart greeted me from a mission-style armchair upholstered in dark red chintz. "Forgive me for not rising, Professor Pelletier," she said, "but standing up is simply too much of a chore these days. I hope you had no trouble finding us." Dr. Hart's tone was polite but formal. From her expression of appraisal, I could tell she didn't quite know what to make of me; Mrs. Northbury's great-granddaughter was clearly not altogether enthusiastic about this unknown scholar's sudden interest in her ancestor's work.

"Your directions were perfect, Dr. Hart. And this place is wonderful." Although she appeared to be somewhere in her eighties and seemed frail, Edith Hart was still a beautiful woman. White hair clipped modishly short framed a high-cheeked, square-jawed face. Her damask-rose sweater, worn with pleated gray wool slacks, accentuated deep-set gray eyes and dark brows. She looked serious and intelligent, and I liked her instinctively. But, as I said, she didn't seem at all certain about me.

As she'd informed me on the phone, Dr. Hart was a retired physician who had spent her long career in Manhattan, working at inner-city hospitals and clinics. Now, ill with diabetes, she had given up her New York apartment and lived year-round at Meadowbrook, the Northbury family home in the Massachusetts hills, with the assistance, she told me, of a "young man, a family connection."

"Meadowbrook was built by my great-grandmother," she'd said. "I'm not certain there's a great deal I can tell you about her, but you'll probably enjoy seeing the house. It's really quite unusual. I don't get around much, but Will could give you a tour before you leave."

Dr. Thorpe, only a few years younger, but far more robust than Dr. Hart, got me settled on a love seat, and once Edith Hart was satisfied I was comfortable, she turned to her friend. "Will, do make certain the professor gets some tea." Dr. Hart was of the generation—and class—that takes the tea ritual seriously, and in a recessed window nook of the sunny, cherry-paneled room, a lace-covered table was elegantly set with a silver tea service and rose-patterned china. I was intimidated. The last time I'd handled bone china was at a funky little tearoom in Greenwich Village where the pots came in the shape of bulldogs and thatched cottages, and afternoon tea was served with more than a spoonful of parody. But for this lady the ritual was purposeful; any awkwardness between strangers was to be smoothed away in the time-hallowed courtesies of the tea table.

As I sipped the strong brew and gazed around the room at the marble mantel, glass-fronted bookcases, floral still lifes, and quaint half-keyboard piano, a tall man with frizzy blond hair carried in a silver tray holding a plate of scones and a small cut-glass bowl of strawberry jam. He set them precisely in the center of the small table. This, I thought, must be the "family connection" who takes care of Dr. Hart.

"Ah, Gerry," Edith said, "let me introduce you to Professor Pelletier, who is interested in ah . . . my . . . illustrious ancestor Mrs. Northbury. Professor Pelletier, this is Gerry Novak. Gerry makes it possible for me to live here."

The frizzy-haired man nodded in my direction, but didn't make eye contact. He fussed with the table arrangement, moving spoons and realigning damask napkins. Then, without speaking to anyone, he left the room.

Edith Hart sighed and glanced over at Dr. Thorpe. He shrugged. When she turned to me, her smile seemed forced. Placing her cup on a mahogany side table, she sat back in her large chair. For a moment I feared she was going to say, "Good help is *so* hard to find these days." But, of course, she didn't. Rather, she regarded me again with cool appraisal.

"Professor Pelletier, I'll be frank with you. I'm astounded that a literary scholar—especially one from Enfield College—would show any interest at all in my great-grandmother. From what I understand, everyone thinks Mrs. Northbury's books are trash."

"Please call me Karen, Dr. Hart. And I *love* Mrs. Northbury's novels."

"Can you tell me why?" This was a woman who was used to asking questions and who expected to get reasoned answers.

It was the first time I'd been forced to think seriously about my eccentric interest in this much-maligned writer, and I took a minute or two to respond. Edith was a patient woman. She lifted her cup, sipped her tea, waited.

Finally I ventured, "She's the only novelist I know from that era who writes about the kind of courage it takes to get through life day by day. No white whales. No uncharted forests. No scarlet letters. No great heroics at all. Just food and drink and perseverance. And ordinary kindness. And ordinary love." A totally banal literary exegesis. If anyone in the English Department at Enfield heard it, I'd be drummed out of the profession, offered a final drag on a cigarette, blindfolded, and stood up against a wall.

But Edith was smiling. "*Ordinary love.* I like that. But nowadays ordinary love doesn't seem to suffice. Everyone is looking for *extraordinary* love, aren't they?" She laughed. "I know *I* always have been."

I could feel my eyes widen. *Extraordinary love?* But this woman was *old*.

Willis Thorpe was watching his friend. "But surely ordinary love isn't ordinary, at all," he said, quietly. "Ordinary love *is* extraordinary." Could I be imagining the wistful expression in his gray eyes?

Edith laughed again. "Maybe so. But I've always had more of an affinity for the Cathy-and-Heathcliff kind of love—dark, passionate, forbidden."

"And dangerous," added Dr. Thorpe. Perhaps age had etched something resembling a frown into the permanent lines of his face. Certainly experience had; Willis Thorpe had the weary eyes of a man who had seen more than his share of human pain and folly.

"Maybe." Dr. Hart's response was quick. "And, God knows, in my work I've seen enough of the danger. I wouldn't be surprised if the Emergency Room isn't the court of last resort for that kind of love. But, nonetheless, it's always appealed to me." She looked directly at Thorpe. "As you well know," she said.

I felt uncomfortable, as if I were eavesdropping on a very old, very complicated conversation.

Then Edith seemed to recall my presence. "I hope I'm not embarrassing you," she said, turning to me and breaking the mood. "But if an eightysomething woman can't talk honestly about love and sex, I don't know who can." She gazed at me a moment, her head tilted. "And besides, I have a strong feeling you understand what I'm talking about."

I smiled, without committing myself. Maybe I didn't; maybe I did.

Dr. Hart took the small plate Dr. Thorpe handed

her. He had given her buttered dark bread, I noticed, rather than scones. Willis Thorpe was very careful of his old friend's health.

"But you didn't come here to talk about love, Professor Pelletier—Karen," Dr. Hart continued. "What is it, exactly, you want to know about Mrs. Northbury?"

Mrs. Northbury, I thought. She calls her great-grandmother *Mrs. Northbury.* Delightfully old-fashioned for a woman who seems so comfortable talking about sex.

As Edith nibbled on a triangle of bread, and Willis Thorpe roamed restlessly around the room, I told them about my plans to write a biography of Serena Northbury. "Not a great deal is known about her life, at least by scholars," I concluded. "So anything you can tell me, any papers you might have, would be useful. And her library. Do you have any other books that belonged to her besides the *Jane Eyre?*"

"Books and papers, eh?" She thought for a moment. "When I inherited this place, I donated the family papers to Enfield College. But that was mostly documents: deeds, birth certificates, wedding certificates, account books, a few letters. I thought those would be of historical interest because we're such an old family, and one that was fairly influential locally."

"Really? Beyond Mrs. Northbury?"

"Oh, yes. The Pinkworth family was—"

"Pinkworth?"

"Didn't you know? Mrs. Northbury's father, Edmund Pinkworth—the *Reverend* Edmund Pinkworth—was a cleric of some note in his day. I gave a book of his sermons to the college, as well as some manuscript sermons. . . ."

"Really?" This place must be a treasure trove.

"Mrs. Northbury's book money built this house; it wasn't the Pinkworth ancestral home. But the Pinkworth family papers were stored here. My great-grandmother inherited them, and then, eventually, I did. And since the Reverend Eddie was—"

I laughed. "The Reverend *Eddie*?"

If I hadn't already taken to Edith Hart, her responding grin would have endeared her to me instantly. "That's what my sister and I called him when we were girls. We hated him. The one portrait we had was ghastly; the poor man looked like an ogre. It sat right there on the mantel," she gestured to the ornate fireplace, "and scowled down at us as if he had known a hundred years in advance just exactly what naughty little children we were fated to be. As soon as I decently could after my father died, I bundled it up with the family documents and hustled them all off to Enfield. The librarians seemed grateful; he was, after all, a founder of the college."

"He was?" This, too, was news to me. I hadn't been kidding when I'd said I knew very little about Serena Northbury's life.

I wished I could pull out a notebook and jot all this information down, but the atmosphere didn't seem conducive. This was a friendly conversation, not a formal interview. Maybe that could come later, after I was certain I'd won Edith's confidence.

"Oh, yes. Quite a mover and shaker in his time, was the Reverend Eddie. And an orthodox education for young Christian men *in these parlous days*," her tone was mocking, "was dear to his heart. I remember my grandmother—Mrs. Northbury's middle daughter, Josie, was my grandmother—saying that her mother had never forgiven the good reverend for refusing to send her to school. Instead, Pinkworth poured all his energies—and money—into assuring a proper education for the young *men* of New England, although he had no sons himself. Reverend Eddie claimed college would *unsex* a woman, my grandmother said."

"*Unsex* her?" I laughed.

"Yes. When I was little, I tried to figure out what

that meant. If she learned Latin, would her breasts drop off? Would she sprout whiskers if she memorized the botanical phyla? Those were pretty bizarre images for a young girl. Come to think of it, that may be what drove me into medical studies." She grinned. "Trying to reassure myself that, even if I did use my brain, my breasts would remain firmly attached."

Over by the piano, where he had arrested his prowling to listen, Willis Thorpe snorted. "You never told me that story, Edie." He looked enchanted. As if, I thought, this woman would never cease to surprise him.

"Well, why would I?" She glanced over at him, laughing. "I'm certain *you* had far more humanitarian motives for becoming a physician."

"Of course I did." His voice deepened an octave in self-derision. "They probably had to do with how splendid I would look in a white coat and stethoscope." He was still chortling as he began to sort through the framed photographs displayed on the piano's top. Then he zeroed in on a picture in a red frame and carried it over to the Tiffany floor lamp. He gazed at it for a long time before returning it to the piano. When he glanced over at his old friend, as if to make some comment, his expression immediately became concerned. I looked at her more closely. Edith appeared exhausted. Pouring a fresh cup of tea, Dr. Thorpe sat next to her and urged her to drink it. For the first time I realized how very ill this woman was. Time for me to make my exit. I rose and thanked her for her hospitality.

"May I come back when you're feeling better, Dr. Hart? To talk to you some more about your great-grandmother? I've learned so much today, but I'm sure there's a great deal more you can tell me."

"Certainly, Karen. I've enjoyed talking to you. And you haven't seen the house yet. Could we make that tour another day? This damn disease gets to me every once in a while, and I don't think I can spare Will right now."

"Of course," I said, feeling a pang of guilt about having worn her out.

"And there's a great deal of family memorabilia in the attics—junk, mostly, I imagine. I've been meaning to go through it before . . . well . . . soon. I'll ask Gerry to start bringing things down. There's at least one box of papers that belonged to Mrs. Northbury, but when I packed up the Pinkworth things, I didn't think Enfield College would be interested in her. I couldn't bring myself to throw her stuff out, though. And I seem to recall seeing a bundle of papers that might be some kind of a manuscript. But that was a long time ago; God knows where it's all gotten to by now. I'll call you when—and if—Gerry finds anything of interest."

"Terrific! I mean, ah—that would be very useful. Thank you. Thank you *so* much." On my way out of the room, I passed the piano, and a framed black-and-white snapshot in a distinctive red frame caught my eye. I picked it up; I was fairly certain this was the photograph Willis Thorpe had singled out earlier. The shot was of a laughing, dark-haired Edith Hart. Cigarette in hand, wearing a short, wide-shouldered dress, with ornamental braid around the square-cut neck, she was young, beautiful, and sexy. And there was a glamour about her that belonged to a pre-feminist era—the cigarette, the dark lipstick, the frank sensuality. I felt a strong pang of politically incorrect envy.

"Beautiful," I murmured, indicating the photo in its bright red frame.

"Yes," she replied, with an enigmatic smile. Fifty years later, this woman's beauty still gave her private satisfaction.

Then, thinking about photographs, I remembered the picture in the old copy of *Jane Eyre*. "Dr. Hart—"

"Do call me Edith." It seemed that she'd made up her mind to trust me.

"Edith." I reached into my shoulder bag and retrieved the baby's photograph. "Do you know who this is? I found it in the Brontë that belonged to your great-grandmother."

She took the picture, held it close to her eyes. Of course, I thought. Diabetes. She probably has problems with her vision. She lowered the photo, then shook her head. "I've never seen this before." Then she turned it over. Her eyes widened; for a brief moment she appeared stunned. Then her face shut down, her expression became neutral. *"Carrie?* Nobody in the family by that name. And *1861?* I seem to remember that Mrs. Northbury was living in New York then. Maybe it was the child of a friend. Who knows, she may have lent the book out and someone used the photo for a bookmark, then forgot it. It could be anyone. Sorry I can't be of more help." She was speaking just a little too rapidly. Suddenly she was pale and sweaty, drained of energy. What's *this* all about? I wondered. Again, I remembered the diabetes. Maybe she was going into insulin shock. I felt another guilty pang.

"Interesting picture, though," Edith said, wearily. "May I keep it? Since it was in a family book?"

"It's yours," I replied. But I felt a sense of loss: I'd become fond of the beautiful child. Edith looked closely at little Carrie's picture once again, and then, as she leaned her head back against the pillow Willis had provided for her, she tucked the photo between her chair's cushion and its frame—for safekeeping, I assumed.

As I left Meadowbrook, the late-afternoon sun cast long shadows on the lawn and on the immaculate shrubbery. I turned right at the stone pillars and began the trek back down the mountain. When I'd gone a half mile or so, a shiny black Chevy Suburban whizzed past me, going at least sixty miles an hour on the twisting dirt road, and forcing my little Jetta as far over to the right as the mountainous terrain would allow. I wasn't certain, but I thought the light-haired man behind the wheel was probably Gerry Novak, Edith Hart's taciturn "family connection."

Five

" '*And now, reader,*' " I read aloud to my American literature class, a week after my visit to Meadowbrook, " '*I come to a period in my unhappy life, which I would gladly forget if I could. The remembrance fills me with sorrow and shame. It pains me to tell you of it; but I have promised to tell the truth, and I will do it honestly, let it cost me what it may.*' " I looked up from my copy of Harriet Jacobs's *Incidents in the Life of a Slave Girl* at the sober faces of my students. "Now, what we have here," I said, "is a tale of attempted rape and illicit sex told by a black woman to a white audience, an audience Harriet Jacobs is well aware reveres sexual chastity above any other feminine quality. This is a difficult story for her to tell, because of the personal humiliation involved, and also because there are no narrative conventions available in which to tell it. Sexual harassment and sexual liaisons were not the stuff of polite literature. Listen to her language here: '*It pains me to tell you of it,*' she says, '*but I have promised to tell the truth—*' "

"I don't think she *is* telling the truth," Tibby Brewster asserted from the back row. Today he was wearing a bright green golf shirt with his khakis. His curly hair was freshly clipped. His lips were set in a determined line. "How could she be? Her master *owned* her; that was a legal and economic reality. He had a right to rape her." At the collective gasp that arose from the class, he held up his hand. "Hey, wait a minute. I'm not saying it was *morally* right. But it was an economic and legal fact: She was his property. He could do whatever he wanted with her, and the law sanctioned it. She says she resisted him, but I don't believe it. How could she? The law was on his side. And would it have even *been* rape?"

"Damn right it would have been rape." Emily Hannon's blond, shoulder-length hair bobbed with indignation. "Moral law supersedes civil law absolutely. And rape is a violation of the implicit moral right of each person to the integrity of his or her own body."

"Yeah, Brewster," Steve Nagler affirmed, "haven't you ever heard of individual moral responsibility?"

In the heated debate that followed, Tibby Two was roundly chastised. Surprisingly, Shamega Gilfoyle, the only black student in the class, sat mutely through the discussion. And I could see why; it must be exhausting to constantly be the sole representative of your race in a class at a cushy, white institution like Enfield. Still, this silence wasn't at all like Shamega. And neither was the unreadable expression in her dark eyes as the furor raged around her. *Poor kid,* I thought. I remembered the two years I'd spent as a scholarship student at Smith College; I'd gotten sick of being the token working-class student. In my junior year, I recalled, I'd infuriated one professor by calling *Huck Finn* a bourgeois fantasy of boyhood, totally out of touch with the hard realities of degradation, illiteracy, and homelessness that actual poverty visited on disadvantaged children. It was the only course I ever got less than an A in, and after that I'd learned to keep my mouth shut. Academics don't like to have their dream lives intruded upon.

I concluded the class discussion of Jacobs's *Incidents* by stressing the author's courage. "It's almost as if we have a social contract to be silent about rape. No one wants to talk about it; no one wants to hear about it. And in the 1800's, things were even worse; sex of every kind was barred from literary expression. Harriet Jacobs was breaking a powerful code of concealment and risking her hard-won identity as a respectable woman in recounting her sexual experience." The dry abstractions didn't even begin to summarize the painful dilemma faced by a former slave telling her story to a white audience.

Shamega's silence nagged at me, and I tried to catch up with her, but she vanished the moment class let out.

Tony and I were making love in the big bed in the Upper West Side apartment I'd left when I took the job at Enfield. He had just kissed the back of my neck so sweetly it gave me shivers, when I heard the baby cry. I rolled to the edge of the bed, reached over to the cradle, and pulled back the hand-knit lavender blanket. The frantic screams turned into the loud clamor of a telephone, and I woke from the luscious dream. I fumbled for the light, glanced at the green numbers on the bedside clock: 11:52 P.M. *What the hell?* The phone rang again; I grabbed it.

"Professor Pelletier?" The voice coming over the line was small and frightened. "Professor Pelletier, you said I should call you if I was having any problem with . . . well . . . with . . . with anyone in the class. . . ."

"What? Who?" I sat up in bed, blinking in the glare of the lamp. "Shamega? Is that you?"

"He was in my room."

"What?"

"He was in my room at least I think it was him I was coming home from work—the late shift—and the room was dark and I turned on the light—" She was jumbling

it all together as if separate sentences would be too difficult to articulate. "But there was no light just the glow
from the hall and someone threw me on the bed and
before I could see who it was he had disappeared down
the hall and . . ."

"Was it—Tibby Brewster?" I remembered the open
antagonism between Shamega and my troublesome student.

"I don't know." There was silence again on the
other end of the line. Then she whispered, "I think so."

"Shamega, did you call Security?"

"No! And I'm not going to—"

"You must—"

"No. No, I can't—"

"Why not?"

"I can't." She was crying now. "Look, I shouldn't
have bothered you. He didn't hurt me. He just scared
me. I'll be all right. I'm sorry I woke you. Just forget I
called."

"Shamega—don't hang up. *Don't. Hang. Up.*
Shamega!—" But she was gone.

I was already out of bed, stripping off the extra-
large Enfield T-shirt I sleep in. As I slipped into jeans and
a sweatshirt, I rifled through my desk for the Enfield
College Directory. Shamega answered her phone on the
eighth ring, just as I bent to tie the laces of my battered
white Nikes. At least I assumed it was Shamega; she
didn't say anything, but I could hear her frightened
breathing.

"Shamega, it's Karen Pelletier—"

"I am not calling Security." Each word was a small,
hard fist.

"Okay. Okay. Listen, stay in your room. I'll come
there. We need to talk."

"No!"

"No? Then why did you call me?"

"I mean, no, don't come to the dorm. The guard

would have to let you in, and I don't want him to know. I'll meet you, somewhere—On the library steps, okay?"

Although an unseasonable daytime warmth had lingered through the final week of March and well into April, the night air felt cold as I belted myself into the driver's seat. I wasn't optimistic about the permanence of spring. This was New England, and each morning I checked the crocuses that had poked their purple and gold heads through the melting piles of gray snow, each time expecting to find the perky flowers frozen into limp clumps of unidentifiable plant matter. I was shivering in my wool jacket as I turned the key in the ignition, and I was absolutely certain the poor, naked flowers would be dead by morning.

It was after midnight, and the back roads leading to Enfield from my house in the country were empty of traffic. Still, after I braked for the first deer, a young skittish buck with budding horns, I kept to a reasonable speed. I would get to the campus in twenty minutes. It was the best I could do. And I couldn't help feeling a little resentful. Why me? There were counselors at the school. Why hadn't Shamega called one of them? Or the dean? Or a friend? Or her parents?

English teachers—*female* English teachers, in particular—tend to be recruited as unofficial counselors in a goodly percentage of student crises. It has something to do with all that raw literary emotion we handle so coolly every day. I remembered Harriet Jacobs's *It pains me to tell you of it* and the class discussion that very morning. Then the memory of Shamega's haunted eyes flashed into my mind.

Any residual resentment vanished the moment I set eyes on Shamega. She sat shivering on the library's top step, huddled against the base of a two-story-high marble pillar. Wearing only a sweatshirt and baggy pants, she looked even smaller and more insubstantial than normal. Her eyes, though, seemed twice their usual size—like those of the frightened deer I'd just seen. I sat and put my arm around her shoulder. "Tell me about it."

"I told you everything that happened. Really. I worked the late shift—at Starbucks—and took the last bus home. The dorm was quiet when I got in, no one in the hall—and I don't have a roommate. I opened the door and reached for the light, and he grabbed me and threw me. Then he was gone. It was so unexpected, and over so quick. By the time I got to the door, there was no one in the hall."

"The guard would know if there was an intruder—"

"It wasn't an intruder. Professor, there's at least as many men as women in my dorm. It could have been anyone."

"But you think it was—"

"Yes. He lives in my dorm."

"Then, why—"

She clutched my arm. "Shhhh!" Then she whispered, "Do you see someone over there?"

"Where?"

"There." She pointed toward Dickinson Hall, the boxy brick building that houses the English Department.

Pools of light surrounded the campus buildings and swam with shadows as the tight red buds of early spring shook in the cold night wind. I peered through the gloom. Between the lighted areas, random blocks of darkness hid anything a midnight imagination could conceive. I saw nothing but the usual goblins.

Shamega shuddered. I stood up and pulled her to her feet. "Come on," I ordered crisply. "We're in full view here—if anybody *is* there. And without a coat, you must be freezing. Listen, neither of us wants you to go back to the dorm. Do you have a friend you could stay with?"

She shuddered again, shook her head. *No friends. Please.*

"Okay," I said, "then we've got two options. Either

we can inform Security, or you can come home with me."

All the way home, in spite of the heat pouring into the interior of the car, Shamega shivered. Since she wouldn't talk, I did. I told her all about my daughter, how Amanda was in her sophomore year, studying premed, which made me happy, because she used to say she wanted to study criminal science, and I didn't want her to be a cop, because I had lived with one for years and it was a really hard life, and dangerous, and how she was on the chess team at Georgetown, which really surprised me because in high school she had been the captain of the basketball team and I'd expected her to play for the college, and how she had come home at Thanksgiving her freshman year with magenta hair. And on and on. I was talking to keep the silence at bay. If I were Shamega, I would have detested my daughter by the time we got to my house. But she didn't seem to. Amanda's funky room, with its lime walls, black curtains, and pro-choice posters intrigued her—especially the music collection.

"Cool," she said, browsing through the racks of cassette tapes. "Okay if I listen?"

"Sure." I tossed her a flannel nightshirt of Amanda's. "Enjoy." I turned and headed for my own room. It was two A.M. If Shamega didn't need me to play Mother Confessor, that was cool, too; maybe I could get a few hours sleep.

"Professor Pelletier?"

I pivoted in the hallway. "Yes?" My eyes had already begun to droop.

"You know I appreciate your help. I just have a few things to think about."

"I know you do." I'd known a great many young women over the past few years—Amanda, her friends, and scores of students—and I was fairly well versed in the late-adolescent female psyche.

Through the wall from my daughter's bedroom I

could hear the melancholy strains of R.E.M. God, I was thankful I wasn't that young anymore.

When I woke at eight, Shamega was making pancakes in my kitchen. She had sliced a banana and was laying a banana spiral in each large cake. I poured coffee and sat at the round oak table.

Shamega set a plate of the thick browned cakes in front of me, then tucked into her own. She seemed calmer.

"So?" I asked. I cautiously examined the plate in front of me. College students tend to be loose cannons in the kitchen, but these pancakes looked good. I spread butter, drizzled syrup. Suddenly I was ravenous.

"So," she replied. "Thank you. This was just what I needed—a real home and a real kitchen." Her smile was wan, but resolute. Then she continued, "You know what I want to do with my life?"

"What?" I cut a wedge of pancake and nibbled. Then, not believing what I was tasting, I forked the entire bite down and reached for another. These were the best pancakes I'd eaten in my entire life. I couldn't believe how good they were. I hefted my coffee cup and glanced over at Shamega.

"Cook."

I *knew* it. "I'm not surprised. These pancakes are terrific."

She smiled hesitantly. "Thanks. So, you think that's okay? I mean—to cook? To cook for a living? My folks would freak out, you know. They sacrificed so much to send me to this expensive school. And my grandfather spent his life flipping burgers in a greasy spoon. They don't want that for me."

"Well, of course they don't. But have you ever talked to them about a culinary institute?"

"No. No, I haven't. Two things they've always made clear to me: I have to marry black, and I have to be a doctor, a lawyer, or a professor. *Uplift the race,* you know."

"You could talk to them." I wiped up the last of the syrup with the last of the pancakes. "There's nothing more uplifting than great food. Are there any more of these?"

She jumped up, retrieved a plate of golden cakes from the oven, where she'd been keeping them warm. We each helped ourselves to another cake. "Yeah, I could—I *could* talk to them, couldn't I?" She looked thoughtful for a moment. Then she changed the subject.

"Don't get the wrong idea, Professor Pelletier. My parents are good people. And one of the things they taught me was never to be a victim. So, in my senior year of high school, when I was raped by two members of the basketball team . . ." She tried for a casual tone, but my exclamation of horror threw her off just a little.

"Shamega!"

She raised both hands, palms outward. "Just let me tell this, okay?"

"Okay. But, oh, Shamega . . ." I was no longer hungry. I laid the fork and knife crosswise on my plate.

"When I was raped, I decided not to be a victim. I reported the rape, I pressed charges, we went to court." She paused as she spread butter.

"And?"

"And—I lost." She put her knife down, but neglected to pick up the fork. "Insufficient evidence of resistance. White boys, black girl. Young woman not a virgin to begin with. Young men with promising lives ahead of them. One's now at Harvard; one's at Brown." Shamega finished her coffee, then pushed her plate away.

"I know it's a cliché, but it was like being raped all over again. Once in Bobby's living room, once in my hometown's courtroom. And the second time was almost worse, because it was so public. And last night when . . . whoever it was . . . grabbed me, it felt as if it were happening a third time. That I was being violated again. That's why I got so hysterical. I *won't* go through that again. The cops weren't so bad. But the lawyers . . ." She shuddered. "And the jury. And the looks from my classmates . . ."

So this was why Shamega had looked so distressed in class yesterday; the discussion of rape was too painfully close to her own experience. And this must be why she'd called me, instead of a counselor. I'd talked with some understanding about rape; she knew she could trust me.

Shamega cleared dishes from the table, and scraped the uneaten cakes into the garbage. I ran hot water into the sink, squirted the dish soap. This old house doesn't have a dishwasher. I really should move somewhere more civilized. With my hands deep in soapsuds, I pondered Shamega's dilemma. Enfield was a small campus, and gossip spread like wildfire. If she reported an intruder in her room, it would be public knowledge by dinnertime. I understood her desire to keep it quiet. On the other hand, if there was any danger of it happening again . . . I really didn't know how to advise her.

"I didn't tell you," she said, "but he got into my underwear."

"What?"

"I mean he got into my drawers."

"What!"

"My *dresser* drawers, I mean."

"Oh . . ."

"There was underwear thrown all over the room— and I think some of it was missing."

She dried my cast-iron griddle, then rubbed vegetable oil onto it with a paper towel. I watched, fascinated. I didn't know you were supposed to do that.

"If it *is* Tibby Brewster, I think it's a sex thing, not a race thing. But it's so odd, Professor. This—*thing*—he's got with me . . . this fixation, or whatever it is, it's something sort of *new*."

"What do you mean, *new*?"

"Well, I was in classes with him last year, and he never paid any attention to me. It was like, you know, I didn't even *exist* for him. It's like that with some white people. They see *black,* then they don't see anything else. And that was fine by me; I never had the slightest desire to attract the attentions of Thibault Brewster the Second. And I had an Irish poetry course with him in the fall. Same thing for most of the semester: I didn't exist. Then—" She paused to pour a last cup of coffee. "Then we come back from Thanksgiving vacation and suddenly I'm visible; he can't take his eyes off me. Since then he's made it clear— Well . . ."

I slid the glass pot into the soapy water and scrubbed it in silence. Shamega took it from the drainer and spoke. "The kind that's into underwear, Professor: You can imagine. But I don't think Tibby's really danger-ous. It was just that he didn't expect me to be there—in my room; I surprised him, and he reacted. But he didn't *attack* me."

"Shamega . . ." I admired this young woman's in-dependence and courage, but, even more, I wanted her to be safe.

"I *trust* you, Professor. I trust you to keep this to yourself." She folded the dish towel and hung it on the wooden rack. "Please?" Her brown eyes implored me.

I sighed. "Okay. But on two conditions: one—that you'll let me know if there's any more trouble, and two—if it goes any further you'll talk to Earlene John-son."

"That sounds fair." Shamega flashed me a bright smile. "Okay. And thanks. Thanks for bringing me home with you last night, and thanks for the use of your kitchen. And by the way, Professor Pelletier, you really need to do something about your cookware. All that cheap, thin-bottomed stuff . . . How do you ever get a decent sear on anything?"

A decent *sear?* I guess I've got a lot to learn about the culinary arts.

·   ·   ·

While I got ready for work, Shamega sat cross-legged on the hard oak floor by the glass-front bookcase where I keep the old books I scout out at flea markets, estate sales, and antiquarian bookstores. The two shelves of Northbury novels intrigued her, and by the time I'd loaded my bookbag with corrected exams and was set to go, she was deep into the second chapter of *The Abandoned Innocent*. "Can I borrow this?" she asked. "I won't be able to sleep tonight if I don't find out what happens to Esmeralda's baby."

"Sure. I'd love to know what you think of it." And on the winding trip back to school I told Shamega about my visit to Meadowbrook and about meeting Mrs. Northbury's great-granddaughter.

"Wow. And she's going to let you look through Mrs. Northbury's papers?"

"If she finds any."

"That is *so* fascinating. I'd *love* to do something like that."

"Well, maybe you could help. If there's a lot of material, I'll need an assistant."

"Cool."

I dropped Shamega off at her dorm and parked in the Dickinson Hall lot. When I entered my office, I stopped dead. The room looked as if it had been hit by a windstorm—books pulled off the shelves, file cabinets yanked open, papers strewn around. Weirdest of all, a bright array of women's underwear had been spread across the surface of my desk. Colorful cotton briefs, flimsy pastel bikinis, flowered silk jockey shorts. The first thing I did was call Shamega. Then, after talking to her, I picked up the phone again and called Security. I could merely tell them about the break-in at my office; as Shamega had pointed out, I didn't have to mention her.

Six

The note from President Avery Mitchell was brief and polite, but it packed a wallop. *Dear Professor Pelletier. The Collegewide Curriculum Revision Committee and the President's Office invite you to attend a planning dinner at the President's House on Thursday, April 18 at 7 P.M. Cocktails will be served at 6.* It was signed by Avery in his aristocratic, flowing script.

"Damn," I said. "Damn, damn, damn, and *damn!*" At its contentious luncheon meeting, the Curriculum Committee must have decided to throw a few junior faculty members into the volatile mix of department chairs and college administrators. Lots of entrenched animosity there; committee members probably thought fresh blood would diffuse the explosive potential. *Fresh blood:* a good metaphor; I'd been chosen as a lamb to the wolves. *Oh,* damn. I envisioned the interminable meetings ahead of me, the pious arguments, the ostentatious demonstrations of obscure knowledge, the patronizing attitudes, the small, mean, erudite digs. I dropped my head into my hands and groaned. But I had no choice. An invitation from the President's Office meant a command appearance. I noted the date in my appointment book—in ink—and marched myself over to Greg Samoorian's office. The least my good buddy could have done was to have given me some advance warning.

Greg's door was open, and he sat at his desk deeply absorbed in the contents of the small paperback book in his hand. He was so intent on his reading that he didn't hear my tentative rap on his door frame. As he concentrated on the text, he ran his fingers through his curly dark hair. I knew intellectual problems could be all-consuming for Greg, but I had never before seen him quite so intent. I knocked again, cleared my throat, said "Greg?" He jumped—I swear it—six inches. The wheeled chair skittered back from the desk.

"Karen!" He was as disoriented as a man waking from an intense dream.

"Jeez, Greg, you're in another world. *What* are you reading?"

"Oh—nothing." He dropped the book, covered it with the latest issue of *Social Text,* rubbed his eyes. It took a few seconds for his gaze to focus. "Long time, no see, Karen." He motioned me into the room. "What's new?"

"You tell *me.* Why have you been keeping the good news from me?" I was just pissed enough about being on the Curriculum Committee to feel good and sarcastic.

"You *know?*" His eyes widened. "How?"

"I just got the note—"

"The *note?*"

"From Avery."

"Avery? . . . What the hell? . . . How does *he* know? We weren't going to tell anyone until—"

"Greg, *I'm* talking about the Curriculum Committee. What are *you* talking about?"

"Oh," he said, "ohhhh. The Curriculum Committee. I forgot. I've been so distracted by . . ." He let his voice trail off. His eyes slid toward the book hidden under his copy of *Social Text*.

What could it be? I wondered. Pornography? Had Greg taken to indulging depraved sexual fantasies during office hours? A vision of scantily clad young blondes and vicious German shepherds, each wearing wide, brass-studded leather collars, encroached upon my imagination. Something that had seeped into my mind by osmosis, no doubt—probably while I was waiting for my car to be lubed. "Greg, *tell* me!"

His expression was sheepish as he retrieved the book and showed me its cover: no dogs or scantily clad blondes; just a little blue-diaper-clad baby and a little pink-diaper-clad baby. Framed in blue and pink ribbons, the title read: *Names for Your New Baby*.

He swiveled from side to side in his desk chair, smirking like a Cheshire cat on weed.

"Ohmigod, Greg. That's wonderful news." I bent and kissed his cheek. Then I paused. "At least I *think* it's wonderful news."

"Oh, yeah," he said. "*Oh*, yeah. Karen," he asked, glancing down at his little book, "what do you think about *Clarissa*? I mean, as a *name?*"

The living room of the President's House was festive with spring flowers. A vase of bright red hothouse tulips sat on a leather-topped mahogany side table next to a cream brocade-covered wing chair. The long table behind the sea-green sofa held an enormous bouquet: daffodils, poppies, tulips, iris. A few stems of white narcissus in a crystal bud vase decorated the piano top. I was early, having arrived at six, as the invitation said. Of course, no one else was there. You think I'd know better by now, but in Lowell, where I grew up, when you were invited for six o'clock, that meant the macaroni-and-beef casserole would be on the table at six sharp, and if you wanted it hot, you'd better get there on time.

I wandered around the room, touching beautiful things—the gleaming crystal of a Waterford vase, the textured silk of the upholstered sofa, the warm, smooth ivory of the piano keys. There was no mistress in this house; Liz, Avery's wife, had run off six years earlier with a junior member of the Music Department. But someone had chosen the furnishings with care, and the room, in spite of its elegance, had a warm and lived-in feel.

"Do you play?" Avery stood in the doorway with a bottle of sherry in one hand and a cordless phone in the other.

I was startled into indiscretion. "No. Music wasn't part of my education."

"Really? No talent?"

No money, I thought, but said, instead. "Do you? Play, that is?"

In response, Avery handed me the wine and the phone, sat down at the piano, and lilted through the first bars of "Begin the Beguine." "If you call that playing," he said, as the last notes died away.

"Sounds good to me."

"You *really* don't know music, do you? I play the piano as I do everything else, in a competent but facile manner. A consummate dilettante, I guess you could say." He was smiling, but there was a wistful undertone to his words.

"Well, we can't all be Elton John," I retorted inanely, immediately realizing I should have chosen a far more cultured example.

But Avery laughed. "And it's a good thing, too, isn't it?"

This was the first time I'd been alone with Avery since an awkward encounter one cold night the previous year. In the shadow of the library building he'd told me firmly that there was absolutely no future for a personal relationship between a college president and an un-tenured professor. Since I had never aspired to such a relationship—not outside my fantasies, anyhow—I'd been a little shaky around him ever since.

Avery is not my type. He's a lady-killer—and I'm no lady. I've always gone for big, bulky men—like Tony. *Real* men. *Working* men. Not slender, effete intellectuals like our distinguished president. I'd despised Avery from the moment I'd met him until the moment he'd first turned the blue spotlight of his gaze in my direction. Then I'd despised *myself*—for being such an easy mark. But the man was irresistible. Sandy hair, cut conservatively, but not so short that a beguiling strand couldn't flop now and then over his cerebral brow. Ice blue eyes, a long, slender face, and thin, expressive lips completed an inventory of features straight out of a Ralph Lauren advertisement. And he knew how to dress. Tonight Avery wore an off-white jacket over a black golf shirt, black linen pants, and oxblood loafers. And he reeked of Eau de WASP.

Rising from the piano bench, Avery retrieved the wine and the phone. Placing the sherry on the antique sideboard that served as a temporary bar, he turned to me solicitously. "I understand you had a distasteful experience a week or so ago."

I paused, mystified. Then I blushed. Of course he would have heard about the intruder in my office. He was the president; he knew *everything* that happened on campus. And *now* he knew about the panties.

I'd kept Shamega out of the account I'd given Security. They'd found my first-floor office window closed but not locked. In the semifrozen earth outside, they'd discovered several boot prints. "You know the kind the kids wear now," Paul Dermott, Enfield's security chief, told me. "Those heavy boots, with the ugly soles?"

"Lug boots," I said.

"Yeah—lug boots. Well, two were full prints—not large, but not real small either. You have any idea who they could belong to?"

I thought about Shamega in her street garb, the lug

boots so incongruous on her small feet. *Shamega? Could she have done it herself?* Then I thought about all my other students. Who ever noticed what they were wearing on their feet?

"Could be anyone," I replied. And that was as far as it had gone.

"Well," I said to Avery, "these things happen. Probably some student who'd gotten a bad grade on the midterm or something."

"Security's going to keep a close eye on your office."

"So they told me."

He started to say something else, but only got as far as "I hope," when he paused and looked levelly at someone behind my back. "Thibault." His tone was restrained.

I turned, curious. I wouldn't have recognized this man as Tibby Brewster's father. Thibault Brewster had the same pale skin, but that was as far as the resemblance went. Where Tibby's nose was prominent and his mouth soft, Brewster's features were as chiseled as anything on Mount Rushmore—straight nose, square jaw, brown hair and thick eyebrows. Brewster wore his fifty-odd years well; the bulky frame had been well toned on the handball court, the thick hair streaked with sun on the eighteenth hole. Only the hard vertical lines adjacent to his mouth gave a clue to his age—and, I suspected, to his character. Thibault Brewster wore a navy blazer, khaki pants, and loafers identical to Avery's. I was suddenly aware of the frivolity of the flowery blue dress and white sandals I had charged that very afternoon on my Filene's card.

"Tib, have you met Professor Karen Pelletier of the English Department? Karen, this is Thibault Brewster, Chairman of our Board of Trustees."

"We haven't met. Karen." Brewster's two-handed grasp of the hand I extended was more of a courtly clasp than a handshake, as if he had been trusted with some infinitely precious, infinitely fragile object. "But I've

heard a great deal about you—from my son." His speculative gaze was as hard as the handshake was gentle.

I'll bet you have. "Thank you, Thibault," I replied,
ambiguously. "And it's very nice to meet you, too."

Then Jill Greenberg came in, dressed in lime green
paisley-patterned leggings and a long, baggy turquoise
sweater, and I was released while Avery introduced her
to the Board Chairman. I wanted to ask Jill if she was
feeling any better, but when Brewster moved off in
search of bigger game, Jill took Avery by the arm, and
began flirting with him in her easy manner. I stifled an
impulse to rip her gorgeous orange-gold hair out by its
roots, slunk away, and watched the pair covertly from
the sanctuary of the window seat. Avery was laughing at
some outrageous comment, when my gaze suddenly focused, not on him, but on Jill. Something was different
about her tonight, but what? I took a rapid inventory:
same wild hair, in pigtails tonight; same slender, com-
pact body; same wacky, mismatched clothes. What had
changed? But my attention was deflected from Jill by the
arrival of Miles Jewell and Greg. *Let the games begin,* I
thought. As I rose and began to move toward Greg, my
eye settled on Jill again, and a half-formed, nonsensical
thought drifted through my mind: *Jill doesn't look quite
so unfinished any more.*

Unfinished? What the hell did that mean? Jill still
looked fifteen years old rather than the ancient twenty-
five she actually was. And, if flirting with Avery was any
indication, she hadn't become a heck of a lot more inhib-
ited since I'd first met her. *The strain of the semester
must be getting to me,* I decided. *I'm beginning to imagine things.*

We were quite a group around the dinner table. The
committee had decided to go for inclusivity. Every element of college politics and population was covered—
including students. I was surprised when Shamega

showed up—seeming a little unnerved in this gathering of faculty and administrators. But, of course, they would need a student representative, and she fit the necessary demographics—black, female, and smart as hell. Over the appetizer of broiled, stuffed Portobelo mushroom, I surveyed my fellow committee members. Avery, of course, and Greg, both centerists, vs. Miles, his crony Phillipe Le Croix from Philosophy, and the senior Thibault Brewster to represent Tradition. Latisha Washington from Black Studies, Jill Greenberg, and I constituted the moderate left—all female, recent hires, and untenured. But I really hadn't expected to see the infamous Professor Sally Chenille of T.V. talk show fame there—representing the Crazies, I guess.

Sally was an exotic at Enfield College. Indeed, she'd be an exotic anywhere—except maybe in some high-fashion whorehouse. Bone thin, with the protuberant cheekbones that come with systematic self-starvation, Sally had dark hair, clipped severely close to her head. Today it was bleached neon yellow. But, then, Sally felt it imperative to keep up her appearance; she was, after all, a national celebrity. Her notoriety stemmed from shameless self-promotion and from her off-center notions about sex. Sally urged women to turn the tables on men: to blatantly exploit their own sexuality for advantage and profit in a masculine world.

Sally's latest book, *Writing on the Body,* had had a brief notoriety in the media as exemplifying everything that had gone wrong with postmodern intellectual discourse. She'd gotten an NEH grant to write this study of the textual significance of body piercing, tattooing, scarification, and personal branding, and now the Christian Right was up in arms about the debased use of their sacred tax dollars. With Sally involved, curriculum revision meetings were certain to be explosive.

Conversation during dinner was guarded, as might be expected with such a polarized group. I sat between Greg and Miles, and my Department chair spent the entire meal glowering into his roast lamb. Obviously he hadn't forgotten our little contretemps over the Dickinson seminar. The only comment he volunteered during the entire meal was when he overheard me telling Greg about my visit to Mrs. Northbury's great-granddaughter.

"She wrote trash," Miles fumed. "Serena Northbury was nothing but a sappy sentimentalist, one of that 'damn mob of scribbling women' Hawthorne hated." He thumped his fist on the table once: Bang. He had spoken; it was true.

"Have you *read* any of her novels, Miles?"

"Don't need to; Hawthorne's word's good enough for me."

"But I don't think Hawthorne ever actually *mentioned* Northbury—"

From the corner of my eye, I could see Greg shaking his head. "Don't confuse him with the facts, Karen," he muttered into my ear. "He's on the losing side, and he knows it."

Fortunately, it was time to settle into the plush living-room chairs with coffee and petits fours. I chose a seat on the far side of the room from Miles. Sally Chenille had somehow maneuvered Avery onto a love seat, and she was possessively curled up next to him, buffing her acid green fingernails.

"I see this meeting as exploratory," Avery said, getting right down to business, "an opportunity to begin a dialogue about what the college considers to be the true meaning of a liberal education." Next to me, Greg groaned softly. I squeezed his arm. This was going to be a scene.

"Such a dialogue," Avery continued, "is an essential preliminary to any informed decision-making. I know it will be difficult to reach a consensus," he looked pointedly at Greg, "but re-drawing the college curriculum without such a discussion would be like shooting an arrow without a target."

"Well," huffed Miles, "I would have thought the 'target' was perfectly clear—a solid command of essential knowledge."

"Yes," his pal Brewster affirmed. "The college's historic mission has always been to immerse students in the treasures of the humanistic tradition." *Mixed metaphor,* I thought. "Socrates, Homer, Dante—"

"Ahhh," Latisha broke in, shaking her dreadlocks, "but there's the problem. Who determines what constitutes *essential knowledge?* Or *the* humanistic tradition. Take the literary canon, for instance. Would you consider a 'command' of Native American oral narratives *essential knowledge?* Would you place them on a must-read syllabus for a course in world literature?"

"Of course not—" Brewster looked appalled.

"But *why* not?" I jumped in here. "Why are European classics any more essential than the myths and traditions of our indigenous forebears?"

"Because they're the fundamental basis of the Western tradition." Miles was beginning to sputter. "And I am sick to death of all this talk about the canon. The scholarly world is being held hostage to trendy theoretical and political agendas. Literary tradition mandates excellence—"

"*Eurocentric* excellence, you mean," Latisha continued, with the indignation of the righteous. "And as for the contributions of African-American culture—"

"*That's* the problem," Brewster interjected. "Self-interested ideological assaults on fundamental knowledge—"

"But," Sally Chenille's tongue ring clicked against her front teeth, her quarter-inch-long neon yellow buzz cut seemed to bristle, "we must acknowledge the fundamental instability and relativity of *all* knowledge and evaluation. Postmodern feminist standpoint epistemology—"

"But what about the post*feminist* position," Jill interrupted, in a girlish voice. For some reason—I couldn't imagine *why*—Jill didn't like Sally, and she took every opportunity to provoke her. "The issues of *young* women are consistently elided by the institutional hegemony of a generation of older feminists—"

"Older!" The syllables were squeezed from Sally's throat.

And so it went. I'd heard the arguments before. We all had. One group ascribed to a theory of solid, traditional knowledge; the other to a concept of relevance and inclusivity. What constituted the "higher" education our students would get here at Enfield depended on the conclusions we reached in this debate. But, like me, everyone in this room had long ago made up his or her mind. And no one was about to be persuaded differently. I was surprised to see Greg taking notes, but he had pulled a scrap of paper out of his pocket and was jotting down what seemed to be fairly serious reflections. When the stormy discussion ended after a fruitless two hours, he turned to me with an intent expression, glancing down at the paper in his hand. "Karen, what do you think of Portia?"

"Portia? Who's Portia?"

"I mean—as a name? For the baby? Or Rosalind? Kate? Juliet?"

As soon as I could without being rude, I gathered up my jacket and briefcase and headed out the door. On the top step of the President's House, I paused and breathed in the balmy spring air. An irrelevant notion wafted through my mind: It was a perfect night, I thought, to fall in love. Tony's upcoming marriage came instantly to mind, and I suddenly slipped into a slough of desolation. Shaking my head to rid myself of the unexpected rush of emotion, I started down the granite steps resolutely; I had far more important things to do than fall in love.

Shamega had been mute during the debate, but she'd obviously been paying close attention. By the time I reached the sidewalk, she was at my side. "So, Professor Pelletier—when we change the curriculum are you going to offer a senior seminar in the novels of Mrs. Northbury?"

I laughed. "Yeah. Right. I had to fight to schedule a course on *Emily Dickinson* next fall."

Shamega's mention of Mrs. Northbury reminded me that I hadn't heard from Edith Hart since my visit to Meadowbrook two weeks earlier. Nor had I called her, not being certain if she was up to talking to me. I'd drop her a thank-you note, I decided; that would at least remind her of my existence. But I was so busy, with exams, papers, and now this damn committee, I didn't know when I was ever going to have time to get back to Eastbrook.

"I've signed up for your Dickinson course next fall," Shamega told me.

"Good," I replied. "I'll be glad to have you in class again. You liven things up. How *are* you, anyhow? Everything okay?" Shamega looked tired—everyone did at this time of the semester—but she also looked good. This was the first time in months I'd seen her in a dress instead of the baggy hip-hop clothes she wore to make her point—whatever it was. The soft beige cotton looked terrific against her dark skin. The buzz cut had grown out a bit, re-framing her delicate features in curls. When I looked at her now, I thought of pixies, and brownies, and elves.

"Yeah. I guess. No more nastiness, anyhow." She shrugged. "Just a lot of eyeballing on Tibby's part. But, listen," she obviously didn't want to talk about Tibby Two, "I was only kidding about you teaching a Northbury seminar, but really I did enjoy the novel you lent me. I knew from the start that Esmeralda would eventually find her lost daughter, but I was glad when it happened."

"That's called," I intoned in my most scholarly voice, "the gratification of gendered genre expectations." In normal tones, I went on, "And when Northbury's in good form, she does it well. But, of course, she's not a *classic of the Western tradition.*" I mimicked Miles Jewell's deep pedantic cadences.

Shamega grinned. "I'm glad she's not. I had fun—for a change."

"Karen, wait up!" Greg was behind us as we turned onto campus. He nodded at Shamega, then turned to me. "What do you think of Cordelia?"

I stopped, and chewed my lower lip as I contemplated. Then I winked at Shamega, but spoke directly to Greg. "What do *you* think of Esmeralda? I mean, as a name?"

As I cruised past the President's House on my way home, Jill walked down the front steps, alone. The porch light turned her red-gold hair into a spun-gold halo. I was about to honk, wave, and pass her by when I noticed Sally Chenille lurking by the gate, watching Jill intently. Sally's heavily made-up face was expressionless, masklike. Shuddering inexplicably, I slammed on the brake and screeched to a halt. "Hey, Greenberg, can I give you a ride home?"

Seven

"Let me know if you find anything interesting." Edith Hart twisted the small locket she wore on its thin gold chain. "I'm going to have to put these old bones to bed for a while." It was Easter Sunday afternoon. In the door to the large storeroom off Meadowbrook's kitchen, Edith leaned on Willis Thorpe's arm and watched as Amanda, Shamega, and I began the job of sorting through piles of dusty boxes Gerry Novak had lugged down from the attic. "If you come across any treasures," she continued, "you can show them to me later. Right now I'm a little—fatigued." And she did look fatigued, gray and drawn, as if some plug had been pulled and whatever vital energy she'd mustered for our visit was visibly draining away.

Edith had responded to my thank-you note with a telephone call: She was sorry she hadn't gotten in touch earlier, but she'd been ill. She was feeling stronger now, and would I come to brunch on Sunday? I could spend the afternoon going through boxes. "There are a great many," she'd said hesitantly, "and I'm not certain which ones have Mrs. Northbury's things in them. But you could at least make a start at sorting them out." Amanda was home for Easter break, and my offer to bring her along was met with enthusiasm. "Lovely. I can't begin to tell you how much I miss young people. It would be such a treat for me to have your daughter here. And any other helpers you care to bring." So on this rainy Sunday in late April I'd brought Amanda and Shamega to Meadowbrook, the former interested in talking to Dr. Hart about her long medical career, the latter now deep into her third Serena Northbury novel and head over heels with delight about meeting the author's great-granddaughter.

Edith had gone all out with brunch—or, rather, Gerry, her cook and general factotum, had. Our hostess, pale in a high-necked lavender dress of some filmy, floaty fabric, did nothing more strenuous than sit in her cushioned chair and preside over the feast. The dining room table was spread with Irish linen and a lavish Easter buffet of baked ham, cheese soufflé, green salad, tropical fruit salad, jelly roll. Accustomed to college food-service fare, the girls fell on the meal as if they were famished, and I wasn't far behind. Edith ate little, picking at the abstemious selection of ham, dark bread, and greens Will Thorpe had chosen for her. But she entered into the mood of the party with undisguised pleasure: talking to Amanda at length about the practice of medicine, sending Shamega to the kitchen to get the Northbury jelly-roll recipe, laughing at the repartee between the girls. As I'd expected, Amanda and Shamega had liked each other immediately.

"I can't tell you much about Mrs. Northbury," Edith responded to Shamega's questions. "I didn't know her, of course—she died years before I was born—but my grandmother, her daughter Josie, talked about her a little. It was odd: My grandmother always referred to her as Mrs. Northbury, never as *Mother,* as if the public woman were more important to her than the private woman. And she didn't tell many personal stories." She paused, and her eyes took on a meditative look, as if she were attempting to come to some kind of a decision. Then she continued. "Maybe that was because—Gerry!" Then, after an awkward silence, "Listen, why don't you join us? Surely you don't need to spend the *entire* afternoon in the kitchen?"

Gerry Novak stood silently in the arched doorway, an enigmatic figure. Although so far Novak hadn't said much in my presence, his taciturn manner radiated dissatisfaction. Was it because he'd had to put together a lavish meal for us? Or was there some friction in this household I didn't know about? Most likely, I decided, noting the dour lines etched into his face, Gerry Novak simply had a permanent chip on his shoulder. Edith had referred to Gerry as a family "connection"—whatever that meant—but he insisted on behaving like a servant. At the moment his stiff posture and stilted manner seemed less like the behavior of any actual modern American domestic employee than like a stage performance of proper servitude.

"No, thank you, Dr. Hart. I merely need to know if you desire anything else at the moment." His formal demeanor was calculated to throw cold water on any attempt at familiarity.

"No, Gerry." Edith's tone was resigned. "We're fine. Thank you."

When he left, she raised an exasperated eyebrow at Will, then turned to me. "Gerry has lived here all his life, was born on the estate to a family that's been at Meadowbrook since Mrs. Northbury's time. I think of him as—well—one of the family. But there are moments when he insists on being—"

"Difficult," Will broke in. "*Difficult* is the only word describing Gerry's attitude. And after all Edie's done for him, sending him to college, supporting his work—"

"Karen didn't come here to talk about our domestic

problems, Will." A repressive glance from Edith's dark eyes silenced her friend. "She's interested in my great-grandmother. We should use what time we have to discuss Mrs. Northbury." She turned back to me.

"Really, Karen, those old boxes are your best hope for biographical information. To the family, at least by the time I came along, the most significant thing about Serena Northbury was her money. Before she stopped writing so abruptly in her forties, she'd earned a fortune—at least by nineteenth-century standards. But there's really no one left who has much interest in this— white elephant." Edith gestured around at her gracious, old-fashioned room, implying by extension the entire sumptuous phenomenon that was Meadowbrook.

Will had given us a tour when we'd arrived. The grounds were green and sloping, with a large pond, a white brick barn and stables, and the small tenant cottage Gerry Novak lived in. And the house *was* a bit of a white elephant, a three-story, hip-roofed, brown-shingled "bungalow" few modern families could afford to maintain. But it was elegant. Double parlors, connected by paneled pocket doors, overlooked the wide, white-pillared, wraparound veranda and manicured grounds. A library, dining room, butler's pantry and commodious kitchen completed the layout of the first floor. Ten bedrooms—large rooms for the family and cramped ones for the staff—made up the two top floors. And the multiroomed attic in itself would have provided adequate housing for a not-so-small modern family. The Northbury family money obviously had survived the decades, because the house was modernized and well maintained. From the first-floor landing, I'd looked down the curving staircase to the wide center hall and wondered who would inherit this fine home after Edith's death. Now she was saying there was no family—at least I thought that's what she was saying. Sad, I mused. Mrs. Northbury's legacy would come to an end.

"Although they were grateful for her fortune," Edith

continued, "I think the family was always a bit embarrassed by its relationship to Serena Northbury; everyone said her novels were such trash—"

My exclamation of impatience stopped her. She examined me curiously. "You really care about Mrs. Northbury, don't you?"

"I care about women's lives and writing." I was on my soapbox now. "So many women's stories have been lost to readers in this country. What's come down to us from the nineteenth century? Alcott's Jo March and Stowe's Little Eva—that's about it. But in reality, a goodly number of accomplished women writers were publishing, and they created some fascinating characters."

Edith played with her heart locket and listened attentively. Encouraged, I continued. "Mrs. Northbury was a terrific storyteller. So, she *wasn't* Herman Melville—or Ernest Hemingway. So what? Do we need more stories about big fish?"

The elderly woman laughed. "No, I don't imagine we do. So, you're telling me my great-grandmother wasn't an embarrassment."

"No, she wasn't. Certainly she didn't write the kind of books in vogue today, but she has intriguing things to say about being a woman."

"Then why do you think her work vanished so completely?" It wasn't a challenge; she really wanted to know.

"Northbury—ah—*Mrs.* Northbury, that is—was writing women's novels at a moment when the literary establishment was undergoing a kind of—how can I say it?—a kind of masculinization, I guess. In the late 1800's, magazine editors decided what was quality literature and what wasn't. And they were mostly men. And by the early twentieth century that job had been given over to the academic establishment, white male intellectuals who didn't have much tolerance for women's literature. And it wasn't just white women writers who were disregarded; black literature, immigrant literature, working-class literature: Whole genres of writing were *disappeared,* I guess you could say. Just totally written out of literary history with a few scornful remarks. Poof! There goes Charles Chesnutt. Poof! There goes Serena Northbury. Never to be taken seriously again."

"Hmm," Edith said, looking thoughtful.

The pause gave me an opportunity to hear myself—I was preaching. Again. "Sorry," I said, sheepishly, "I get carried away. It was a much more complicated process than you want to hear about. But I think a lot was lost . . . all those stories about women's lives—and loves."

"That's what you meant in class, isn't it," Shamega broke in. "When you were talking about *eradicated female subject positions.*" In this social situation the words sounded pretentious, but it was nice to know someone had been listening.

"Did I really say that?" I laughed. "Well, yeah. That's when *universal* experience—in other words, the stuff literary scholars think is worth being written about and taught—came to be defined by rafting down the Mississippi or being bricked up with a cask of Amontillado, rather than, say, giving birth or raising a family."

"Really?" Edith seemed absorbed by what I was saying. "And you're doing something to change that?"

I shrugged. "A number of scholars are. And a biography and literary study of your great-grandmother would help."

"Hmm."

"Edith." Will Thorpe was observing his friend with concern. "Don't you think you're overextending yourself? Remember—"

She waved a dismissive hand at him, but the light had indeed gone out of her eyes; she looked bone-weary. "Karen, I'm truly interested in what you're telling me, but Will's right—I need to rest now. Why don't you start sorting through the things from the attic? We'll talk later."

•   •   •

Mountains of dusty boxes and suitcases topped leather-strapped steamer trunks. The storeroom was full, but, according to Edith, Gerry had emptied only two of the attic rooms. I had a daunting task ahead of me. "Okay, kids," I directed, "there's a lot of old stuff to go through here, and it would be easy to get sidetracked. But remember, I'm looking for things that have to do with Serena Northbury and her books. So focus on stuff that looks as if it comes from the mid- to late nineteenth century. The rest isn't any of our business. We'll stack the Northbury artifacts over here outside the door, and the rest . . ." But neither girl was paying attention.

Amanda pulled an orange beaded flapper dress out of an old leather valise. "Look at this thing. Wow!"

"Wrong period," I said. "Northbury died long before the Roaring Twenties."

"Yeah, but this is super." A pair of white spats was next out of the suitcase, and Amanda buttoned them around her ankles atop her Nike high-tops. I sighed. I didn't know if she was going to be any help or not.

I tackled a battered blue hatbox stuffed with old envelopes, and was thrilled to find Serena Northbury's careful, rounded signature at the close of the first letter. I placed the hat box and its treasures in the hallway to sort through later, atop a dusty cherrywood lap desk monogrammed with the initials S.N. I was tempted to pull out letters and read them right on the spot, but efficiency demanded we organize the material first, separating the Northbury artifacts from the rest of the family belongings. If we didn't, we could be stuck in this storeroom for months.

"Ohhhhh—this is cool." Shamega wafted a red feather boa through the air, wrapped it around her neck, then struck a pose. In spite of her baggy pants, she looked exotic and decadent. She *didn't* look like someone who was ready to spend hours poking through musty old papers.

Firmly, I closed the top of the dilapidated suitcase she and Amanda were plundering, fastened the tarnished clasps, and hefted it over to the far corner of the room. "This is a serious endeavor we're engaged in here, kids. There's no time to mess around. Who knows if I'll ever have an opportunity like this again. Concentrate on Mrs. Northbury." A pasteboard stationery box caught my eye. I opened it. Eureka! Neat stacks of letters addressed to Mrs. Serena Northbury at an address on Fifth Avenue in Manhattan. My Northbury pile was growing.

At the end of two hours, Amanda, Shamega, and I had separated out a modest heap of Northbury belongings and were sprawled on the hall carpet, looking through boxes.

"Excuse me."

The voice was flat. I glanced up to see Gerry Novak carrying a glass pitcher of iced tea. My throat was dry from breathing in dust, and I smiled at the welcome sight. Gerry didn't smile back. "Dr. Hart thought you might like a cold drink in the parlor." His thin lips were pinched with disapproval. Had I done something wrong? Were you not supposed to smile at people who thought they were servants? I sighed. As always, the ways of the rich were a mystery to me.

Shamega and Amanda were deep into the contents of the hatbox, sorting out letters and organizing them into separate piles, but I welcomed a break.

Sitting in her armchair in the late afternoon light, Edith appeared refreshed by her nap. The vitality was back in her expression, and color had returned to her cheeks. She had changed from her flowered dress and wore dark green wool pants with a white knit pullover sweater open at the throat. The gold chain of her locket still circled her neck. Even though she was clearly not at her strongest, this lady managed to present herself with style. When she saw me, Edith smiled ruefully. "The most frustrating part of old age is that the body refuses to keep up with the mind," she said.

"That's better than the other way around," Will responded.

"Oh, absolutely." Edith's tone was fervent. "I don't even want to imagine what it would be like if the mind went." Her next words were only half in jest. "Don't *ever* let that happen to me, Will."

He took her thin hand between both of his. "You can count on me, Edie. You've always known that." Next to Edith he seemed robust, his body stocky, his shoulders wide.

She smiled up at him. "You're right; I always have." The look they exchanged spoke of decades of shared experience, and I realized that—in spite of Edith's prickly treatment of her old friend—the affection between these people was mutual and warm. I sighed, enviously. A random thought flitted through my mind. *Oh, Tony . . . What have I done?*

I'd been so interested in the scene before me that I'd forgotten about Amanda and Shamega and was startled when they burst into the room. "Professor Pelletier," Shamega cried, "look what I found!" The sheet of paper she waved at me was covered with the careful rounded penmanship I'd seen on the two or three Northbury letters I'd looked at.

"Mom," Amanda cut in, indicating a bundle of identical pages snug in the bottom of the blue hatbox she carried, "we think this is the manuscript for one of Mrs. Northbury's books."

"You're kidding!" I took the sheet Shamega held out to me. They weren't kidding. It was the opening page of a novel or story. *"Child of the North Star,* by Mrs. Serena Northbury," I read aloud. "Chapter One." I looked up. "I don't remember a book called *Child of the North Star.* Do you suppose the publisher changed the title?"

"Read. Read," Amanda said. That had been one of

her first commands when she was a toddler. *Wead, Mommy, wead.*

"Do, Karen," Edith Hart urged.

I settled back on the love seat and began to read aloud. *"The shrouded furnishings of the small attic room lent a dark and desolate air to Emily's sanctuary, for sanctuary it was, in spite of webs which hung the windows with filmy drapes of poverty and desperation. Poor Emily Westford. To have fallen so far, and all for love. Yet she was grateful even for this gloomy room in this forsaken mansion. Soon the time would come when no woman could bear to be alone, and here at last, Emmy had found a friend. But such a friend! In such a time! In such a place!*

"This doesn't sound familiar." I broke off, staring at the paper in my hand. "And I've read all of Northbury's novels, or at least all I could get my hands on—they've been out of print so long. And I've never even *heard* of *Child of the North Star.*" I raised my eyes to my small audience. Will sat in a straight chair he had pulled up next to Edith. Amanda leaned against the archway. Shamega had plopped down on the green Axminster rug.

"Go on. Go on." Edith seemed as enthralled by the tale as the girls were. Will simply looked bemused.

"Yes, Professor Pelletier, don't stop now," Shamega pled. Amanda nodded vigorously.

"You want me to read this to you? Aloud? Now?"

"Please do," Edith said, settling herself more comfortably in her chair. "A lost novel. What fun!"

I slipped a second sheet from the loosely tied string securing the packet of pages. "Well—here goes.

"There was a hesitant tapping at the ponderous door of Emmy's gloom-filled chamber. 'Enter,' Emmy called, and a small, dark girl came through the door carrying a cumbersome valise. With care, the weary child—for a child rather than a woman she seemed in this dim light—placed the bag on the clean but threadbare cloth covering a table by the narrow bed.

" 'Mrs. . . . ah . . . Mrs. . . . Westford, in your delicate condition you should not be standing. Let me help you off with that wet cloak and into clothes more suitable for this trying moment.'

" 'Call me Emmy, my dear girl, for who but you should have a sister's right?'

"The color rose on the young girl's dusky cheek. She stammered, 'But Miss . . . Mrs. Westford . . .'

" 'Emmy,' restated our fair heroine. 'And from this moment you alone know my true name, a name not now to be spoken otherwise than in this quiet room.' Her tone was firm. Her fate was clear, and she would live with love and courage the hard, hard life that lay ahead. 'And, perhaps,' she continued, 'nevermore in this terrestrial life to be spoken save but in a whisper. And never, never, to be borne by the poor innocent to be brought into the harsh world this very night.' With those words she fell, insensible, to the bare garret floor.

"My God," I said. "I believe this *is* a lost novel. Maybe one that was never published. And I think it's about an illegitimate birth. *No one* wrote about that in the nineteenth century. At least not respectable women like Mrs. Northbury—"

"Edie?" Will rose abruptly from his chair. "Are you feeling ill?" Edith was staring at me, her face ashen and blank of expression.

"Karen," Will directed, "quick. Get Edith some orange juice. I think she's going into insulin shock." The old pages flew from my lap as I jumped to do his bidding.

When I burst through the kitchen's double doors, Gerry Novak was seated at a well-scrubbed pine table, deeply engrossed in writing in a small spiral notebook. He looked up, startled. "Yes?" His voice was not welcoming.

"I need orange juice—for Edith. She's going into shock."

He leapt up, knocking his notebook off the table, and grabbed a tumbler from a glass-fronted cabinet. He poured the juice, and I reached out to take it, but he pushed past me into the hall. Before following him, I retrieved his notebook from the floor. The small page was covered with the much-reworked lines of what appeared to be a poem. In the brief glance I gave it before I replaced the book on the table, the block-shaped verse looked like a sonnet. *Huh,* I mused, *Servant Gerry is a poet. Who would have thought?*

Edith had recovered by the time I returned to the parlor. With Will's help, she slowly pushed herself to a sitting position on the chintz-covered couch where he and Gerry had carried her. Her color was better, having progressed from gray to merely pale, but I knew our presence was tiring her. It was time to go.

Sipping at the glass of juice, Edith said, "Karen, don't let this incident frighten you away. Will overreacted a bit. I wasn't really in shock; it was just a bit of a blood-sugar dip. Terrifying if you don't know what's happening—but manageable. And, as you see, Gerry knows just what to do for me. Don't you, Gerry?" She smiled up at him, and, when she received no response, turned back to me. "You've brought a new interest into my life, Karen, and I so much want you to continue your work on Mrs. Northbury."

"You just let me know when you feel up to having me here again, Edith. I am anxious to begin my research." I glanced over to where Gerry was gathering up the scattered pages of Mrs. Northbury's manuscript. "And—I'd love to have a copy of that manuscript. It sounds like such a departure for Mrs. Northbury—a sensation tale rather than a sentimental novel. Maybe it would even be publishable. Do you remember a few years ago there was a huge hue and cry made about a newly discovered Louisa May Alcott manuscript, *A Long Fatal Love Chase?*"

Edith nodded. Gerry stacked the manuscript pages neatly on the leather-topped side table.

"Well, it sold for something in seven figures and was published by a commercial press with a good deal of fanfare. And then two more manuscript novels were found. The most recent was *The Duke's Daughter,* which turned up in an attic in Concord. I've met Earl Wiggett, the guy who found that one, and edited it. He's a researcher, a kind of 'literary sleuth' he calls himself. And he made a bundle on the sale of that manuscript—two million dollars, I think. So there *is* a market." I laughed. "Of course, Serena Northbury doesn't have Alcott's ready-made twentieth-century audience. But, still—an unpublished sensation novel should attract *some* attention—a university press, at least."

"You've got me so intrigued, Karen," Edith replied. "I'd like to finish reading this story before you take it to copy. Then—of course you can have it; it would be absolutely lovely if you could get it published." She gave me an enigmatic smile. "A voice from the grave, so to speak. Telling the truth about a woman's experience, after all this time."

I glanced back into the parlor as I shepherded Amanda and Shamega into the wide front hall. As Will bent over Edith with a second glass of juice, Gerry Novak was deep in perusal of Mrs. Northbury's manuscript pages.

The final weeks of the semester descended on me with their heavy load of papers and exams, and it was three weeks before I could take a deep breath and think about Serena Northbury again. I handed my final grades to the Registrar on a showery Tuesday morning, then strolled back to my office, taking time to savor the faint perfume of spring, the delicate mid-May green of leaves beaded now with rainwater. The wonderful, long academic summer was at hand and I was about to do what I loved best—dig into the long forgotten past and tease it into coming alive again. I had two phone calls to make.

"Tess? It's Karen Pelletier."

"Karen! How *are* you?" Tess Holmes was my editor at Oxbridge University Press. Oxbridge had recently published my book on American writers and the constraints of class, and, so far, the reviews were good. Tess said the reviews were "glowing," but, of course, I'd never be immodest enough to repeat that to a living soul.

"Tess," I ventured, when we'd gotten past the greetings and the gossip, "I've got a project in mind that I'd like to run by you." And I told her about my idea for a Northbury biography. "A cultural biography, of course," I said, "looking not only at her life, but also at contemporaneous print culture and conditions of authorship."

"Hmm," Tess said. "Hmm. I like the idea. I like it a lot. Write up a proposal, Karen, and I'll run it by the Press Review Board."

I hung up with a smile. Tess Holmes always got what she wanted at Oxbridge; I had a publisher for the Serena Northbury biography. I picked up the phone again. Now I had good news for Edith Hart. The manuscript of *Child of the North Star* was enticing me back to Meadowbrook, but I was also looking forward to seeing Edith again; even in the short time I'd known her, I'd come to think of her as a friend.

A flat male voice—vaguely familiar—responded after two rings. "Hart residence." The greeting was abrupt. I remembered Gerry Novak's rudeness.

"Gerry? This is Karen Pelletier. Is Dr. Hart, ah, Edith available?"

"*Dr. Pelletier!*" The voice now sounded even more familiar—and absolutely astonished. "*What* on earth?—" Then silence. With dawning, horrific recognition, I realized it wasn't Gerry Novak who had answered the phone; rather it was someone I'd never—ever—expected to encounter in my life again.

"Lieutenant Piotrowski?" I was as flabbergasted as he was.

I had called the home of my new friend Edith Hart, and who had answered the phone but my old acquaintance, Lieutenant Piotrowski of the Massachusetts State Police, Bureau of Criminal Investigation. Homicide.

Eight

"I got your note about that radio program, Dr. Pelletier. I was pleased you remembered me."

At six foot three and a good eighth of a ton, Lieutenant Piotrowski would not be easy to forget. Even in his deliberately low-profile dark blue windbreaker, jeans, and Red Sox cap, he drew attention as he stopped at my booth in Fran's Kountry Kitchen outside of Greenfield. The flat, high cheekbones, the watchful brown eyes, the cropped hair, the massive shoulders, and some far more intangible essence—the general air of attentiveness and physical power, I guess—all clamored *police*. I liked the lieutenant, but I hadn't expected to run into him again. Ever. Academic life may be characterized by cutthroat competition, but I don't habitually require the services of a homicide cop.

"Hello, Lieutenant. Have a seat." I dabbed at my eyes with a paper napkin; I'd cried all the way up Route 2 on my way to meet Piotrowski. Edith Hart was dead. She'd died at home, in her sleep, apparently of natural causes. That's all Piotrowski would tell me on the phone. But there had to be more to it than that, or I wouldn't have found my old pal the lieutenant on the scene.

Piotrowski squeezed his bulk past the speckled orange Formica table and onto the orange vinyl bench. His gaze was speculative. "You were fond of the old lady, huh?"

"Yes, I was. I'd only known her a short time, but she was a wonderful woman. So, tell me—what were *you* doing at Meadowbrook? Is there some question about the way Edith died?"

But the lieutenant wasn't giving anything away. "How'd you come to be acquainted with Dr. Hart?"

I told Lieutenant Piotrowski about my plans to write a Northbury biography. "Edith was so interested—and so alive," I concluded. Tears squeezed past the eyelash dams. I mopped at them, futilely. "I know she was sick and very old; I know we all have to die sometime. . . ." I wiped my eyes again. The soggy napkin was disintegrating. I reached for another from the metal dispenser, but Piotrowski got to me first with a small cellophane packet. I'd never known him to be without tissues; for a homicide investigator, tissues must be a professional requisite. "I don't know why it's hitting me like this, Lieutenant; I really barely knew the woman. But I felt such an affinity with her. I just couldn't help thinking—if I'd had someone like her for a mother, my life would have been totally different."

"Yeah? Better?"

"Who knows? Maybe better. Different, anyhow. She was so alive, so certain, so experienced. So—unafraid."

"Your mother was afraid?"

Where was this conversation taking me? Nowhere I wanted to go. Especially not with this big cop. I sniffed, patted my cheeks dry with the tissue, made an attempt to pull myself together. "But I don't understand, Lieutenant, what *you* were doing at Meadowbrook? And why do you want to talk to *me?*"

Without responding, Piotrowski beckoned to the waitress, a skinny, raddled-looking woman in her early thirties with blond-streaked hair and an arrow-pierced heart tattooed on the back of her hand. The black letters on her white plastic nametag spelled *Lucy.* "Coffee," Piotrowski said, "cheeseburger, fries." He turned to me. "You had lunch, Doctor?"

"No. But I couldn't eat, anyhow."

"The same for her," he informed the waitress. "Coffee right away."

"Piotrowski!"

The waitress concentrated, her tongue between her teeth, as she laboriously recorded the order.

"Ya gotta eat," the lieutenant told me. "Ya can't go around on nothing but beer."

I followed Lucy with my eyes past the knotty pine paneling and the wall-mounted wagon wheels. She was still writing as she disappeared behind the counter and through the kitchen door.

"What's got into you anyhow?" Piotrowski demanded. "I never remember you drinking beer. And in the middle of the day . . ." The expression on the broad, square face was disapproving: Nice ladies don't get boozed up before sundown.

"It's none of your business what I drink, Lieutenant!" Now I remembered how annoying this man could be. I was about to tell him in rude language to *butt out,* when my gaze fell on the cellophane tissue packet, and I realized I didn't need tissues anymore. Piotrowski had me where he wanted me, irritated—and tear-free; I was now ready to talk rationally.

"Lieutenant, please don't keep me in suspense. I assume there must be something suspicious about Edith's—ah—Dr. Hart's death. What is it? Why are *you* involved?"

"You know anyone else in that house?" He still wasn't answering my questions.

"Well—yes, I met a couple of people. Gerry Novak; he's kind of a—I don't know—handyman and house-keeper. And maybe a bit of a nurse as well. Edith said he made it possible for her to live there in spite of her diabetes, so I assume he took care of her. You know—medication and stuff." I paused. "But he's weird, this guy. Quite weird."

"Really?" Piotrowski's expression was impassive. Only the infinitesmal lift of his beige eyebrows revealed any interest in what I had just told him.

"The only other person I met there was Will Thorpe, her former medical partner. He seemed to have been staying at Meadowbrook indefinitely."

"Thorpe hasn't been there for the past coupla days. Says he's been in Manhattan—working at some clinic. But he's the one who called us. Showed up at the house late last night and found the . . . er, and found Dr. Hart. Or so he says." He shrugged. "We'll follow up on all that, of course. So—this Novak guy's 'weird,' huh? What d'ya mean by that?"

"Piotrowski! I'm not saying another word until you tell me why you're in on this!"

The waitress deposited a heavy brown ceramic cup in front of Piotrowski. Steam curled off the surface of the coffee in a ghostly swirl. In front of me, she placed a second sweating mug of beer.

"You're on your second already?" Piotrowski's tone was sharp.

I looked at the glass in confusion. "No," I said. "I didn't order that."

The brown eyes were skeptical. *Right.* The lieutenant beckoned the waitress back to our table, then pointed at the beer.

"Yeah?" she queried. "Ya want another beer?"

"*Another* beer?" I responded. "No. And we didn't order that one."

"Oh, yeah, ya did."

"I did *not*—"

"Not you. Him. He ordered it for you." Lucy pointed a two-inch-long blue fingernail at Piotrowski. "He said, *the same for her*. I wrote it down." She yanked the green order pad from her apron band and consulted it. "Burger, fries, coffee for him. Beer for you. The same. The same as before."

"No, I meant . . ." Piotrowski straightened out the order—burger, fries and coffee for me, as well as for him. "Leave the beer," he said. "I'll drink it." The waitress departed, then returned almost immediately with a third mug of beer, which she placed in front of me.

"What's that for?"

"Well—if he drinks that beer, then you don't have your second one."

"Jeez," I said, when Lucy walked away carrying the third beer, shaking her head, still confused. "No tip for this one."

"Come on, Doctor." Piotrowski's words were indulgent. "She's a single mother with three kids, just trying to keep off welfare."

"You *know* her?"

Again he didn't answer my question. Instead, he said, "You, of all people, should be sympathetic."

The lieutenant knew all about my years of hustling burgers in truck stops as I'd struggled to support Amanda and put together a college education for myself. As a matter of fact, he knew far too much about me. He'd investigated my background a little over a year before when I was a suspect in the "unpleasant incidents" at Enfield College—i.e., the homicides. Thank God, I thought, that I wasn't involved in any way in Edith Hart's death—and that Enfield College was also free and clear.

"At least I was competent," I retorted. "When someone ordered a burger and coffee from me, they got a burger and coffee—not beer."

"Yeah, well, and now you're a college professor. . . ." His voice trailed off. He seemed preoccupied with his thoughts. "You know anything about medicine?" The question was abrupt.

"Medicine? Me? No. Amanda's taking some premed courses, and she talks about what she's studying. But that's all I know."

"Would you be able to give an injection?"

"No! Of course not! Why?"

"I shouldn't be telling you this, so keep it to yourself, will ya? That's maybe how your friend Dr. Hart died. By injection. Overdose of insulin."

"That could have been an accident—"

"Could of. But the Medical Examiner doesn't think so."

"Why not?"

"A lotta reasons. But mostly because she handled her own medication and she was so knowledgeable—a medical doctor and all."

"Suicide?" I hated to think of the possibility, but, being a physician, maybe she was all too aware of the physical deterioration ahead—the pain, the humiliation, the dependency.

The lieutenant raised his eyebrows. "No note. She seems like the kinda lady that would of left a note."

"Do you have any hard evidence of," I hesitated to say the word, "of—*murder?*"

"So far, just an injection mark in her arm, where there shouldn't been one."

"What do you mean?"

"The M.E. says her usual injection site was the abdomen, which he tells me is preferred for insulin shots 'cause absorption's faster. They don't do it in the arm anymore. In the M.E.'s preliminary opinion—and mine, too—we're dealing with a homicide here."

I was horrified. "And you think *I* might have given her an overdose?"

"No, not really." His voice was rueful. "You know I

gotta ask these questions. But I gotta tell you, Doctor, it was a real shock when I heard you on the phone. My first reaction was, oh, for God's sake, not again. When I think about how . . ." he searched for a word, "how—*embroiled*—you were in those homicides at the college . . . But I can't see anything here that would connect you. What motive could you possibly have? You say you only knew her a little while? Tell me about that."

The waitress slapped our burgers and fries on the Formica tabletop. "Anyone want another beer?" she asked.

Piotrowski carefully thanked her and said no. Lucy favored the lieutenant with a long, slow smile, before she turned on her heel and walked away. He noticed. Then he noticed me notice. A deep pink suffused his complexion. He became extremely businesslike, asking brusque questions, taking detailed notes, both on my acquaintance with Edith Hart, and on my observations about the members of her household.

We'd finished the burgers, and the lieutenant was making his way through a slice of apple pie and his third coffee, when, uncannily, an echo of Edith's voice encroached upon my memory: *Gerry knows just what to do for me.* And then, immediately, I recalled an intriguing piece of information that had, at the time, almost glanced off my brain. "Lieutenant, two things I just remembered. Gerry Novak *must* have been able to give injections." No visible response from Piotrowski. So I recited Edith's words, *Gerry knows just what to do for me,* and then continued, "And Dr. Thorpe said something about Novak that surprised me. He said Dr. Hart had put Novak through college, and that she supported his 'work,' whatever that might be. Poetry, I think. He said it in that solemn tone of voice people use when they talk about—um—starving artist kind of stuff. You know what I mean—*woorrk.*"

"Yeah? This old lady had cash, huh, a lotta dough?"

"Dr. Hart seemed to be a well-to-do woman." I told

him about Serena Northbury's best-sellers and the obviously well invested Northbury fortune.

"Money's good." Piotrowski looked up from his note-taking. "It's as good a motive for murder as anything. Along with family squabbles, sex, revenge, money's right up there on the top of the list. I guess I gotta look into this lady's financial situation, huh? And that stuff about Novak's interesting. What's the Thorpe guy's relationship to the victim? Aside from being her former partner, I mean."

I thought carefully about what I'd observed between Edith and Will. "He was in love with her. I think he always had been. For decades."

"Oh, yeah? At their age, huh? That's nice. Real nice." The lieutenant's expression grew sentimental. Then his beeper sounded, and he jumped up, all business again. When he came back from the phone, he threw some cash on the table. "Gotta get back there, Doctor. Thanks for the info. It was real helpful. Listen, don't let me worry you. In my opinion, you're completely clear here."

"Well, of *course,* Piotrowski!"

He grinned his rare thousand-megawatt grin. "Of *course,* of course." He slipped his wallet into his back pocket. "Ya know—it's been good seeing you again, Doctor. Talking to you is always, ah—different. Interesting, like."

"Yeah, you, too." I smiled back at him.

He stood in the narrow aisle, turning his Red Sox cap in his hands. The lieutenant seemed to be in no hurry to leave. "So, ya ever see Miss Warzek?" Sophia Warzek was a student I'd taken under my wing the previous year after a suicide attempt motivated by the death of a professor with whom she'd had an affair.

"I see her once in a while—mostly when Amanda's around. They've gotten to be really good friends. Sophia's doing okay. You knew she dropped out of school to take care of her mother?"

"Yeah. Too bad."

"Well, I know she'll finish. She's working full-time at the Bread and Roses Bakery, but she manages to schedule a course each semester. She'll graduate next year."

"Good. And how's Amanda?" The lieutenant had run into my daughter on several occasions the previous year. "You said she's planning on medical school? She'd be good at that. Coolheaded. Smart."

"Yeah—well—she's thinking about other things, too."

"Yeah?"

"Like—criminal justice . . ." My voice trailed off. I was not thrilled about this possibility.

"I knew it!" He slapped his hand down on the table. "I just *knew* it! She was so interested last year. Kept asking questions. And she'd be *damn* good."

"Yeah. I'm afraid she would."

He gazed at me, knowingly. "You've had enough of living with cops, huh?" When I didn't respond, he continued, "So—how *is* Captain Gorman? If ya don't mind my asking?"

"Tony's getting married." My curt tone put a twist on the statement I hadn't intended. The lieutenant instantly picked up on it.

"Oh, yeah? Whaddya know?" He knew not to take the discussion any further. "Well, if we don't run into each other again—hope things go real well for you, Doctor."

"Yeah, you, too, Lieutenant. *Real* well." I've always had a soft spot in my heart for big lugs like Piotrowski. Especially when they're as good at their work as he is— as single-minded, effective, and inescapable as a smart bomb.

And especially when I don't have to take them home with me.

On the way home, I pulled the car over by a roadside creek still swollen by melting mountain snow and scrambled down a rocky bank to the water's edge. Perched on a broad, flat boulder, hugging my knees, I stared at the swiftly moving stream and pondered the dilemma of life and death. *Our deepest feelings are animated clichés*, I thought, as the icy water bore its transient burden of leaves and twigs to the ocean's oblivion. The particular self that was Edith Hart was now gone. The elegant configuration of neural pathways that constituted a wise and well-lived life—gone. The experience, the memory, the compassion—gone. When another sudden spring shower sent me scuttling back to my car, I was no more enlightened than I'd been to begin with. Just a good deal wetter.

Nine

"You've got to *swear*," Jill said between sobs, "that you won't tell another living soul what I'm going to tell you."

"Jesus, Jill. What *is* it?" A frantic call on my home answering machine when I'd returned from the visit with Piotrowski had brought me speeding recklessly from my way-out-in-the-country house to Jill's Enfield apartment. *"Karen, where are you?"* was the message Jill had left in a high, quavering wail. *"I've got to talk to someone. Call me. Ohmigod, Karen. Call me—right away."*

"What *is* it, Jill?" I repeated, leaning back against the apartment door I'd just closed. I like Jill's place, with its funky retro furniture. It suits her—as if her whimsical, carefree personality had materially reproduced itself in purple lava lamps, lime green fiberglass drapes, and orange amoeba-shaped ashtrays. But I didn't notice any of that now.

"Swear you won't tell."

"Okay. I swear. I swear. What *is* it?"

Jill's eyes were huge and dark in a bone white, tear-streaked face. A firestorm of orange-gold curls fell across her shoulders, unrestrained by the usual flamboyant barrettes and ribbons. Even her normally crimsoned lips were bone-pale. She looked both terrified and sick. First I thought she must have suffered a death in the family. Then I wondered if maybe she'd contracted some horrific, life-threatening illness; she looked as if she might vomit at any moment, or faint.

I took her arm to lead her to one of the overstuffed chairs. As soon as she felt my touch, Jill flung herself into my arms and broke out in a shrill, prolonged, penetrating wail. There were words to it, but the only one I could make out was *father*.

"Your father, Jill? Something's happened to your father? Your father's dead?"

"Nooooo." She pulled away, collapsed into an aqua armchair, and dropped her head in her hands. Great racking sobs and another semiarticulate wail followed. This time I made out the word *baby*.

"A *baby's* dead?"

"Nooooooooo." She was furious enough now at my stupidity to raise her head and shriek at me: *"The father of my baby's been arrested for murder!"*

"What!" Then, "Shhh!" As baffled as I was by Jill's revelation, I was savvy enough about survival in Enfield to shut her up immediately. "Hush," I instructed firmly, as if I were talking to my daughter. "Hush, Jill. The neighbors don't need to hear this. You know what a gossip Kenny is."

Jill lives in what's known as the faculty ghetto, the dense concentration of college-owned housing in the heart of residential Enfield. Her sprawling apartment is made up of half the first-floor rooms of a converted Victorian on Josepha Street, two blocks from campus. Kenny Halvorsen of Phys. Ed. lives in the other half.

As I'd climbed the five steps to the spacious porch, I'd wondered, not for the first time, why I live where I do—in a small, characterless house on a nondescript road in a township that's lost whatever sense of community it once had, twenty minutes drive from the town of Enfield. When my knock on Jill's door instantaneously brought Kenny's face to a window overlooking the shared entrance, I remembered why. That twenty-minute drive kept me out of the fishbowl that is Enfield's social life. In my remote and charmless location I could do whatever I wanted without notice or comment. Too bad my life didn't include anything that would warrant notice or comment.

"Jill, let's go in the kitchen and talk about this. We'll have more privacy there, and I can make you a cup of tea."

Jill sat white and silent as I boiled water and brewed the tea. Sliding the yellow Fiestaware mug across the royal blue enamel tabletop, I took her cold hand and commanded, "Tell me about it."

Jill began sobbing again, in great hiccupping gasps. "I'm four months pregnant," she wailed, "and Gerry Novak is the baby's father, and the cops have just arrested him for murder." She ignored the mug of tea.

"What!" Edith Hart's Gerry Novak? I was stunned by each element of Jill's bombshell revelation: that she even *knew* Novak, let alone had had an affair with him; that she was pregnant; that Novak had been arrested. "Gerry Novak! How the hell do you know *him?*" And, oh, my God, *I* was the one who had sicced Piotrowski on him!

"I met him at the Iron Horse. He gives readings there sometimes. He's a poet. He's *very* good." This last assertion was made with defiance. "I've been seeing him since December—just before the holidays."

"Gerry Novak!" I couldn't get my mind around it; this vibrant, vital, young woman and that . . . *difficult,* I remembered Will Thorpe saying with a hint of asperity . . . *difficult* and dour man. "Why didn't you tell me?"

"Gerry didn't want anyone to know." She dabbed at her eyes. "He's a very private person. He told me he'd met you, but— Well—I wasn't supposed to say anything to you. Gerry hasn't had an easy life, Karen. He . . ." Then she seemingly thought better about saying anything more.

Sitting across the table from Jill, I realized I'd seen very little of her lately; the day she'd given me the copy of *Jane Eyre* was the last time we'd talked at any length. Other than that, there were just the usual public encounters—Women's Studies meetings, Curriculum Committee meetings. Come to think of it, I'd called her a couple of times, but she'd always had some reason not to get together, and the end-of-semester craziness had kept me so preoccupied I hadn't thought about her at all.

"What—are you going to do, Jill?" It was a delicate question, and I asked it delicately.

She stopped sobbing, gave me a straight, serious look. "I'm going to *keep* the baby, if that's what you're asking, Karen. I'm not so sure what to do about Gerry. He doesn't want a child. Said something about *another unwanted brat* and *history just repeating itself*. I love him, but he's . . ." She struggled for a word.

"Difficult?"

"Yes—he's difficult—very complex and pained." She wiped at her eyes. "But he's *not* a killer. He wouldn't have killed Dr. Hart; she was his—" This time she shut her mouth firmly, protecting Gerry Novak's privacy. Her eyes teared up.

"Drink your tea, Jill." Anything to keep her busy; I didn't want to have to deal with another attack of hysteria.

But she rubbed the tears away with a knuckle, and concentrated on tugging cotton threads from her fluffy pink bathrobe. When she spoke again, she was calmer. "Karen, to tell you the truth, I don't know if I want to spend my whole life with Gerry; that may be more of a challenge than I want to take on. But I *will* have his— our—child; I can certainly raise it by myself. And my baby's father is *not* a killer."

"What did he mean, Jill, when he said that about *another unwanted brat?*"

"It's not *unwanted;* I want it. I've been carrying this baby for four months; I love it—him, her—already."

"But what I mean is, he said *another . . .*"

But Jill wasn't answering any questions about Gerry; her mind was set on convincing me of his innocence. I wondered if perhaps she wasn't working on convincing herself.

I spent the night at Jill's place; she needed someone with her, and she refused to call her parents or her brother. And certainly, no one needed me at home—or was even expecting me. It was two years now since Tony and I had separated, and Amanda had gone off to Georgetown, but I still wasn't used to not having to report in. It should feel liberating to be that free, but, instead, it felt—incomplete. No partner, no daughter—just bumping around all by myself. Nothing wrong with that, I guess; I just wasn't used to it.

Jill did call *someone*—her shrink. She spent an hour and fifteen minutes on the phone with him, while I made scrambled eggs and toast, and she swallowed them down with the cordless phone tucked between her shoulder and her ear. She slept after that, and so did I—she in her big water bed and me on a lumpy gold plush sofa that hit me in awkward places with its small, hard upholstered buttons. I woke shortly after three A.M. with all my nerves jangling. Everything struck me at once: Edith was dead, probably murdered; Jill was romantically involved with Gerry Novak; Jill was pregnant with Gerry's child; Gerry had been arrested for killing the elderly physician—and possibly because of what I'd told Piotrowski. I was such a witless blabbermouth. I lay awake on the uncomfortable couch until dawn, fighting grief and anxiety. In the very short time I had known Edith, I had come to admire and respect her. Now she was dead. Jill was my friend, and I had unwittingly betrayed her. At dawn, I sat up on my unyielding bed and watched five programs of *Headline News* in a row.

When the phone rang at 9:10, Jill was in the shower. "Hello, Jill Greenberg's residence. Karen Pelletier speaking." The silence on the other end of the line was so extended I almost hung up, deciding that the caller was either a slow-off-the-mark telemarketer or a heavy breather. Then Lieutenant Piotrowski spoke: "I don't *fucking* believe this. Karen Pelletier! Again! I thought you told me you had nothing to do with this case."

"Piotrowski! For God's sake! What are you doing calling Jill?"

"What are *you* doing at her house?"

"I asked you first." I sounded like a six-year-old.

"It's not really your business why I'm calling Professor Greenberg, is it? But it *is my* business to know about suspects and their associates."

Of course—Gerry and Jill. Poor Jill; I'd been so stunned by her revelation, I hadn't thought of any implications of her situation other than how she was going to raise a child alone. "Piotrowski, listen to me, take it easy on Jill, she's—" I stopped. *She's trusting me to keep her secret—that's what she is.*

"What? She's *what?*"

"She's—in the shower. Take it easy on her, will you; she's very young." Jill wouldn't be able to hide her pregnancy forever, but I wasn't about to spill the beans.

"Weren't we all? Young, I mean. She'll get over it. And what d'ya think I'm gonna do, anyhow—stick lighted matches under her fingernails? You ought to know me well enough, Dr. Pelletier, not to jump to the conclusion that I *terrorize* people."

"Sorry, Lieutenant." And I was. When he'd dealt with my student Sophia the year before, I'd seen how gentle Piotrowski could be with vulnerable people. "I didn't mean to imply that. It's just that . . . there are special circumstances here."

"Yeah—I'll say. Homicide. Wouldn't you say homicide was a *special circumstance?* And you didn't answer my question: What are *you* doing there?"

"I'm a friend of Jill's, Lieutenant. And she got hyster—very upset when she found out about Gerry Novak. I hope you didn't arrest him solely on my word—"

"*Arrest* him? We haven't arrested anyone; we're just *interviewing* him. Novak wasn't cooperative on the scene, but, like we thought, a few hours in detention made him a little more—er—vocal. *Arrest* him? Jeez, Doctor! Now put Professor Greenberg on, willya? Please? And," the lieutenant cleared his throat before he said the next words, "looks like you and me are gonna have another chat, Doctor. I believed you, ya know, when you said you weren't involved in this, and now, look at you—smack dab in the middle. Again."

"I guess it's time for me to grow up now—isn't it, Karen?" A good night's sleep seemed to have given Jill a new sense of resolve. She couldn't tell me what Piotrowski wanted, other than that he was on his way to "ask her a few questions." As she prepared for his visit—and I prepared to get the hell out of the way—Jill wanted to talk about babies.

"It's just that I feel so young to have the responsibility of a child. How old were you when Amanda was born?" She pulled her hair back in a ponytail and secured it with a purple scrunchy.

I hesitated. I'd never talked to Jill about my past. I knew she couldn't even begin to comprehend life on the wrong side of the tracks in Lowell, Massachusetts, in the 1970's. "Nineteen," I replied, running a borrowed hairbrush through my hair, and securing the dark mess with a borrowed clasp.

"Nineteen! For God's sake, Karen; whatever possessed you to have a baby that young?" Her green eyes were incredulous. As if I'd had choices.

"I had sex. I got pregnant."

"But why didn't your parents—"

"I've got Amanda, Jill. She's the best thing in my life. That's all I care about. I don't want to talk about anything else. Especially not about my parents."

"But—"

I gave her a cold, level stare. No one was going to get me to talk about my early life. No one.

"Okay—don't get huffy." She grinned at me; I was relieved to see a little spunk. "Nineteen, huh. Well, if you could do it, I can do it. My folks'll help out financially; there's day care here at the school . . ." And she was off, making plans for the future. This was going to be one hell of a privileged single-parent family; I could see that already. Jill would probably have the kid enrolled in Harvard before it was born.

When I left Jill's place and was crossing the wide, white porch with its hanging pots of fern and ivy, the door to Ken Halvorsen's apartment opened, and Jill's neighbor emerged. Ken was as blond and solid as usual, and his customary outfit of blue Enfield sweats did nothing to detract from the air of physical strength and prowess that had earned him, among student athletes, the nickname of The Incredible Blue Hulk.

"Is Jill okay, Karen? Last night I couldn't help but hear her crying. She sounded so—upset, I almost came over, but then I saw you arrive. I knew you'd take care of her."

It was all I could do to keep from sighing with exasperation. Kenny took a lively interest in the doings of his faculty fellows; the gossip mills would be churning today: Jill Greenberg hysterical, Karen Pelletier spending the night. But, at this moment, he looked genuinely concerned.

"She *was* upset over something, Kenny; but she's fine, now." I paused, then decided to appeal to his worried frown. "I know I can count on you to keep this to yourself, Ken. Jill needs a little time to get over—well, whatever—and nobody needs to know she was so—distraught. You know?"

"I hear what you're saying, Karen. I hear you. And I'll keep an eye out for her; Jill's a bit of a nut, but she's always been awful nice to me."

"Thanks, Ken." I took another look at this blond hunk; maybe behind the muscle and the macho and the well-filled blue sweats lurked the contours of a decent guy.

Ten

"I was in the neighborhood, Doctor. Didn't have a chance to let you know I was coming. Sorry."

Lieutenant Piotrowski wasn't alone as he strode brusquely through my front door two days later at the rude hour of nine A.M.; he was accompanied by an extremely plain young woman wearing black jeans and a forest green twill jacket. I'd lived with a cop long enough to note instantly the slight bulge of the shoulder holster concealed under her loose-fitting jacket. I brushed Piotrowski's introduction aside; I knew this woman right away.

"I remember Trooper Schultz," I said.

"It's Sergeant Schultz now." Her rejoinder was curt. Felicity Schultz, working undercover on a protection detail, had saved my life the previous year, but I knew she didn't like me. On the trail of a killer, she had shadowed me for a few days. Since Piotrowski hadn't seen fit to inform me he had protection on me, I'd become annoyed by the persistent little busybody who seemed to show up everywhere I went. And, unfortunately, I didn't hide my irritation; Officer Schultz had found me "arrogant and rude," Piotrowski had later announced.

So what was she doing here now?

And why was Piotrowski here? When he declined my offer of coffee, the creeping fingers of trepidation began playing up and down my spine. I make good coffee, and he knows it. And I'd never seen the big cop turn down *any* offer of sustenance.

When the lieutenant lowered his bulk onto the worn black recliner in my living room, Sergeant Schultz perched on the edge of a straight oak chair and pulled out a notepad. She began writing immediately, and I knew she was recording the date, location, and purpose of their visit. This looked increasingly like an official interview. The fingers of trepidation ceased their creeping and clutched—hard. What in holy hell was going on here? I was instantly sorry I had chosen a seat on the couch. The soft cushion sagged under me, and I seemed to be sitting at least six inches lower than either of the police officers. I felt like a little girl in the presence of stern adults.

"Lieutenant?" I queried, apprehensively. "You're scaring me. What do you want?"

Piotrowski leaned forward in the large chair, his hands clasped lightly between his knees. He was more formally dressed today than he'd been at Fran's Kountry Kitchen, wearing a gray tweed jacket, black flannel slacks, and a blue Save the Children tie. Despite his size, he looked fit, as if he worked out on a regular basis. Piotrowski had been on a diet when I'd known him the year before, and although there was still a great deal of poundage there, the word *fat* didn't come to mind.

"One," he said, holding up a forefinger, as if he were about to tick off items on a list. "Your call to Meadowbrook on the day of Dr. Edith Hart's death." He tilted his head and granted me a straight, unblinking stare.

I shrugged.

"Two." A second finger came into play. "Your presence at Professor Jill Greenberg's apartment the morning I called to arrange an interview with her about her—er—boyfriend's activities." The beige eyebrows rose, the tilt of the head became more suggestively pronounced.

I shrugged again.

"Three—"

"Three?" I sat up as straight as I could on the soft couch. "How can there be a three? Nothing else has happened."

"Three," he repeated, firmly. His ring finger joined the other two digits. "Dr. Edith Hart's last will and testament."

I could feel my eyes widen. "Her will?"

"Her will. Of which we found a copy in her papers." His three raised fingers repositioned themselves contemplatively at his lips. "Yes. Quite an interesting will, as a matter of fact. Have you seen it?"

"No. Of course not."

"Did Dr. Hart speak to you about it?"

"No!" I was getting annoyed now. "Why the hell would she? I hardly knew the woman."

"So you said." The words came from Sergeant Schultz, sitting upright on her straight chair. I'd forgotten she was there, recording everything in her little book. "So you said."

I turned in her direction. "Yes? So I said. Is there a problem with that?" Even I could hear the edge in my voice.

"No," Piotrowski chimed in. "No problem, Doctor." He gave Schultz a hard look. "Is there, Schultz?" She dropped her eyes to her notes, and began writing again. Her lashes were long and dark in an oval face. A slow flush brought color to her cheeks, prompting me to take a prolonged second look at Piotrowski's new sidekick. Hmm, I thought, with a little makeup and the right clothes, this woman could be quite attractive. But given the brutal way her chestnut hair was chopped off and the stark plainness of her wardrobe, Sergeant Felicity Schultz seemed determined to fade into the woodwork. In her line of work, invisibility was probably far more useful than beauty. I wouldn't have forgotten the presence of a beauty the way I'd allowed the unremarkable Felicity Schultz to slip from my mind. But all the time she'd been sitting there, upright on her uncomfortable chair, observing, coming to conclusions, taking notes. And—it would seem—distrusting me.

"What about Dr. Hart's will, Lieutenant? Why do you think I might have seen it?"

"Tell me again about your relationship with the victim." Piotrowski was expert at evading questions. "Begin at the beginning and tell me everything."

I sighed, sat back in my soft burrow of cushions, and began to talk. I told the detectives about Mrs. Northbury's copy of *Jane Eyre* in great detail—even to the photograph of the baby stuck between the pages.

"Can I see it?"

"The book?"

"The picture."

"Why?"

"You know me: just nosy."

"I gave it to Edith."

"Really?" He swiveled toward Schultz. "Sergeant, we come across anything like that at the victim's place?" I flinched at his casual use of the word *victim*.

"No." In the single syllable, the sergeant managed to convey absolute skepticism about my story. *No, sir, we sure didn't.*

I glanced at her out of the corner of my eye. Ms. Prim and Proper. Butter wouldn't melt. Etc. Etc.

"I visited Edith twice, Lieutenant." My best option was to ignore the sergeant completely. "We talked about her great-grandmother; we talked about women's literature; we talked about Mrs. Northbury's manuscript. By the way, what'd you do with that manuscript, Lieutenant?"

"What manuscript?"

"Mrs. Northbury's book manuscript. *Child of the North Star*. A bulky thing, handwritten, tied with string. We found it in one of those ancient boxes—a blue hatbox. Edith was going to pass it on to me when she finished reading it. I thought it might be publishable."

"Sergeant? Sound familiar?"

"No." But Schultz looked thoughtful. "There were a few handwritten pages in her bed—under the blankets. Four . . . maybe five. Six? We didn't know what to make of them. Old paper. Brownish ink—"

"That's right," Piotrowski broke in. "Six pages—but not consecutive. Bits and pieces of something."

"Were they part of a novel?" I was leaning forward now, anxious. Edith's death was bad enough. The loss of her ancestor's novel would compound the tragedy. "A story of a woman about to give birth?"

"They didn't make any sense to me." Piotrowski was gazing at me contemplatively, his expression impenetrable. "And there's so much stuff in that house—we didn't pay much attention to a few loose pages. At least I didn't. How about you, Sergeant? You look at those documents closely?"

She spread her hands, shrugged. "But being as they were found with the body, they're in Evidence."

Piotrowski rose abruptly. "Okay, Doctor. Come along with us."

"Where are we going?"

"Headquarters."

I froze. Headquarters? Were they arresting me? "I want to call my lawyer." I rose from the saggy couch with a futile attempt at dignity. "I'm not going anywhere until I call my lawyer." I was bluffing; I didn't have a lawyer.

"Dr. Pelletier," the lieutenant's smile was slow and amused, "you don't need a lawyer. Not unless you want someone real pricey to look over some manuscript pages with you."

. . .

Six sheets of paper in Serena Northbury's careful, rounded handwriting lay in front of me on the long, scarred table in the BCI Evidence Room. They were numbered in the top center of each page, and I arranged the pages in order: 23, 24, 179, 180, 432, 434. Centered under the half page of script on 434 were the words *The End.*

"This is it, Lieutenant," I said. "At least these pages look identical to those in the manuscript I saw. The handwriting is Northbury's; the paper and ink look the same; there was a character in the novel named Emmy."

" 'Zat so?" Piotrowski ruminated. "So—maybe we did overlook this manuscript. That possible, Schultz?"

Her expression was implacable. "It's a big place. Lots of stuff there. A whole room full of boxes of dusty books and papers on the first floor alone. I s'pose it's possible we missed it." An unspoken message passed between the two officers, then the sergeant left the room. I watched Schultz's retreating back. I would have bet anything she was making ready to head back to Meadowbrook to do a follow-up search.

"Or," the lieutenant continued, more to himself than to me, "maybe somebody took it." His gaze raked over me, then slid to the pages in front of me. Then he glanced up at me again. "Look 'em over, Doctor. Then we can have a long talk. A long, literary talk." He leaned backward in his battered wooden chair; the front legs rose from the floor. For a second I was riveted; would two spindly legs hold the policeman's great weight?

"Read," he said. "I don't have all day."

—23—

. . . in a leafy copse on the hillside.
The child's eyes widened with wonder at the

sight of the vine-covered summerhouse. "Pitty," she said. "Pitty. Lizzie want go in."

Emmy placed her hand lovingly on the golden haze of her young daughter's curls. If ever a child was loved by nature, it was surely she. The amber hue of her skin in the summer sun and the halo of scarce more golden curls: Yes, surely she was as much nature's child as if all of nature's benison had gone into her begetting.

At the thought, it was as if a morsel of sky detached itself from the general cerulean and fluttered toward the pair waiting in the leafy arbor. "Butta-fwy," cried the child. "Oh, catch it, Muvver, do."

The ethereal winged creature evaded Emmy's grasp, but circled little Lizzie's head, as if inscribing a halo of blue around the airy golden one, brushed briefly against the rounded cheek, then vanished at the cherub's joyous laugh. "Muvver, Muvver. The sky give kisses, jess like you."

Emmy clutched her daughter to her throbbing breast while tears fell like Niagara. If only . . .

I came to the end of the page and looked up, the leafy bower vanished, replaced by the institutional green walls and the metal shelving of the BCI Evidence Room. Piotrowski was staring at me. "Doctor? You all right? You look like you're gonna bawl."

"I do *not*. And don't use that word; I never *bawl*."

Page 24 swam just a little as I dropped my gaze back to the old manuscript pages. But I'd be damned if I'd let this, this—yahoo—see me misty-eyed. I read on: *she were mine to glory in before the world, I would die a happy woman.*

"So, what'd ya think?" The detective's question cut through my sentimental haze.

"I've read one page, Lieutenant. I don't think anything yet. Except, maybe . . ."

"Maybe what?" He was still leaning back in his chair, and with Sergeant Schultz out of the room his expression seemed to have relaxed a little. But he was still sharp with his questions.

"Well, this is stupid, I know . . . But here goes." Piotrowski nodded in encouragement. "This seems to be a sensation novel—"

"What's a sensation novel?"

"In the nineteenth century that would have been a story about—well, illicit happenings—you know, dark, wicked deeds: adultery, murder, theft, opium fiends, wrongful imprisonment—"

The policeman snorted. "Reality. A story about *reality*."

"Yeah," I responded, with a wan smile, "right. It must seem that way to you. And, although I've only read a few pages, I'd bet my buttons that this book is about an illicit love affair and an illegitimate child. What they would have called a *love child*."

"So? That stuff's on the best-seller list all the time. Why would anyone want *this* manuscript?"

"Now this is where it gets a little shaky. But—you remember I said this novel might be publishable?"

"Yeah?"

"When I talked to Dr. Hart about that, I was thinking of maybe publishing it with a university press, for circulation among scholars and students. Interesting—but no big deal. Very little money in the academic world, you know? But then I got to thinking—"

"Yeah?"

"Lieutenant, do you follow publishing at all?"

"You kidding?" He looked as astonished as if I'd queried him about a passion for exotic orchids.

I told him about the three recent Alcott publications

I'd mentioned to Edith. "I met the editor of one of them once—Earl Wiggett, his name is. He's always on the lookout for old manuscripts with commercial value. Spends his time poking around in libraries and attics for anything he can edit and sell. And he really hit pay dirt with Alcott's *The Duke's Daughter*. Got a two-million-dollar advance for it. He got me thinking—I mean, *thinking* about him got me thinking, I mean—well, anyhow—I *suppose* it's possible there could be some real money involved."

"Two million, huh?" Piotrowski's eyes widened. "Like I said before, money's always good. Who would benefit from the sale of this here Northbury manuscript?"

"I don't know. You're the one who's seen Edith's will. Who inherits?"

Piotrowski's expression shut down abruptly. Then the door flew open, and Sergeant Schultz stood framed in its blocky shadow. "Lieutenant, may I have a word?"

The front legs of Piotrowski's chair clattered on the gray tile floor, and he rose with a surprisingly fluid motion for such a large man. "Keep reading, Doctor. I'll be back."

With the lieutenant gone, I settled into the story again. Northbury's sentiment always gets to me, and she was in rare form here.

Emmy lingered at the airy summer house, pierced by memory, then, resolutely, she took the trusting little hand and led Lizzie away, toward the great house so far below.

"Muvver, must you go?" The child's forlorn words lingered, hung heavy in Emmy's heart, as the stage wended its route down the treacherous mountain road away from Brookside. There were tears in Emmy's eyes, tears for the beautiful soul she feign must leave behind. Alas, an-

other long year must pass while she labored in the vineyards of the wide, wide world before the bright face of her dear child would light her pathway once again.

The flaming beauty of the autumnal country through which the four great horses carried the fragile coach with its human freight of hope and sorrow did nothing to distract the destitute mother's thoughts, until, passing slowly through a quaint, neat village of the kind so frequently found in our New England countryside, her eyes happened to fall upon a small group of foot-weary, travel-worn wayfarers headed resolutely northward. Emmy's involuntary exclamation of surprise drew the attention of a tall, stalwart figure in the group, whose dark gaze was drawn magnetically to Emmy's hopeful stare. A stern look from the black eyes of the wanderer, a near imperceptible negation in the movement of his dark head, and the troubled woman dropped her eyes, retreating into her customary silence, and the stage passed on. But, reader, is this a look of glee we see in—

Here the page ended, and I looked up, frustrated. *Was it glee?* I'd bet anything it was. But why? Unless I found the rest of the manuscript, I'd never know. Dammit! Maybe one of the remaining pages would give me some clue. I was reaching for page 179 when Sergeant Schultz entered the room and plucked it from my hand, then briskly swept the other pages up from the table in front of me.

"Okay, Dr. Pelletier. That's enough for today."

"Sergeant, you dragged me all the way down here. The least you could do is let me finish reading this thing."

She shook her head. "Nope."

"Why not?"

"I'm not required to give you any reasons." Her plain face was expressionless.

"Couldn't you let me have photocopies?"

"Nope."

"Where's Piotrowski?" By now, I was furious.

"Had to rush off. This isn't our only case, you know." This woman really knew how to hold a grudge; the chip on her shoulder must have weighed twenty pounds. "And in the lieutenant's absence, I'm in charge here."

Oh, Jeez!

"And," she continued, "while I am not free to disclose factors of the case which would make it clear to you why I think it is procedurally inadvisable for you to have further access to this evidence, I do feel it necessary to advise you that, in spite of your—ah, acquaintance— with the lieutenant, you are not free and clear in this investigation."

I sputtered, but she overrode my protest. "As a matter of fact, I'm requesting you give us consent to search both your house and office—"

My exclamation of outrage cut off her words. Impassive as a statue, Schultz loomed over me, clutching the document envelopes. "If for some reason, Dr. Pelletier, you don't wish to give us permission to search, I can easily request warrants. Just let me know if that's the case, and I'll get on my way." Any minute now, she was going to start tapping her foot like an impatient schoolmarm.

"Just tell me, Sergeant." I rose from my chair and stood directly facing her. She squared her shoulders, and I had a sudden impression that my additional height— about two inches above her five six—intimidated her. The sergeant stuck her chest out, displaying to maximum advantage the gun bulge under her green twill jacket. "Just tell me, does Piotrowski know about this?"

It was the first smile I'd seen from her, and it was smug. "The lieutenant says you are so *impassioned*," she paused so the term would have time to sink in, *"impassioned* about literature, that he couldn't one-hundred-percent guarantee that if an old manuscript just happened to come your way you wouldn't *for all the best reasons in the world,* he said, avail yourself of the opportunity to acquire it. Thus," she concluded, "tampering with evidence."

I groaned. "Sergeant, I'm not stupid; if I was going to do that, I'd never have told you about the manuscript in the first place. And why the hell don't you search Meadowbrook? You're much more likely to find it there—where it belongs."

"For your information, Dr. Pelletier, no one thinks you're stupid. Quite the opposite. And we haven't forgotten Meadowbrook. Now I'd appreciate if you'd sign these," she picked up two printed consent forms from a small table and waved them at me, "then find yourself something to do until we've finished looking through your house and office." The sergeant's words were cool, but her cheeks were flushed. It must be awfully difficult to be a cop when you color up so easily.

"I'll sign your damn forms." I snatched them from her hand, and scrawled ferociously with the ballpoint she handed me. "But I have every right to be in my home and office while you're there, and I absolutely insist—"

Sergeant Schultz shrugged. "Come along." Her attitude implied, *No skin off my butt.*

"You're not going to find anything other than stacks of boring scholarly notes, but I want to go on record as protesting this."

"Oh, you will, Dr. Pelletier." She waved the forms in the air, drying the ink. "Believe me, you will."

I spent the afternoon in doorways, raging inwardly, watching with a hawk's glare as uniformed officers combed through my desk and file cabinets, my dishes and lingerie, for anything that might possibly resemble a missing novel manuscript.

As they drove away from my house, I watched from

the front porch until the cruisers were out of sight. My hand was on the doorknob before I remembered Piotrowski's questions about Edith Hart's will. I'd been so engrossed in the problem of the missing manuscript and in my anger about the search, I'd completely forgotten the will. I turned to call to Schultz, but her blue sedan had already backed out of the driveway, and the sergeant's eyes were on the road ahead of her. I considered jumping into my car and following her, but a wave of exhaustion swamped me. Instead, I sank into a chair at the kitchen table, lowering my head into my hands.

I have to admit that, after working so closely with Piotrowski when murder had last struck Enfield College, I was more irritated than frightened to find myself on the other end of the lieutenant's investigative efforts. I knew I had nothing to do with any homicides—and I was certain he knew it, too. But his new partner had it in for me, and she was in a position to make my life miserable.

Eleven

The bedside clock read 9:47 A.M. as I awoke and grabbed for the phone. " 'Lo?"

"Am I speaking to Karen Pelletier?" The voice was cultured and familiar—and thick with some indefinable emotion.

"Yes?"

"Karen, this is Willis Thorpe. Are you planning on attending the services today?"

Services? My brain had not yet begun to function.

He must have sensed my confusion. *"Funeral* services? For Edith?"

"I didn't know about them." I was conscious enough now to feel my heart suddenly weighted with sorrow. The ceremony made Edith's death more final.

"Gerry was supposed—" The elderly doctor clicked his tongue in annoyance. "Oh, well, no matter. I do hope you'll be able to come? A *small* funeral . . ." He said *small* as if it would make the event more bearable.

"Of course, I'll come—"

"With a few people to the house afterward. It would

be nice if there could be one or two Edith actually liked. You'll come, then? She would be so pleased." He sounded burdened—with grief, I thought. Poor man; he had truly loved her.

"Willis, I'm so sorry for your loss. I know how much she meant to—"

"It's for the best." His tone became unexpectedly brusque. "The life ahead of her was not a quality life. She wouldn't have been able to bear it. Not Edith. Not given who she was, what she needed. Better she go now—with dignity."

"But still—it's so sad. And the police say—"

"The police don't know what they're talking about. I'll see you at Maguire's Funeral Home in Eastbrook, then, at two?"

To my astonishment, a small Enfield College contingent occupied white folding chairs in the funeral parlor chapel. A bank of roses, gladioli, and lilies flanked the open casket where Edith Hart lay. I'm not certain if it was the sight of my new friend lying there so white and still that choked me, or the scent of flowers heavy in the air, but I had to pause in the doorway a second or two before I could bring myself to enter the room. Then, as I passed through the open double doors, my eye was caught by a blaze of vivid color in the muted palette of the congregation. Jill Greenberg? What the heck? And dressed in sober gray, with only the flame of her bright hair to make her usual flamboyant statement? I blinked to clear my vision. Yes, there in the front row, Jill Greenberg sat next to Gerry Novak, who sat alongside Dr. Thorpe. The closest thing Edith had to family, I mused. So sad. But it wasn't only Jill's presence that stunned me; if I'd thought about it at all I might have expected to find her there. What really blew my mind was the Brewster family. Directly behind the Novak-Thorpe row sat Thibault, Tibby Two, and Mrs. Brewster, black clad, and as straight and solemn as crows on a fieldstone wall. What in hell were the Brewsters doing at Edith Hart's funeral?

As I stared at them speculatively, a strong hand gripped my upper arm. A deep voice murmured, "Karen? What on earth are *you* doing here?" I jerked around and came face to face with—Avery Mitchell, for God's sake! The chapel organ began the sonorous tones of "Abide With Me," and Avery quickly steered me to a seat in the back row. Then, with a practiced twist of the wrist, he flipped open a hymnbook. As his rich baritone boomed out "Aaaa-bide with me-ee, fast falls the e-ven-ti-i-ide," I struggled to keep my eyes front forward. I was here to pay my last respects to an accomplished and passionate woman, not to gawk at Avery. He poked the hymnbook in my direction; evidently I was supposed to sing too. *Oh, God.* Taking a tentative grip on a corner of the scarlet book, I was quavering, "Cha-ange and decay, in all around I see-ee," when Lieutenant Piotrowski slipped quietly into the row ahead of us. *Jesus!*

At the sight of Piotrowski, Avery, who had met him during the Enfield incidents, glanced at me questioningly. My shrug was intended to suggest profound existential bafflement. The frown lines between Avery's eyebrows deepened. He was too smart to assume this cop was simply a member of the family.

Will Thorpe's eulogy was short and heartfelt. He'd known Edith for over fifty years, since they'd met in medical school. She was a woman ahead of her time, a committed care-giver whose passion for the deprived had carried her safely through some of the most dangerous decades and neighborhoods of a hazardous time in a hazardous city. "At a time when birth control was illegal in New York," Will said, "Edith risked her professional credentials to assure that women in her care had access to basic contraception. More than one young family owed its health and well-being to Edith Hart, and in some cases her care went well beyond the medical. A number of the women and children who benefited from her concern have kept in touch with her. Some are here today."

Listening to him speak of his old friend with such quiet emotion, I recalled Will's tender treatment of her during my short visits. I remembered the full-blooded vitality of the youthful Edith in the photograph he had scrutinized so wistfully. Then his half-teasing debate with Edith about ordinary love versus extraordinary love came back to me. Suddenly I grew cold with horror. This subdued but moving eulogy was motivated by a deep passion and abiding love. How far would Will Thorpe have gone to save his beloved old friend from the degradation and humiliation of pain and dependency? How *extraordinary* was his love?

My gaze was drawn to the back of Piotrowski's sturdy neck. Could he be entertaining the same speculations? If he was, the massive spread of gray tweed in front of me kept its own counsel. I sighed; there was no keeping anything from the lieutenant. If I'd thought of it, he had, too.

My eyes slid back to Avery. He listened attentively to the eulogist, the cool blue gaze clear and thoughtful. I still didn't know what he was doing at this funeral, but I found this man's physical proximity all the more alluring in the presence of the hard reality of death. The cold body at the front of the chapel; the warm, lean body so close I could reach out and run a hand down—I yanked my attention back to the funeral rites, clasped my hands demurely in the lap of my dark blue dress, and concentrated fiercely on the service. Some hungry little voice whispered: *But life is so very short and the perfume of flowers so rich in this sweet, close air.* I ignored it.

When Gerry Novak rose to give the final eulogy, the small group shifted and murmured. This man was the son Edith Hart had never had, and she had treated him well. What more fitting occasion for him to express his love and gratitude? Gerry's frizzy blond hair was pulled back into a short ponytail. He was dressed in an old khaki suit. It was the first time I'd seen him wearing anything other than jeans, and he had a sort of shabby dignity as he moved to the lectern.

"All the bastard world," Gerry began, "cries out to the child of innocence."

Avery's head jerked; he stared, first at Gerry, then at me, startled by the breach of decorum.

"He's a poet," I muttered.

Avery's expression registered instant comprehension. *Oh, Christ. He's a poet. God knows* what *he's going to say.* I could almost see his Episcopalian soul cringe. I was brought up Catholic; nothing fazes me.

Gerry placed both hands on the lectern and repeated the first line.

> *"All the bastard world cries out to the child of*
> *innocence.*
> *Railroad ties and the long scaffolding of*
> *trestles*
> *Serve baptism, and confirmation*
> *waits. Give me my name."*

He stood braced against the lectern for an excruciating ten seconds after he'd finished declaiming the brief verse, gazing enigmatically at his shocked audience. Then he returned to his seat next to Jill, his pale face impassive.

The congregation took a unanimous breath, the first since he'd begun speaking.

As we filed by the flower-flanked coffin to say a final farewell, my attention was caught by Edith's gold filigree locket. She'd worn it on one of my visits, and I had the same sense then that I had now: This heart-shaped trinket reminded me of something I'd seen somewhere else, but, frustratingly, the memory wouldn't shake itself loose.

• • •

Since Avery hadn't been to Meadowbrook before, I rode with him to show the way. Dark gray Volvo sedan, leather interior, CD player, Mozart sonatas: The man had taste as well as money.

Avery had learned just that morning that Enfield College had received a bequest in Edith Hart's will. "I'll get the details later, Karen, maybe even this afternoon, but from what her attorney told me, it's a sizable sum. I thought it only right for me to attend the services and pay my respects."

"Now, why would she leave money to Enfield College?" I wondered aloud. "It must be because of her great-great-grandfather." Avery cut a mountain curve sharply, and I grabbed hold of the door handle.

"Sorry." He favored me with a rueful grin. "And who was her great-great-grandfather?"

"The Reverend Edmund Pinkworth."

"Ah—a founder. Yes. That makes sense, then. I had no idea what the connection was—this bequest from out of the blue. Not that we can't use the money. . . ."

"Enfield College? Having financial problems?" My smile let him know I was joking; the college is noted for the amplitude of its endowment. We turned the corner to the Meadowbrook drive.

"Well, not so you'd notice; our financial base is quite solid. But every once in a while something comes up. . . ." His vague tone told me that was as much insider information as I was going to get. Then he exclaimed, "Christ! This is magnificent!" We had just topped the ridge and gotten a glimpse of the house. "Is that Meadowbrook?"

"Yes." The woods were in first leaf, now, and daffodils dotted the fiery verdancy of early spring grass. Meadowbrook rode its sea of green and yellow like a stately ship voyaging through time rather than through ocean waves.

"Very, *very* nice." Avery's assessing gaze as he pulled up under the porte cochere and allowed an attendant to open the car doors impressed me with its air of acquisition. Was it possible Edith had left Meadowbrook itself to Enfield College? True, she had mentioned no living relatives, but that didn't mean she had none. And why Enfield? She hadn't showed any particular fondness for the school—or for the Reverend Mr. Pinkworth—in our brief conversations. She'd been much more interested in what I'd told her about Mrs. Northbury's work—and about women's writing in general. Walking up the steps to the porch, I sighed. Them that has, gets: business as usual. And college presidents, by job description, were in the business of getting. Avery held the front door open for me, and I gave him a long, appraising look; occasionally my rational mind pierced the erotic cloud, and I realized how very little I really knew about this gorgeous man.

The Brewsters had preceded us to Meadowbrook, and Thibault met Avery and me at the door. "Avery. Karen." His expression was guarded. "I wasn't aware either of you were acquainted with Aunt Edith." *Aunt Edith? Brewster was Edith Hart's nephew?* Well, that would explain the Brewster family presence at the funeral, but, still, it was almost impossible for me to conceive of a family connection between this stiff patrician and the vital woman I had come to know. "How very nice of you to attend the service," Brewster continued. His words were not a welcome, but a coded interrogation: *What the hell are you doing here? Is it possible either of you has your hooks in dear old Aunt Edith's estate?*

Avery smiled coolly at Brewster. "Hello, Thibault. Sorry for your loss." If he was just now learning of the family connection, it didn't show. I emulated his WASP aplomb, nodded, offered soft condolences.

Brewster introduced us to his wife, who, strained and pale under her hostess demeanor, motioned us toward a table in the dining room. Mrs. Brewster was even thinner than the time I'd seen her in the college coffee shop with Tibby. Was this wan emaciation the newest wrinkle in Fifth Avenue chic? Or did this woman suffer from something more severe than trendiness? Perhaps an eating disorder? I shrugged. The afflictions of the elite were of no concern to me.

Before Avery and I reached the dining room, Thibault waylaid my companion with a hand on his arm, and I went into the room alone. There I found Tibby, loading a plate with small triangular ham sandwiches, and salmon mousse on wheat bread fingers. "Professor," he said in cool acknowledgment. He had earned a C-minus in my course, and grades had been mailed yesterday. Had he gotten his yet? One of the first pieces of wisdom I'd been offered at Enfield College was that, in this fortress of intellectual prestige, a C was a "suing grade." And, indeed, Enfield students were a bright lot; I hadn't been obliged to give anything lower than a B-minus in my four semesters there. Until now. And that to the son of the Chairman of the Board. This could be a problem.

Tibby moved away without saying anything more, and I was left alone. The lace-covered table was laid as it had been on my first visit, with a proper English afternoon tea, a ritual Edith seemed to have followed with both elegance and appetite. And why not? Life is difficult, and if small rites smooth the way . . . I poured myself the clear, flower-scented tea and added a splash of cream. Whose rituals get to be considered valid, I wondered. If you could down a dram of whiskey in remembrance of the dead, why not a cup of tea and a buttered scone? I sliced the scone, slathered it with butter and jam, and raised my thin china cup in silent tribute: *This one's for you, Edith*. She was beyond her illness now; she could have anything she wanted—even a scone and strawberry jam. But, then, of course, she was also beyond desire.

We were a group of almost a dozen when everyone had gathered: the Brewster family trio; Gerry Novak; Willis; Avery; Kendell Brown, a woman in her forties whose multiracial appearance gave her an intriguing ethnic ambiguity; Mary and Hector Menendez, a married couple of the same age as Kendell who had taken over Edith's inner-city medical practice; and William Margolis, Edith's attorney—a stocky, graying man in an impeccable blue suit. Piotrowski wasn't there, but he might as well have been. His big, ghostly bulk hovered beside me, looking everyone over twice, suspecting everyone.

My eye snagged on Gerry Novak as he carried a plate of cream cakes from the kitchen. Where was Jill? She'd sat with him at the services, but here, at Meadowbrook, Novak was as enigmatically solitary as ever.

Mrs. Brewster—Joyce, was it?—came up beside me at the tea table in her size three black linen. "Are you finding everything you need?" she murmured, fussing with the placement of the sugar bowl and the creamer. Her hair formed a stiff blond parenthesis for her pale face.

I nodded, smiled. I know the social rules. Then Joyce Brewster turned from rearranging the table setting and looked directly at me. Something in my vision shifted; the large, dark eyes and hollow cheeks suddenly became symptom rather than style. Was it possible this woman was ill?

"About Tibby," she began, earnestly. "I—"

Kendell Brown, in her floaty green Indian print, appeared beside us. Her unanticipated presence silenced whatever Tibby's mother had been about to confide. Kendell watched curiously as the dark-clad woman moved abruptly away. Then she turned to me.

"Did I interrupt something?"

"I have no idea what that was all about." Then, perhaps in reaction against an entirely unexpected spurt of sympathy for this elegant matron, I went on to say,

"Maybe she was counting the silver teaspoons." Sometimes I can be really nasty.

Kendell laughed. "Well, anyhow," she gestured toward the table, "this is a perfect setup. Just as Edith would have wanted it."

"I was thinking that exact thing."

"She loved doing this," Kendell said, with a reminiscent smile. "When I was a kid in the city, she'd have me and my cousins and some others over on a Sunday afternoon, maybe once a month, and she'd put out a spread like this. I remember the first time—my eyes were bugging out of my head. I'd never seen anything like it; East Harlem isn't given to afternoon tea. But on those Sundays, the sandwiches would be a lot thicker than this, and the cakes a good deal heftier—and there'd always be enough left over to take home." She shook her head, sadly. "I'll miss her."

"She was a terrific woman."

"*Woman?* Well, yeah. And a *lady,* too." She poured tea, stirred sugar into it.

I cocked my head at Kendell. She understood my look. "Yeah, I know, I know. *Lady:* a complicated word. But Edith was a complicated person. After my mother died, Edith saw me through a rocky childhood—and made certain I got to college, too. Even though I didn't really want to go at the time." She laughed. "I was gonna run to Hollywood, be the first biracial Charlie's Angel, ya know? But I'm not the only one Edith bullied into higher education. You see Mary over there? And Hector? She put them both through med school. We keep in touch. And there's others, as well. But, Edith could be pretty high-handed about getting you to do just exactly what she thought was good for you. Like me— she just *knew* that teaching in an inner-city school was what I should be doing with my life." Kendell laughed again. "And she was right—as she usually was. But she could be pretty damn lady-of-the-manor about it. I loved her, but, like I said, at times she was *infuriating.*"

Kendell lifted the cup to her lips. "Here's to you, Edith Hart," she said, "a great lady."

"To Edith." I raised my teacup again.

"Are you one of her hardscrabble kids, too?" Kendell's question caught me off guard.

I laughed. "I wish. I could have used a patron, believe me. I only met Edith this spring, but I liked her right away."

We were interrupted by a somber announcement from Lawyer Margolis. "Ladies and gentlemen. We are here this afternoon to pay tribute to one of the great ladies of twentieth-century America."

Kendell's eyes met mine, and we both looked down before we disgraced ourselves with giggles. In Kendell's mouth, *lady* had been a vivacious tribute; in Margolis's, the word dripped with pomposity. But what he said next, jolted me into instant sobriety.

"As each of you has, in one way or another, been mentioned in Dr. Hart's last will and testament, I would ask you now to gather in the parlor for the reading of the will."

Me? Mentioned in Edith's will? Couldn't be. I'd scarcely known the woman. An image of Piotrowski's guarded expression flashed through my mind. He must have *known* about this. Flabbergasted, I followed the buzzing crowd into the parlor and chose an inconspicuous seat in a corner. I felt excited. Had Edith left me something for the biography? The Northbury papers, perhaps?

On the chintz-covered sofa, the Brewsters spaced themselves widely apart, Thibault at one end, Joyce as far at the other end as possible, and son Tibby smack in the middle. Idiotically, I resented the trio's appropriation of the piece of furniture upon which Edith had reclined the last time I'd seen her. Gerry and Willis sat on the love seat. The Menendez couple and Kendell grouped themselves together on chairs by the French doors. And, at the last minute, Avery slipped into the room and sat by the door. As Margolis began the reading, " 'I, *Edith Leonore Hart, being of sound mind . . .*'" Thibault Brewster scanned the inhabitants of the room with a sharp, calculating eye.

Edith had left the following: to Gerald Novak, five hundred thousand dollars and lifelong occupancy of the tenant house (an enigmatic scowl); to Ms. Kendell Brown, five hundred thousand dollars (a shriek of joy); to Dr. Willis Thorpe, her gold filigree locket, the photograph in the red frame, and whatever other memorabilia he wished from among her possessions (a wistful smile, a tear dashed from the eye as Will received the locket, taken from Edith after the ceremony); to Drs. Mary and Hector Menendez, ten million dollars to set up an inner-city medical clinic specializing in family medicine (smiles and a satisfied inclination of the head; they had obviously known of the bequest in advance); to Enfield College, the Meadowbrook house, contents, and grounds and an endowment of ten million dollars, to establish a permanent library and research center to be called the Northbury Center for the Study of American Women Writers. This bequest was offered on the condition that Professor Karen Pelletier be appointed Director of the Northbury Center for as long as she chose to serve. From Avery, a discreet whistling intake of the breath, followed by a gratified nod and a speculative glance in my direction. From me a stunned, frozen silence.

The lawyer hesitated, then went on: to her sister's son, Thibault Jameson Brewster, " *'whose expectations have previously been fulfilled in numerous ways,'* " the residue of the estate. A choked exclamation from Brewster drew the eyes of everyone in the room, eliciting what seemed to be an involuntary *tsk* from Avery in his chair by the door: *A public expression of anger over a financial disappointment: such ungracious behavior!* But something about Thibault Brewster's expression didn't precisely strike me as *angry.* In the brief glimpse I got of Mr. Brewster's reaction before the patrician mask fell, I thought I discerned something a good deal more like cold, pale shock.

But I didn't pay much attention to Thibault Brewster; I was too stupefied by the implications of Edith's will for *me*. I was a legatee! Or almost as good as one. So that was what Piotrowski had meant by the number *three!* Now I had been endowed with a motive for the murder of Edith Hart. A good solid ten-million-dollar motive. Money: the best incentive for homicide, according to Piotrowski. *Edith, how could you do this to me?*

Twelve

Edith's letter arrived the next morning.

Dear Karen,
I have done something impulsive. I do hope you have no objection, but, as I have not been feeling at all well, I wanted it done and over with before anything could interfere. Would you please come see me—very soon. You have brought me a new interest, one about which I feel quite excited. It's time for restitution, I believe—in any number of ways. Mrs. Northbury's novel is quite wonderful! I can't wait for you to read it. That dense, brooding, Victorian storytelling brings back my childhood pleasure in fiction. And you have given me an ancestor of whom I can be proud.

With gratitude and best wishes,
Edith Hart.

The letter had been sent to my home address, and I sat at the kitchen table and stared at this message from the dead until the quavery handwriting on the thick cream paper began to blur. A tear splattered down before I could grab for a paper napkin, causing a fat gray blotch right over the words *come see*. A passionate, imperious woman to the end, this Edith Hart. And I had landed smack in the middle of one of her passions.

Avery had expected me to be thrilled with the terms of Edith's bequest, but I wasn't—not by a long shot. Oh, I was happy about the Northbury Center—it's time there were more serious resources for studying American women writers—but I didn't want to *head* it. I was a teacher and a scholar, not an administrator. If a few committee meetings could make me as irritable as, say, Curriculum Revision meetings did, I could just imagine what day-after-day center organizational activities would do to me. Now I understood what Kendell Brown had been telling me about Edith: She was the kind of woman who would do you good—even if it killed you.

The thought of *killing* temporarily distracted me from my quandary by reminding me of Piotrowski. I should let him know about this letter.

"Whew," the lieutenant whistled through his teeth when I showed it to him. He had responded with almost frightening immediacy, showing up at my house within twenty minutes of my call. And this time he had come by himself. That, I chose to interpret as a good sign. If he seriously suspected I was a killer, he wouldn't have showed up alone. Would he?

The clear May sunshine fell at an angle through the kitchen window, illuminating the left side of Piotrowski's face as he stirred his coffee and pondered the note in front of him. Again, I was reminded that the lieutenant was an interesting-looking man, not classically handsome in the manner of Avery Mitchell, but rugged and big-boned with high, flat Slavic cheekbones, deep-set brown eyes, and beautifully molded lips he was right now chewing in contemplation. His half-lit face and the intensity of his concentration gave him the air of an enigmatic seer, and he contemplated Edith's last words as if they were runic messages from the dead. If he read any occult meaning in them, however, he wasn't about to share it with me.

"May I take this?" he asked, cautiously, motioning toward the letter.

"Certainly," I responded, with marked composure. "But I would like it back when you're done."

"Of course."

This was an exquisitely polite interaction; the police search of my premises two days earlier shadowed each word. If I didn't voluntarily give this document to the lieutenant, he could get a warrant, and we both knew it. But I was still furious about having had my privacy invaded.

As if he could read my mind, Piotrowski spoke. "Doctor, I'm really sorry about the other day. I know it wasn't nice for you. But, you gotta understand, we had to do it. And it was all for the best—now you're in the clear."

"Does the sergeant think so?" I strove for a complete lack of inflection in my tone. I failed.

The lieutenant's gesture was complicated: half dismissal, half apology. There was a *third* half, too, but I couldn't quite read it.

"The sergeant was thinking within the framework of information we had received about Dr. Hart's will," he replied, stiffly. "We weren't free at that time to tell you what it was, but I understand now you know. So you can see her point, can't you?"

I shrugged.

When he didn't get any further response, Piotrowski continued. "We hafta have *evidence,* Doctor; you know that. Everyone's in the clear until we've got good forensic evidence that'll hold up in court. There was no sign of a manuscript—or anything of Dr. Hart's—in your belongings. So you're clear. Okay? Ya got that?"

I nodded, reluctantly. I don't easily give up a grudge. And I suspected Felicity Schultz still had it in for me.

The lieutenant finished his coffee. Taking Edith's letter and its envelope by their edges, he inserted them carefully into an evidence bag, which he slipped into the pocket of his Red Sox windbreaker.

With his hand on the doorknob, Piotrowski stopped. "By the way, Doctor, congratulations on your good fortune. No one deserves it more than you do. I mean that." Then he gave me one of his infrequent supercharged smiles, squeezed me lightly on the shoulder with a large hand, and was out the door and gone before I had a chance to tell him that his congratulations were misdirected.

I watched his shiny red jeep pull out of my driveway. This was the kind of inarticulate, musclebound, good-hearted man I'd been brought up to love; why the hell was I wasting my time mooning around over that effete intellectual snob, Avery Mitchell?

That effete Avery Mitchell sat at the polished conference table in the president's office with the rest of us intellectual snobs, not quite at the head of the table, but close enough to matter. I sat somewhere toward the foot, next to Shamega and across from Jill. Other committee members completed the group of curriculum reformers. It was our first working meeting, and probably the last full session before school broke up for the summer recess. We were forming subcommittees by specialization, and Jill and I exchanged rueful glances as she rose from her chair and followed half a dozen male colleagues to the Social Sciences corner. Along with Miles Jewell and Ned Hilton from English, Latisha Washington from Black Studies, Joe Gagliardi from Romance Languages, Sally Chenille from Comp Lit, and Shamega, I was a member of the Literature Subcommittee. Our goal was to see if subcommittee members could meet at least once during the summer months to sketch out divisional priorities. Miles sat scowling at his date book as Sally attempted to fit in a two-to-three-hour meeting between book tours, TV interviews, and publicity photo shoots.

"Perhaps June fourteen or fifteen," she speculated, as she brushed a thin, beringed hand over the quarter-inch pink stubble that bristled from her skull, "if the *Sonya Live* thing doesn't come through. Other than that, Miles, I don't know *when* I can find time. I'm a very busy woman; what can I say?"

I knew what *I* could say, and if I'd been tenured, I probably would have said it. But junior faculty walk a very fine line between discretion and integrity, and I was learning to go with discretion. One never knew *who'd* be sitting on the College Executive Committee when one came up for tenure. And, in meetings like this, one found oneself using words like *one* a hell of a lot more than one would care to; maybe it was time for one—me—to begin rethinking one's—my—career.

So I was well behaved—for the most part. But when Sally overrode Latisha's motion to schedule the meeting for later this week, saying scornfully, "Well, that's all right for ordinary faculty, who have no other obligations, but *distinguished* professors can't be expected to linger on campus after classes are over," I lost it.

"Sally," I said, jumping up from my seat, and mother's milk would have curdled at my tone, "surely we *undistinguished* members of the Enfield faculty—" But a hand on my arm brought me to a halt. Avery stood at my side with an amused glint in his eye.

"Karen," he said, "may I have a word?" As we walked over to the window alcove, he muttered, "Believe me, Karen; I understand the impulse. But, around here, you've got to watch your back, and our distinguished colleague has some powerful allies." Startled by his uncharacteristic frankness, I stared up at him speechlessly. He laughed. "What? What's that look all about? You didn't hear me say anything; I'm the soul of discretion. But, seriously, we need to confer about the Northbury Center. There are a multitude of complications—as you can imagine." I glanced over Avery's shoulder to where Thibault Brewster glowered at us from the doorway. Yes, I could imagine. After that one shocked exclamation during the reading of Edith's will, Thibault had stalked out of the room, trailed silently by Joyce and Tibby. I wondered if Avery's "complications" might not eventually include a lawsuit contesting the will. But Avery continued without alluding directly to Brewster.

"I know how surprised you were by the bequest—and by the stipulation that you direct the center. And now is not the moment to discuss that. But once I begin to address the—ah—complications, I want to take you out for a long, working dinner—somewhere quite special. Surely the college owes you that much." He reached for the date book on his desk, and the amused glint returned to his eyes. "That is, Karen, if you can find the time in your busy schedule."

God, he was charming, and there was nothing I would like better than a long, lingering dinner with him, somewhere *special,* but I sensed I was being manipulated into something I wasn't at all certain I wanted to do.

"Avery, I do know that now is not the time to talk, but I need to make it clear that I'm not happy about this situation. Yes, I liked and admired Edith Hart, and, yes, I'm thrilled about the center, but I've got to say I resent being thrown into this position without being consulted. I'm no administrator—"

"I know, Karen." Avery had turned so he could keep an eye on the dispersing group of colleagues. "You made that very clear as we were leaving Meadowbrook."

"And my feelings haven't changed."

"But the terms of the bequest stipulate—"

"And there was something very high-handed about that. I never agreed—"

"We'll talk about this further, Karen." His guarded expression told me I was compounding an already "complicated" situation. "And please remember that this bequest has not yet been publicly announced—" We spoke in undertones, and Avery was still keeping a watchful lookout on our fellow committee members. "So, discretion . . ." His eyes hardened as Thibault Brewster moved to within hearing distance. "Thibault," he said, and his greeting would have frozen molten lava.

Why is Sally Chenille following Jill? I wondered, as I exited Emerson Hall. From my vantage point at the top of the flight of limestone steps, I couldn't help but notice my celebrated colleague's odd behavior. As Jill crossed the campus common, lugging a commodious canvas bag loaded with books, Sally trailed after her, pink hair a bright beacon. When Jill paused to shift the bookbag from one hand to another, Sally loitered before a poster affixed to an outdoor bulletin board. When Jill halted to pull a small notebook from her pocket and consult it, Sally dawdled in front of the art museum, checking out the list of exhibitions. When Jill picked up her pace and headed in the direction of the Sociology offices, Sally quick-stepped after her. I'd been planning on going directly to the library, but something about this scenario didn't sit right. I flashed on the memory of Sally lurking by the gate of the President's House as Jill came down the steps.

"Jill!" I yelled. Both women jerked around, startled by my voice. "Jill," I called again, bustling after my friend. "Hey, Jill! How about a cup of coffee before we get to work?"

Sally changed her course, veering off abruptly toward the parking lot.

•   •   •

Later that afternoon, I found myself the sole occupant of the gleaming oak tables in the Enfield College Library Special Collections Reading Room. With classes over, I was eager to begin the biography. And I could think of no better place to start researching than right here, where Edith Hart had deposited the Pinkworth family papers. After the librarian brought me three large gray pasteboard manuscript boxes and a pile of shabby books, she must have gone on an extended afternoon coffee break; I'd seen no sign in at least fifteen minutes of her comfortable figure in its gray cardigan and denim wraparound skirt. I was in my element here, surrounded by these ancient books and papers. After a long assessing look at the daguerreotype of the Rev. Edmund Pinkworth, I had propped it against a volume of his published sermons; when I needed a reminder of just whose letters I was reading, I could glance up from the precise, angular handwriting for a glimpse of the tight, thin lips, the heavy brow puckered into what appeared to be an immutable frown, and the wild graying hair. As Edith had told me, Reverend Eddie looked like an ogre. I could well imagine how Pinkworth's disapproving scowl would have intimidated little girls. It intimidated me, and I was far from being a child. But perhaps it was the minister's resemblance to Thibault Brewster that unsettled me the most. The straight nose and chiseled jaw had been genetically transmitted from generation to generation for a century and a half.

I'd come to the library hoping to escape into a kinder, gentler era by reading through the papers of Serena Northbury's illustrious father. But there was nothing either kind or gentle about the man I discovered in these letters and journals. No one knows better than a historical researcher how superior the present is to the past, but even I at times succumbed to the mythologizing of the past as a Golden Era of good times and good people. Once again the human records were disabusing me of that notion.

> *Daughter,*
>   [read the Reverend Pinkworth's letter of 11 October, 1836,] *It is with the utmost dismay and disapproval that I find you again insistent upon following your willful Desire to attain an educational level suitable only to the Superior Sex. I cannot render strongly enough the Dangerous Position in which you place yourself by such overweening Ambition. Where have I Failed in my Duty to you, my Only Child? Our dear Saviour alone knows how many long, perilous nights I have struggled in prayer with your obdurate and selfish Disobedience. As I have relayed to you on far too many occasions, Providence has approved for you only such aspirations as Divine Providence itself has rendered Appropriate to the weak and vulnerable Female Disposition. Now I feel myself driven to extreme actions. I must inform you, Daughter, that if you do not cease—*

"Interesting reading?" inquired a deep voice, and Thibault Brewster slid into a chair across the table from me. I glanced up, startled, and for a single heartbeat it seemed as if the writer of the missive in my hand had returned from the grave to confront me: same long nose, same square jaw, same scowling brow. I shuddered and dropped the letter as if it were crawling with maggots.

"Mr. Brewster. How are you?" I tried for a level tone.

"So," he leaned across the table, his hands folded in a parody of paternal benevolence. "So, *Professor* Pelletier . . ." The word *Professor* was stressed scornfully, as if my claim to the title were something of a joke. "My Aunt Edith seems to have taken a great liking to you."

Brewster's slate-gray eyes examined me. I wasn't prepared for the disdain I saw there, and it unsettled me. I swallowed hard and kept my gaze steady. "As I did to her," I responded, evenly.

"I'll bet you did." His condescension was laced with sarcasm. Thibault Brewster sat back in his chair, stretching his legs under the wide table until I was forced to shift my feet in order to make room for his. This school was his, goddammit, and he'd take up as much space as he wanted. When I didn't drop my eyes in face of his penetrating stare, he went on.

"So, tell me—what mode of undue coercion did you use on my senile and vulnerable relative in order to entice her to leave the family fortune to some fly-by-night pseudo-academic venture?"

I laughed. I didn't do it on purpose, but Thibault Brewster flushed, and I knew immediately this was the most disconcerting response I could have made to his implicit threats. And it *was* funny. *Undue coercion; senile and vulnerable relative; pseudo-academic venture:* Brewster's words had no relation to reality—my hesitant approach to Edith, her tough-minded willpower and intelligence, the much-needed scholarly resources the Northbury Center would provide. His language was the stuff of TV melodrama.

He jerked himself upright in his chair, the motion surprisingly spasmodic for such a seemingly self-controlled man. "You think it's funny, *Professor?* You won't think so for long, not after my attorneys get through with you. Particularly after the pattern of harassment my son reports you've perpetuated against him, with absolutely no provocation." Brewster's right eye twitched. His voice squeaked twice, on the words *harassment* and *provocation.* Clearing his throat, he stood up as abruptly as he'd sat down. Then, both hands flat on the table, in control of himself again, he leaned toward me. I glanced around for the librarian. Nowhere to be seen. I sat forward, ready to spring out of my seat if I had to. That brought Brewster's face even closer to mine.

"The unfair course grade you gave Tibby—a student who's never earned below a B-minus in his three years at the college—that's documented evidence of persecution. For some reason, Ms. Pelletier, you have a grudge against our family. And now Aunt Edith's rash and ill-judged bequest makes the origins of that grudge clear. But by the time I get through with you, *Professor,* you won't have a leg to stand on. You won't even have a job."

He straightened up, turned on his heel, and stalked out of the room, passing the returning librarian. She glanced at me curiously. "Everything okay, Professor? You look a little pale."

I nodded. *Oh, yeah. Sure. Everything's okay. Everything's just dandy.*

Thirteen

The wooded yard of the Samoorians' multilevel contemporary on the outside of town was set up with long tables of food and drink. Greg and Irena were hosting their annual end-of-the-academic-year-monster-blowout-potluck picnic and barbecue. Friends and colleagues clustered in small groups on white plastic molded chairs, sipping wine and chatting; Neil Young sang "Transformer Man" just under the buzz of conversation; and faculty kids chased the Samoorians' yellow Labrador pup, Misty, from one corner of the yard to the other. After the frenzied hassle of finishing up courses, reading papers, grading exams, and dealing with hysterical students, frazzled professors were delighted to have a little downtime. Greg only invited people he could tolerate, so we were a select group, and the mood was mellow, without the posturing that goes on at most College gatherings.

A plate of ribs and potato salad on my lap, I relaxed on the deck, leaning back against the redwood siding of the house and basking in the late afternoon sun. Almost myself again, after the stress of end-of-semester pressures, the sadness of Edith's death, and the nastiness of Thibault Brewster's threats three days earlier, I guzzled a Sam Adams ale and laughed at one of Greg's silly-student stories. Greg was a happy man; Irena's pregnancy was no longer a secret, and a sonogram had confirmed that the couple was expecting twin girls. This party was a double celebration.

Ned and Sara Hilton—Ned's in the English Department—and George Herman from Anthropology joined Jill, Irena, and me on the deck, and Greg continued with his tale. "And then this young woman—would you believe it?—after not showing her face in class for a good eight weeks, has the nerve to appear on the last day of class with a final paper in her hand."

"Jeez," George interjected.

Greg held up a hand. "Oh, but it gets better. She says, 'Professor Samoorian, my roommate said you're looking for me?' 'Well, yes, Annie,' I say. 'You've missed more than half a semester of classes. I wondered what the problem was.' 'Oh, there's no problem,' Annie says, looking up at me with childlike eyes, trustingly certain I'll sympathize with her dilemma. 'You see, Professor, I just didn't *like* the course.'"

A roar of laughter greeted this statement. "What did you do?" Ned asked.

"What did I do? I gave her an F, naturally—especially after I recognized the paper she turned in as one I'd read the previous year. It must have been circulating in the dorms."

I gnawed a remnant of sweet pork from one of the denuded ribs on my plate, slurped down the last of the ale, and sighed with contentment. Good food, good booze, good talk: What more could I want?

Avery Mitchell strolled around the side of the house. He wore a navy-blue golf shirt and khaki shorts, and he carried a bottle of champagne in one hand.

I snatched a handful of paper napkins to swipe the

barbecue sauce from my mouth. Sitting next to me, Greg reached over with his own napkin and dabbed at my cheek. "You missed a spot, Karen." He winked.

Irena, glowingly beautiful in a loose denim jumper, rose to greet Avery. "Congratulations, you two," Avery said, kissing her and greeting Greg with a slap on the back. "Why am I always the last to hear these things?"

"It's your exalted position, Mitchell," Greg responded. "Gossip simply doesn't pierce the higher levels of the academic stratosphere."

Avery chuckled. Greg was one of the few faculty members who felt comfortable joking with him, and the president seemed to like it. "Right," he said, "sure." He handed the champagne to Irena. "This is for *after* the babies are born."

"I *know*," she said. Her honey blond curls haloed in the slanted late-afternoon sun, Irena radiated the aura of a Renaissance Madonna. Jill stared at her fixedly, no doubt fascinated by the image of maternal beauty. This party had to be difficult for Jill; as far as I knew, she had told no one but me about her pregnancy. Irena's impending motherhood rated a public celebration, but Jill was still hiding hers, clutching it to her like an invisible scarlet letter. I took a closer look at her strained expression, realizing how lonely she must feel. I smiled at her and received a wan smirk in reply.

Irena took Avery's arm. "Let me get *you* a drink, oh mighty one," she said with mock seductiveness. Avery grinned and rolled his eyes at Greg—*hey, I'm only human*—and allowed Irena to lead him toward the drinks table. I began to breathe again. Greg gave me a sharp sideways look.

I jumped up from my bench against the sun-drenched wall. "Anyone want dessert?"

"I'll come with you." Jill, in black leggings and a loose open-weave cherry shirt over a black shell, laid a hand on my arm as we went down the steps. "Thanks for being such a pal, Karen. I'm not going to be able to keep this—well, you know, the kid—a secret much longer, but might as well let Greg and Irena bask in their glory for a while. Sophisticated as everyone claims to be around here, people are gonna kinda freak out when I announce my little unwed blessed event."

She glanced back at the deck where Greg sprawled on a lounge and Irena stood, laughing with Avery, a glass of milk in her hand. "God, I envy them. Grown up and together. I've got a feeling me and the tadpole here are gonna be all by our lonesomes."

I stopped in the middle of the yard. "Where's Gerry?"

"Probably fishing." Her tone was acerbic. "He doesn't like social events. He'd rather spend his life in a boat on the Meadowbrook pond. A regular Tom Sawyer, Gerry Novak is." In the background, Neil Young was crooning "Helpless." The acerbic tone intensified to caustic. "Or else, he's off with—"

"What I mean is, where's Gerry in the long run?"

"I honest to God don't know, Karen." She nudged me toward the dessert table, and stacked a plate perilously high with lemon squares and chocolate fudge cookies.

I chose a brownie and began nibbling at its corner. My jeans were starting to feel just a bit tight around the waist. "You guys break up?"

Jill sampled an oatmeal cookie. "I don't know if we were ever really *together*. I *thought* we were a couple, but then Gerry got so pissed when I showed up for Dr. Hart's funeral. . . . All I wanted was to be there for him." She looked wounded as she recounted the incident. "After the service he gave me hell. I cried all afternoon. And then—well—I haven't seen him since." Her eyes hardened. "I don't need this shit, Karen. I didn't even bother to remind him about this party tonight."

Before I could respond, Sara Hilton arrived at the table, towed by three-year-old Hilary and four-year-old Nancy.

"Sara," Jill said, brightening her mood, seemingly without effort. "I didn't get a chance to tell you before, but I'm thrilled about Ned winning his tenure appeal." The year before, a powerful—and, now, deceased— member of the Executive Committee had sabotaged my departmental colleague's tenure case. Ned Hilton had appealed to the College Tenure and Renewal Committee, and had, just this month, been granted his well-deserved tenure. He was still depressed, though—at least I thought so; his movements seemed listless, his lanky frame still slumped. In a profession where the granting of tenure is a mark of legitimacy, the initial denial seemed to have branded Ned a failure—in his own eyes, if in no one else's.

But bubbly Sara more than made up for Ned's gloom. "Thanks, Jill. I can't tell you how much it means to me to get to stay here in Enfield. The girls and I love it—Girls, girls, *no*. Not so many. You may choose *one* dessert apiece. Hilary, I said *one!* That means o-n-e." She tugged the three-year-old's plump hand away from the tray of peanut butter fudge, and grinned at us. Then she turned back to her children. "Okay, Nancy, that's it. If you take the chocolate-chip cookie, you *can't* have blueberry pie."

As she helped one small towhead pour a glass of milk, she added, laughing, "Irena and Greg have *no* idea what they're getting themselves into."

Jill tittered politely, then we moved away toward the edge of the yard where an old-fashioned park bench sat up against a fenced-in garden plot.

"Neither do I," Jill groaned, sinking down on the bench. "Neither do I." Her face was a study in tragedy.

I put an arm around her shoulder. "It'll be okay, Jill. Really it will. If I could do it, you can."

"Yeah, but you're a grown-up." She picked up a lemon square, began chewing.

"For Christ's sake, Jill, I was *nineteen* when Amanda was born. You're *twenty-five*. And *you've* got a means of support. You grow up damn fast when you're a mother."

"I'm not certain I want to grow up." Jill chose a second lemon square. "I'm Generation X, you know," she continued, sardonically. "We're terrified of commitment." She munched at the edge of the confection, then dropped it back on the plate. "I just remembered—too much sugar's not good for the tadpole." She set the plate down on the edge of the bench, picked up the cakes one at a time, and pitched them into the trees. *"Something* will eat them," she said.

I shook my head at her. "Jill, *you* are something— something *else.*"

"Yeah, but just exactly *what?*"

We sat, silent for a moment or two, listening to Neil sing "Like a Hurricane."

"Karen, can I confide in you?" In this secluded nook, we were out of sight of the rest of the party, and Jill seemed to feel safe speaking intimately. "I need some advice."

"There's *more* to confide?"

"Oh, yeah. You know, part of what attracted me to Gerry in the first place was his poetry, the pain in it. I thought I could help him, that I could make it better for him. I still do, if he'd let me. Oh, I get furious at him, but, then, sometimes I think all he really needs is someone to love him, to believe in him. And, then, other times I think it's hopeless. That he's incapable of commitment. Actually, I think he's been seeing—" Jill broke off, swallowed hard, and continued on a different tack. "I told you he's had a rough life?"

"Yeah?" *And who hasn't?*

"Well, he was brought up poor, you know?"

"Yeah?" *And who wasn't?*

"His parents were tenant farmers for Dr. Hart, and she was pretty good to the family. His father came from Czechoslovakia, but his mother was born right there on the Meadowbrook farm, so Dr. Hart knew her all her life. Mrs. Novak was like some kind of—well—family retainer, I guess. Anyhow, she—Edith Hart—paid Gerry's way through college, right here at Enfield. And he did beautifully. Everyone expected great things from him. But, when his father died in the middle of Gerry's senior year, he dropped out. He says he didn't see any reason to get a degree if all he was going to do was run a farm and support his mother. Dr. Hart begged him to finish, told him she'd get someone else to run the farm. She'd send him to grad school. But Gerry didn't want to take any more of her money. Said it was a matter of integrity—"

"But she did that for a lot of needy people," I broke in, "—sent them to school, supported them as they began their professions."

"Did she? Gerry didn't tell me that. Maybe he doesn't know he wasn't the only one. Well—anyhow—he had a special reason for—what he did. . . ."

"Oh?"

"Yeah." Breaching confidence didn't come easily to Jill. A strand of bright hair had fallen down from her demure topknot; she chewed on it contemplatively as she considered what she was about to say.

"Don't tell me this, Jill, if it's going to be a problem for you."

"Well, you're the only one I can talk to, Karen. I think I'll go crazy if I keep it to myself." Jill took a shaky breath, then spoke very fast. "Gerry thinks the Novaks were not his real parents. He thinks he was adopted at birth. He thinks Edith Hart was his real mother, and that she gave him away so she could get on with her medical career without being bothered with him."

"*Jesus,* Jill!" I was stunned. "Do you think that's true?"

She shrugged. "I have no idea. But *he* believes it. He's got this humongous chip on his shoulder. He thinks he's been deprived of his birthright—that's what that poem was all about at the funeral. You've got to understand, nobody ever told Gerry this, and he's got no proof. But he *believes* it. He says all his life there's been this sense of some sort of family secret, and when his mother—his Novak mother, I mean—was dying, she started to ramble on about Gerry getting his birthright. What else could it be?"

She was crying softly now, and I shook the brownie crumbs out of my paper napkin and handed it to her.

"What really freaks me out, though, Karen," she went on, "is that he seems to want to do the same thing to our child. Just walk away, and let me bring it up by myself." She dabbed at her eyes.

My head was spinning with this news. A family secret. Another motive for murder. I blurted out, "Does Lieutenant Piotrowski know about this?"

Jill's head shot up. "No! And you're not going to tell him. Remember, Karen, this is all in confidence. I only told you because I wanted some advice on what to do. Should I stay with Gerry and try to make a family? Or should I simply assume he's too damaged to ever be a real father?"

I stood up from the bench, wiping brownie crumbs off my blue-jeaned legs. One fat crumb stuck to my finger. I conveyed it to my mouth. *Dump the jerk*, I thought. "Jill, I don't give people that kind of advice. All I can tell you is that I'll help in whatever way I can. If you need a good obstetrician, I'll give you my gynecologist's name. If you need a labor coach, I'll be there for you. If you need help shopping for baby supplies, I'll come along. But I will not tell you whether or not you should spend the rest of your life with Gerry Novak. That decision is solely up to you. Do you love him?"

"Yes. No. I don't *kno-o-w*. How does anybody know if they love somebody else? He sure does know how to make me wild—but maybe that's not enough."

"Maybe not." I looked back to where the festive sounds were coming from. Was that Avery Mitchell's laugh I heard? Someone had changed the music. Nina Simone was singing "Every Time We Say Good-bye."

"Maybe I'd better call my parents. Let them know."

"Maybe that'd be a good idea."

Jill jumped up from the bench and threw her arms around me. "You're such a good friend, Karen. I don't know what I'd do without you."

I hugged her back, and Misty, the yellow lab, came galumphing around the corner, followed by the Hilton girls. The children stopped when they saw us, Hilary with a finger in her mouth, Nancy with her hands on her hips. The four-year-old stood watching Jill and me with our arms around each other.

"Are you the kind of ladies who marry each other?" Nancy demanded.

Jill broke into startled laughter. "Oh, honey, I wouldn't be in this predicament if we were."

We walked back to the group, arm in arm, and Jill said, with wonderment, "I just realized something. This baby's going to be as real as that nutty little girl. This baby's going to be a *kid*."

"A little Jill," I ventured.

"Or a little Jack," she replied. She paused for a moment. "But not, I think, a little Gerry. No, not a Gerry." Her tone was resolute. "I—we—won't need that kind of turmoil in our lives."

Good, I thought, breathing a little easier. *Thank God.*

Greg met us halfway to the house. His expression was puzzled. "Jill, there's someone here looking for you. Tall blond guy? Frizzy hair?"

Jill's face lit up. "Gerry," she cried, and took off for the house on the run.

Fourteen

"Greg," I said, "I got the weirdest e-mail this morning." We were gossiping over coffee at the Blue Dolphin after having met at the college pool for a mid-morning swim.

"Yeah? Who from?"

"From *whom*, Greg." Grading freshman compositions has ruined me for ordinary conversation.

"You English types . . ." Greg hates it when I get prissy about grammar. "I got my meaning across, didn't I?"

I ignored him. "You ever hear of Earl Wiggett?"

"Wiggett?" Greg's eyes narrowed as he consulted the data banks of his amazing brain; Greg never forgets an iota of information. "Wiggett? Wiggett? Oh, yeah. Isn't he the guy who found that Louisa May Alcott manuscript? *The Duke's Dastardly Deeds* or something?"

"*The Duke's Daughter*, yeah. And he sold it to a commercial publisher for what's euphemistically called *seven figures*."

Greg whistled through his teeth. "Good for Wiggett.

You have a lead on an Alcott manuscript?" He beckoned to the waitress for a refill on his coffee. The Blue Dolphin makes great coffee.

"I wish." I held out my ceramic mug for another shot, then I slid a printout of Wiggett's e-mail across the table top. "Take a look at this, will you? Tell me what you think."

Greg read it out loud:

"Professor Pelletier: I am making so bold as to remember myself to you via this electronic medium. I have been a great admirer of your work on women writers. As I will be in Enfield the first week in June to do some research into the life and work of Mrs. Serena Northbury, I would much appreciate the opportunity to meet with you and discuss our joint project of recovering the treasures of the past. Earl Wiggett (earwig@ucla.edu)"

"Joint project?" Greg inquired. "You working on something with this guy?"

"No! I mean, I've *met* him. And I was actually talking about him recently—to Edith Hart. But I don't really know him. And suddenly we're engaged in a 'joint' endeavor? I have no idea what to think."

"Well, he admires your work. You should be flattered."

"No, that's not it. Not with Wiggett. He's not really a scholar. As a matter of fact, his university e-mail address surprised me; I had no idea he had any academic affiliation. He calls himself a 'literary gumshoe.' I dug out the business card he gave me a couple of years ago, and it actually says that: *Earl Wiggett, Literary Gumshoe.* He searches through archives and attics for manuscripts that well-known authors—you know, Alcott, Poe, Hemingway, Twain—either discarded or lost interest in—for the most part, with good reason. Then he tries to peddle them to commercial presses as sensational new literary finds. He's in it for the money."

"So? There's nothing wrong with that, is there? What's the problem?"

"It's just that the *'treasures* of the past' part's got me nervous. Most literary 'sleuths' work at uncovering lost material because of a genuine love for the past; that's how a number of the Alcott works have been found. But Wiggett's different. I've always thought of him as some kind of a literary bottom-feeder, out to devour whatever crumbs he can find."

"Seven figures—that's a pretty big crumb."

"Yeah, it is. And for the most part the things he finds aren't really *lost* manuscripts; scholars have known about them, but didn't think they had much literary or historical value. But now Wiggett's operating at the margins of the whole new literary recovery thing—"

"You going to start trashing the DWM's again?"

"Greg!" In the academy, the term Dead White Males has become such a cliché for what used to be called "major" authors that people jokingly use the acronym alone. "Get serious."

Even though Greg's an anthropologist, he knows a lot about what's going on in American literary scholarship right now. When minority scholars and women scholars first entered the academy in the 1970's and 80's, their research began to uncover fascinating books, stories, and poems from the past that earlier academics had either ignored or even ridiculed. These were texts by, for the most part, (surprise, surprise), women and minority writers. And, because of this research, many of those "lost" works have gotten reprinted and are now available for reading and teaching. So, in the 1990's, American literature courses are much livelier than they used to be. Instead of being restricted to the sober musings of Emerson and Thoreau, you can also read the comic novels of Emma Southworth and Fanny Fern. Instead of getting only the fictional Huck Finn's story of freeing the slave Jim, you now can read both Frederick Douglass's and Harriet Jacobs's true accounts of freeing themselves from slavery. And now the lusty imaginings of Nathaniel Hawthorne's cousin, Elizabeth Stoddard, can spice up discussion of *The Scarlet Letter*. It's not that professors have dumped the DWM's; it's just that the DWM's have a lot more company now.

"So," Greg asked, handing me back the printout, "what's got you 'nervous'?"

"Remember I told you about that manuscript?"

"The Northbury novel manuscript?"

"The one I thought might be publishable? Well, the problem is—it's missing."

"Missing?"

"The cops found only a few pages after Edith died. And—"

"And you think Wiggett might be after that?"

"Do you think I'm paranoid? How would he even know about it? Unless . . ." I thought for a moment. "Well, maybe somebody got in touch with him. Maybe Gerry Novak. He was there when we found the manuscript."

"Novak? Really? Anyone else?"

"Well, Will Thorpe, but he'd never—"

"I thought you always said there was no money in academic reprints, anyhow."

"Not much—at least not the kind of money Wiggett's interested in. So it's silly to worry, but—"

"But you're going to keep an eye on this guy. Right?"

"Right." We sat in silence for a few seconds. Greg finished his coffee and set the fat ceramic mug on the table with a clunk.

"Karen?" Greg's expression had turned uncharacteristically serious—and a little tentative.

"Yeah?"

"There's something I want to talk to you about, but

I'm afraid you'll bite my head off." He rubbed a hand over his dark beard.

"Jeez, Greg. We're pals. You can tell me anything." Greg's reticence surprised me; he generally has no problem saying what he thinks.

"Yeah? You sure?" He chewed his bottom lip. "Okay, here goes. It's about Avery Mitchell." Greg took a deep breath. "The other night at my house, I saw how you looked at him—"

"Greg!" My face was suddenly hot enough to glaze fine china.

"I told you you'd snap at me! But, listen, just let me say this, and then I'll shut up. Avery's an attractive man, and he's lonely, but there's a hitch—"

"Greg, I don't want—"

He plowed on. "I know Liz was gone before you came to Enfield, so you never knew what they were like together. When she left Avery, we all thought he was going to fall apart, but he pulled himself together and got on with his life. But, you know, Karen, Avery never really got over Liz. It's obvious he finds you, ah, interesting, but you should watch out. He's the president, you're untenured—I know you understand the complications. But the main problem is—Avery's not really free. Oh, he's divorced, but his *heart* isn't divorced, not completely, if you know what I mean."

"I have absolutely no idea what you're talking about, Greg." My face was still burning. "And even if I did . . ." I paused to pull myself together ". . . it's none of your goddamn business anyhow!"

"Uh-huh," he said, "uh-huh. Got it." Then he hesitated. "Karen . . . we still friends?"

I mopped my forehead with a paper napkin. Thank God we were sitting in a back booth where no one but Greg could see my red face. "Of course," I replied, with an attempt to recoup some dignity. "Of course. And I thank you for your concern. But there's really no problem." I stuffed the napkin into my empty mug and changed the subject. "So, tell me—how's Irena? She looked great the other night, positively glowing."

Greg gave me an empathetic smile. "She's really good." Then he winked. "So—what do you think about Lucy and Maud? As names?"

"How about Hester? And Prynne?"

"Don't be such a wiseass."

"How about Wise? And—"

"Karen!"

The interview room was as gloomy green as the last time I'd entered it, but the welcome was a good deal warmer. That may have been because Sergeant Schultz was busy on another case, and Piotrowski met me there by himself. He wore a suit, not the gray elephantine suit of the previous year, but one in blue that fit rather nicely. This time his Save the Children tie was scarlet, with yellow and blue drawings of kids. He looked neat and fit, in spite of his bulk; he looked like a man who didn't think badly of himself.

"You're a smart woman, Doctor, and knowledge-able," Piotrowski began, without preliminaries. "And, even though we don't always see eye to eye, I know you can be real helpful to me. On that Enfield case, you—"

"Okay, Lieutenant, cut the flattery. What do you want?" In my denim shorts and Enfield T, I felt at a sartorial disadvantage, but it was a warm day, heading for hot, and my house isn't air-conditioned. I suppose I should have changed into something more professional when the lieutenant called, but he seemed in a hurry, and, besides, I thought, it's only Piotrowski, I don't have to bother. Now here he was, so nicely dressed that I perceived myself, stupidly, as somehow—grieved. What is there about this man . . . ?

But he was in an expansive mood. "I've sent out for some good coffee, Doctor—Starbucks—and a coupla scones in case we're here longer than I expect. I want ya to be comfortable—"

Scones? "What is it you want, Lieutenant?"

"And if we go till lunchtime—"

Lunchtime? "Lieutenant? Just tell me what you—"

The door opened and a uniformed trooper entered. Piotrowski jumped up, grabbed the officer's cardboard tray of coffee containers, began fussing with napkins.

"Lieutenant!"

"All right. All right. I need your help." He peeled the plastic lid from a coffee cup, checked out the contents. Black and bitter. He handed it to me, reached for another. Peeled. Checked. Light and sweet. He sipped, then slurped.

"You said that on the phone."

"Yeah, well, we went over the victim's place with a fine-tooth comb—" Images of cops and cooties flashed through my all-too-literal imagination. "—and we found nuthin' like that manuscript you were talking about—" When he placed the coffee cup neatly in front of him it was already half empty. I know, because I checked.

I must have made a *tsk* sound, because Piotrowski broke off to say, "Yeah, I get real suspicious when something is missing, no matter how unlikely it looks for a motive." He finished off his coffee. Reached for another cup.

I scowled, untangling his syntax. But he misinterpreted my scowl.

"I know you're a busy woman—"

"It's okay, Lieutenant. Just put me out of my suspense. I liked Edith. I want to help. Tell me what you want me to do."

Piotrowski put his second coffee down without opening it. From a manila envelope on the table he extracted the six extant manuscript sheets in their plastic sheaths.

Yes!

"You remember these documents?"

"Well, yes, I do." *Let me at 'em!*

"Will you—"

"Certainly." I leaned forward, elbows on the table, fingers loosely cradling my Starbucks cup, the very model of amiability. "Happy to assist you, Lieutenant."

Piotrowski loomed over my shoulder as I set the first two sheets aside and picked up the third.

—*179*—

The great port was abustle as Emmy disembarked with her heavy valise. She had no other baggage because notice had been short and the message urgent. He was here! He was safe! He was awaiting her! A lively urchin with a tousled head of dark curls pushed his way through the crush of porters and tram men.

"Please, lady, do you want your carpet bag carried?" And before Emmy could protest, the ragged child—he couldn't have been more than twelve years old—grabbed her bag and flung it onto a barrowlike cart, glanced at her with a pair of mischievous, dark gray eyes, and said, "Where to, lady?"

Trams and coaches rushed by, and the clamor and filth of the city were as Emmy recalled. Where to, indeed? A dozen grand mansions within the metropolis would have opened their doors at Emmy's request with joyous and bounteous welcome, but not for her this day the refuge of the genteel and substantial citizens of Gotham. Not on this—of all errands. Not today, and perhaps never again. The bar that lay between her and the well-bred circle of her acquaintance would, if known, close all doors to her—forever!

Pressing a silver coin in the hand of the little "prince of rags and patches" . . .

I grabbed for the next sheet.

—180—

who stood, first on one foot in its ragged shoe,
then on the other, in his impatience to be gone,
Emmy said, "Take this bag to the Astor House,
boy, and book a room for me there in the name
of . . . Mary Smith of . . . oh, New Hamp-
shire. Tell them I will arrive by dinnertime to-
night." Then, with lilylike hands, she lifted her
skirts, and set off on foot, dodging carts and
cattle, in the direction of a more modest area of
the town.

"If she's Mary Smith," the urchin muttered,
"I'm the heir to a great fortune. But, say, crikey,
she give me a whole dollar by mistake, she can
be Mary Smith if she wants ter." And the raga-
muffin set off at a smart pace for the Astor Ho-
tel.

The door at which Emmy knocked, when,
footsore and exhausted, she reached the desig-
nated spot, opened readily and the woman of
the house, her dust cloth still in hand, glanced at
our fair heroine with dark, suspicious eyes.

"The North Star rises tonight," said Emmy,
as she had been directed. With a whoosh of its
brass rings, a heavy curtain was swept aside
from a door adjoining the small but immaculate
entry, and Emmy, sobbing through her cries of
joy, was in his arms at last!

"Hmm," I said to Piotrowski, who'd been reading along
with me, "if this is what I think it might be, it's truly an
amazing find."

"Well, what *do* you think it is?" He tapped his
meaty fingers on the scarred table top.

"Let me read the rest, then I'll tell you." I skipped to the two end pages: 432 and 434.

—432—

the heartbroken pair.

"Are you my father?" the young girl asked. "My mother wears your likeness in her locket." Lizzie's sallow hand, no longer golden from the unbiased rays of the summer sun, reached out and grasped the dark, strong hand of he whose care and adoration had been denied her by the bars of an un-Christlike world.

Armand allowed his tears to flow unchecked upon the child's pale forehead in both baptism and farewell. In the quiet room a wan beam of light shone through a pane upon which a fly buzzed in impotent desire to be free.

Emmy looked upon the joined hands, one so fair and one so dark, and avowed that the passion of her life would not be in vain, that, although a great earthly wrong had been done to this small family, they would indeed rise and gather together in Heaven's happy home.

As the sun slipped beyond the green mountains of old Quebec to the east, the promise of the North Star was realized at last. The three, alone around the fever-dampened bed, formed a momentary circle of devotion. Lizzie glanced up from her bed of pain and smiled wearily at her progenitors. Outside, an ax thwacked thick branches of the felled oak. A calf bawled somewhere in the distance. The scent of boiled cabbage wafted in from the lean-to kitchen. But the room itself, save for the droning of the entrapped fly, was still, as the tearful family, together at last, awaited the onset of Death.

The wan shaft of sun lingered long on the

locket around Lizzie's throat, where the inter-
twined strands—

The page ended. "I was right," I said to Piotrowski.

"Right about *what?*" he demanded.

"Shh. Let me finish." I picked up the final sheet. It was half covered with Mrs. Northbury's curlicue script.

—434—

Armand circled Emmy with his strong arm, as they looked from the ship's deck back at the receding land of both their births. She took one final glance at that receding green where the child of her heart slept the long, deep sleep, then turned to her protector, blue eyes gazing deeply into brown.

"A great wrong has been done to us, my dearest love. A nation has turned its back upon a people of feeling strong and deep. You and I, Armand, will share our love in exile, and our children will shun the native shores to dwell with more compassionate races in the older world."

"With you, my Emily, no place is exile. As the poet has said, 'The world is all before us.'" He bent his dark head to her fair, and their kiss sealed a bond of passion fated to endure.

The End

"Amazing," I murmured, eyes on the precious page of manuscript. I thought that now I understood, both why Northbury didn't publish this novel, *and* why Earl Wiggett might be interested in it.

"What's so *amazing* about it? Like you said before, it's a love story."

"Yeah, it's a love story, all right; but it's an *interracial* love story. Emmy is white. Armand is black—probably a fugitive slave. That's what's so astonishing. Historically, interracial sex happened all the time, especially in the South, but it was taboo as far as literature went. No other novel—or even short story—that I know of from the antebellum era—"

"Antebellum?"

"From before the Civil War. No other novel centers on interracial lovers who are allowed to survive and go off together to live happily ever after—"

"This doesn't seem like a happy ending. They lost their kid—"

"Yeah, but that *had* to happen." My mind was clicking away on the symbolism of all this. "Their child had to die because she represented the fate of interracial union in the U.S.—which Northbury sees as cruelly denied. But their *future* children—"

"Would thrive in Europe?"

He *was* quick. "Yeah, don't you see, this is a truly subversive text; it figures the centrality of amalgamation to the continuance of a just American polity."

"Huh?"

"Yeah, you see, the concluding kiss figures sexual congress as compensation for a political congress that denies citizenship—indeed, denies humanity itself—to races legally marked as chattel, for commercial exploitation, or for extinction. Hence, the necessity in the U.S. of Lizzie's death. But in an idealized Europe the continuance of a mixed-race—"

"Right, Doctor," Piotrowski said. His expression of baffled disgust snapped me out of my flurry of lit-crit theorizing. "So let's cut to the bottom line here. Who benefits from this book? Would anyone kill for it?"

"Jeez." *I* was baffled now. "I don't know why." The detective pried open the lid on a second cup of black coffee and handed it to me. He opened his own cup and eyed the scones. He selected a raisin scone and slathered it with butter from a foil packet in the Starbucks box. Crumbs fell on his trousers, and he brushed them off with care. "Piotrowski?" The e-mail message from the literary gumshoe was niggling at me. "Have I mentioned Earl Wiggett to you?"

"Wiggett? Maybe. Refresh my memory."

"He calls himself a literary sleuth. He edited Alcott's *The Duke's Daughter*—"

"—For two million bucks. I remember now. Why do you bring *him* up?"

"Just the question of profit. Of how much is enough to kill for."

"This guy's a killer?"

"Well—no! Don't be silly! It's just that his name popped into my mind. This manuscript could conceivably sell for a pretty penny, if it was marketed right—as a transgressive text about a forbidden interracial love. It depends on how good a *story* it is, whether it would go to a commercial press or a university press. But, at the very least, in the current politicized academic climate, it would get a *zillion* course adoptions." I mused a bit on the idea. "Yeah," I said. "There could be money in this. And it's the kind of thing Wiggett would be interested in. But—well—forget about Wiggett, Piotrowski. How the hell would he even *know* about this Northbury thing?"

"So, you think this story might be worth money, huh? Enough money to kill for?" Piotrowski was nothing if not persistent.

I laughed. "How much is enough to kill for?"

He shrugged. The massive shoulders underwent a process resembling seismic upheaval. My agile mind raced on to something else.

"Piotrowski, here's another thought. Have you considered Thibault Brewster? As a suspect, I mean? In the murder?"

"Why do you ask?" He had that still look he sometimes got, as if all faculties were suspended except for listening and thinking.

"Because he's a nasty man."

The lieutenant snorted. "Dr. Pelletier, if we arrested

all the nasty men in the world, the planet would be paved wall-to-wall with correctional facilities."

"I know," I insisted. "But he's *real* nasty." And I told him about my encounter with Brewster in the library. By the time I'd finished, the lieutenant's eyes had a sort of unseeing, inward look, as if the reality in his mind had superimposed itself indelibly upon the reality of the grim green room. As if he wasn't really seeing me any more, I thought, but was cogitating upon what might possibly happen to me in the worst of all possible worlds.

I shivered, and clasped both hands tightly around the cup of lukewarm coffee. Once, a long time ago, when I was eating chicken à la king in a school cafeteria, I chomped into a bit of the gallbladder a careless cook had failed to remove. That was exactly the taste I had in my mouth now.

Fifteen

I rounded the corner of Kinney and Whitlow streets, and the scent of lilac assaulted me. Local rumor had it that the ramshackle three-story Victorian dominating this block was owned by an eccentric recluse who hadn't shown her face in public since a romantic disappointment fifty years earlier. Helen Whitlow, it was whispered, lived alone with a dozen cats, cared for by a mysterious man who came and went under the cover of darkness. I didn't believe the gossip, but I loved walking on Whitlow Street because occasional glimpses of the mysterious yellow Italianate mansion were available behind the hedge of overgrown yew. Once I even caught sight of the recluse herself, tending her roses, surrounded by felines sunning themselves on the spacious lawn. Disappointingly, she had been garbed in baggy khaki pants and a man's plaid shirt rather than the filmy white dress local myth clothed her in. In the spring I often took this route—a long-cut rather than a shortcut—from campus to town; walking down the quiet street made me feel momentarily transported, as if the scent of lilacs were the eternal reality here, transcending time and weather, eliciting the same sensuous response now as it had in a past so dim that only mere traces of its vitality survived. The scent of lilacs or roses, or the weight of snow on the yew.

But today I was not transported by the lilacs. Today was Tony's wedding day. This very afternoon my former lover was marrying someone named Jennifer. Amanda said Jennifer wore her blond hair in a French braid. I'd never met Tony's bride, but I hated her anyhow. As I passed the Whitlow house with its tales of old passion thwarted, the thick fragrance of the heavy purple blooms squeezed at my heart. I picked up my pace; the Whitlow route had been a mistake.

The night before, Tony had called, waking me from a restless sleep in which I was dreaming about a house with endless rooms. Each time I thought I'd gotten to the end of this beautiful house, a new door appeared, and carpeted halls led off to chambers unknown. I descended a curving staircase into a spacious living room furnished in the bulky greens and chintzes of a 1930's English country house. French doors led through a bower of lilacs to a swooping expanse of country lawn. In the dream I had just stepped out of a bath, wrapped my scented body in a silk dressing gown, and was descending the stairs in delicate gold-embroidered Chinese slippers, when the phone rang. I had a vague notion that Winston Churchill was on the other end of the line.

"Karen? I know I shouldn't be doing this." Tony's voice had the texture of lilacs, lush, sensuous. I think he was a little drunk.

I stumbled over my response, struggling with surprise and a sleep-thickened tongue. He was silent then, and I used the moment to test whether or not I was still dreaming. "Tony? Is that really you?"

"I'm getting married today, Karen."

"Amanda told me."

"I thought I should let you know that you . . . you still mean a lot to me."

"You, too, Tony. To me." I swiped at a tear. Damn allergies.

"It's just—you know, I want . . . I need . . ."

"I know, Tony. You want a home and children. You want someone there for you all the time and dinner on the table. You don't want a flighty, self-involved academic type who's only around when she hasn't got anything better to do. I understand, believe me."

"You have a right to your life, Karen. I know that."

"Yes. You, too."

Then there was a long silence. Tears coursed down my cheeks. Those damn lilacs.

"Karen, are you still there?"

"Yes, Tony."

"Have a good life, Karen. I hope you get everything you want."

"Oh, Tony . . ." But he'd broken the connection.

Miles's house was a comfortable late-Victorian within walking distance of campus, and I'd taken the Whitlow Street route as a delaying tactic. The annual English Department garden party was an obligatory festivity for the twenty or so members of the department and their domestic partners and hangers-on. I had stopped for a bottle of chardonnay at a liquor store on Field Street, one of the few locally owned businesses left on Enfield's trendy main shopping thoroughfare. Over the past decade, upscale mall franchises had discovered the marketing potential of Enfield's concentrated population of students and professors. The previously functional downtown with its food markets and dry cleaners was now tenanted by self-consciously low-key versions of The Gap, Banana Republic, Baskin-Robbins, and Pottery Barn. Even McDonald's had gotten by the zoning board, but without the golden arches and with an enormously discreet sign. It was easier to buy a pair of safari pants in downtown Enfield these days than it was to buy a quart of milk.

Most of the students had left for home, and the village, with its white churches, brick storefronts, and green common, lay basking in an idyllic spring sunshine that lent it the aura of some eternal haven of peace and quietude. If I hadn't known the real Enfield, with its petty quarrels and incestuous intrigues, I'd have thought I'd died and gone to Norman Rockwell heaven.

In Miles's yard, clusters of men and women in pastels and whites—there were carefully delineated shades of white in these wardrobes: Coconut, Ivory, Bwana—perched picturesquely on wicker chairs, expounding on the evils of Eurocentric literary imperialism. In the glass panes of a French door I caught a fleeting glimpse of myself, a long, almost lean, stripped-down figure in a sleeveless black tank top and brightly colored Indian skirt. Dolores Jewell, Miles's wife, met me at the back door and directed me to the kitchen. I like Dolores. She's a saggy, comfortable, gray-haired woman who has always made me lust for cookies and milk. The Jewell household was more complicated than Dolores's grandmotherly appearance would suggest, however. The third member of the Jewell ménage greeted me in a kitchen sweet with the odor of recently smoked cannabis. Luke Bierce was a portly man of uncertain age whose tough-skinned tan and network of fine wrinkles belied his mop of wind-tossed, auburn curls. He wore off-white pants I couldn't tell if they were Tarzan-white or Bwana—and a mint green safari shirt with a pattern of elephants. I took a deep sniff of the redolent air. Like his hair, Luke's recreational habits remained amazingly youthful.

Luke, a gentleman of private income, had made his home with Miles and Dolores ever since he'd been a ravishingly handsome Enfield undergraduate thirty-five years ago. Deciding whether he was Miles's special friend, or Dolores's—or, maybe, the lover of both—had been a favorite parlor game of the Enfield community for almost four decades now.

Luke relieved me of my wine, glanced at the label, and hastily slipped the sweating green bottle behind a thicket of finer vintages. I gave a mental shrug; I had more important things to do with my life than learn the delicate nuances of choice booze.

"I've been hearing rumors about you, you naughty girl." Luke raised his tinted eyebrows at me as he poured an undoubtedly superior wine into a Waterford goblet.

"You have?" I was baffled. I wished I'd been doing something—anything—to justify Luke's arch tone. He handed me the diamond-like glass with its clear blond contents. I sipped. It tasted like wine.

"Dear Miles is *quite* upset." The gleam in Luke's aquatinted eyes was positively gleeful. The last time I'd seen him, his eyes had been green. The time before that—amber.

"What?" I didn't want to play this game.

"Oh, my dear." His hand on my arm had the substance of a moth. "I am sworn to secrecy."

"Oh, well, then . . ." I detached his hand and headed toward the patio. I passed through the open French doors and stopped dead in my tracks.

Gerry Novak slouched on a white wicker love seat, hands shoved deep in the pockets of his worn black jeans. He seemed intently involved in a muted conversation with Ned Hilton. Gerry Novak? What the hell was *he* doing here? I glanced around for Jill. She was nowhere to be seen—which was no surprise, since she wasn't a member of the English Department. But if Jill wasn't at this party, why was Gerry? And—I looked a little closer—what was that object he was slipping to Ned? Something small enough to fit in the palm of the hand? Some kind of envelope? When Gerry glanced up and caught me staring, he scowled. I shuddered, turned hastily toward the buffet table—and ran smack into Miles Jewell.

"Karen—a word, please," he said, grabbing my arm to steady me.

"Certainly, Miles." I detached my arm from my chairman's firm grip. His carefully balanced gin and tonic sloshed over the side of its tall glass.

Miles led me to a curved marble bench by a birdbath, but didn't avail himself of the opportunity to sit. "I feel," he said, a white shoe braced on the bench beside me, "that it is only fair for me to warn you that I intend to protest this situation formally." He was deeply serious, and his words had the weight of anvils.

"Really?" I responded. Whatever was he talking about? Oh—must be my decision to proceed with the Dickinson seminar. My heart sank: This was all I needed, a battle with my department head over course listings. And me still untenured. But, goddammit, everyone else in the department got their choice of seminar topics—Ned had just completed one called *Satanic Verses: Transgressive Milton;* Nicole Gottesman was scheduled for a seminar on *Queen Arthur's Court: Queer Texts in Medieval Contexts;* Fred Finney of Art had cross-listed a course on *PoMo in Soho:* Why not a seminar on Emily Dickinson?

"Well, you couldn't expect otherwise, could you? The college will be the laughingstock of the Ivy League!" *What? Because of an Emily Dickinson seminar?* "I haven't poured my life's energy into creating a department that—with a few exceptions—" he glared at me, "reflects the heights of legitimate academic achievement, only to see its reputation tainted by—" His face grew red. I began to fear for his heart.

"Miles, darling." Dolores was at his side, her plump hand on his pale, hairy arm. "Miles, that promising young poet you invited is about to leave. Wouldn't you like to say a few words to him before he goes?"

"Gerry's leaving? I rather hoped he'd stay long enough to read us a few works-in-progress."

So *that's* why Novak was there: his poetry!

"He seems restless, says he's going to take off."

"In that case . . ." But before Miles followed his wife toward the cluster of guests, he turned back to me. His mouth opened, but he must have found himself speechless because no words emerged. Instead he lifted an admonitory finger, and wagged it at me twice. Then he spun on the sole of his white mesh shoe and hustled after Dolores.

Why did Emily Dickinson make this man so angry? I lifted my wineglass, forgotten until now, and followed Miles with my eyes as I sipped. Dolores led him to Gerry Novak, standing awkwardly by the side of the house, hands deep in pockets. Miles kept up on young poets, and he must have heard—or read—some of Gerry's work and invited him to give a reading. Gerry Novak? But not Emily Dickinson? I simply didn't get it.

More than a little unsettled by my encounter with Miles, I turned gratefully to Ned Hilton when he approached carrying a plate of crudités. I selected two carrot sticks from the proffered vegetables, and smiled at my colleague. "I'm glad to see you, Ned. Miles was just giving me an earful. I seem to have offended him, but I'm not certain why."

Ned was not interested in my griefs; he wanted to talk about his own. The gloomy expression on his long, sallow face did nothing to cheer me. Nor did the aroma of pot that clung to his wrinkled cotton sahib shirt and white linen pants. *Someone's been in the kitchen with Lukie,* I thought. And neither of them had gone there to strum on an old banjo.

"Who knows, Karen?" Ned carped. "The ways of the mighty are inexplicable to mere mortals such as we. I just found out that the college denied my request for a merit increment this year—in *spite* of my position on the Editorial Board of *English Literary Renaissance*. Those pricks in the Dean's Office are so fucking shortsighted. . . ." And he was off on the imbecility and moral turpitude of college administrators, a topic dear to the heart of all professors.

I said little; I'd just that morning gotten the letter awarding me my merit bonus—pittance though it was. And besides, I intended to keep my mouth shut about everything until I knew for certain what had gotten Miles's shorts in such a twist.

After five minutes I'd had it with Ned's melancholy. His tirade, which I didn't listen to, had allowed me time to brood over Miles's narrow-minded bias against one of America's greatest poets. I'd become angry. Furious. Goddammit, who did Miles think he was anyhow to pass judgment on Emily Dickinson? Sexist old fart: I'd tell *him* a thing or two. Quitting Ned in midsentence, the word *asinine* just emerging from his lips, I marched back toward the house where I could see Miles deep in agitated discussion with Edmund Brooks, another departmental dinosaur.

"Miles," I began speaking in a tone so resolute it must have taken my chairman by surprise, because he cringed a bit. The whites of Ed Brooks's eyes expanded, and he scurried away with a mumbled excuse. "Miles," I repeated, "I must say I resent your assault on my intellectual autonomy."

"What assault?" The distinguished white head jerked; Miles was taken aback.

"Your opposition to my Dickinson seminar represents an unwarranted imposition of power—"

"What do you mean—Dickinson?" His tone was incredulous. "I wasn't talking about *Dickinson*. I was talking about Serena Northbury. *And* the so-called *Northbury Research Center*." He began to sputter. "The college will be a national laughingstock if it associates itself with this wrongheaded venture. A literary study center at Enfield named for the author of those witless sentimental novels! Positively humiliating! *And* funded with the money earned from schlock fiction! I won't be able to look my fellows in the eye at the next meeting of the MLA." Miles pulled a linen handkerchief from his pants pocket and wiped beads of sweat from his forehead. "Call it the *Emily Dickinson* Center, if you wish. *Or* the Eudora Welty Center. Or even—God help us— the *Gertrude Stein* Center. But *not* the Serena Northbury Center.

"As soon as this gathering is over, I intend to sit down and write a letter of protest—in the strongest possible terms—to the president and the Board of Trustees. I will insist, in the name of all sanity, that they turn down this ludicrous bequest. I simply cannot allow the college to mortify itself in this fashion! And I'm appalled that you—even given the radical bent of your literary politics—would acquiesce to such an endeavor. To the profession at large, we shall look like absolute fools." He stormed off toward another gin and tonic.

So much for Avery's attempt to keep the Hart bequest under wraps until he had resolved the legal problems. Nothing—I repeat, *nothing*—remains confidential at Enfield College for more than forty-five seconds. And now another problem was about to land in our president's—mailbox. I was about to say in his *lap*, but I didn't want to think about Avery's lap. Especially not after what Greg had told me about President Mitchell's feelings for his ex-wife.

The blinking red light on the answering machine was the only sign of life at my house that evening. Avery's sonorous tones greeted me. *Karen, can we talk? I'd like to arrange a walk-through of the Hart property. Although there are, ah, complications regarding the bequest, Dr. Hart's executor has given permission for us to make an initial assessment of the house with its suitability as a research center in mind. Would you give me a call,*

Karen? So we can set up a time? And he left me his private number at home. It was after ten, too late to call, but I played the message over again. Twice. The hell with Greg and his warning. There was something about Avery's voice that reminded me of the scent of lilacs.

Sixteen

I should have been ashamed of myself, but when I entered the library's Special Collections room a week after Thibault Brewster had accosted me there, I peeked around the doorway first, as if I were a child; I was half-convinced Brewster would be lurking inside, waiting to pounce. But no. Nothing there but the golden oak tables, the librarian's elevated desk, the glassed-in bookcases containing the college's collection of Edwin Arlington Robinson first editions and related works. Robinson had some association with the school, I could never remember what—had he taught here?—and he'd been given prominence on the shelves. *Miniver Cheevy, Child of scorn,* I recited to myself every time I entered this room, *Grew lean while he assailed the seasons; Da dum, da dum, da dum dum dum. Da dum, da dum dum.* It was that kind of poetry.

Gazing around at the floor-to-ceiling shelves with their packed-together, multicolored books, Robinson's and others, I tried to visualize a Serena Northbury book collection here. Perhaps I could donate my books to the college; then they wouldn't have the excuse that Northbury's books were simply too hard to find.

"Professor Pelletier?"

I gasped, startled; I hadn't realized anyone else was in the room. "Shamega? I thought you'd gone home for the summer." My student had let her hair grow, and stubby dreadlocks now haloed her delicate features. She was back in street garb, slender body almost overwhelmed by the baggy khaki shorts and oversize orange-and-green striped T. She looked tired and even thinner than usual. Her usually melodious voice sounded strained.

"I didn't really want to go home. I'm a bit out of favor there at the moment." She tightened her lips, as if to repress further words on the subject. "So," she said, "I got a room off campus, and a prep job in the kitchen at Rudolph's. And, at the last minute, the library found work-study money for me; I'm here as a runner until the fall. But . . ." She broke off, her brown eyes uncertain. Then she looked directly at me. "But staying in Enfield may have been a mistake."

"What's the problem, Shamega?"

Shamega had invited my question, but the return of the desk librarian, garbed today in a wraparound army green skirt and a flowered blouse with a Peter Pan collar, prompted an abrupt change of subject.

"So, Professor Pelletier," my student said, "I'm spending the summer working in Special Collections here. Whatever you want, I'll get it off the shelf for you."

"Well, good," I said, catching on. "You can help me track down material related to Mrs. Northbury." I explained to her about the Pinkworth family papers.

"Cool," she said, and when I'd given the call slips to the librarian, Shamega gathered them up and headed toward the closed stacks where the noncirculating material was kept. She hadn't referred again to her earlier remarks, and I didn't press her. I was concerned about

Shamega, but I could talk to her later. Right now I was eager to get back to the letter I'd had to stop reading when Thibault Brewster had so rudely interrupted me, the one from the Reverend Eddie to his daughter Serena. By the time Brewster had slammed out of the reading room, I'd been too upset to continue my work.

I didn't know what to do about Brewster's threats. Avery was the logical person to mention them to, but I hadn't seen him since that encounter. When I'd returned his call about scheduling a visit to Meadowbrook, Avery had been in the middle of a meeting, so our conversation had been short and brisk. And what was I going to do? Call President Mitchell again, solely to tattle on the chairman of the Enfield board? And, then, what about Miles's showdown with me about the research center? Surely Avery would have received my department chairman's irate letter by now. I'd mention both incidents on Friday, when I met Avery for the tour of what Miles thought of as The House That Mrs. Northbury's Ill-gotten Gains Had Built. But, oh, good God. How had I gotten into this complicated mess?

Shamega unloaded the Pinkworth boxes from her book cart, and I began sorting through the reverend's correspondence. The letter I wanted—October 11, 1836—was in the middle of the batch.

> *It is with the utmost dismay and disapproval,* [blah, blah, blah. Okay, here we go]— *the weak and vulnerable Female Disposition. Now I feel myself driven to extreme actions. I must inform you, Daughter, that if you do not cease—*

[This was where I had broken off.]

> *If you do not cease to follow your Disastrous and Blasphemous course I will find myself compelled to disclaim all Responsibility for*

*you. I think you will not find it comfortable to
supply your wants and needs in the manner to
which you have been accustomed when you
are reduced to Earning your own Living. I repeat, if I hear, from you, yourself, or from any
other, that you have proceeded with your Intention to enroll at Oberlin Collegiate Institute, or any other institution of Higher
Learning, you will not see One Red Cent Of
Support from he who has stood so staunchly
and so lovingly in a Paternal relationship to
you.*

> *Your father,
> the very reverend Edmund Pinkworth.*

Fatherly love Victorian-style! But the rhetoric sounded
familiar, not so very different from my own father's response to me when I'd walked out of my abusive marriage. *Not one penny,* my father had said on the phone,
*not one goddamn penny. You made your bed, now lie in
it.* And then I'd stood outside the phone booth at the
McDonald's in North Adams that winter day sixteen
years ago with fifty-seven cents in my pocket, no job,
and nowhere to feed or shelter my child.

The Reverend Pinkworth's words swam on the page
by the time I got to the end of the letter. With Tony's
marriage, Edith's death, and the shock of finding myself
smack dab in the middle of a ten-million-dollar-plus
brouhaha, I was just the *teensiest* bit overwrought these
days. The quiet scholarly life I'd so carefully con-
structed—teaching, research, writing—had proved insufficient defense against the messy demands of love, death,
and money. No matter how hard I tried to keep my feet
on the high road of intellectual detachment, the slippery
slope of human need tripped me up every time. And,
now, just look at me—bawling over words uttered in
anger a hundred and fifty years before.

Returning the letter to its folder, I rose from the table. "Coffee break time," I chirped to Shamega, who pushed a cartload of file boxes toward the front desk. She gave me a complicated look, but I didn't know how to read it, so I headed for the door.

Shamega caught up to me in the coffee shop, just as I took the first sip of the steaming black brew. She slid into the seat across from me, and without saying a word slapped an envelope on the table. My questioning glance resulted in a firm nod toward the envelope. It was addressed to Shamega at her college post office box and had been sent through campus mail. From the envelope, I extracted an eight-by-eleven-inch lined notebook sheet folded in half, then in three. I smoothed it open and immediately went cold with anger: It was a twin of the racist cartoon I'd found weeks ago on my classroom floor. Only this time the image of the pickaninny had been circled with a black magic marker and then slashed across boldly with the same marker. And—I looked closer—the figure in this ugly sketch was dressed only in underwear: a huge, pointy bra and enormous flowered panties.

I glanced up at my student. "You think . . . ?"

She nodded. "Tibby's noted for his cartooning skills; as you can tell, he's good at it." And, indeed, there was undeniable graphic skill apparent in the clownish sketch.

"Do you want to take this to—?"

"No!"

"You could have a legal case against him. I think this could be considered hate speech; it was mailed to you and was obviously intended as a message."

"I don't ever want to go to court again." Her lower lip trembled. "I just want to understand *why* someone would do something like this. I thought maybe you could help me figure it out."

"He's a racist pig."

She shook her head. "That's not good enough, Professor. I've been living with racism since I was born; it's in the air I breathe. There's something more going on here. Some peculiar twist . . ."

Three students with varying degrees of African-American heritage appropriated the table next to ours. The dark, slender young man I'd seen with Shamega earlier in the semester grinned at her, made a fake gun out of his fingers, and pulled the trigger. She stuck her tongue out at him. "See you, later?" she called to him.

"You bet!" All three young men at the next table were garbed in the baggy apparel of the streets. An in-your-face style statement directed at the more typical preppy types of the dominant white student population.

She turned back to me. "My break is over, Professor. Can we talk another time?"

"Sure. How about later this afternoon? Right now, I've got to get back to those papers."

I spent the rest of the workday reading through sermon drafts, account books, and dutiful family letters. None of them bore any signs of the passion Pinkworth had shown in that one letter to Serena. It was tedious and boring work, and I was relieved when I came to the end of the material in the last file box. But that final document jolted me awake.

6 November 1860

Father,
    Word of your condition has reached me here in New-York, and I am reluctant to allow the breach between us to remain unmended into Eternity. You are a cold, hard man and I—as you have made quick to inform me on a multitude of occasions in my unhappy youth— am a passionate and willful woman, even so far beyond your imagining. Yet, Father, I am willing to tender forgiveness on the edge of the

grave, and do so with a whole heart despite both our failings. If I were sufficiently well to travel, the first cars would see me on the way to Enfield and to the long watch love would not begrudge. But I am—[Here she had scratched a word out, and I was unable to decipher it under the heavy scoring of the dark brown ink.]—ill, and my position is precarious. Nonetheless, did not my children depend solely upon my efforts for their earthly support, I would risk the journey, and happily so. Its consequences in any other case might prove a welcome reprieve. But my duties lie more with the living than with one soon to be gathered to his own Father's divine bosom.

Go peacefully, my father, and think upon your prodigal with some slight fondness in the end.

> *Your Daughter,*
> *Serena Northbury*

Whew! Twenty-five years between his letter and hers. Had the estrangement lasted that long? And had the letter reached Edmund Pinkworth in time? I wanted to know more—much more—about the family tragedy unfolding here after a century and a half of oblivion.

"Millie," I said to the librarian, "there's no more Pinkworth material listed in the computer. And nothing at all by the reverend's daughter, Serena Northbury, even though she was a well-known writer. Is there any possibility you've got more secreted away somewhere in the collection? Maybe filed under some other heading?"

Millie's nostrils flared, as if I'd impugned her cataloging abilities. "Everything I know of has been listed, Karen. Of course, there's no saying what might have been misfiled in the past. As you, yourself, know," she added, portentously, "from your unfortunate experience at Harvard."

"Yes," I replied, "I do know." A misfiled document at Harvard's Houghton Library had led to murder during the previous year's "incidents" at Enfield College. I shuddered as I reluctantly recalled the peril I myself had faced because of some anonymous librarian's long-ago oversight. I didn't particularly want to gossip about that occurrence with Millie, so I changed the subject. "Is Shamega still around? There's something I want to ask her."

"She left at four. That poor girl works two jobs, here and as a cook at Rudolph's."

"That's right. I'd forgotten," I said. There'd be no talking to Shamega until tomorrow morning.

Back at my office, I checked my mailbox before heading home for the evening. Three envelopes, one delivered by U.S. Mail, the others by campus mail. I opened the official Enfield College English Department envelope first. I thought I knew what it was, and I was right: a copy of Miles's letter to the Administration requesting a reconsideration of the college's acceptance of the Northbury Center bequest. Naming a research center after *a subliterary hack*, he wrote, would *valorize mediocrity and demean the historical reputation of the college for excellence, integrity, and rigorous scholarship.* He recommended that the Board of Trustees *gratefully but gracefully decline the generous but misguided gesture* of Dr. Lydia Hart.

In your dreams, Miles, I thought. A fabulous property with a ten-million-dollar endowment? The college would do back flips over a bed of burning coals to keep the bequest. In his letter Miles listed all the reasons he'd outlined to me two days earlier, only without the sputtering. I shrugged, and laid the letter on my desk. This was Avery's problem, not mine.

I reached for the second business-size envelope with its Manhattan return address. Once again, a copy of a letter to Avery about the center—this one from Dr. Willis Thorpe. While his old friend Edith's bequest of Meadowbrook for use as a resource for studying women writers seemed to him to be a particularly appropriate use of the property, he would like to suggest that the college consider the possibility of a name change. Rather than simply the Northbury Center for American Women Writers, the new research library should be called the Northbury/Hart Center. This renaming, he felt, would honor the generosity of the donor as well as the literary accomplishment of her ancestor. *Hmm,* I thought. I liked the idea, but was it legally possible? I'd talk it over with Avery.

Preoccupied with Will Thorpe's suggestion, I reached for the final envelope with minimal concentration, slit it open, and pulled out a sheet of lined notebook paper. One look, and my eyes were riveted. The paper in my hand contained a cartoon sketch. A ludicrous caricature of a tall, skinny white woman with a long, thin nose, and straight dark hair falling over scrawny shoulders. Me. And, like Shamega's caricature, mine, too, wore nothing but an enormous pointy bra and huge flowered panties. The only difference was, instead of being circled in black, my image was circled—and slashed—in red.

Was this some kind of a threat? I could call Security, I could call Earlene, and I intended to do both. But first I had to talk to Shamega. I checked my watch. Six-ten. The dinner rush. I wasn't hungry, but I headed for Rudolph's, nonetheless. Maybe I could catch her for a few minutes between peeling carrots and boning trout.

Shamega was inexorable. Wrapped in a huge white apron and standing in front of a half dozen tightly lidded garbage cans in the alley behind the restaurant's kitchen, she lashed out. "Professor, you can't do this to me! I showed you that ugly thing in confidence. I refuse to be dragged into another sex scandal! If you tell anyone else about that cartoon, I'll tear it up, burn it, deny I ever got it. I swear I will! I just want to get through my last year of college and graduate without any humiliation. I deserve that, don't I? I'm sorry I ever trusted you with this, and I *won't* go to the authorities. No. No. No. *No!*" Her dark skin had taken on a grayish cast; her lips had paled.

I reached out and placed my hand on hers. "Okay, Shamega, okay. I should have known you would feel strongly about this. I've been insensitive, I suppose. But I'm angry, and that makes me want to do something about this—harassment. And it *is* harassment—"

"One stupid cartoon!"

I'd forgotten she didn't know about the one I'd found weeks ago in my classroom, and I didn't want to tell her; she was upset enough already. "Well, I got one, too, so there's more than simply *one*. And—who knows—maybe he's sent them to other people as well. I'm going to show mine to Earlene Johnson. As Dean of Students, she should know. . . ."

"Go ahead," Shamega said, shoving both hands in her shorts pockets underneath the apron. "And I hope dear little Tibby Two gets what's coming to him. Just don't involve me."

"Okay," I replied. "If that's the way you want it." More concerned for Shamega than I was for myself, I knew I wasn't going to take the nasty sketch I'd just received to anyone in authority. I'd file it with the crumpled caricature I'd found in my classroom and hope that nothing further developed.

We were awkward now, standing in the alley. The scent of grilled salmon mingled with the redolence of day-old garbage. "Well," she said, jerking her thumb in the direction of the kitchen, "I better get back."

"Yeah. Let me know if anything else happens, Shamega. You *can* trust me, you know."

"I know. You're okay." She grinned at me. "Okay, that is, for a bony white lady with *really* bad hair."

Seventeen

My name is Emily, I wrote, then scratched the words out with heavy strokes of the pen. I was trying to reconstruct the first two pages of *Child of the North Star,* the pages I had read aloud in Edith's parlor on Easter Sunday afternoon. Piotrowski had given me photocopies of the six manuscript pages in police custody, and I'd thought I could add to my understanding of Mrs. Northbury's unpublished novel if I could remember how it began. *Call me Emily,* I wrote, then scratched *that* out. Surely Northbury wouldn't have begun her story with such a bald statement. I put my pen down. I had to face it; I couldn't remember much at all about the opening pages of the lost Northbury novel.

The maples and birches were in full leaf as I drove up the steep mountainside to meet Avery Mitchell at Meadowbrook. It was a beautiful evening, and I was relieved to get away from Enfield and its environs for a few hours. I turned up the sound on the Jetta's cassette player, rolled the window down, and breathed greedily of the warm spring air. This time, confident of finding my way to the Hart/Northbury place, I could relax and enjoy my trip through the roadside greenery. The prospect of being alone with Avery for a few hours was titillating, in spite of Greg's caution. And I was the only one who needed to know that my oh-so-casual chambray shirt and denim skirt were top-of-the line, ranch-hand-in-Ralph-Lauren chambray and denim, purchased just that morning at the mall—and at full price, too.

The higher I traveled on the road from Eastbrook, the fewer working farms and lived-in houses I found. With the decline of the New England agricultural economy, the stony subsistence farms of these steep mountainsides had been abandoned one by one by their impoverished owners, until only showplaces like Meadowbrook remained, playthings of the rich, tax write-offs for city farmers. And now, a new use—a research center for an already sufficiently well-endowed educational institution. I don't know why I felt so resentful of Enfield's good fortune; the Northbury Center would butter *my* bread quite nicely.

As I wended my way up the mountain, Springsteen sang "Born in the U.S.A." on my cassette player. I bawled along in as deep a tenor as I could muster.

Avery's Volvo was nowhere to be seen on the Meadowbrook grounds when I pulled into the circular drive. Neither was Gerry Novak's big Suburban. Perhaps he'd locked it away in the commodious white brick barn. I pulled the Jetta into a position facing the house, and turned the ignition key to auxiliary power so I could continue listening to The Boss.

Avery's secretary had arranged with Edith's attorney for us to tour the house and grounds, so Avery had the keys and the code for the security system. I settled back comfortably in my seat and waited. As Bruce began "Cover Me," I surveyed the building. Meadowbrook was spacious and somewhat grand, but nothing about it was pretentious. The brown shingle siding, modest third-floor dormers, wide, white-pillared porches, French doors leading to the sloping lawn, elegant, arched porte cochere—all was pleasingly married to the landscape. It was a house designed for a person of sensitivity and restrained taste—a person I knew I would have liked. For the first time I felt a smidgen of genuine enthusiasm about the task that had fallen to me—turning this beautiful property into a place where people could come and learn about the women whose books had played such an important role in shaping our culture. Women like Serena Northbury.

Where *was* Avery? I checked my watch: twelve minutes late. I turned the sound up on the cassette and tapped my fingertips against the steering wheel to the beat of the music; I really liked this song. *"Covah meee,"* I sang, *"Come on, baby, covah me-ee."* It was early evening, and the June sun was still only halfway to the horizon, but the slanted light transformed the house windows into molten gold. As the sun sank, my voice rose: *"Well, I'm lookin' for a lovah who will come on in and covah me-ee—"*

"Karen?" Avery bent to peer at me through the open car window.

"Wahhhhhhhh:" I had started to shriek it along with The Boss, but the shriek ended in a horrified croak. My hand flashed out; the music stopped.

"Avery!" My voice was still croaky as I opened the car door.

Avery was a gentleman, but, even so, he had trouble keeping the laughter out of his eyes. "I hope I didn't keep you waiting long?"

Did he intend the *double entendre?*

"Just sitting here thinking . . ." I cleared my throat, and spoke in my most academic manner, ". . . about how best this lovely property could fulfill its function as a research center." I hurrumphed again, slammed the car door decisively, and walked briskly toward the house. "Now, if we utilized the double parlors as a main reading room and the dining room as a reference area, we could control traffic flow. . . ." Even to myself, I sounded as if I knew what I was talking about. And a good thing, too; I was still hot with embarrassment.

Avery was uncharacteristically silent as we wandered through the big, echoing house. Although all was as I remembered it—the massive Victorian furniture, the heavy Oriental carpets on the first floor, the bamboo matting of the upper levels—Meadowbrook seemed lacking in life with Edith's vivacity gone. *Dormant,* I chastised myself. *The house isn't lacking life, it's simply dormant. I'll have these old rooms alive and hopping again. Just as Edith would want it.* Unexpectedly, I was beginning to warm to my task of turning this place into a vital center of learning. As I expanded on my ideas, Avery took occasional notes in a small spiral book, but mostly he trailed after me and listened.

"Now our space needs," I said, "will be varied. These smaller second floor bedrooms will function well as offices, the larger as seminar rooms. Housing for resident scholars can be established in the servants' rooms on the third floor. Book storage . . ." I was determined to make up for the humiliating scene in the car with a spectacular display of efficiency.

When we came to the front parlor, I felt, for the first time this evening, Edith's presence in the house. There was the chintz-covered mission chair where she'd sat and related her family history. There was the flowered sofa Will and Gerry had carried her to when she'd gone into insulin shock. There was the odd little half-keyboard piano covered with framed photos of family and friends. The twilight gloom of the room seemed perfect for conjuring up the spectral proximity of generations of Northburys and their descendants. I recalled the young Serena Pinkworth, disowned by her father because of her burning desire for an education; I imagined her older, a

successful author now, recounting to her daughters in
this very room the deadly struggle with her father; I envisioned Edith as a child, cowering with her sister under
the disapproving daguerreotyped gaze of the Reverend
Mr. Pinkworth. Suddenly the room swarmed with
ghosts—generations of them, all here because of the
courage and determination of one intrepid woman.

Then an incongruous image flashed into my mind—
the portrait of a Victorian infant. What *had* Edith done
with that photograph? I'd love to have it back. Perhaps
I'd find it when I went through the boxes of family memorabilia. The attic rooms were still crammed with boxes
and barrels of books, papers, clothing, and worn furniture. And I wouldn't be allowed to resume my investigation of the stuff in the small room off the kitchen until
the will was probated and the title was clear. It was all
very annoying.

When we'd finished our tour of the house, Avery
suggested we save the outbuildings and grounds for another day. In the twilight gloom, we stood in the kitchen
with its eclectic outfittings—painted wainscoting from
the 1800's, sinks from the 1920's, stove from the '70's,
state-of-the-art refrigerator—summing up the pos-
sibilities the house offered. "You know what I can see
here, in this room?" I asked, rhetorically. "A restored
nineteenth-century kitchen. Can you picture it?" A flourish of my arm lacked only the magic wand to make it all
materialize. "Icebox, coal-and-wood-burning stove,
pitcher pump—a material reconstruction of nineteenth-
century domestic conditions. *And* . . ." I was really getting carried away now. "*The* foremost collection of
American cookbooks and domestic advice books in existence. Historians, domestic scientists, anthropologists
would come from the four corners of the globe to research and practice under actual nineteenth-century material conditions. *And*—"

But Avery held up a hand to stem the flow. "Your
enthusiasm is contagious, Karen." He was smiling at me

oddly. "And let's hope you get to put your ideas into practice. But before we go any further with plans, I'd better bring you up to date on certain situations that have developed since we last spoke. Do you think we might muster up a cup of tea while we talk? I didn't manage to get any dinner this evening." He looked helplessly around the large kitchen.

That seemed to be a cue for me to do the mustering. I located tea in a white enamel canister with a red cover and filled the kettle with tap water. Avery perched on a tall kitchen stool; his khakis stretched fetchingly tight over muscular thighs. I set out two porcelain mugs and busied my hands with spoons and loose tea. My companion was silent. He appeared tired and stressed. Although he followed my movements while I prepared the tea, I had no idea what he was thinking. Even though he was usually a fluent conversationalist, Avery was always a difficult man to read. This time when he spoke, his words were slow and deliberate.

"As you can imagine, Karen, when ten million dollars and a property such as this one are at stake, people can get a little . . . exercised." *Translation,* I thought, *the jackals have begun to gather.* "And, in addition, there's not only money involved here, but . . . ah . . . philosophies, as well." *Translation: the old boys are freaking out over a center devoted to women's issues.*

I nodded, and poured boiling water over Darjeeling leaves in a fat brown earthonware pot. It was dark enough now for me to need a light on over the sink. I hesitated a moment before I flicked the switch; it was cozy in this homey room. In the twilight. With Avery across the table. It had been a long time since I'd been alone in a kitchen with a man. Kitchens can be—I flicked the light switch and shattered the spell.

"I received a copy of Miles's letter, Avery, so I know what 'philosophical' differences you're talking about, but . . ." I let my voice trail off. The ball was in his court.

He fielded it skillfully. "You know, of course, that you have my full support as regards the focus and function of the center. Although Miles's concerns are understandable given the . . . ah . . . traditional perspective he brings to literary . . . ah . . . traditions. . . ." Avery was the consummate diplomat; I was not going to come away from this conversation with any sound bytes slamming Miles or his reactionary views. "Recent epistemological speculation affirms a more . . . differentiated . . . and . . . ah, relevant . . . field of investigation for advanced scholarly study. . . ." *Translation: Don't sweat it, Karen; the fogey is mired in the intellectual Stone Age. We're going ahead with this center.* "So," Avery concluded, "Miles's caveats would not seem to pose a significant barrier to the affiliation of the college with a Center for American Women Writers."

"Good," I responded. *Damn* well *better not.*

"However—"

"I thought there was going to be a *however.*"

Avery granted me a weak smile and took the mug of tea I handed him. *"Oh,* yes. There's a *big* however." He stirred sugar. I followed suit. It was quiet for a long, long time—maybe sixty seconds.

The sound of a car motor broke the silence; lights swept the kitchen window, then dimmed, disappearing in the direction of the barn. Must be Gerry Novak coming home to the tenant house Edith had willed him lifetime use of. Was he returning from seeing Jill? I wondered if they were still an item. She was almost five months pregnant; she wouldn't be able to hide her condition much longer. Soon the only secret would be the identity of the father. I lifted the mug. Sipped. Turned my attention back to Avery.

That wasn't hard to do. In his navy blue golf shirt, khakis, and boat shoes, Avery was dressed for a casual evening in the country, and the attire became him. But, then, *any* attire would become this man: the long elegant bones of his body, the aristocratic contours of his face, the thick, floppy, light brown hair. Tony had been so different, with his stocky frame and dark Irish coloring. They both had blue eyes, though. Tony's were a warm blue, like an August sky. Avery's were—I examined them dispassionately, just to make sure—*fjord* blue. Yes—like a Norwegian fjord in April. Or, like I *imagined* a fjord would be—deep, cold, and invigorating, full of submerged life. Just like a picture in *National Geographic*.

A car door slammed in the distance.

"I wonder exactly what Novak's place *is* in this petting zoo?" Avery's unexpected comment startled me.

"Jill thinks—" I bit my tongue to shut myself up.

"Jill *Greenberg*? I wanted to ask you about that, Karen. She was sitting with Novak at Edith Hart's funeral. How does Jill know Novak?"

"Oh," I waffled, "she heard him read his poems at some club, and they became friends."

"Oh?" Avery waited, head cocked, for me to finish my statement. When I didn't, he prompted me. "Jill thinks . . . ?"

"She thinks . . . he's . . . a brilliant poet."

"Humph. I didn't think much of that—er—*poem*— he read at the funeral."

I shrugged. Neither had I.

It was dark now, and my tea was cold. Suddenly I was ready to leave. I slipped off my stool, gathered up the cups, took them over to the sink.

Avery watched me in an abstracted manner. As I dried the cups, he finally spoke. "But, Karen, here's the real problem for the center—not Miles Jewell, but Thibault Brewster." His sandy eyebrows were raised in the classic "it-couldn't-get-much-worse-than-this" elevation. I waited him out. "I am telling you this in strictest confidence, Karen; you understand that, don't you? You can imagine how bad it would be for the college if word got out that the Chairman of the Board of Trustees was about to institute a lawsuit against the school." His lips were tight with—was it anger? "Anyhow, Brewster claims Dr. Hart's estate by rights belongs to him; as closest living relative, he's threatening litigation."

"I'm not surprised." I told Avery about my nasty encounter with Thibault Brewster in the library. He listened without interrupting, nodding at certain of Brewster's more outrageous statements.

"Then it won't come as a shock to you, Karen, when I tell you he's claiming that you, as an agent of the college, exerted undue influence on his incompetent elderly relative."

"Uhh." I dropped like a stone into a rocking chair in the corner. "You mean he's going to sue *me?*"

"*And* the college—unless we renounce the bequest. He told me he's going to take us for *every penny we've got.*" Avery's eyes were hard.

My laugh was short. "In my case, that wouldn't amount to much."

A sound from the dining room—as if in the dark someone had bumped into a chair—startled both of us. I jumped up from the rocker; Avery slipped off his stool. The scuff of Gerry Novak's feet heralded his entrance. Avery's eyes sought mine: *Had this guy been eavesdropping? Had he overheard our conversation?*

"Thought you people'd be gone before this." Aside from his poem at the funeral, this was the longest statement I'd ever heard from Gerry. He pulled out a chair from the end of the table and plopped down in a proprietary manner.

"We were just leaving," I said, gathering up the clean cups and restoring them to the cupboard. "We were discussing options for the center while the tour was fresh in our minds." Why did I feel the need to explain to him? This wasn't Gerry's house. He was only a factotum; he'd made that quite clear. But his attitude made our presence here extremely awkward. I felt a bit like Goldilocks, caught in the act by the three bears.

"Oh, izzat right?" Novak's laconic manner seemed designed to insult, but I couldn't tell why. Then I remembered what I had almost let slip to Avery—that Gerry believed he was Edith's out-of-wedlock son. Good God—would there be yet another claimant to this estate? Startled by the thought, I glanced up at Avery. He was watching Gerry with a mystified, but not overly concerned, expression. But then, of course, he didn't know what I knew.

As we left the house, Avery and I were quiet, both preoccupied, I thought, with the complications of what had initially seemed to be a trouble-free windfall. It was full dark now, and the air had a chill to it. My chambray shirt was sleeveless, and I hugged my arms to preserve a little warmth. My car was parked closer to the house than the Volvo, so Avery stopped and stood with me as I opened the door. This high on the mountain, the stars were clear and bright in a perfectly black sky. A thin rim of moon hung just over the horizon. What was that song I used to sing to Amanda? *The moon is the North Wind's cookie. He bites it every day. Until there's just a rim of scraps, that crumbles all away.* I smiled at the memory, and turned impulsively to share it with Avery. He was standing next to me, hands stuffed in his pockets, staring at the ground. He looked like a worried man.

"You must be sorry I ever got us into this situation." I laughed, hoping he would deny it. Avery glanced up at me, without responding. His aristocratic features were strained and he suddenly looked enormously exhausted. Impulsively I reached out and placed my hand on his arm. "Avery," I said. His skin felt warm to my chilled fingertips. *What the hell did I think I was doing? This man was in a position to destroy me. Emotionally and professionally.* I moved to snatch my hand back, but Avery grabbed it, pulled me to him. My elbow jabbed him but that didn't seem to matter. He kissed me long and hard, then held me away, breathless, at arm's length. He gazed at me enigmatically for an endless moment, then dropped his hands from my arms. "That was stupid, Karen," he said. "On both our parts." His expression, in the dim light spilling from the car interior, was infinitely sad. "Do you think maybe we could both just go back five minutes in time and erase that impulsive act from our memories?"

"I don't think it works that way, Avery." Tears stung my eyes; I was so lonely.

"Then we'll just have to work around it, Karen." His expression was resolute. "Because it's not going to happen again."

He opened my car door wider. I got in. He slammed the door shut and strode over to his own car. I started the Jetta and began the long descent to Eastbrook. All the way down the mountain, I watched for Avery in my rearview mirror. It was a wonder I didn't go barreling off the edge on one of the hairpin turns. At the stop sign, I even turned my head around to check for his automobile somewhere on the long road behind me. But in all that darkness, the lights of the Volvo were nowhere to be seen.

The words of the Springsteen song kept running through my head: *Well, I'm looking for a lover who will come on in and cover me-ee.*

Eighteen

The attic room was sparsely furnished, I wrote, *but immaculately clean. Emmy closed the door behind her and stood for a brief moment, the glass knob cold and solid, like an immense diamond in her hand. It was the only solid fact in a world that seemed to be dissolving around her. Another pain assailed her, began as a tight, hot fist in the center of her bowels, seized and spread until her entire being was contracted in agony. She groaned, dropped the carpetbag, fell to her knees. Thank God she had managed the stairs; now, at least, the culmination of her shame would be concealed from the eyes of any who might have thought they were acquainted with a good woman, a woman who knew the boundaries between pleasure and decency, between love and the marriage vows. With a clatter of brass rings, a dark-eyed young girl pulled the curtains back from around the bed. "Mrs. Westfall," she cried, "your time has come." "Call me Emily," the afflicted woman gasped. "For who but you should have that right?" Then she fell, insensible, to the floor.*

I threw the pen down in frustration. That wasn't right, and I knew it. If only I could remember the opening pages of Northbury's novel, I might be able to piece together a rudimentary version of the story. But *this* attempt was nothing but trash; it didn't even sound like nineteenth-century language. I ripped the page off the pad, crumpled it up, tossed it at the wastebasket. Missed. Jeez, I couldn't even do that right.

Okay, I'd try again, using words that sounded as if they might have been penned a century and a half earlier.

The attic door was heavily timbered with oak and studded with iron spikes. The rust on the ponderous ironwork looked more antique than anything else in the new world. Rooted almost at the threshold was a wild rosebush—a rosebush? In an attic? Pelletier, you are definitely losing it. Rip. Crumple. Toss. Miss. *I am dangerous*, I thought; *I should not be licensed to carry a pen.*

Once upon a midnight dreary, while I pondered weak and weary—Rip, crumple, toss, miss.

I had returned from Meadowbrook hours before, and it was now well after midnight. I couldn't sleep, and was setting myself the task of reconstructing Mrs. Northbury's mammoth of a novel from a few leg bones and a sliver of tusk. Anything was better than lying sleepless in my bed going over and over Avery's kiss in my memory. What *had* he said? *Couldn't we just wind back the clock? Pretend it never happened?* No way! Yet he was right; it *would* be better if it had never happened. Anything other than a totally professional relationship between Avery and me would be a disaster—for me, especially. He was the president of a prestigious college; I was a second-year untenured assistant professor. He was a scion of the WASP aristocracy; I was a half-Canuck mill-town girl. He was a man; I was a—

My pen moved over the lined yellow sheet again: *I's wicked*, I wrote—*I is. I's mighty wicked. I can't help it.*

•   •   •

Avery called three days later at nine A.M. He was all business. Would it be possible for me to come in that afternoon to discuss my intentions regarding the directorship of the Northbury Center? Good. Would four P.M. be convenient? Good. He and Marc Compton, the college attorney, would be waiting for me then.

An attorney? *Good,* I thought, in turn. He was interposing a lawyer between us; there would be no opportunity for any awkward scene. God, but that man was smart.

A warm rain fell fitfully as I left the house, and I threw a hooded yellow rain jacket on over my jeans and white cotton knit shirt. My sneakers skidded on the flagstone path, and I would have gone down if I hadn't grabbed a sturdy branch. I should have worn my reliable old Nikes, but the retro red-and-white Keds were brand-new. Aside from that one smidgeon of vanity I hadn't given a single thought to my appearance.

I rubbed the Terrifically Tawny blusher more deeply into the skin over my cheekbones, and shook the spill of newly washed hair back off my shoulders.

The clouds were beginning to rise from the Enfield valley as I approached the town. By the time Lonnie, Avery's secretary, greeted me in the president's outer office, a pallid ray of sun fell wanly across the thick green carpeting. "Karen," Lonnie told me, "Avery will be just a few moments. Can I get you something to drink? Coffee? Some mineral water?"

He kept me waiting twenty minutes. This from a man who was noted for his promptness. Was he making some kind of point? At four-seventeen I checked my watch and decided I'd give him until four-thirty; then I'd be out of there. But three minutes later he emerged from his office effusive with apologies. "*So* sorry to keep you waiting, Karen. Marc and I were just considering certain contingency plans."

Marc Compton was a medium-brown black man with crisp, dark hair and a well-trimmed graying moustache. He stood examining a group of black-and-white nature photographs in the alcove behind Avery's desk as I entered the room, but turned to me with a practiced smile. "Karen," he said, coming forward with his hand extended, "I don't believe we've been introduced."

"Good to meet you, Marc." His grip was strong without being painful. A firm, reliable, lawyerly handshake. Like his smile, it was practiced.

"Coffee, Karen? Or perhaps a drink?" Avery examined the contents of a cabinet by the clean-swept fireplace. "I've got Glenfiddich here, some bourbon, a little Harvey's—"

"No, thanks, Avery. I'm fine." Going through the liquor cabinet meant he didn't have to shake my hand when Marc did. I noted the evasion.

Avery gestured to a maroon leather chair. When I was seated, he adjusted the chintz drapes so that what little sun there was no longer shone in my eyes.

"Cigarette, Karen?" Marc was at my side with a pack of Dunhills.

"Thank you, but no."

Avery moved a crystal bowl of hard candies to the table beside my chair. I ignored it. These two minions of the college were fussing over me far more than was seemly, which sharpened my paranoia about their agenda. At last, Marc got down to business. Edith Hart's will, of course, was currently going through probate, but a facsimile had been made available to him. He had read through the language, he said, and had found a troubling loophole. The terms of the will, seemingly cobbled together in a hurry by a less-than-meticulous lawyer, had bequeathed Meadowbrook and its endowment to the college on the condition that I be appointed director. No alternative had been considered should I refuse the directorship.

"So you see, Karen," Marc summarized, "the college finds itself in a position where it needs to have your intentions clarified . . ." I glanced over at Avery; he nodded, smiled, smooth as silk. ". . . because, an, er, situation has arisen—about which, I do believe, Avery has briefed you."

"You mean—Thibault Brewster's threatened lawsuit?"

"Well, er, yes. You *could* put it that way. That's *one* element of the situation." Marc leaned forward in his black Enfield College captain's chair, his hands flat on gray summer-weight wool knees. His expression was earnest, his gaze intense. Avery had assumed a similar posture in his leather armchair, hands flat on khaki, cool blue eyes trained directly on my face.

Whoa, I thought, as it hit me. *These guys are in desperate need of my cooperation. I am in the catbird seat today.* If I were a different kind of person, I would have flashed a shit-eating grin right then and there, and declared, "Okay, boys, tell me what you're gonna do for me," and they might have doubled my salary, granted me early tenure, promoted me to full professor. But I've never been one to play games, and I wasn't about to start now.

But I was no patsy either. "So? What are the implications here? In particular," I glanced over at Avery, "since our talk the other evening, I've been wondering about my liability should Brewster proceed to press a suit against me."

Avery opened his mouth to speak, but his mouthpiece got there first, all assurance and very little information. "In the extremely unlikely instance, Karen, that you should choose to refuse the directorship of the center, the probability exists that, rather than suing you or the college directly, Mr. Brewster would petition the

court to have Meadowbrook and its endowment revert
to the estate, to which he, as Dr. Hart's closest living
relative, would then lay claim." Marc ceased speaking,
waited for my response. I gave him a *go ahead* nod.
"Now, it is my understanding that you initially ex-
pressed some, er . . . reluctance . . . to undertake the
responsibilities of this position. . . ." His voice trailed
off. Once again I nodded: *Go ahead.* "Ah, since your
inclinations regarding this directorship might well impact significantly upon the future direction of the institution's response to any challenge legally instituted by Mr.
Brewster, we feel it imperative at this point in time to
ascertain your, er, definitive disposition in this matter." I
nodded again. "And I am empowered by the Office of
the President to assure you that, should you allow yourself to be named director—say, even in a somewhat
nominal capacity, such as, perhaps, *Executive* Director
or Chairman of the *Board*—as an agent of the college
you would, of course, be immune to any personal liability should the lawsuit proceed." Avery's head was bobbing in affirmation. "And, I believe, you would find the
compensation more than adequate. Now, at this point in
time—"

At his attorney's second *this point in time,* Avery
winced. "Karen," he inquired bluntly, "do you or do
you not intend to accept the directorship of the
Northbury center? That will make a great difference in
how we decide to proceed."

"Oh," I replied, all innocence, "I do intend to accept
it. Given the proper compensation, and a written assurance of legal immunity, of course, and with the understanding that, after an appropriate period, I would be
free to retire from the position and go back to teaching."

Marc glanced over at Avery. Both men sat back in
their chairs, as if their spines had simultaneously unstif-
fened. The sense of relief was almost palpable. Clearly
the president and his minion had anticipated some seri-

ous resistance. But I'd already made my decision before I entered this room. I didn't have to *marry* the job. I could do it for a year or two, get the Northbury Center going, and then go back to full-time teaching. Which I definitely *would* do; I did *not* relish the prospect of a future composed primarily of board meetings and fund-raisers.

Walking through Meadowbrook with Avery the other evening, envisioning reading rooms, seminar rooms, archives, maybe even nineteenth-century flower gardens, had brought the center to life in my imagination. And, as annoyed as I might be at Edith Hart for saddling me with an unanticipated responsibility, I owed it to Serena Northbury to do this for her. To Mrs. Northbury and her contemporaries, women who had braved the censure of their culture to write about their lives and dreams, many of them with names that had vanished in the mists of the past. I was truly psyched about the Northbury Center—but with these two potentates of institutional power I intended to play it cool.

And, anyhow, a vague question was beginning to niggle at my mind: How long had Avery known about this particular complication in the Hart bequest? Had he known about the college's need for my cooperation the evening we toured Meadowbrook? The evening he—*No*. I refused to think . . . Oh, Jesus. What was going on here?

While the two administrators plotted their next moves in the legal game of chess the college was about to play, I stared thoughtfully out a small-paned, leaded window. It was raining again. An azalea bush, its pink flowers just past their peak, drooped under the weight of the intermittent drizzle. I knew that by the time the shower had passed, a circle of brown-edged blossoms would surround the azalea's base. From the bowl of candy at my elbow, I chose a cellophane-wrapped peppermint and untwisted the wrapper. The mint was sharp and fresh on my tongue. Sweet, too. An almost breath-taking sensation.

The men's voices had ceased. I glanced back at them. Marc was shuffling through some papers on his lap. Avery was examining me with an unreadable expression on his features. "Thank you, Karen," he said, when my gaze met his. Then, after a silence measurable only in heartbeats, he continued. "I can't tell you how much I, personally, appreciate your decision."

My expression as unreadable as his, I also chose to pause enigmatically. "That's not why I'm accepting the directorship, Avery," I said, finally.

He appeared startled. "No, I didn't mean—"

"I'm doing it for Serena Northbury. I'm doing it for my students. I'm doing it because Edith Hart wanted me to."

"Of course," he said, hastily. "Of course."

Marc jumped in here, "Brewster will probably sue, anyhow, Karen, but you've saved the college a great deal of legal hassle."

"I am so glad," I said. "So very glad."

The rain had let up by the time I left Avery's office. Strolling past the now-denuded azalea bush, I bent down impulsively and scooped a handful of limp petals from the wet grass. Really, I knew nothing at all about Avery Cabot Claibourne Mitchell except what he wanted me to know. I fingered the damp blooms. He had a reputation as a brilliant administrator and fund-raiser. A breeze came up as I reached the portals of Dickinson Hall. I released a few petals, watched them flutter toward the grass. Was it possible his kiss that night at Meadow-brook had been part of some devious plan to get me to go along with his agenda for the Northbury Center? Who knew? And, anyhow, could he possibly think I would be that easy to manipulate? Well, he was wrong.

Just because Tony was no longer in my life didn't mean I was vulnerable to any smooth talker who chose to play kissyface with me. I felt my lips tighten. Not on your tintype, I wasn't. I opened my hand and freed the remaining blossoms into the wind.

Nineteen

I sat at Rudolph's bar, licking salt off the rim of a frozen margarita, and waited for Dr. Willis Thorpe to arrive. In a far corner, Miles Jewell and Thibault Brewster huddled in close confab. The old guard girding their loins over martinis, straight up.

Will slipped onto the high caned seat next to me and ordered a double martini, straight up. Well, there's old guard, and then there's old guard.

"Have you heard about Gerry's coup?" he asked.

"No-oo." I didn't think he was referring to Jill's pregnancy.

"He has a publisher for his book of poems."

"Really?"

"Yes. Helen Whitlow just told me. Some independent press, somewhere in Vermont, I believe. Small, but respectable." Will grimaced. "Book's title, believe it or not, is *Bastard*. He dedicated it to Edith."

"Oh." A mixed message to give about someone you believed was your mother.

Will smiled, wistfully. "I do wish Edie was still

around; she'd have a good laugh." He paused. "I can't begin to tell you how much I miss that woman."

"I can imagine." I laid my hand on his arm in sympathy. "I miss her, too, and I hardly knew her."

"She liked you, you know. Said you were a no-bullshit kind of person. And that you . . ." The martini arrived in its stemmed glass; and he drank it in three gulps, like a man downing medicine. That much gin would put me under the table, but it didn't seem to affect him at all.

"What?"

"Well," reluctantly, "she said you had a huge untapped reservoir of passion."

"Jesus!" I could feel the blush rising.

"She talked like that, you know. Like a character in a D. H. Lawrence novel. Edie was the only person I ever met who was totally candid about what she thought. It got her in trouble more than once."

"I'll bet it did."

While Will ordered another double martini, I took a closer look at him. Tonight he wore his nearly eighty years like a heavy coat. He looked far more stooped and elderly than he had when I'd first met him, earlier in the spring. His broad shoulders slumped noticeably, and a gray tinge had replaced the ruddy tones of his complexion. Edith's death had hit him hard.

Will had called that morning—to tell me he was staying with an old friend in Enfield while he tied up a few loose ends in Edith's affairs, and to ask if I would have dinner with him. He'd like, he'd said, to apprise me of Edith's thinking about the Northbury Center. When he'd told me Helen Whitlow was the friend he was visiting, I'd exclaimed in surprise, "But I thought—" Helen Whitlow the recluse? The crazy woman in the big house behind the overgrown yew hedge? The house on Whitlow Street where I liked to walk. The house with the scent of lilacs.

"I know." Will had laughed. "You've heard the rumors. You think she's a crazy lady, don't you? A cat-ridden recluse. Well, Helen's distinctly odd, and she does have a number of cats, but she's . . . well, she's *sane*. And—she's an old friend. I've known Helen as long as I've known Edith. They were friends as girls."

"I didn't know that."

"Then they had a falling out over . . . Well, they had a falling out, and I've been . . . a rather sporadic link between them for over forty years." He'd chortled. "And, believe me, it hasn't always been easy."

"Tell me, Will," I asked as I sipped the last of the margarita, "how did Helen Whitlow know about Gerry's book?"

Will pushed away his half-finished second martini. "If I drink any more of that, I won't find my way back to Whitlow Street. Well, it's quite a story—about Helen and Gerry. Let's get a table, and I'll tell you."

With the Enfield students gone, Rudolph's is quiet in the summertime, its clientele a mix of locals and academics, with a few tourists thrown in for the money. So, as we passed the table where Miles and Brewster conspired, they had a difficult time not seeing us. "Hello, Tib," Will Thorpe said. Brewster nodded, without making eye contact. Miles grumbled unintelligibly in my direction. His spiky white eyebrows needed a good combing. As I walked with Will Thorpe into the dining room, I could feel the eyes underneath those brows burning into my back. What new wrinkle does it portend, the old guard must be wondering, my presence here with Edith Hart's good friend?

According to Rudolph's highly cosmopolitan menu, the grilled breast of local free-range chicken I ordered would be served with Ceylon mango salsa, Moroccan couscous, broiled Holland tomatoes au gratin, and New Jersey asparagus bundles wrapped in paper-thin Parisian pastry. This was one of the ironies of eating at Rudolph's: My food would be more well-traveled than I could ever hope to be. Will ordered porterhouse steak—

rare—baked potato with sour cream, early corn on the cob, and a carafe of burgundy. "Unhealthy," he told me. "Especially for a man with a history of heart disease. But I might as well. Life's not much fun without Edith, anyhow. God, I loved that woman." The alcohol was beginning to take hold. I hoped he wouldn't get maudlin.

While I tucked into my salad, Will broke open a roll and slathered it with butter. "I fell in love with Edith in med school, you know—the first day of anatomy class. It was in the middle of the Depression, and we were a fairly threadbare crew, we medical students. My family had suffered serious reverses in '29, and overnight I'd been transformed from a privileged adolescent to a frightened young fellow, terrified to open my mouth for fear I'd jeopardize the only chance I had to keep a toehold in the middle class. Well, here were these rows and rows of stone-faced young men—not many women in medicine in those days—and the lecture began. I was scribbling in my notebook, when the auditorium door flew open and this dark-haired vision in a gray wool suit, high-heeled sandals, and a full set of fox furs walked in. Everyone gaped, and Professor Lowell halted in mid-sentence. 'Young lady,' he said, 'I believe you're in the wrong classroom.' 'Is this Human Anatomy and Physiology?' she asked. 'It is,' he responded. 'Then I'm most definitely in the right classroom.' She swept in, taking a final drag on her cigarette, and, granting me a dazzling smile, she slid into the seat next to mine." Will placed the buttered roll on his plate, and poured himself another glass of burgundy. "I was her slave from that moment on." He took a gulp of the wine and fell into a meditative silence.

Following his example, I poured wine and sipped at it. Unaccustomed to more than one drink, I was getting pretty loose myself. "Tell me, Will," I ventured, "were you and Edith, well . . . ?"

"Lovers? Of course. For decades. But it was an off-and-on kind of thing. Always *on* for me, but *off* for her a good deal of the time." He nodded at the waitress who'd arrived with our meals, then poked his steaming baked potato with a fork. Just as the silence threatened to prolong itself beyond the comfort level, he met my eyes. "She preferred a more—*heightened*—kind of experience than I was able to give her. I was always too . . . *safe* . . . for Edith."

"Oh," I said. "Oh."

He shrugged. "But she always came back."

"It must have hurt a great deal." I didn't know how else to respond to such unguarded revelations. I cut into the chicken breast, and piled mango salsa on the slice.

"It hurt like hell," Will replied. "But in some ways she was always mine. What hurt even more was seeing her deteriorate these past few months. *That* broke my heart." He reached in the pocket of his seersucker jacket and pulled out the fine gold chain and heart locket I remembered Edith wearing on Easter Day, the keepsake she had left him in her will. He began sliding the chain through his fingers, as if it were a set of worry beads—or a rosary. His sigh bespoke a deep, almost somatic resignation. "The police believe I killed her, of course."

At my exclamation, he laughed. "Oh, I don't blame them. And it wasn't as if we hadn't talked about it, she and I. About playing the role of Dr. Death for each other, I mean." He cut off a bit of steak, checked it for rareness, chewed. "Look at it this way. The police have three obvious suspects: Tib Brewster, Gerry Novak, and me. We're the logical candidates for *perp*." He gave the final word an ironic twist. "Tib for the inheritance he expected. He'd approached Edith several times in recent months for loans. She couldn't understand how he could possibly have gotten himself in such a shaky financial position so suddenly. Finally she said *no*. So, *there's* Tib: greed and anger.

"Now, Gerry. Gerry also needed money. Edith paid him a generous salary, but he was always broke. We'd begun to suspect that he had expensive habits." Will rubbed his thumb and forefinger together underneath his nose. "And he had an attitude problem. It's hard to define, but there was always an . . . underlying resentment in Novak's relationship with Edith." Will paused, contemplating some particular incident, I thought, then continued without sharing his memories. "So, *there's* Gerry: greed and resentment.

"Now, me. Euthanasia, of course. Because I loved her. It wouldn't have been a *bad* death, you know, as deaths go. She would have become weak, maybe confused; she'd have experienced a declining level of consciousness and gone into diabetic coma. And, without medical intervention, that would have been it. There are worse deaths." He shrugged, as if he'd seen a few. The burgundy came into play again. "And of course, I would have done it had she asked. But—she didn't. And I didn't."

"And you told them that—the police I mean?"

"Of course, I told them; I have no desire to spend my remaining days in incarceration. That large officer . . . the one in charge . . . ?"

"Lieutenant Piotrowski."

"Yes, Piotrowski—he's quite intelligent, isn't he?— well, I got the feeling he wouldn't have blamed me if I *had* confessed to euthanasia. He told me his father's in advanced Alzheimer's. He has to have round-the-clock care for him. He thought, if his father could have predicted his present state, he would have wanted someone to do something. I was surprised to hear him say that, officer of the law that he is. And I was almost sorry not to be able to oblige him by confessing. The only problem is—I didn't kill her."

"Of course you didn't, Will." But I wouldn't have blamed him either. And—Piotrowski with a father? Well, why was I surprised?

"No *of course* about it. All she had to do was give the word."

"Oh." What could I say to that? Fortunately Miles

Jewell attracted my attention at that point, stalking by our table with a disgusted glance at me. I tried to catch Will's eye, but he had begun eating in earnest and seemed not to have noticed Miles. Will worked his way through the entire meal with a kind of stolid determination, finished off the carafe of wine, then ordered brandy with his coffee. *Pretty composed,* I thought, *for a man who had just coolly provided himself and two longtime acquaintances with compelling motives for murder.*

I ordered caffeine with my coffee—I had a twenty-minute drive ahead of me—and sat back to listen as Will Thorpe, having pushed his empty plate away, began to relate Edith's vision for the Northbury Center. As he relayed it, her thinking pretty much matched mine: a research center with a major library of women's literature and an archive concentrating on authors whose papers had previously not been thought worth collecting. Authors such as Serena Northbury. "Edie was extremely enthused about it," Will related. "It had been a long time since I'd seen her look to the future like that." He tilted his head toward the bar, where Thibault Brewster still sat—by himself now. *Lingering alone in bars,* I thought. *Not the healthiest of pastimes.*

"That piece of work in there was expecting to get everything," Will continued. "And Edie never felt very good about that—" He broke off, and looked thoughtful.

"You know, Tib's mother—Edith's sister Lydia—was diabetic, too. And she lived with Tib until she died—maybe fifteen years ago."

"Oh . . . ?"

"He would know how to administer insulin." He shrugged, let the statement die, and went back to his previous topic: Edith's plans for the research center. "Afternoon tea," he said, laughing. "She thought that would be civilized. Around four-thirty every day, researchers would have tea and sandwiches available in the dining room, so they could meet each other and share ideas."

"What a good idea," I replied. "I'll remember that." But I was thinking about Brewster's experience with diabetes. From Tony I'd learned the three fundamentals of criminal investigation: motive, means, and opportunity. As I'd told Piotrowski, Thibault Brewster was a nasty man. And I'd known he was a nasty man with a major motive: Edith's fortune. Now I was learning he was a nasty man with the means: a probable knowledge of insulin and its administration. Now—what about *opportunity?* I wanted to talk this new possibility over with Piotrowski; I'd call him in the morning.

It wasn't far from the restaurant to Whitlow Street, but I decided to walk my dinner companion home. Will was from a drinking generation, and didn't appear more than slightly muddled by all the booze. I am from a more Puritanical generation—at least when it comes to alcohol—and couldn't quite believe someone who'd consumed that much of it was capable of putting one foot in front of the other for a space of five or six blocks without the help of a designated walker.

We paused at the bottom of the restaurant's steps; Field Street was fairly well lit, but, after the brightness of the restaurant, the evening shadows seemed dense. With my first breath of the scented June air, Edith's assessment hit me: *A huge untapped reservoir of passion.* Jeez! The woman didn't know what she was talking about. I had a good life. A great job. A wonderful daughter. I was *fine.* And what business was it of Edith Hart's, anyhow? No wonder the good doctor's outspokenness had so often gotten her in trouble.

Will broke into my musings as we turned off Field and onto Whitlow Street. "You did get a copy of my letter to President Mitchell, Karen? About naming the center?"

"Yes, Will, I did. But I haven't talked to him about it yet. So many other issues have come up." Just in time I recalled Avery's injunction to keep silent about the impending lawsuit. "But I do think it's a good idea—*the*

Northbury/Hart Research Center. Edith deserves to be remembered for her generosity, and besides—*Northbury/Hart*—it's got a wonderful ring to it. You can count on my support." And, in the end, I wouldn't have been surprised if soliciting my support for the new name hadn't been the primary purpose of our dinner.

At the gate to the Whitlow house I remembered something my companion had mentioned earlier. "Will, what's the 'long story' you were going to tell me about Helen Whitlow and Gerry Novak?"

His hand on the half-opened gate, Will turned back to me. "I forgot about that, didn't I? Well, come in and let Helen tell you herself."

I was astonished. "Oh, I couldn't—it's so late. And, besides, she's not expecting me. I—"

He took my arm. "She'll be up, believe me. Helen never sleeps. It'll do her good to see someone besides Gerry."

"Besides *Gerry*—?"

We passed Will's maroon Lincoln in the circular driveway, then climbed the stairs to the ornate, peeling double doors. Will fumbled with a key. "Helen," he called when he'd gotten the door open. "Helen, you've got company." We were standing in a wide central hall with a curved staircase heading up into the darkness.

"I don't want company." The quavering voice floated down from the top of the stairs. "Tell the young woman to go home."

"Karen's not going home, Helen, so you'd better come down. If you don't, I'm going to bring her upstairs." Will was grinning, as if this were not an unfamiliar exchange. He lowered his voice as he turned to address me. "She's been watching us from the upper hall window. She's got a chair there. When the weather's too cold or wet to garden, she spends hours reading and looking out the window."

"Willis, I feel very uncomfortable about barging in on Miss Whitlow like this. Don't make her come down if she doesn't want to." And, really, weren't we bullying this poor old woman?

"Pshaw." I'd never actually heard anyone say that before. "She's better off not giving in to her notions. She'll be down in a minute; just you wait. And she'll be happy to visit. In her own style, that is. Why don't you sit in here," he motioned to a parlor reminiscent of Meadowbrook's, but smaller and far less well cared-for. Horsehair tufted from one corner of a green velvet love seat, and tattered rose-colored wallpaper gave a Gothic ambiance to the high-ceilinged room. Cat hair covered everything. "I'll just go get us a nightcap."

"Willis, I don't want—"

But he was gone. After three or four minutes of restless waiting on the hard settee, I rose and roamed the room. A fluffy gray cat strolled in from the hallway and wound itself around my ankles. It was followed by a yellow tabby, who shot me a contemptuous glance, then proceeded to sharpen his claws on the fraying love seat. As I shooed him away, a dusty photo album on a side table caught my eye. I took it back to the settee and opened the embossed front cover. The sepia photographs commenced with a formal wedding portrait in which a tall, thin man and a tiny, pudgy woman dressed in fin-de-siècle serge and flounces stared somberly at the camera. A number of years later, to judge by the dress styles, an infant made her appearance, then grew to pony-riding size, dressed for Easter services, went away to college in a flapper-style suit, rode out the Depression in a small dark coupe, donned short patriotic skirts during World War II, then, sometime in the fifties, vanished abruptly as the gallery of pictures ended with an empty rectangle where the last photo in the album had been ripped from its black adhesive corners.

"I've seen you before." The voice from the doorway was creaky, as if with disuse. "You walk by here. You look at my flowers."

The heavy album cover slammed shut as I started at

the unexpected words. A tiny, white-haired woman walked toward me, followed by Will with a tray of delicate, stemmed glasses and a bottle of sherry. The woman wore decrepit rolled-up jeans and a boy's plaid flannel shirt. Her face was the face of the photographs, only freeze-dried.

"Yes, I do," I replied. "Is that all right?" My sense of trespass was becoming irrationally strong.

"Will says you want to know about Gerry. If I tell you, will you go away?"

"I'll go away now, if that's what you want—"

But she had perched on a crewel-worked ottoman and begun talking. And, then, I didn't think she would ever shut up.

An hour later, in response to my casual question about how she was acquainted with Gerry Novak, I knew enough about Helen Whitlow to write *her* biography when I'd finished Serena Northbury's. Will had sat patiently through a tale he must have heard a hundred times before, and I wondered again about his relationship with these two passionate women.

Helen had met Edith at Smith College in the late twenties, and then had spent a few heady years living with her in Greenwich Village. While Edith studied medicine, Helen pursued a career in dress design, specializing in scaled-down fashions for the newly impoverished rich. With her mother's death, she had come back to Enfield to care for her ailing father. Years later, when Helen was in her early forties, she'd fallen in love with a handsome, brooding, immigrant handyman named Karl Novak. Edith had strongly disapproved of this unsuitable liaison. Her interference resulted in Karl's removal to Meadowbrook and his hasty marriage to the daughter of Meadowbrook's resident farm manager. Almost immediately, Gerry had been born. Helen's revenge against Edith for breaking up the romance of her life had been to win the affections of Karl's son away from her. Edith, it seemed, during the few weeks in each year she was in residence at Meadowbrook, had taken a great liking to the winsome child.

"She may have had Karl and his son there at Meadowbrook, but I had Karl's heart. He never said so, but I knew it. And, then, when Karl went away and didn't come back . . ."

Korea, Will mouthed at me.

". . . I won *Gerry's* heart. I saw to it he learned all about Edith and her conniving ways. Gerry learned to hate her and to love his Auntie Helen. And to this day he takes care of me like a son, does my shopping, takes out my garbage, helps me with the flowers. Does anything I ask him to do. Gerry's a good boy, and he loves me more than anyone," the old woman concluded triumphantly, in her rusty voice. I glanced back at Will: *This woman is sane?* Will shrugged.

My mind was racing. Wasn't this long-inculcated hatred another nail in Gerry Novak's coffin? If Gerry *had* murdered Edith, he'd certainly had a wealth of powerful motives—a half-million-dollar inheritance, a belief that Edith was his mother and that she had abandoned him at birth, possibly the stolen Northbury manuscript—and, now, a lifelong hatred of his benefactor.

Helen's creaky voice broke into my thoughts. "Will, bring me that picture," she commanded, pointing to a black-and-white snapshot in a silver frame sitting alone on the mantel. Posed with a curly-haired child in a cowboy suit, a younger Helen beamed at the camera. "You see that outfit? I bought it for him, the suit, the guns, the boots, the spurs, everything. He loved it; he'd get on that old pony of Edith's and ride and ride." The light in her expression dimmed. "I never forgave Edith, though. I thought she was my friend. But she stole the love of my life—"

"She *stole* him?"

But Helen Whitlow's face had taken on a sour, uncommunicative expression. The story was told; this book was closed.

•   •

I left the Whitlow house sometime after eleven, befuddled by aged sherry, exhausted by aged passions. As I traversed the lawn with its variegated flower beds, the scent of roses hung thick in the air. *A huge untapped reservoir . . .* Damn that woman, anyhow!

Twenty

"Karen," Jill said as soon as I picked up the phone, "it's a girl."

"Oh," I said. "Great." I paused. "Tell me, Jill: Am I supposed to say *great*? Are you happy about this?"

"Happy? Karen, I'm *thrilled*. Oh, I admit I was shattered when I first knew I was pregnant. But then you and I talked—remember? About Amanda? And how you were only nineteen? And I figured if you could do it, I could do it. And then I saw the sonogram." Her laugh bubbled. "Karen, she's so beautiful: all gray and fuzzy, with a little round head and a little round tummy. And *toes*. Karen, she's already got *toes*. Her name is Eloise, and—"

"You saw that on the sonogram? You saw the name *Eloise*? Where was it written? On her little round forehead?"

"Don't be snide, Karen; I'm ecstatic." And, indeed, she sounded over the top with happiness. "*And* I'm giving a party. Tonight. To make the announcement. Can you come? Can you bring food?"

"A party? Jill, are you sure this is how you want to let people know about your pregnancy? There are more discreet ways—"

"The hell with discretion. I'm a grown-up woman; I'm going to have a baby; I'm perfectly capable of taking care of her. This kid deserves as much of a celebration as any other rug rat. There's just one thing. . . ." Her voice abruptly went flat. "Gerry definitely won't be in the picture. He doesn't want to have anything to do with this baby."

"Jill—"

"So, I told him I never want to see him again. Ever. He's not the person I thought he was." Her tone grew bitter, as if her natural ebullience had snagged against a particularly distasteful fact. "As a matter of fact, he's a real *jerk*. I just found out that the whole time I was seeing him, he was balling someone else."

Jeez. "Jill, I'm so sorry—"

"Karen, it's not your fault that I'm so stupid. But, listen, no one else knows who the baby's father is. I didn't even tell my parents. So . . ." she phrased it casually, but it was a plea, "here's an occasion for your famous discretion."

"Sure. Teeth buttoned. Lips zipped."

"Thanks." Then she was bubbling again. "So, I'm gonna make a huge salad. What can you bring?"

"How about my *infamous* Serbian spinach casserole?"

"Ohhhh. The one that's made of nothing but butter and cheese? Terrific! The doctor said I can eat as much as I want to."

Jill had put out an all-points bulletin about the party, and by eight P.M. that evening her apartment was packed with Enfield faculty and administrators, their families and friends. A mid-June heat wave had sent the already-warm temperature soaring, then a fast moving thunderstorm had swept through, driving partygoers off the wraparound porch and into the close, nonair-conditioned quarters of Jill's three-and-a-half rooms. The doors and windows were thrown wide open, but the air was stifling. The mood was festive, anyhow; a college town is a dull place in the summer, and the impromptu Saturday night party seemed to delight Jill's friends and colleagues. As I handed out icy bottles of Michelob Lite and Pete's Wicked Ale from the open refrigerator, my face was cool enough, but a rivulet of sweat trickled down my spine. Between the clamor of voices and the melancholy angst of R.E.M., the decibel level was high, but nowhere near as high as it was about to be.

"Boys and girls," Jill called, as she climbed on a kitchen chair she'd dragged to the middle of the living room. "Boys and girls! Gather round please. I have an announcement to make."

That was my cue. I positioned myself by the CD player.

"Jill. Careful!" Big, blond Kenny Halvorsen elbowed his way out of the crowd. "You don't want to fall, do you?" He grabbed her arm. Smiling at him, Jill steadied herself on his more-than-adequate shoulder. Kenny glanced over at me and shook his head, disapprovingly. I wondered if The Incredible Blue Hulk, neighbor that he was, knew more about what was going on with Jill than his stolid jock persona revealed.

When the laughing crowd had hushed, Jill looked over at me and commanded: "Hit it, Karen."

"Yes, Jill," I replied, dutifully. I was not thrilled with this scenario, but pressed the button and started the Madonna track of "Papa, Don't Preach." From his position at Jill's side, Kenny Halvorsen scowled. His expression grew grim. Just as I'd thought—he must have suspected all along that Jill was pregnant.

With her flushed face framed by the wild golden-red hair, Jill was radiant. Her long white sundress was gathered loosely under the bosom; she looked strikingly like a Pre-Raphaelite angel. A gold heart locket on a long, thin chain gleamed against the filmy white fabric of her dress. *I've seen that locket somewhere,* I thought, *and not too long ago.* Then it struck me: This was Edith's locket! The gold heart I'd seen in Willis Thorpe's hand the evening before. But, how on earth did Jill get it? And when?

"Boys and girls," Jill proclaimed, "just about midterm, when most of you dear people will be deeply immersed in the manifold pleasures of grading mid-semester exams, I will be approaching the end of a very different kind of term. *So*—I'm holding this party to-night to announce—ta dah!—the impending arrival of Eloise Karen Greenberg, at Enfield Regional Medical Center, sometime in late October."

My gasp of astonishment—that she was giving the kid my name—was drowned in the general uproar. Kenny, with a grave look on his habitually cheerful face, helped Jill down off the chair, and she was immediately lost to sight in a mob of curious well-wishers. While Madonna wailed about havin' his baby, Sally Chenille stood at the fringe of the crowd, and stared enigmatically in the direction of Jill's disappearance. Then Sally looked around, spotted me.

"So, Karen," she made her way to my side with a hard, unreadable smile, "who's the lucky man who got to father this brat?"

"What's the matter, Sally?" I responded, "you've never heard of immaculate conception?"

I didn't catch Sally's reply. The figure suddenly out-lined in the doorway behind her distracted me. "Excuse me, Sally," I said. Surely that couldn't be . . . ? I brushed past my scowling colleague and made my way through the crowd to the apartment door. Surely it wasn't . . . ? Surely . . . ? But with the dusk at his back, and the porch light throwing dense shadows on his heavy, sweating face, it surely was. "Hello, Lieutenant," I said, "I suppose you caught that announcement."

"I did," he replied, mopping at his face with a blue bandanna. "I did, indeed. And it's particularly—distressing—in light of my—er—errand here this evening." Wearing khaki shorts and a black Willie Nelson T-shirt, the lieutenant looked as if he'd been dragged away from a low-key day at home. His arms and legs were brown and solid. His eyes were intent on Jill, laughing now as she reset the Madonna CD.

I'd called Piotrowski's office that morning. I'd wanted to tell him about Thibault Brewster's experience with caring for a diabetic. I'd decided to keep my suspicions about Gerry Novak to myself—at least for the time being. Jill was my friend, and I didn't want to interfere in her personal life any more than I already had. When the dispatcher said the lieutenant was off duty until Monday, except for emergencies, I'd decided my bit of gossip didn't fall into that category. I'd left my name and a message that I'd like to talk to the lieutenant at his convenience. When he materialized in the door of Jill's apartment, I assumed, stupidly, that he'd gotten the message, wanted to talk to me immediately, and had tracked me down. "Lieutenant, you really didn't have to come all the way out here. I could have told you on the phone."

"*You* could have told *me?* On the *phone?*"

"Yes, it's just a little piece of information. You probably know about it already, anyhow. But I thought just in case you didn't—"

"Doctor," he grabbed my arm and drew me out onto the porch, "you and me, we gotta talk."

"Well, yes, of course. That's why I called you."

"Oh, you called? I guess I didn't get that message."

My fingertips grew cold. "Then why are you here?"

He ignored my question. "What did you want to tell me?"

"It's probably nothing. First I want to know why you're here."

"My business is with Dr. Greenberg, not with you."

"Oh, for God's sake, Lieutenant, don't harass Jill tonight. She threw this party to celebrate her pregnancy."

"So I heard." A troubled expression crossed the lieutenant's face. He leaned back against a pillar and crossed his arms. He looked as if he were there for the duration. "What's your info?"

I sighed. For once, I'd come up against someone more obstinate than I am. "Well, Lieutenant, I had dinner with Dr. Thorpe last night, and he happened to mention . . ." But when I'd finished telling him about Thibault Brewster's diabetic mother, Piotrowski showed no response. None at all. The "info" had gone into that great data bank of a brain for processing, and that was all I needed to know—at least as far as the lieutenant was concerned. He was in that kind of mood.

The porch light didn't reach into the corner where we stood, and the few partygoers who'd deserted the house for the minimally cooler porch must have assumed our tête-à-tête was private. Piotrowski leaned back against the white pillar, chewing his lips—very nice lips, I'd always thought, full and sensuous. I decided not to interrupt his meditations. Finally he looked up at me and asked, "Doctor, do you know anything about Gerry Novak you haven't told me?"

Gerry Novak? Helen Whitlow's bitter tale came flooding into my mind. I could hear the funny, rusty voice: *Gerry takes care of me like a son . . . he does anything I ask him to do.* "Why do you ask, Lieutenant? Have you arrested Gerry?"

Piotrowski's brown eyes were absolutely still. "Do you know something about Novak that would make you think I might have a reason to arrest him?" Carefully selected and carefully articulated, his words thickened the darkness in our remote corner of the porch.

"Noooo. Well, I *have* heard some things about him, but nothing that would count as—you know, evidence of any wrongdoing."

Abruptly the lieutenant uncrossed his arms, clapped his hands back against the porch railing, and pushed himself into an upright position. "Come on, Doctor, we're going for a walk."

"A walk? Piotrowski, there's a party going on here."

"And don't I know it."

Protesting all the while, I was tugged along in the big cop's wake as he navigated the small group by the porch steps and headed toward the sidewalk.

"Dr. Pelletier," he said, as soon as we had gotten out of earshot of the house, "sometimes I think I have the shittiest job in the world."

"Lieutenant?" I was flabbergasted, by his words, but even more, by the vehemence with which he'd spoken them.

Piotrowski sighed. "Ferrinstance, Doctor, you and me—we go back a ways, right? And I gotta admit I like you—as a person, I mean." He paused for a second. "That's okay to say, right? I mean, that's not—like, er— sexual harassment or anything, is it?"

"No, of course not!"

"With you academic types, I'm never sure—you know, all that PC stuff. Anyways, so you're basically a decent person, and I know that. But, you're all the time pissed at me. Holdin' out on me. Accusing me of harassment. And all just because I'm tryin' to do my job. I mean, c'mon, Doctor—give me a break! We're talking about a homicide investigation here. I gotta ask obnoxious questions, and you know it. But I don't *harass* anyone—unless they deserve it, of course. Give me credit for having some brains, willya?"

I winced at his words. "Sorry." We were walking fast in the direction of downtown Enfield. My legs are long, but I had to hustle to keep up with Piotrowski's rapid stride. "You know I respect you, Piotrowski. And I do know how hard your job is. Living with Tony was no . . ." The heavy fragrance of roses in the air alerted me that we were passing the Whitlow house. "Anyhow, it's just that I, well, I guess I have conflicted loyalties—"

"Tsk. How could you have conflicted loyalties when it comes to homicide?"

"No, it's not that. It's just that a lot of the stuff I hear, you know, couldn't possibly be relevant. . . ."

"Tsk." The lieutenant came to an abrupt halt at the door of Moccio's, a dingy bar at the near end of Field Street. He peered in the door. "We won't likely run into any of your colleagues here, will we, Doctor?"

"Hardly. I'm probably the only faculty member on campus who'd be caught dead in a place like this."

By the yellow light above the entry, I saw Piotrowski wince. His voice was somber as he said, in all seriousness, it seemed, "Well, let's hope it doesn't come to that, Doctor." Then I remembered, for this man death was more than simply a figure of speech.

A blast of cold air hit me as I pushed open the door. My sweating face went clammy. Avoiding the bar, the lieutenant led me to a table in a back corner. "Order something stiff," he said.

"My God, Piotrowski." My fingertips went even colder than my face, and the sudden chill had nothing to do with air conditioning. "What's going on?"

"You drink bourbon?"

I nodded.

"Two Jack Daniel's," he called over to the bartender. "Doubles."

"Another shitty part of my job," he continued, once the drinks had been delivered, "is that I occasionally have to deliver really bad news, sometimes to really nice people."

"Me?" Had something happened to Amanda? Was he trying to break it gently? Something seized up in my chest. I think it was my heart. *Was that why the booze?*

"No," he said, and reached out to squeeze my hand. I almost choked on my drink, I was so surprised. "Thank God, no."

My heartbeat picked up again. "But, then, why are we here?"

He looked down at his hand, pulled it back. His expression remained grim. "I'm gonna need your help, Doctor. I gotta tell your friend Dr. Greenberg that the father of her child—I assume Novak is the father of her child—was found dead this afternoon."

My shocked intake of breath sounded like something between a hoot and a cry of pain. A couple of chivalrous UPS drivers at the next table glanced up, concerned, saw they couldn't take Piotrowski, even if he was brutalizing me, and, wisely, decided to ignore us.

"What? How?"

"Drowned."

"*Drowned*? Where?"

"In that big pond at Meadowbrook. Down behind the house a ways."

"Yes. I've seen it. He goes—went—fishing there, Jill said. All the time. Oh, my God, poor Jill! What a horrible thing! It was an accident, right? Please tell me it was an accident."

"*Maybe* it was an accident—" The bulky shoulders moved fractionally up, then down.

"Maybe?" My voice came out in a horrified squeak.

"Or maybe it wasn't."

"Lieutenant!"

"Drink your drink." I sipped, obediently. "The other options are homicide—or, of course, suicide—"

"Suicide!" Maybe because Jill had broken up with him? Could she live with it, if that turned out to be the case?

"So you see, Doctor, why I need you to tell me anything you might possibly know about Gerry Novak, whether you think it's *relevant* or not."

I knocked back the rest of the bourbon, then began to talk in a rapid, mechanical, manner—about Gerry's belief that Edith Hart was his real mother, and had given him up at birth, about Helen Whitlow's long-ago passion for Gerry's father, her bitter hatred of Edith, her statement that Gerry would do anything she asked him, about the other woman he'd been sleeping with at the same time as Jill, even the fact that Jill had just ended her relationship with the father of her child-to-be. I wasn't breaching any confidences with that last piece of information; Piotrowski'd find out soon enough.

As I spilled it all out, a story began to form, a nice, neat narrative package. I couldn't resist explicating it to the lieutenant. "Don't you see? It must have been suicide. Under the influence of Helen Whitlow, Gerry had come to hate Edith. Whether or not she really was his biological mother wouldn't matter." I recalled Helen's claim that Edith had *stolen* Karl Novak. Given what Will had told me about Edith's—*heightened*—sex life, a hot affair with the handyman was a not-inconceivable scenario. So I threw that supposition into the narrative brew. By the end of my tale, I had Gerry guilty of killing Edith, and then, in a state of repentant remorse, deciding to end his life by drowning himself in his murdered mother's lake. It was a good story, positively Faulknerian, and I told it vividly and compellingly. By the end of the tale, I had myself utterly convinced.

When I glanced over at Piotrowski for a reaction, he was sitting back in his chair with a wry half-smile on his face. "Well, Dr. Pelletier, that's real good. That sounds just like one of those stories your Mrs. Northbury woulda written." His response jolted me back to reality.

"Piotrowski, don't mock me! And, anyhow, why *couldn't* it have happened that way?"

"Oh, it might of, and I'll keep the possibility in mind. And I'm not mocking you. It's just that—well—unlike you literary types, I hafta provide evidence when I put together a story like that."

"And a good thing, too." I was just a little muzzy from the bourbon. "But I can't bear to think that he was *killed*, Lieutenant! Two murders at Meadowbrook in the same month? It *is* just like a book! The place must have a curse on it. A long, dark, sinister curse."

Piotrowski gave me a straight look. "You really shouldn't drink, Doctor."

"But you . . ."

He pushed back his chair and stood. "C'mon, I gotta get back to Dr. Greenberg's. The sergeant's probably there by now."

"Sergeant Schultz? What's she doing at Jill's?"

"I thought a female officer might provide some comfort—"

"Comfort? That woman would provide about as much comfort as a pit viper."

"Yeah—and she likes you, too. C'mon, upsy-daisy, Doctor. Ms. Greenberg is gonna need you. You wanna hold onta my arm?"

Twenty-one

Gerry Novak had been a pack rat. What's more, he had come from a long line of pack rats. Not only was the dining room table he'd used as a writing desk piled high with stacks of meticulously dated and labeled drafts of poems—"Bastard I," draft one, "Bastard I," draft two, "Bastard I," draft three, "Bastard II," draft one, and so forth—but two of the three small bedrooms in the house his family had occupied for over a century were stacked five feet high with papers and magazines dating back at least to the 1930's, long before he was born. In the kitchen, under the stony gaze of Sergeant Felicity Schultz, I leafed through the topmost issue of a pile of *Reader's Digest*s from the 1950's—"My Most Unforgettable Character," "Humor in Uniform," "Life in These United States." No clues there.

"What is it you want from me, Sergeant?" The night at Jill's house had been a long, sleepless vigil. Then, as soon as I had gotten Jill to agree to rest for a few minutes, the call had come saying Piotrowski wanted me at Meadowbrook. I left Jill under the solicitous care of

Kenny Halvorsen and trekked out to Eastbrook, exhausted—and sick to death of cops. I plopped down into a red vinyl-covered kitchen chair and surveyed the chaos around me. "It would take weeks to go through this junk," I told Felicity Schultz, "and I wouldn't have any better perspective on it than your greenest rookie would."

The sergeant remained standing; that way she was taller than me. Intimidation. I hadn't lived with Tony for six years without learning stuff like that. Today, as hot as it was in this musty little house, Felicity Schultz wore a beige poplin jacket over a rust-colored camp shirt and khaki pants. Her scrubbed face shone with a fine layer of sweat. I was better off in the lightweight white pants and sleeveless blouse I'd worn to the party, but just marginally. Only a few windows in the Novak house would open—the rest had been painted shut long ago—and the kitchen was stifling. In order to tolerate life in this airless atmosphere, any permanent occupant would have had to be totally impervious to discomfort.

"The lieutenant and I—" she stressed *lieutenant,* "—did not ask you to come out here to look at *Reader's Digests,* Professor Pelletier. We are fully aware of the limited range of your professional expertise"—*ouch*— "and it is within that range that we require the assistance of your knowledge." *The assistance of your knowledge:* That's probably how she thought you were supposed to talk to college professors; I resisted the impulse to inform her that I spoke English, and she could simply ask me to *help.* Striding over to the open kitchen door, Schultz barked, "Demarest!" The tall, thin uniformed trooper had to stoop to enter, the old-fashioned door frame was so low.

"Yeah, Sarge?"

"The box the lieutenant gave you? You got it in the van, right?"

"Which one?"

"That round box? The blue one?"

Round box?

"Right. Should I bring it in?"

"On the double."

Hmm. Round blue box. I wonder . . .

"Right, Sarge." Demarest turned hastily and cracked his head on the low lintel. I winced when he did, but Schultz remained stone-faced. Tough guys don't sympathize. Hey, maybe I'd get a T-shirt made up and give it to her.

Officer Demarest walked back in, ducking carefully. He carried a large brown paper bag. Placing it on the red enamel tabletop, he opened it and revealed—*yes!*—Serena Northbury's battered blue hatbox. The one I'd seen in Edith's pantry. The one that held the manuscript of *Child of the North Star*. I shrieked and lunged for it. Schultz grabbed my arm; her grip was the kind that leaves bruises.

"Don't touch, Professor."

"Yeah. You, too, Sergeant. That hurt."

"Sorry." She didn't look in the least bit remorseful. "Guess I don't know my own strength." *Yeah, right.* "But this here is evidence; I can't let you touch it. The lieutenant says to tell you that later on you'll have your chance. We just want to see if you recognize this before it goes in for testing."

"Yeah, I recognize it. That's the box I told you and Piotrowski about, the hatbox Serena Northbury's novel manuscript is in."

"Not any more it's not." Slipping on a pair of latex gloves, the sergeant lifted the ornate lid with her fingertips. Inside, a jumble of yellowing envelopes half-filled the round pasteboard hatbox. No sign at all of anything resembling a manuscript.

I looked up at Schultz, imploringly. "Tell me you took the manuscript out separately. Tell me it's stowed away in a nice, clean evidence bag on some nice, safe shelf in some nice, secure evidence room."

Her eyes were hooded. "We didn't see hide nor hair of any manuscript, Professor. Just these old letters."

"Yeah. They were in the box when I found it. I recognize the handwriting. It's Northbury's. Can I at least look at those?"

She slid the box out of my reach. And enjoyed doing it. "First we got to check for forensic traces."

Traces, I thought. *That's what I'm looking for, too. Traces of a lost life. Serena Northbury's life.*

The sergeant replaced the hatbox top and motioned with an abrupt jerk of the head for Demarest to return the precious box to the van. I watched the officer's back until he was out of sight. . . . All those letters. They could tell me so much. Folding my arms on the table, I pillowed my head. I could go to sleep right there. Then a thought struck me.

"Sergeant!" I jerked my head up. When she thought I wasn't looking, Felicity Schultz had dropped her guard; her eyes revealed exhaustion, the muscles of her face were tight with anxiety. The instant I spoke, however, she jammed the stone mask back over the human features.

"Yeah?"

"When you found the box, was there anything else with it?"

"Why?" My question had hit some kind of nerve. Stone turned to iron: the plain, round face gave nothing away. "What *kind* of anything are you talking about?"

"Well, more papers, of course."

"Oh." The flatness of her tone let me know that this was not what she had wanted to hear. I plowed on, anyhow.

"Because when Shamega and I went through those old boxes at the big house, there was another cache . . . er . . . bunch . . . of letters, right next to the hatbox. Did you see it? A gray pasteboard box? So big?" With my hands I indicated a rectangle a foot long. "If Gerry took the hatbox and brought it here, for whatever reason, maybe he took the other letters, too."

Schultz wasn't really interested. "There's so much stuff here. . . ." She obviously didn't want to admit the possibility of having overlooked anything. "But, we've got an—er—team of specialists coming in; by this evening they'll have gone through everything."

For what? I wondered. But that wasn't my business. I was interested only in the Northbury papers. "Could I look around a bit? I might recognize the box; it was the kind stationery comes in."

"Well, I suppose." It was a grudging concession. "You can look, but you can't touch. You understand? And I go along, too—to make sure you don't get carried away." *And thank you* so *much, Professor,* I thought, snidely, *for your commendable willingness to assist.* But I did find the second box of letters. Under a pile of twenty-year-old college textbooks in the corner of Gerry's bedroom. Schultz wouldn't let me touch the box, let alone read through the letters inside, but after I identified it as Northbury's she thanked me, thus practically sending me into shock. The new sergeant was finally happy: She had something to take back to her boss; she had done good.

Jill's parents had arrived at her place, so I headed for home. I wanted nothing more than to sleep all afternoon, but, as I unlocked the front door and pushed it open, the aroma of fresh coffee hit my nostrils. *What the heck?*

"Mom!" My daughter bounded out of the kitchen. "Where've you been? I've been waiting for hours." She grabbed me in a mighty hug. "I was starting to worry."

"Amanda!" I hugged back. "Where on earth did you come from?" I peered out the window. Her little red VW Rabbit was nowhere to be seen. "How'd you get here?"

"Oh, I went to Boston for the weekend with a guy from school, and he dropped me off. He's going on to Montreal for a couple of weeks, and I'm gonna take the bus back tomorrow."

"What guy?" I worry about my beautiful daughter.

"Just a guy. Don't freak out. It's nothing."

"Who was freaking out?" I was. I stroked her cheek. "But you do remember to be careful, don't you?" I was thinking of Jill.

"Mom! I'm twenty years old!"

"Yeah, I know. That's what worries me. I was a mother before I was twenty."

"Well—that was *then*."

"And female anatomy has changed?"

"Mother, I *work* for Planned Parenthood."

I grinned at her, and ruffled her short, chestnut hair. "God, I miss you, kid. We always have the best conversations."

"Yeah, but I'm not coming home again if you don't feed me. Do you know there's absolutely no food in this house?"

"Let's go to Bub's. I'm hungry, too." The flashing red light on the telephone answering machine tempted me as I walked past it, but Amanda was already out the door.

Bub's Coffee Shop is a shabby eatery on 138, five miles from home. I'd become a regular after Lieutenant Piotrowski had introduced me to its hearty, homey fare the year before. I liked the good food and the working-man's prices, but what really attracted me to Bub's was its location, so far from Enfield that I never had to worry about running into any of my colleagues there.

Amanda pushed open the restaurant's glass front door, still chattering about her internship at Planned Parenthood, and crashed into a behemoth of a man on his way out. As she staggered from the impact, the big man grabbed her by the shoulder to steady her. A famil iar voice said, "You okay, lady?" Then, "Amanda Pelletier? Is that *you?*"

Before she could reply, another, far more familiar, voice succeeded his, "Karen?"

"Lieutenant Piotrowski?" Amanda queried.

"Tony?" I echoed.

It *was* Tony, standing just behind and a little to the left of the big lieutenant, his blue eyes wide and startled.

"What on earth . . . ?" I gasped.

"I never expected to see . . ." He seemed to choke on the words.

"For lunch?" the teenaged waitress asked. "How many? Two? Four? Smoking or non?"

I sat across the table from Tony, his square, clean-shaven face as familiar to me as if I'd woken up to it that very morning. He looked good, wearing jeans and a gray golf shirt, his shoulders as broad, his black hair as curly as ever. Well, what did I expect? I walk out on a man, and he shrivels and dies? Then, in the light from the big window by our booth, I saw that the hair at Tony's temples was threaded with gray.

"So?" It was hard work to keep from reaching out to stroke his hand. "What brings a big-city cop like Captain Tony Gorman to the backwoods of New England?"

Tony and Piotrowski exchanged glances. Piotrowski raised his eyebrows. Tony shrugged. Evidently that constituted an agreement, because the lieutenant said to me, "Captain Gorman and me, we been talking quite a bit lately. About . . . about some stuff you really don't need to know. And . . . and . . . you're not gonna believe this, Doctor—"

"No?"

Piotrowski glanced at Tony again. Tony nodded. The lieutenant continued, "Interestingly enough, Gerry Novak's name came up."

"Gerry?" I was flabbergasted. Tony specialized in

the New York City drug trade. He didn't investigate homicides. I stared across the table at my former boyfriend. He was fiddling with the plastic daisy in its milk-glass vase. The dark, curly hair on the back of his big, square hands was peppered with gray.

"We're pretty sure Novak was doing a little trafficking in drugs," Piotrowski said. So that's why Tony was involved. *Drugs!* I recalled Schultz saying that a special team was coming in to go over the Novak cottage. Tony's unit?

"Novak wasn't big-time," Tony interjected. "He just worked the New England corridors a bit. He'd come into Manhattan on errands for his employer. Use the opportunity to make himself a little cash. Looks like he was dealing a little literary weed."

Piotrowski picked up the story. "Novak knew a lot of—you know—artsy types. All that poetry stuff—makes for a good clientele. We looked at him for Dr. Hart's death, but couldn't get anything on him. But he *smelled* wrong, so we kept on him. Then Captain Gorman contacted us about some big-time dealers, and Novak came up connected. But, like I said—small potatoes. Then, last night—"

"Do you think Gerry killed Edith?" I interrupted.

Piotrowski shrugged. "You know I can't say nothing about that, Doctor."

"Do you think maybe he was killed by drug dealers, Lieutenant?"

He looked over at Tony, then replied, evasively, "All I can tell is—the guy was basically your high-class scumbag. When he wasn't hanging with the local literatzi—"

"Literatzi?" I queried.

He looked at me blankly. "You know, poets, scholars, that type."

"Oh." I had a hard time repressing a grin. "You mean *literati*." *Literatzi.* I'd have to remember that; I knew a few.

"Whatever. Anyhow, when he wasn't hanging with

them, he'd be in Springfield associating with some real, er, interesting boys. And it's really them the captain here is looking at. You know, the big picture. As to whether the homicide is drug-related . . ." He shrugged again. That was all I was going to get from him.

"Poor Jill," I said. "Poor Edith . . ."

Piotrowski glanced at me warily; was I going to start bawling? "Well, anyhow, yesterday, when we went back to Novak's place—"

"That's all she needs to know." Tony's abrupt tone startled me; he'd been so quiet. "She understands why I'm here, now," he was talking to Piotrowski but looking at me, "and that's—enough." The waitress brought coffee for the men, and hot turkey sandwiches for Amanda and me. I wasn't hungry anymore; sitting across from my ex-lover had done something to my appetite. Tony went on. "And you know, don't you, Karen—you, too, Amanda—how important it is that you keep this information to yourselves?"

"Sure thing, Tony," Amanda assured him, between mouthfuls of stuffing and gravy. She was wired with excitement; I could feel it radiating from her body like an electric charge. I'd been keeping her up-to-date on the Hart case by phone, and, on the way to the restaurant, I'd told her about Novak's death. She'd been interested in the Enfield College investigation the previous year, and I hadn't seen how talking things over with her could hurt. Now here she was, right in the thick of things again. Her eyes were shining. I groaned; medicine was so much *safer* a career than law enforcement.

"Karen?" Tony queried. I nodded, *sure thing, Tony, sure thing.* I sliced a small corner off the soggy turkey sandwich. I couldn't keep my eyes off his hands, cupped around that white ceramic mug. My fork clattered as I dropped it on the plate. Even one bite would be a bite too much.

"If you're not gonna eat that, Dr. Pelletier . . ."

I shoved the platter of bread and turkey across the

table to Piotrowski. "Tony, how about we go for a walk while these guys finish eating?" As soon as I slid out of the booth, Amanda began to question Piotrowski about homicide investigation.

Tony and I scuffed along the dusty roadside, kicking up miniature clouds of fine brown dust. We each had our hands firmly ensconced in our pockets.

"How you doing, Karen?"

"Fine," I responded. "And you?"

"I'm fine. Just fine." He inspected his Nikes, then scuffed up a particularly impressive dust cloud. I looked down, too. My white Keds were now the color of sand.

"How's . . . ?"

"She's fine."

"Any signs of . . . ?"

"Not yet. But we're working on it."

"Good. I know you've always wanted—" No matter how fast I blinked my eyes, I could hardly keep the tears back. I looked over at Tony; he had the cop face on, deadpan, emotionless. Abruptly, I stopped walking. "Tony, I'm sorry. This is a mistake. Let's go back."

Tony glanced back at the diner, then turned toward me and took my hand. "Karen, I miss you. Every day I see or hear something I want to tell you, something that makes me think of you."

"Me, too, Tony. There's no one like you." I seem to have given him both hands. He squeezed them tight.

"But what I have with Jennifer is good, Karen. And with kids—well—it's what I want. What I need."

"I know, Tony. I know." I squeezed his hands, kissed him on the cheek. His skin tasted of salt. "And what I have is what I need. My work—" I pulled my hands away, pivoted abruptly, and strode back to my car.

Miles's phone message awaited me on my machine. *"Karen, some members of the department are planning a quiet memorial service for Gerry Novak, a young local poet, who's been cut off in his prime. Such a tragic loss—a fine new poetic voice, foreshadowing the anxious postmodern morality of the approaching millennium . . ."*

I pushed the rewind button, and spun Miles's voice off into oblivion.

Twenty-two

If Miles Jewell had his way, he would have spun *me* off into oblivion. At ten-fifteen the next morning, Miles stopped by my office as I was going through the accumulated mail and voice-mail messages of the past hectic week. Four publishers' catalogs, three pleas for letters of recommendation from recent graduates, two requests from academic presses to review scholarly manuscripts for publication, and one reminder from *American Literature* that a book review I'd promised them was two weeks overdue. All I needed now to compound my work load was a partridge in a pear tree. And there was Miles, partridge-shaped, clearing his throat just outside my open door.

"Karen—if I may have a word . . . ?"

"Come in, Miles." I gestured toward my green vinyl armchair, and, to my dismay, he shut the door behind him before plodding across the office, sinking into the chair, and pulling out a white handkerchief to wipe his florid face. No one shuts doors in this department unless they're about to dish the dirt—or give you hell. And, from his sour expression, I didn't think Miles had any gossip to monger. "Karen, I have an extremely touchy issue to discuss with you." *Oh, God.* But it was in my best interests not to sound as panicky as I felt.

"Really?" Cool as a mango snow cone.

"This puts me in an extremely difficult position, especially now that you seem to be in the president's confidence."

"I'm not in—"

He waved my protests away with an irritated hand. "There's been a complaint."

A complaint? What the hell? "Oh, really?" Cool as a Ben & Jerry's Peace Pop.

"Yes, you've been charged with gender bias—"

Cool as—"Huh?" *Gender bias?*

"Gender bias—and personal animosity. And Thibault Brewster, making the complaint on behalf of his son—"

Ah. Tibby Brewster.

"—claims he can provide witnesses to support a consistent antimale bias in both the content and the style of your teaching. *Male bashing* is how he put it. The grade of C-minus you submitted for Tibby's course work, he claims, is documented evidence of harassment. Mr. Brewster has requested that you file a change-of-grade form with the registrar by the end of June. If you refuse to do so, he says, he will present a formal complaint to the Dean of Faculty, charging pernicious pedagogical sexism and a personal vendetta against his family—"

Pernicious pedagogical . . . ? "You've got to be kidding!" My attempted nonchalant laugh emerged as a nervous titter.

"There's nothing frivolous about this, Karen." Miles's chest swelled with indignation. "These kinds of cases get national attention—especially when they occur at a prominent school such as Enfield. If Brewster goes ahead with this charge, it would constitute a slur on the department's reputation. And you must realize that for a junior member of the faculty, these would be extremely serious charges. Now, I'm speaking to you as one who has your best interests at heart when I recommend that you seriously consider changing that grade."

"But, Miles, Tibby's work was appallingly bad, and his attitude was arrogant—"

Miles was shaking his shaggy head ponderously. "There are no signs of substandard work in the boy's other courses. He has consistently earned a three-point-zero—not a brilliant GPA, to be sure, but respectable. Now, may I report to Mr. Brewster that you will consider changing Tibby's grade?"

"No." Suddenly I was so angry the pounding of my heart just about deafened me.

"No?" Miles's expression was incredulous. "You *are* aware, aren't you, of the influence Thibault Brewster is capable of bringing to bear on the administration of this institution—"

"Are you threatening me, Miles?" I stood up from my desk and strode over to him. Having once broken free of an abusive marriage, I tend to react to intimidation with knee-jerk hostility. Even when it might not be prudent to do so. Like at this very moment. As I advanced, Miles rose from the vinyl chair. The white handkerchief came into play again. He was sweating far more copiously than the humid day would seem to warrant.

"*Threatening* you? Far from it, Karen. I'm merely pointing out the perilous position you could be placing yourself in, in the not-too-distant future, when your teaching contract comes up for renewal. Even if at the moment you seem to have the inside track with the administration because of that Northbury thing—" he flicked the research center away with his thumb and all four fingers, "you've still got to consider your reputation within the department. When is your contract renewal scheduled? Next year? And then tenure, in three or four more years—"

"Miles," I said, my voice frigid, "has the concept of abuse of power ever been explained to you?"

"Miss Pelletier! I . . . I . . . I . . . assure you, I have no intention—"

But I was guiding him toward the door, my hand far more gentle on his arm than it wanted to be. "Good-bye, Miles." Even after I'd closed the door, I could hear him sputtering in the hallway. Then I shot the bolt; I didn't want anyone stumbling in on me while I was sobbing in fury at my suddenly imperiled desk.

"I don't know what's happened to Miles." Greg paused to detach the wedge of lime from the salted rim of his margarita glass. "He used to be good people. Oh, he was always a bit stuffy and old-fashioned. And he's passionately opposed to what he considers to be *invidious ideological assaults* on his precious Great Writers. But I never would have suspected him of stooping to intimidate an untenured professor." He squeezed the lime juice into his drink, spraying the table, then plopped the rind in after it. "After all, department chairs have ethical responsibilities to nurture and protect members of the junior faculty." Since the previous year when Greg had been voted chair of the tiny Anthropology Department, he'd become extremely vocal about the rights and responsibilities of academic chairship.

"And he's got to know," he continued, after a long, frosted sip, "that you don't go in for *male bashing*. He's read your work; he knows it's historically grounded and objective—if we're allowed to use that word anymore. He'll come around."

When I'd pulled myself together after Miles's departure, I'd called Greg for advice. Now we sat on his back deck in the humid air, sipping tall, frozen drinks. The long shadows of late afternoon provided some relief from the heat. The margaritas provided more. Irena, wearing a two-piece brown-and-yellow-polka-dot bathing suit, reclined on a wicker chaise on the lawn, her beautiful, rounded belly browning in the sun. As soon as she'd heard we were going to talk shop, she'd groaned, scooped up her bottle of Evian, and departed for more golden climes. But she couldn't fool me; she relished Enfield gossip. She had positioned the chaise well within earshot.

"You've only been department chair for a year, Greg. It's all fresh and new to you—including your sense of the responsibilities of the position. Miles has headed the English Department for a *quarter century*, and I have a funny feeling that's the issue. Miles wants to protect the department he knows against the department he's afraid it's about to become."

Greg grabbed a handful of pretzel nuggets from a bowl on the glass-top table and began munching. "You mean he wants to save a department that specializes in traditional courses, like *Introduction to the Major American Writers,* from becoming one known for trendy stuff, like that *Body in the Library* course Sally Chenille has cross-listed for the fall?"

I laughed. "Well, of course," I said. "I can understand that. But he also seems intent on preventing us from turning into a department that offers senior seminars in Emily Dickinson. *That's* a problem. There's got to be a happy medium between trendiness and ossification."

"Miles is frightened," Greg ventured, flicking a pretzel nugget in my direction. "Change is coming too fast for him, and he can't see the woods for the trees. But I don't imagine that, even as chair, he has enough influence left in the department to give you any real trouble. And I can't help thinking that once he has time to reflect on the situation . . ." He let the thought trail off. "It's Brewster you've really got to worry about. Somehow you've got to devise a way to get around the Brewsters. . . . How about poisoned pretzel nuggets?" He flicked another of the small, salt-crusted chunks in my direction.

"Don't even *joke* about that," I replied, sending it back. "I've seen more than enough homicide since I've come to Enfield." Suddenly, my career problems diminished in importance. There were worse things than the denial of tenure. Death, for instance. And, after all, there *was* a world *outside* academe. I wouldn't starve; I could always go back to waiting tables. "Any margaritas left?"

Greg rose. "Margarita," he mused, then grinned at me. "That's a nice name. How about Margarita and Daiquiri?"

I snorted. "How about Pink Lady and Gin Blossom?"

Irena rose majestically from the wicker chaise. "Sounds like if Miles Jewell had the naming of these kids they'd be called Old-Fashioned and Horse's-Neck."

As Greg headed for the kitchen to freshen up the drinks, Irena donned a short terry robe and lowered herself into his vacated chair. "Karen, have you talked to this kid?"

"Kid?" For a wild moment I thought she was referring to one of her babies.

"The Brewster kid? Have you tried to find out what's going on with him? Why he's so hostile?"

"Well—there's the grade. He got a C-minus in my course."

"Yeah, but I remember you saying over a month ago that he was disruptive in the classroom. That was before the grade." She picked up a pretzel nugget, examined it, popped it in her mouth. "Maybe if you talked to him, you know, just informally, you might find out what's *really* troubling him. The root cause." Irena's gone into therapy, and it's taken. Nothing escapes the fine-tooth comb of psychotherapeutic analysis. "It would seem to me," she continued, "that if this kid's exhibited a sudden marked change in behavior, something traumatic might have occurred to initiate it."

"You mean, it's possible he might not simply be a natural-born dirty, rotten human being?"

"Now, Karen," she responded earnestly, "you know that nobody's simply a natural-born . . ." Then she threw back her head and laughed. "Oh, you're teasing me."

Greg caught the end of this conversation. Grinning, he ruffled his wife's golden curls. "Irena refuses to believe in the Puritan doctrine of Innate Depravity, Karen. No matter how often I preach Original Sin to her, she keeps babbling on about individuation, repression, and primal psychic wounds." He raised his eyebrows in mock incomprehension. "I honest to God don't know what she's talking about."

Earl Wiggett was as I remembered him, a tall, skinny man with a lock of long, thin side hair slicked over an otherwise shiny pate. The rust brown polyester pants with the slight flare to the bottoms and form-fitting beige polyester-knit sport shirt suggested either that he was on the cutting edge of men's style or that he'd been wearing the same outfit for the past twenty years. Wiggett's general air of scuzziness and the snag in the left knee of his bells led me to the latter conclusion. When he'd announced his arrival in Enfield by phoning to invite me to lunch—to "pick your brains" he'd said, with an attempt at a worldly chuckle—his high-pitched laugh had set my teeth on edge. Now, over a shared table, his effusive prattle hammered at my brain like the pecking of a nervous sparrow. I had reservations about the presence in Enfield of a man who had peddled an Alcott manuscript for two million dollars, but it would have been churlish not to talk to him. At least I'll get a good meal out of the encounter, I'd thought; but, then, I hadn't expected that we'd be lunching at McDonald's.

Wiggett had ordered my Arch Deluxe burger, fries, and Diet Coke with all the flair of a connoisseur. He'd paid for them with much fingering of bills and counting out of change. I'd cringed at the prospect of being obligated to this man, even if only for $6.14 worth of chemicals and fat. How much of my time would $6.14 buy?

"So, Karen—I may call you Karen, mayn't I—it seems we have an interest in common." He bit into his burger; tomato seeds and mayonnaise dribbled down his chin onto the little notebook computer he'd placed carefully in front of him on the restaurant table, and from there onto his lap. Grabbing a wad of paper napkins from the dispenser, he hastened to wipe the greasy drips from the computer. He didn't bother with any of the drops that had reached his person. I replaced my sandwich hastily in its cardboard shell and nibbled on a salty fry. Salt is reputed to be good for nausea.

"Oh, yes?" I responded.

"Serena Northbury—or, should I say *Mrs.* Northbury, as she was most often referred to by her readership—is an author in need of some serious reconsideration. And the grapevine has it that you are in the process of a biography?" It was a question.

"Oh, does it?" *The grapevine sure works fast,* I thought. *It's only been two months since I decided to begin the book.* "Where'd you hear that?"

"Oh, I was at the ALA. . . ." His voice twittered off inconclusively. He continued to wipe at the top of his little black computer.

"How was it?" The American Literature Association is a cozy conference, far less painful than the annual Modern Language Association with its ten thousand frenzied participants.

Wiggett pursed his lips, miming deep contemplation. "Useful," he murmured. "It was useful. Not too much of this postmodernist garbage. Good, solid, historical work. Useful." Then he changed the subject, as if he didn't care to pursue it. I had a niggling suspicion he hadn't really been at the ALA. *Based on what?* I wondered. *Just because the man repulses me doesn't mean he's a liar.* Then I suddenly knew why I didn't believe Wiggett—I've been to the ALA any number of times: *Plenty* of postmodernist garbage goes on there.

"So, tell me, Karen," Wiggett leaned forward cozily, his half-consumed burger lying forgotten on its paper wrapper, "have you found anything of particular interest in your research thus far?" Although his posture was nonchalant, he couldn't hide the avid gleam in his rust-colored eyes. His fingers tapped nervously on the closed computer.

"Oh," I waved my hand dismissively, "just the ordinary stuff. Family background, mostly."

"Any interesting scandals?"

"Not unless you count a rift with her father. Other than that, Mrs. Northbury seems to have been a paragon of respectability."

"Too bad. Sensation sells." Wiggett rubbed his thumb and fingers together in the universal symbol for *moola.* "A good scandal might get your biography on the best-seller list." His snaggle-toothed smile would have terrified alligators.

I tightened my lips. "That's not what I'm interested in. It is my intention to write a historically reliable account of the author and her times, not some sensational blockbuster." Even I could hear the self-righteousness dripping from my words. But, God, this creep was really getting to me.

Jill Greenberg sailed by our table with Kenny Halvorsen in tow. His tray held enough junk food for three and a half people, but he and Jill seemed to be alone. When she noticed my companion, Jill widened her eyes and raised her eyebrows. The resulting expression would have been hard to misinterpret: *You really that hard up, Pelletier?* I gave her my best *screw you* look. She smiled wanly, then turned her attention back to Kenny.

Kenny and Jill? Hmm. Although he was tall and blond like Gerry, Ken Halvorsen resembled the late

Gerry Novak not at all. Broad shoulders. Straight, floppy hair. Open, earnest face. You looked at this guy and your first thought was *muscle*. Then you looked again and thought, *nice guy*. At no point did you ever think, *tortured genius*. Next to Kenny, slender Jill with her firestorm of hair looked fragile, in need of protection. She also looked like the boss.

"So," Wiggett continued, drawing my attention back to his thin, horsey face. "No surprises, huh? No great unpublished novels or anything?" His twittery laugh was meant to discount the question, but in that moment I knew he'd somehow heard about *Child of the North Star*. But how? Who'd told him? Who knew about the manuscript? Keeping my expression carefully blank, I went over the list in my mind: Will Thorpe, Amanda, and Shamega had been there when we'd found it. And, oh, yes, Gerry Novak. Had Novak contacted Wiggett? I tucked that speculation away to share with Piotrowski. Had I told anyone? Avery, of course, and Greg, and, oh, yes, Piotrowski and Schultz. Regular little blabbermouth, wasn't I? My eyes fell on Jill, sitting with Kenny in front of golden arches painted on a plate glass window. Had I mentioned the manuscript to Jill? Probably—and maybe Gerry had, too. Jill would know. Had Edith told anyone? Her lawyer? The Brewsters? Kendell Brown? The Menendez couple? Who else might she have confided in? The list was endless. But what seemed absolutely certain was that one of those people had sought out Earl Wiggett and asked him a question or two about the going rate for sensational nineteenth-century novel manuscripts.

"Unpublished novels?" I would play it innocent with Wiggett; maybe there was something I could learn from him. *"You're* the expert in that field." I widened my eyes, admiringly. "I don't know anything about unpublished novels." *I don't know nothin' 'bout birthin' no babies.*

Wiggett leered at me, his rusty gaze narrow, knowing, and unmistakably furtive. With the greasy paper napkin, he stroked his little black notebook computer caressingly. I glanced hastily around; anyone watching us would surely think we were involved in some illegal—or immoral—transaction. "It's true," he said, "I *do* know the ropes. If there *were* anything out there," he raised his eyebrows, nodded his head sagely, "if anything just happened, you know, to *surface,* I could make it well worth somebody's while to make the—ah—connections." The skimpy eyebrows were raised almost to the frontmost strands of mousy hair plastered across Wiggett's shiny skull. He tapped his fingers on the closed lid of his computer as if he were entering information then and there.

I was so very sorry to have to disappoint him.

"You see, Lieutenant," I said into the phone a half-hour later, "when Wiggett sold the Alcott book, his name was in all the papers. Someone, maybe Gerry Novak, contacted him about *Child of the North Star,* hoping to make some money from it. If you talk to him, he might lead you to the person who—er—purloined the novel manuscript."

"Thank you, Doctor," Piotrowski said, earnestly. "Thank you. Did you happen to get the name of his hotel?" Earl Wiggett would be receiving visitors shortly.

But unfortunately I hadn't found out where in Enfield Wiggett was staying. Unfortunately, because, even with all the resources at his disposal, Lieutenant Piotrowski was unable to locate the erstwhile literary sleuth anywhere in the area. Messages left at his home phone in California were not returned. And, although an e-mail message to the address he had given me was picked up at his end, probably on his trusty little laptop—cyberspace yielded nary a reply.

Twenty-three

Haunted Mansion Murders! trumpeted the early edition of the *Boston Herald* over a front-page photo of Meadowbrook, shot from an eerie angle with a night-scope lens. "Holy Christ," I breathed, and snatched a copy from the tottering pile by the register. Kelly's Tobacconist and Stationers, the paramount spot for an early morning news fix in Enfield, was almost deserted at eight-thirty on this beautiful Wednesday morning, four days after the discovery of Gerry Novak's drowned body. I'd come to town early for a few hours' work in the library before attending the curriculum subcommittee meeting on literature, scheduled for midafternoon. A heavy storm the previous night had cleared the air of the dense humidity that had plagued us for the past week. My brain, too, felt clearer than it had since Edith Hart's death, and I was eager to finally begin systematic research into Serena Northbury's life. But, now—this headline!

I slapped two quarters on the counter and hustled the scandal sheet next door to the Bread and Roses

Bakery for a cup of black coffee and a quiet corner. *Two Shocking Deaths at Murder Mansion,* elaborated the subhead. I groaned, and opened the paper wide to read the page-three article. *Murder Mansion?* So much for discretion and a dignified beginning for the Northbury center. Under the heading *Murder at Meadowbrook!,* I read:

> The past month has seen two suspicious deaths at Meadowbrook, the posh Eastbrook estate built in the 1800's by schlock novelist Serena Northbury, according to confidential police sources. In mid-May Dr. Edith Hart, an elderly physician who spent her life in the noble work of caring for the down-and-out of Manhattan's East Harlem, passed away almost unnoted by those whose lives she had so richly blessed. Suspicions that the eighty-five-year-old diabetic inner-city physician might have been hastened to her final reward by a murderous hand have not yet been confirmed by the Coroner's Office. But the death by drowning of Dr. Hart's protégé and heir, aspiring poet Gerry Novak, less than a month after the wealthy Edith Hart's private funeral services, reinforces suspicions that foul play may have been involved in both deaths—

"Karen, what on earth . . . ?" Avery Mitchell's astounded tones shocked me out of my appalled absorption in the *Herald* article. Natty in a navy seersucker jacket and charcoal trousers, Avery stood at the far side of my table, balancing a maroon Bread and Roses coffee cup and a copy of the *New York Times,* and staring in horror at the inflammatory headline over the unmistakable photograph of Meadowbrook. Gaze fixed on the journal's front page, he set first the paper cup, then the rolled-up newspaper, on the marble top of the small, round table and slid into the chair across from me. "Oh, dear God, Karen, tell me that's not what I think it is."

"I wish I could, Avery. Here." I scooted my chair over closer to his so he could read along with me. "I just started the article, so I don't know much more about it than you do." The remaining few paragraphs did nothing to reassure either of us. Innuendo, unsubstantiated claims, and provocative speculation, managed to insinuate that a long, dark history of death, mayhem, and sinister secrets surrounded a "brooding Gothic mansion" and had led fatefully and inevitably to current violent death. *Two* violent deaths.

"God," I groaned as I raised my eyes from the final paragraph, "I feel as if I've just finished reading 'The Fall of the House of Usher.' "

Avery's lips were set in a grim line; he was not thinking about Edgar Allan Poe. "At least the college isn't mentioned here," he said. He seemed to be talking to himself. "But I'd better get on the horn to O'Hara immediately, before this rag gets word that Meadowbrook's been left to Enfield." Harvey O'Hara is Enfield College's P.R. person. Having dealt with the fallout from last year's "unfortunate incidents," Avery was obviously concerned with the impact upon the college's image of a link to yet more homicides. "Christ," he muttered, "that's all Enfield needs now: Another public scandal."

Lurid headlines instantly composed themselves in my overheated mind: *Murder Plagues Posh Campus; Classy College Cursed by Killer.* And it was all my fault, I thought; I was the one who'd gotten Edith Hart interested in Enfield College in the first place.

Without thinking, I reached out and touched Avery's hand. "I'm sorry," I said.

He jerked his hand back as if I'd brushed him with a lighted match. Suddenly he was present again. Very present. "Sorry? For what?"

I was confused; his reaction hardly suited my words.

"If it weren't for me," I babbled, "we wouldn't be involved with Meadowbrook at all."

His expression cleared. He laughed. "If it weren't for you, Karen, we'd be out ten million dollars and a fabulous estate. It's my *job* to worry about this . . . er . . . possible complication. You have nothing to apologize for."

He sat, silent, for a few seconds, fiddling with the pages of the newspaper in front of him. Then he glanced around the half-filled café, blue eyes swiftly scanning its coffee-swigging occupants. Aside from my former student Sophia Warzek in her white baker's apron, delivering a heavy aluminum tray of icing-drenched cinnamon rolls to the counterman on the far side of the room, no Enfield College faces were in evidence. Avery turned to me, leaned a little closer, and spoke in muted tones. His gaze was meaningful and direct. "*I'm* the one who owes *you* an apology. I think you know what I'm referring to. This is neither the time nor the place, of course, but if we're going to continue working together on—" The café door opened with a swish; Avery instantly sat back in his chair and directed his voice over my shoulder. "Morning, Miles. Beautiful day, isn't it? It's wonderful to be rid of that beastly humidity. I was just saying to Karen, I was afraid I'd have to start thinking about raising money to air-condition the entire campus if the heat hung on much longer."

"Humph." Miles gave me what I'm certain he would have termed *a speaking look,* then concentrated on Avery. "Mitchell, you have a moment? There's a little item of business I want to run by you." He glanced over at me again. "Something confidential."

I felt my face, flushed already from Avery's comments, turn an even warmer pink; undoubtedly Miles had Tibby Brewster's complaint in mind. Oh, God, what ghastly timing.

Avery was cool; he always was. Folding the *Herald,* headline inside, he slipped the paper over the marble tabletop toward me. I slid it into my canvas bookbag. "Can we finish this conversation later, Karen? Do you expect to be on campus all day?"

Before I could respond, Miles chimed in. "You remember the literature subcommittee meeting this afternoon, don't you, Karen? Three-thirty. Comp Lit lounge." I inclined my head in a general purpose nod— *yes, I'll be on campus, and yes, I'll be at the meeting.* Then I rose from the table. There was no way I could attempt damage control until I knew for certain what Professor Jewell was up to.

"Some real weird guy was in here yesterday, looking through the Pinkworth papers. Tall skinny dude with bad hair," Shamega said. "I thought you'd want to know."

"Really?" I sat at one of the tables in Special Collections, reading through the Rev. Eddie's account ledgers. I'd recovered sufficiently from the shock of the headline to set myself a specific research goal for the day. Intrigued by the letters I'd read between Serena Northbury and her father, I decided to find out everything I could about their quarrel. Pinkworth had kept his account books for over fifty years. He'd documented his frugal expenditures as meticulously as if his entrance into the Great Beyond depended on a well-balanced spread sheet. I'd know exactly when the rift occurred, I thought, if I could find the date Pinkworth had stopped paying his daughter's Manhattan boardinghouse expenses. But I was immediately diverted from my task by Shamega's words.

"So, what was Mr. Bad Hair interested in?"

"He wanted to know if Pinkworth or Northbury stuff was catalogued under any other name."

Hmm, interesting. I had more than an inkling of what this badly coiffed researcher was looking for. "So, what time of day was Earl Wiggett here?"

"Most of the afternoon. And you're right; that *was* his name. You know this guy?"

"Unfortunately, yes." I paused for a moment's reflection. Wiggett must have been sequestered snugly in the bowels of the library at the very moment I was talking to Piotrowski about him. Damn, I should have thought of that. "Tell me, Shamega, did any police officers come looking for him?"

"Noooo." Shamega's eyes widened. "Why? Is he a criminal?"

"No." I shrugged. "At least as far as I'm aware, he's not. I just know they wanted to talk to him."

"Well, now that I come to think about it, he did act kinda suspicious."

Really? "What do you mean, suspicious?"

"He was real jumpy while he was going through the boxes, kept looking up at the door. I watched him kinda close, 'cause I thought maybe he was thinking about pocketing something. He didn't try anything though—at least not when I was around. And he seemed kinda frustrated when he left, shoved his chair back with this real grating screech, then slammed it under the table with a crash." She giggled. "Ask Marian the Librarian. She gave him such a *frown.*"

"Millie," I said. "Her name is Millie, not Marian."

"I *kno-o-ow.*"

"I guess I'm done for now, Shamega. I've got to go make a phone call." I closed the account book, and slipped it back into the file box; I needed to talk to Piotrowski about this. He wanted me to share information with him? Well, then, he was going to get his wish, and he would probably be sick and tired of me before this investigation was over.

Shamega caught up with me as I was going out the door. "Dr. Pelletier, will you be at that subcommittee meeting?"

I nodded. I'd forgotten Shamega was the student rep. "Oh, yes."

She gave me a slanted look. "*I* wouldn't miss it, myself. Just think, another opportunity to meet the distinguished author and cultural critic Professor Sally Chenille in the oh-so-very documented flesh."

"You're *bad*, Shamega." But I was grinning.

The literature subcommittee of the College Curriculum Revision Committee was waiting, seated around the Comp Lit department's conference table, when Shamega and I arrived in the lounge of Anderson Hall later that afternoon. Sally Chenille had managed to locate a few hours in her hectic book tour and lecture schedule to pencil in the meeting. But, as Shamega and I rushed through the door to the air-conditioned lounge, ten minutes late, Sally wasn't in evidence—in the flesh, or on TV, or in any other manifestation.

"Karen?" Miles growled. Yet another black mark in Professor Pelletier's departmental record book. Not only wrongheaded, gender-biased, and sucking up to the administration, but tardy as well. Obviously an excuse was called for. Better yet, a note from my mother.

"Sorry," I muttered. "We were talking to the police."

All heads swiveled in our direction. *The police?*

I waved a hand dismissively; a full explanation would involve far too much information about the recent homicides, and no one needed to know how closely I'd become entangled in the investigation. "Nothing worth talking about. They were just interested in someone who'd used our library. And Shamega and I had both seen him, so they wanted to talk to us."

Piotrowski had grunted when I'd informed him of Earl Wiggett's presence yesterday in the Enfield Library. Then he'd sent Felicity Schultz to talk to Shamega in my office. But I didn't care to go into all that with my nosy colleagues. I sank into one of the blue upholstery-and-chrome conference-table chairs and chirped brightly, "So, are we ready to begin?"

"Sally hasn't come yet." Latisha's lips were pursed with irritation. "We scheduled this meeting for *her* convenience. In *her* department. To suit *her* schedule. And she doesn't even have the good manners to show up."

"She'd better show," Ned complained. "Sara and I rescheduled our vacation to fit this meeting in. The Cape is crowded already, and the house we wanted wasn't available after this week. We had to settle for something smaller." His habitually melancholy expression had taken on an air of truculence. "If it rains, it's going to be hell with the kids." The mood around the table was getting ugly.

"Hey, she's only fifteen minutes late," Joe Gagliardi jumped in. His defense of Sally didn't surprise me; they were buddies. They could have been clones: Joe was as emaciated, as tattooed, and as pierced as Sally was. Today, in spite of the muggy heat, he was clad in skintight jeans and a body-hugging black T-shirt. The sleeves of his T were rolled up to his shoulders, baring fish-belly-white upper arms. A detailed tattoo of a pack of Camel cigarettes adorned his scrawny left biceps. A postmodernist outlaw. A James Dean of the Intellect. A Real Tough Guy.

"Sorry. Sorry. Sorry." Sally Chenille sashayed into the room in her trademark black miniskirt, and flopped into the chair next to Joe. She outdid his postmodern, postpunk, posteverything look only by the cobalt-and-purple thistle tattoo bristling from the cleavage of her form-fitting sleeveless black tank top. The cropped hair was pus yellow today. Bruise-colored blusher sharpened her already angular cheekbones. "Sorry to keep you waiting," she said, "but I was—occupied." Her contusion-tinted lips turned up at the corners, smirking at the double entendre. I winced; but, then, simply *looking* at Sally Chenille was a painful experience.

"So," Sally slapped her hands on the table in front

of her and spread her fingers wide to admire the polished black nails. "So, I assume we're all agreed that this committee's top priority will be to yank the study of literature out of the Dark Ages and expose our students to the age of hypertext and genderbend. Now . . ."

Miles's already flushed face took on the hue of boiled beet.

At the end of two hours of erudite wrangling, my tradition-bound department chair was forced to acknowledge defeat. While not willing to agree to Sally's demand for a mandatory course in Queer Theory, Miles had given in to the pressure from the rest of the committee for a requirement in multicultural literature. The question of whether or not a Shakespeare course should remain mandatory was tabled for discussion at a later time. By the time he closed the meeting, Miles was looking every minute of his close to seventy years. Pale, and sweating profusely, he was obviously exhausted. I almost found it in my heart to feel sorry for the poor dear. Then, as he gathered up his notes, squaring the lined yellow pages meticulously, he turned to me. "The memorial service?" he barked.

"Huh?"

"The memorial service? Friday? For Gerry Novak? Are you coming?" His brusque manner barely covered some quite elemental emotion I couldn't identify. "I thought it would be fitting for a few members of this department to acknowledge his passing."

I sank into the chair next to him. I was curious. "How did you know Gerry, Miles?"

Miles appeared startled that I was actually initiating a conversation. "Known him for years. He was my student."

Ah! "Really?"

"Yes." Stowing the notes in his briefcase, Miles seemed to relax a little; maybe I wasn't going to bite his head off after all. "Years ago. Back in the seventies. Best young poet ever to come out of Enfield. Tragic thing— his dropping out of school like that in his final year. Never did understand why. Something about his mother."

"Really?" *Which mother?* I wondered.

"Yes. Last few years I was gratified to see his poems cropping up in the little magazines. Got in touch with him, and . . ." His gruff voice trailed off. Something was about to remain unsaid. Miles shook his head. "Tragic, just tragic."

"Tsk," I said. *And did you know he hung out with druggies and lowlifes?* But why should I tarnish Miles's fantasies? And besides, the two faces of Gerry Novak were by no means incompatible. Novak might well have been both: a drug dealer and a brilliant poet. Who's to say an addiction to drugs precludes an addiction to language? According to literary legend, Samuel Coleridge was high on opium when he wrote "Kubla Khan": *In Xanadu did Kubla Khan / A stately pleasure dome decree: / Where Alph, the sacred river, ran / Through caverns measureless to man / Down to a sunless sea.* Not bad for a pothead.

I was deep in my thoughts about Gerry, barely paying attention to Miles, when, as he pushed his chair back from the table and stood, I heard him mutter something under his breath—something about "manuscripts in that rat's nest of a house."

"What?" I queried, struck by a sudden, irrepressible, thought. *That's right: Who* knows *what's in that "rat's nest of a house"? Who knows what's been there for years? For a century even.* And even though in the next breath I understood that Miles was talking about Gerry's poetry manuscripts, I knew I had to get into the Novak house—by hook or by crook—and see if I could uncover anything that might elucidate Mrs. Northbury's life or work. For what would be more natural for an author who had a secret—and that unpublished manuscript was surely a secret from her family—than to entrust it to the guardianship of a faithful family servant?

Sally Chenille caught up with me on the way down the stairs from the Comp Lit lounge.

"What's your little friend doing today without her bodyguard?" she queried.

"Little friend? . . . Bodyguard?" I wasn't about to let this bitch fluster me. "Whatever do you mean, Sally?"

"You know very well what I mean, Karen. Every time I tried to get anywhere near Little Mary Sunshine, you showed up to run interference."

"Sally, I have no idea what you're talking about." I knew she was referring to Jill, of course. But why was she speaking in the past tense?

Sally laughed. Then she gave me a long, slow once-over. "You know, you could do a hell of a lot more with yourself, Karen. You really could." Her pale-eyed scrutiny was contemptuous. "You look like a woman running away from her body." She swept off down the hall, stiletto heels tapping fiercely on the polished limestone floor of the Anderson Hall lobby.

I glanced down. Loose khaki pants. Navy blue T. Sturdy leather sandals. I shrugged. There was a body under there somewhere. But what concerned me about this encounter with Sally was not the aspersion she had cast on my sex appeal; my sex appeal was just fine, thank you. I was beginning to worry about Jill. What was this fixation my funky pus-haired, black-nailed colleague had on my young friend, Jill Greenberg?

E-mail; I needed to check my e-mail before I left for home. Schlepping back to my office, I lowered myself into the desk chair, and clicked on the icon. Five messages awaited me, but it was the one titled *hate mail* that drew my attention. I clicked and the words appeared. It was indeed hate mail, and Shamega's screen name *sgilfoyle* was in the address box above my *kpelletier*.

> *babes who think they have brains*
> *are really second-rate pains*
> *they're all really dunces*
> *who think with their cuntses*
> *their heads should be stuck up their anus*

The sender's address box was blank.

I stared at the screen in shock and disgust, tearing my eyes away from the crude verse when I heard the clatter of angry feet in the hallway. Then Shamega stood in my office door, a printout in her hand. She looked furious.

"This is *it*," she snapped. "This is the *last straw*. He's not getting away with another *thing*."

"Good," I responded. "It's about time. You can call Security from my phone."

"Security? Hell, no! I'll take care of Tibby Two myself. I've let this go much too long." Shamega's jaw was set in determination. "I just hope—"

There was a long pause. Long enough for me to picture my petite student lying battered and broken in some deserted alleyway. "What?" I implored.

"I just hope I don't *kill* him!"

Twenty-four

"*Karen?*" President Mitchell's mellifluous tones on my voice-mail seemed to lack their usual composure. Had I not known such an idea was preposterous, I'd have said that Avery, the consummate sophisticate, was a bit shaken. "*Karen? Avery here. Listen, ah—listen, something totally unanticipated has come up. I've got to go out of town for a day or two. Possibly longer. Our talk about . . . ah, about . . . the* Herald *article will have to wait. I just want to reiterate that you are not to be concerned about . . . about the article. I'll be in touch when I return.*" There was a pause. "*See you, Karen.*" Another pause. Then the connection was cut.

I sighed. It was heading for six P.M. on this beautiful summer evening; I had nothing to do, nowhere to go, and no one to see. Shamega, the avenging warrior, had just stormed out of my office and was heading for work in Rudolph's kitchen. I hoped, for his own sake, that Tibby wouldn't go anywhere near the place. I was just a little bit worried about all those knives.

The library was closed; Dickinson Hall, home of the

English Department, was deserted; the campus was emptying out fast. From my open window I could see the last few professors and administrators wandering singly and in pairs to the parking lots.

And Avery Mitchell had headed off for parts unknown.

I sank down onto the green plush cushions of the recessed window seat and breathed deeply of the scent of roses wafting in my direction from the circular bed just outside the building. Big mistake. Along with the perfume of the flowers, an image of Tony's square, battered Irish face drifted unbidden into my consciousness. Was it only three days ago I had seen him at the diner? Would I ever see him again?

I leapt up from the window seat. Nonsense! Tony was married now, and I was *fine* with that. I'd made my choice, and I had a full and rewarding life. Before self-pitying tears could spill over my eyelids, I grabbed my book bag, and headed for the door. I'd get some Chinese take-out, rent a video, and have a terrific evening home alone. Damn it!

Or, maybe—just, maybe—I'd take a run up to Meadowbrook.

Well—it was a gorgeous evening, and, even though I couldn't get into the old house, I could walk the grounds and sketch out some tentative plans for landscaping. An old-fashioned herb garden, I thought, and another garden planted solely with nineteenth-century flowers. And a tea garden. What *was* a tea garden, anyhow? A garden to serve tea in? A garden planted with tea bushes? A garden with blossoms for the tea table? I had no idea, but it sounded lovely. Maybe I'd ask Helen Whitlow. She did a lot of gardening. Yes, I would consult with Helen. And I was definitely going to take a ride up to Meadowbrook.

And I wouldn't even *think* about the possibility of peeking in the windows of Gerry Novak's house. Or of trying the knob to see if maybe the police had left the cottage unlocked. Or of surreptitiously sorting through the decades of stacked books and papers to see if I could find anything related to Serena Northbury. No. That would all be illegal, and I wouldn't even dream of attempting it.

It would be dark in the cottage. Did I have a flashlight in the car? I could stop at Koenig's Hardware and get one.

With my hand on the doorknob, I recalled the open window behind me. Better lock it up; no sense inviting another intruder into my office. As I reached for the old-fashioned casement lock, two figures moved away from me on the far end of the campus common. One—the black-clad skeletal figure—could only be Sally Chenille—unmistakable at any distance. The other person was too tall to be her sidekick, Joe, but something about his height and gait seemed oddly familiar. Skinny and shambling, with a scarecrow's loose pants flopping around his ankles, this distant figure inclined his head attentively, taking in my distinguished colleague's every word. For some inexplicable reason, I couldn't take my eyes off him. Off his pants, in particular. Loose, bell-bottom pants. Rust-colored bell-bottom pants. My God! It was Earl Wiggett!

I threw the window open again. "Sally!" I yelled. "Mr. Wiggett!" But, out of earshot, they didn't even pause, continuing their steady progress toward the faculty parking lot. Slamming the window shut, I sprinted from the office.

By the time I reached the faculty lot, Sally's chartreuse BMW was vanishing down Field Street. I was out of breath, and a stitch in my side reminded me that I was also out of shape. "Shit!" I stamped my foot on the asphalt. "Shit!" I must have said it aloud, because Jill Greenberg's distinctive laugh pealed out behind me.

I swiveled. "Jill! What are *you* doing here?"

"Taking a shortcut home. And you?"

"I had a meeting. But I didn't expect to see you out

and about. You know . . . so soon. Are you up to working?"

"Oh, yeah. Really. I'm fine." And she did look fine, with that glow women often get during the second trimester of pregnancy, her red hair flamboyant in the late afternoon sun, her still-slender body resplendent in a scarlet gauze tunic and orange skirt. So much for a low profile in this, her hour of grief and shame. "You heading anywhere in particular, Karen?"

"No. No!" I let the tempting image of Meadowbrook slide. "What'd you have in mind?"

Jill's kitchen smelled of garlic, onions, and basil. We sat at the blue enamel-topped kitchen table with thick chunks of bread, wiping the last of the take-out sun-dried tomato sauce from her pale yellow Fiestaware dinner plates.

"There was such an *edge* to our relationship," Jill said. "Something really—*dangerous.*" She grinned ironically. "Of course, as the theorycrats would say, *all heterosexual attraction involves complex negotiations of reified biological and cultural binaries.*"

I laughed. "That may well be true, but it does tend to take the *juice* out of the experience." I lifted my glass. "*Vive les binaries!*" I drained my red wine. "*Vive la reification!*"

Jill poured me another glass of wine, then eyed it longingly. "Yeah, well, with Gerry, those binaries sure as hell set off sparks. They weren't only gendered; there were class frictions, as well, and really jagged personality clashes." She paused. "He *thrilled* me." Glancing at me sheepishly, she picked up my wineglass. "Just *one,*" she said, "one little sip. What could it hurt?"

"Jill!" I admonished, and removed both the bottle and my glass from her reach. "Think of the baby."

She sighed, but went on with her love story. "Just

being with Gerry gave me the shivers; anything could happen." She paused thoughtfully. "And *did.*"

I sipped wine and waited. I didn't really want to know what *anything* might be.

"Karen, I hope you don't mind me telling you this stuff." She didn't wait to find out if I did or not. "It's just that, you know, I've always had this need to take risks." Jill stretched across the table, commandeered the wine bottle, took a deep slug.

"Jill!"

"That's the last one, I swear it. Do you want more?"

"No!"

She rose, carried the slender green bottle across the kitchen to the sink, and let the remaining wine glug down the drain. "I think that's why Gerry appealed to me so much." Jill rinsed out the bottle and deposited it in the recycling basket. "My mother and father are good parents, but there was always like this *safety net* for everything I did. My folks know everything about child development, so they gave me all sorts of freedom. Every time I abused it and got myself in trouble, their money, their connections, their know-how got me out of it. Basically, they kept me on track and I whizzed through grad school. And everything was so *safe.*

"Then I met Gerry. There was nothing *safe* about Gerry. How could I resist him? Like I said, he gave me the shivers."

"Hmm," I said. God, was she *young!*

Jill did shiver then, unconsciously, as if sloughing off some kind of outgrown skin. "But when I got pregnant, the odds changed. It wasn't just me, anymore; Eloise—" She grinned like a four-year-old with a new toy. "*Eloise* was involved. So, when I saw that Gerry refused to be a real father, I gave up on him. I may be a thrill-seeker, but I'm not a fool. Can you imagine what kind of life the baby and I would have had with him? What kind of life he would have led us?"

I didn't know if this was a real question, or merely

rhetorical, so I raised an ambiguous shoulder; it doesn't pay to comment too outspokenly on other people's love lives.

Jill continued, "And when I renounced Gerry, it wasn't like giving up a person—because I'd never really had him as a person. I was in love more with who he could have been, than with who he actually was. Giving him up was more like giving up a specific kind of *thrill*. Maybe even an addiction. It was more like *growing* up, than giving up."

"Hmm." A nod of the head. I could be a therapist. This nonverbal affirmation stuff was easy.

"I mean, when I found out he'd been screwing Sally Chenille, that was *it.*" She paused, playing with the gold locket she'd pulled from the neck of her gauze tunic.

"Sally Chenille!" So that's who Gerry had been cheating with! No wonder Sally had been so fixated on Jill. And no wonder she'd been speaking in the past tense when she talked about trying to "get near" Jill; their mutual boyfriend was now dead. I assumed that meant I didn't have to worry any longer about Sally bothering Jill. Right? Or should I tell Jill about my wierd encounter with our funky friend?

But Jill didn't want to talk about Sally. She was fixated on herself. "Am I a coldhearted bitch?"

My ambiguous shoulder came into play again, but she wasn't paying attention.

"You know," she said hesitantly, "it was almost a relief that he died. Terrible for him, of course, but a blessing for me. It got him out of my life completely. And out of the baby's."

"Jill, for God's sake, don't let the police hear you say that!"

"Why not? I mean, I already said it to Felicity, you know, that nice sergeant—"

"Jill! That *nice sergeant* is a hard-assed bitch! You can't *trust* her. She's probably taking down every word you say. As Gerry's ex-girlfriend, you're at the top of her list of suspects."

"Oh, don't worry about it, Karen. I didn't kill Gerry—and cops don't go around arresting innocent people." She slid the gold heart back inside her blouse.

"Geesh, Jill. Don't you ever read the papers?" But her mention of Sally Chenille had jarred me into, among other things, a recollection of having just seen Sally with Earl Wiggett. "Jill, do you have an Enfield College directory?"

Sally's answering machine picked up after the third ring. With Madonna's "Material Girl" as background, Sally's husky voice announced her bodily absence. I hung up without leaving a message. What was I going to say? *Sally, you creep, did you know that the creep I just saw you with is wanted for questioning by the police?*

Piotrowski wasn't in his office—well, it *was* seven-thirty P.M.; he didn't *live* there. I hesitated, then dug out a card he'd given me the year before with his home number on the back. An elderly man's quavery voice answered the phone. "Hello?"

"Is Lieutenant Piotrowski there?"

"There's no *lieutenant* here, girlie. You must have the wrong number; this isn't the army."

"No, I mean—"

"Dad!" I heard Piotrowski's pleading voice in the background. "I asked you *please* not to answer that phone." And I remembered Will Thorpe telling me . . . what? . . . something about Alzheimer's.

"Piotrowski." The gruff phone voice was nothing like the gentle tones just addressed to his father.

"Hi, Lieutenant." This unexpected peep into the investigator's private life had flustered me. "I'm so sorry to disturb you at home—"

"Dr. Pelletier?"

"Yes. Look, I just wanted to tell you that I'm quite certain I saw Earl Wiggett this evening—in Enfield. He was with my colleague, Sally Chenille—"

"The batty one?"

I chortled. "Yeah, the batty one. But I couldn't catch up with them, and no one answers her phone."

"Really? Hmm. Well, I'll send someone out there. She in the book?"

As I read Sally's address and number from the directory, I thought briefly about telling the lieutenant that Gerry Novak had had an affair with my chameleon-haired colleague, but, just in time, remembered that Jill had told me that in confidence. I was just about to hang up when Piotrowski said, "By the way, Doctor, I thought you'd want to know—when we went through the Novak house, we didn't see any sign of a novel manuscript. All sorts of other stuff there, though, going back more than a hundred years: papers, books, magazines, old furniture. The MacMahons were as bad about keeping junk as the Novaks were."

"MacMahons?"

"Yeah, the original family, the one that worked for your Mrs. Northbury. Gerry Novak's mother was a MacMahon."

I wanted to ask the lieutenant if I could look through the house. Even if they *hadn't* found the novel there, there was no telling what else might be useful in my research. But, then, I was afraid that—so close to Gerry's suspicious death—he'd say no. If I was going to do it—and it seemed that I was—I didn't want it to be against Piotrowski's express interdiction.

"Lieutenant, do you have any idea who leaked that sensational story to the *Boston Herald*?"

There was a long silence. Then he said, "I *saw* that."

"That's not an answer, Piotrowski."

"I know," he said. "I know. So—anything else you can tell me?"

There wasn't, and once again I was about to hang up, when the big cop spoke, his voice rough again, but this time with emotion.

"Listen, Doctor . . . I want to apologize about . . . you know . . . my father. He's—er—ill. So—"

"I understand, Lieutenant. Really, I do. And I'm sorry."

"Yeah, well . . . Well, thanks for the tip." He hung up.

I admired Piotrowski's loyalty to his elderly parent. It had been years since I'd seen my mother—not since my father's funeral. I took my hand off the phone and a shudder passed through me. *My mother.*

But I had *nothing* to feel guilty about. My sisters were taking care of her. I sent money to help out. That would have to be enough. They'd all let me down in my hour of need. Well, they could just live with the consequences of that.

Jill and I took a twilight walk around town, weaving in and out of Enfield's narrow back streets until we finally paused in front of the Whitlow mansion, arrested by the perfume of roses and the eerie beauty of the big house behind its hedge of overgrown yew.

"Gerry used to run errands for this woman," Jill informed me, toying once again with her locket on its long chain. "But I never met her."

"I did," I said, and smiled at the memory. "And it was a strange experience. Almost like meeting Miss Havisham."

"You mean, from *Great Expectations*?"

"Yeah, you know, where you walk into a room and nothing has changed in fifty years. I swear I looked around for the moldy wedding cake." Before I could finish telling Jill about Helen Whitlow's disappointment in love, a voice shrilled out from the house: "Girl! Girl! You out there! Karen Pelletier! I want to talk to you. Bring your friend and come on in here." Jill and I stared at each other, wide-eyed. I think she was stifling an impulse to run. I know I was.

"Karen . . ." Jill said, a trifle tremulously.

I pulled myself together and laughed. "Come on, Jill; the lady wants to talk to us. What are you afraid of? You think she's going to eat us?"

"Exactly," Jill replied. We were still giggling when we climbed the steps and entered the now open front door.

Helen Whitlow sat us on the cat-hair-covered love seat, and served sherry in her fragile pink-stemmed glasses. She wore the same boy-size flannel shirt and rolled-up jeans as at my last visit. "My boy is dead," she declared, in her creaky voice. "Did you know that?"

"Your boy?" Jill queried, eyes wide with fascination at this diminutive woman and her dilapidated, romantic surroundings.

"Gerry Novak," I muttered out of the side of my mouth, "I was going to tell you."

"Gerry," Jill wailed. So, she wasn't as composed about his death as she claimed she was.

"Yes, my boy—Gerry," Helen repeated, in her rusty voice. She turned to Jill and her eyes narrowed. "Did you know him?" Helen's gaze slid oddly from Jill's face to her throat, then she looked up at her face again with renewed interest.

"Oh, yes—" But I poked my friend in the ribs before she got any more confessional. If Jill told this eccentric woman about her affair with Gerry, there'd be no keeping the secret.

"We were both slightly acquainted with him," I told Helen.

"He was my baby. My pet." The hooded eyes were dry, dark buttons in a wrinkled-cotton face. She continued to stare at Jill. "And she took him away from me, after all. Even after she was dead, she came for him."

Jill and I exchanged wild glances. "Edith?" I asked, baffled.

"Edith, of course. Who else could have gotten out to that boat in the middle of the lake without leaving any prints?"

"I don't know, Miss Whitlow." My brain reeled at the concept. *Footprints? Fingerprints? On water?* "Maybe Gerry's death was an accident," I suggested. I wasn't about to mention the possibility of suicide.

"Accident! He'd been out in that boat a million times. Accident, indeed!" She paused, still dry-eyed. "Now, who's going to take care of me?" So it wasn't grief that so impassioned her, but the necessary narcissism of the elderly: *Who's going to take care of me?* No devoted Piotrowski for this lady—poor old thing.

"Well, I—I'm sure there are community services—"

"Oh, Will Thorpe has some young whippersnapper coming in to do the shopping. And some busybody social worker—from *elder* services, she claims, was here. Poking around. Talking about medication, regular meals, housecleaning services. As if I haven't gotten along all these years on my own—just me and my boy. *Elder* services! Imagine!" Her creaky voice dripped with contempt.

"I'll come visit you," Jill piped up. She was clutching her heart locket. "You can call me if you need anything, and I'll get it for you. And I can help with the flowers. . . ."

Whaa? I stared aghast at my self-centered young colleague. *What the hell?* Then it hit me: This pathetic old lady was all Jill had left of the father of her child. A mother-in-law, of sorts. A grandmother for the baby— for Eloise.

I sat back and watched them make plans—the weird old woman and the unwed mother-to-be. It should have been a heartwarming scene, but, instead, it gave me the creeps. Why would Jill want such a vivid reminder of the man who had caused her so much pain? And why should this bitter old woman take any interest at all in my impetuous young friend?

Unless somehow she knew that Jill was carrying Gerry's child. Hmm. Could it be?

An hour later, when the sherry was gone and arrangements for a gardening date had been made, Jill and I walked out into the warm, dark night. As the door shut behind us, the last ray of house light glanced off Jill's gold filigree locket.

Jill's locket?

Edith Hart's locket! Jill was once again wearing Edith's gold filigree heart. The locket Will Thorpe had been running through his fingers the night we'd had dinner.

Finally I had a chance to ask her about it.

"Jill," I queried, "that locket? Did Will Thorpe give that to you?"

"Dr. Thorpe? No." She paused. "He's been very nice. After Gerry—" she gulped, "after Gerry died, Dr. Thorpe called to see if there was anything he could do for me. I told him about the baby—he's a doctor, after all—and he's been extremely solicitous. But, no, I didn't get the locket from him. It was Gerry's, and he gave it to me months ago. He said it had been in the family for over a century. It belonged to his mother, and to her mother before that."

Gerry Novak's locket? And Jill had had it in her possession for months? Then what had I seen in Will's hands just a few short days ago? And why did I remember having seen it somewhere else, not too long before that?

Jill paused at the gate. I could feel Helen Whitlow's shoe-button gaze probing into our backs from her perch on the second-floor window seat. "It will be the only thing Gerry's child will ever have that belonged to her dead father," she said. And in the hazy half-light, I could see that this time her dark brown eyes were dry.

We walked hand in hand back to Jill's house. Two or three cars passed by. One looked like Sally Chenille's BMW, the street lights reflecting eerily off its chartreuse surface. The luminous car slowed down when it passed us, as if to take a curious, lingering, look. Somewhere inside my skull, previously detached neurons met in momentary, fleeting synapsis. *If Sally had been screwing Gerry Novak, then she, as much as anyone, should be considered a suspect in his death.* Perhaps Piotrowski, in his investigation of Novak's death, had already ferreted out the fact of that relationship. Perhaps not. I'd tell him next time I talked to him, I decided, but I wasn't about to call him again tonight.

Twenty-five

"This is Joyce Brewster—Tibby Brewster's mother. Am I speaking to Professor Pelletier?"

It was Monday morning. I had just emerged from the shower and was dripping all over the bedroom's oak floor. I tucked the big white towel a little tighter around me and sat down on the unmade bed. "This is she, Mrs. Brewster. How are you?" *And what the hell are you calling me for?*

"Fine." The word had no meaning. "I need to talk to you, Professor. And I don't have much time. Could you tell me how to get to your place?" The vowels were rounded; the consonants were clipped. It was a voice used to getting what it asked for.

I glanced around. Did I want Joyce Brewster in this house? "I'm coming in to campus this morning, Mrs. Brewster. Would my office do?" The bedside clock read nine on the button. "Say at ten o'clock?"

"I'll see you there." Without further nicety the connection was broken. I sat with the silent phone in my hand for a good ten seconds. *You don't have much time?* I thought. *Elitist bitch!* Then I hung up.

I have an olive-green checked DKNY skirt I got for a fraction of its original cost at a Filene's end-of-season sale. It was too good to wear to the office. I stepped into it, anyhow, donned the coordinated cream-colored silk T, and rooted around on the floor of my closet for the block-heeled sandals.

Joyce Brewster was making polite conversation with the English Department secretaries when I walked into Dickinson Hall. I had applied lipstick and blusher, brushed my hair a hundred strokes and allowed it to hang loose.

"My, Karen, don't you look nice today!" Elaine's expression of surprise thoroughly demolished the off-hand effect I was striving for. "You really should dress up more often." I scowled; the matronly secretary misinterpreted my expression. "But you do—you look *really good*. Doesn't she, Shirley? She looks *good*."

"Thank you, Elaine." I said it through gritted teeth. Then I turned to Tibby's mother and was shocked right out of my hostility. *She* looked terrible. Cheeks hollower than ever. Eyes shadowed. Ironed jeans and golf shirt sagging on her emaciated frame. *This woman is sick,* I thought, with an almost audible intake of breath. *Maybe even dying.*

"Hello, Professor Pelletier."

"Mrs. Brewster?" Her name stuck in my throat like a fishbone, I felt so guilty about all my nasty thoughts. "Please call me Karen."

"And I'm Joyce." She glanced around—at the door that opened into the public hallway, at the far-too-interested secretaries. "May we talk in your office . . . Karen?"

"You know, Karen, when I said on the phone that I didn't have much time, I didn't mean it the way it sounded—that I was in a hurry." Joyce Brewster sat, denim-clad knees together, in my green vinyl chair. "I meant it literally: I *don't* have much time. I'm terminally ill with metasticized breast cancer." She waved away my horrified exclamation. "And I have a few things to attend to while I'm still able. One of them is Tibby."

I had settled myself across from her in the black captain's chair with the Enfield insignia. Now I wished I could barricade myself behind my big oak desk—so death couldn't get me.

"You must wonder why I'm here," she continued. "I'm certain my son's recent behavior has not endeared him to you."

As I considered my response, Tibby's mother broke impatiently into my silence. "I want you to know, he's not a bad kid."

I thought about the young man I knew—his harassment of Shamega, his nasty drawings, the obscene e-mail, his father's vile complaint to Miles. I nodded wordlessly.

"I know about his drawings," she continued, surprising me. "I found a number of them in his room this weekend. He broke down then—as if he'd just been waiting for me to ask—and, among other things, he told me about that poor girl he's been bothering. Shamala? Shamona?"

"Shamega," I said. "Shamega Gilfoyle."

She nodded impatiently. It didn't really matter: One ethnic name might as well be another; Joyce Brewster had no frame of reference for any of them. "And then he told me what he'd done to your office. The underwear? And then the nasty verse. He's a troubled boy, Professor. Those are acting-out behaviors."

"Yes?" *Acting-out behaviors?* I remembered Earlene Johnson telling me Tibby had said his mother was a "shrink." She certainly talked like one.

"And then, last week, his *father* announced . . ." she raised an exasperated eyebrow, and I thought, *This woman knows her husband's an ass.* ". . . that he's complained to your department head about Tibby's grade. I *am* sorry about that." She cocked her head, spread her hands: *Men!* "I pressed Thibault to drop the complaint—and I do hope he will." Joyce's voice wavered a little, as if she weren't certain whether or not she had any say in the situation. Then she seemed to gather confidence. "That grade was a reality check. I told Thibault so. It let Tib know his actions have consequences. He needs to be reminded of that."

I sat back in my chair and for the first time took a good look at Joyce Brewster. Her lemon yellow golf shirt was at least two sizes too large for the fragile woman she'd become. The stiff blond do was not her own hair but a wig. Chemotherapy. And it hadn't worked. Oh, God. But the dark eyes were alight with intelligence—and purpose. Joyce Brewster was on a final mission—*to save her son,* I thought, without knowing how I knew.

"Joyce, why are you here?" After all my petty thoughts about this woman, I owed her a response as direct as her own revelations had been.

She smiled, and for an instant I saw what she must have been like as a healthy woman. Smart. Wry. Focused. And—in spite of my sympathy, I had to acknowledge it—arrogant. "I'm here to tell you a story, Karen. And I must have your assurance that you will keep what I am about to say in strict confidence." Without waiting for me to agree, she sat back in the big chair and began talking.

Tibby was an only child, his mother told me, and from the start he had been delicate, and very attached to her. His talent for drawing and painting had exhibited itself early, and she'd had hopes that he would be attracted to a career in the arts. When he reached adolescence, however, his father had begun to pressure Tib to follow him into investment banking. "It's a *man's* work," he'd pronounced one evening at the dinner table during his son's senior year in high school. Then he'd added, "But, then,

I've always wondered just how much of a man you really are."

"Tibby fell in line," Joyce said. "Of course." The strong morning light played across her pale, enervated features.

I shook my head in dismay. To have to die at her age was bad, but to have to leave your only child to the care of an S.O.B. like Thibault Brewster—it was enough to break your heart.

"Joyce, you look exhausted. You don't have to tell me all this."

She raised a thin hand. "But, I do. Edith thought you were a good person. The last time Thibault and I visited, she mentioned you. You'd really caught her fancy with your passion for—what's her name?—Mrs. Northworth?"

"Northbury. Serena Northbury."

"Edith showed us some kind of text—a novel, I think—something you found in the house."

"Really?" This woman had seen *Child of the North Star!* "Do you know what she—?"

"But I don't have time to talk about inconsequentials." Joyce sat up straighter in the oversize chair. "Tibby has agreed to go into counseling, but I wanted someone here at the school to know about the situation—in case of problems in his senior year. I don't expect to be around, and Thibault . . ." Her lips tightened, whitened. "Well, let's just say Thibault is not sensitive to his son's developmental needs. I respect Edith's judgment, and she had confidence in you. She said you had integrity. And at the funeral, I was watching you; you seemed like a caring person. Someone who might intervene for my son."

I sighed; I did *not* want to get immersed in this family's problems. "Joyce, I'm really not certain I'm the one you should be talking to. How about speaking to the Dean of Students?"

Joyce's dark gaze skewed; abruptly she was staring

out the open window, gnawing on her bottom lip. Then she looked back at me. "I've spoken with Ms. Johnson in the past, but I feel awkward about this particular situation—because, well, because . . ." She couldn't get it out.

I took a stab. "Because Earlene is African-American? Like Shamega?"

She shrugged. "It's more complicated than you know."

And it was. Over the Thanksgiving holidays, an investigator Joyce had hired to look into her husband's recent suspicious behavior *(People really do that?* I marveled) had uncovered his long-term relationship with a pricey call girl. The investigator had supplied Thibault's wife with photographs, and also with evidence of lavish gifts and investments made for this woman, with whom Thibault seemed to be obsessed. Tibby, unfortunately, had stumbled in on the resulting marital explosion, seen the photographs, and demanded an explanation. "My son was traumatized," Joyce concluded. "Especially given that I'd only recently informed him of my illness. And since that moment—when he saw the pictures of his father and . . . that woman—his attitude has been . . ." she paused, then concluded delicately, ". . . self-destructive."

"Let me guess," I said, "this, er, call girl—she's black, isn't she? That's why Tibby—"

"He blames *her*—not his father, but his father's, ah, paramour. And he's enraged. And I suppose it would be too difficult for him to direct that anger at Thibault, considering that . . ." Here her voice became very flat. "Considering that—well—his father will soon be all he has."

"Joyce, I'm so sorry."

She flinched at my words, then squared her shoulders; Joyce Brewster wasn't looking for pity. "So he's displacing his anger on that unfortunate girl. But that *will* stop, now that Tib understands the psychological dynamic." She seemed a good deal more certain than I'd ever been about the curative value of psychotherapeutic insight.

"But, Joyce, speaking of consequences—"

The phone rang, and I jumped, startled. I picked it up automatically. "Hello?"

"Karen? Tess Holmes here. Listen," my usually unflappable Oxbridge University Press editor bubbled, "the weirdest thing just happened, and I thought you should know about it: I just got a phone call about Serena Northbury."

My heart sank. "Someone else is doing a biography?"

"No," she replied. "Not a *biography*. This guy was really vague and kind of smarmy—and everything was in the conditional, 'ifs' and 'shoulds' and 'woulds'—but it seems there's some kind of interesting—even scandalous—Northbury novel manuscript floating around out there. He hinted at some kind of *great discovery*. Do you know anything about that?"

"Don't tell me it was Ear—" I glanced up at Mrs. Brewster fidgeting in the green vinyl chair. "Ah, I'm interested, Tess. Can you give me the short version?"

"You've got someone there?"

"Yep."

"Okay. Do you know an Earl Wiggett? . . ."

I was too involved with Joyce Brewster and her evident discomfort to give Tess's tale the level of attention it deserved, but filed away this confirmation of Wiggett's link to *Child of the North Star* under the mental heading of Information To Be Considered Soon.

When I hung up the phone, I turned to Tibby's mother. "Sorry, Joyce. Where were we?"

"We were discussing this Shameeka girl."

"Shamega. Shamega Gilfoyle. You do understand that Shamega has been badly shaken by your son. I think I should let her know—"

"No!" Her tone was imperative. "Don't tell anyone!" Then she seemed to hear herself—the icy, domineering accents. She ran a hand over her eyes, and sank back in the chair. "You will, of course, do what you feel is right, Professor. But I ask you to keep this to yourself as much as you can, especially the bit about Thibault's— ah—indiscretion. I just wanted someone at the school to know about the situation for Tibby's sake, in case—ah— issues arise next year. And you can see why I didn't wish to speak to Earlene Johnson. . . ."

"No, actually, I can't. Earlene is quite capable of handling questions of—" I had been about to say *racism.* Now, considering Joyce's illness, I softened it. "Of, er, racial issues. They do arise once in awhile, even at Enfield, you know."

She gazed down at her hands, white skin wrinkled over bone. "Well, I just wouldn't feel comfortable. I don't know many black people." Her long, thin fingers twisted together. "I don't know any, actually. Socially, that is."

As equals, she meant. Just because this woman was dying didn't make her an enlightened person. And just because she cared so desperately about the fate of her son, didn't make her someone I had to like.

That afternoon I finished going through the Reverend Pinkworth's account books, concentrating hard in order to erase Joyce Brewster's death's-head features from my mind. I learned a great deal about the price of kerosene lamps, chamber pots, and molasses in the 1830's, '40's, and '50's. And—much more to the point—I pinned down the date of the final break between the Reverend Eddie and his daughter Serena: The last quarterly payment recorded for Serena Pinkworth was June 1, 1837, just a month before the letter in which Pinkworth threatened to cut off her support if she persisted in her perverse intention to attend college.

Serena Pinkworth had had moxie; she must have

written right back and told her father to go to hell—metaphorically speaking, of course. In an autobiographical introduction to one of her novels, Mrs. Northbury had briefly mentioned her education at Oberlin Collegiate Institute, but had given no indication of the personal cost at which that education had been purchased.

I jotted a note on my lined yellow pad: *Check Oberlin College student records for the late 1830's*. Oberlin had been the first college in the U.S. to admit black students and women students, and was a hotbed of abolition and women's rights agitation during the years just before the Civil War. I could get all sorts of fascinating historical background for the biography from Oberlin records. Maybe those records would give me some insight into how deeply Serena Northbury had been involved in those activist movements. Her life story was promising to be far more colorful than I could have hoped.

Closing the Reverend Eddie's account book, I sat for a moment with my hand on its speckled cardboard cover. Warm pulsing life was recorded here—hot anger and iron determination—and what endures? Fading ink marks in soldierly rows on blue-ruled pages.

And stories. Serena Northbury's stories.

I'd found out a good deal about this storyteller's life from the spidery entries of her father's financial accounts, and from other archival material. But there was nothing left at the Enfield library for me to research; Shamega had brought me the last of the Pinkworth boxes this afternoon. I was itching to get back into Meadowbrook. I needed to look through all those boxes of papers, but until Edith's will was probated, I was not allowed access to the house. With Thibault Brewster contesting his aunt's final wishes, it could be years before the remaining family papers became available. If Brewster won, I'd *never* get my hands on them.

Damn.

I recalled my earlier thoughts about undertaking a

little—ah—research sortie to Meadowbrook. Well, okay, a little breaking and entering. Too bad Meadowbrook had such an extensive security system; when I'd visited with Avery that night, he'd said the alarms were set to sound in the town police station. So a teensy bit of harmless snooping around in the storeroom and attics would not merely be imprudent, it would be downright impossible.

But Gerry Novak's cottage was a different matter. I couldn't shake loose the memory of all those books, magazines, and papers. What was it Miles Jewell had said? *Who knows what manuscripts might be in that rat's nest of a house?* According to Piotrowski there was no novel manuscript there—well, obviously not, since Earl Wiggett now seemed to have it, or, at least, to know its whereabouts. I really should tell the lieutenant about my editor's call, I thought, fleetingly. But my mind swerved immediately back to the Meadowbrook cottage. Even if no novel had been found there, why couldn't there be other papers relating to the Northbury family? After all, the MacMahon-Novak and Northbury families had lived and worked together at Meadowbrook for more than a century. And surely there would be no security system in that ramshackle little house?

Some annoying internal voice clamored that it would be wrong to sort through the belongings of a recently dead man without family permission. But, then, as far as I knew, there was no one alive who would care about the Novak family effects. The decades' worth of hoarded magazines and papers looked like garbage. They would be crated up and thrown out by whoever eventually fell heir to them. And searching through them would certainly be for a good cause: to further the advance of knowledge about an unfairly ignored American novelist.

I thrummed my fingers on the cover of the Pinkworth account book as I contemplated a scouting trip to the Novak cottage. Yellow police tape had barred the door when I'd been called there by the state police a week earlier. I assumed it still did—but maybe not. The drug unit must be done with the place, and the little house wasn't actually the scene of any crime. Gerry had drowned in the lake, after all, not at home in the bathtub. *And*—if I did find anything related to Gerry's death—or to Edith's death—I'd immediately turn it over to Piotrowski. So it wouldn't actually be *wrong* for me to search the Novak cottage. I pictured myself sorting through all that fascinating junk—

"You really shouldn't be doing that, Professor."

Shamega's admonitory tones caused me to jump guiltily. *What? She can read my mind?*

She slipped the ancient account book from under my drumming fingers. "I'm surprised at you. This is fragile, you know." She inspected the speckled cover for damage.

"Oh, Shamega, I'm sorry. I wasn't thinking about what I was doing."

She laughed. "You did look about a million miles away. I didn't mean to startle you, but I've got to put the files away, now. It's closing time."

"Closing time? So soon?" I sighed. Another long June evening ahead of me with nothing to do.

It was going to be a warm, clear night. Maybe I'd just take that little ride up Eastbrook way.

A message from Sergeant Schultz on my office voice-mail drove any thoughts of an illicit research sortie right out of my mind, however. Felicity Schultz's dry-as-dust tones communicated her displeasure at having to relay the distasteful message that the lieutenant would like to request my assistance. Again. The Northbury hatbox and its batch of old letters had been tested for fingerprints and other forensic traces, and were now available for my perusal. Would I please contact her at state police headquarters as soon as convenient?

Like immediately, I thought, and reached for my desk phone. Although it was 5:23 P.M., Schultz answered the phone right away. *Ha!* I thought, spinning my desk chair around, *clearly this woman has no personal life, or she wouldn't still be in her office.* I tucked the phone between my shoulder and my ear and straightened a stack of manila file folders on my desk. "Sergeant? Karen Pelletier here. You requested my assistance?" Not a note in my cool, even tones betrayed the excitement I felt about finally getting my hands on those letters.

In front of the library Shamega Gilfoyle was talking heatedly to a male student whose back was turned to me. The late afternoon sun transformed her stubby dreadlocks into a spiked ebony helmet. The scene didn't seem to be so much a conversation as a rout, with my young friend as the pursuing warrior. With the pointer finger of her right hand, Shamega repeatedly poked her adversary in the chest. I was too far away to hear her words, but with each poke he took a sharp backward step. Then he raised his head and began to speak in stuttering tones. In profile, the pale face, prominent nose, and weak mouth were those of Tibby Brewster. Shamega heard my gasp and glanced up just in time to note my first step toward her. Dreadlocks bobbing, she shook her head at me in a sharp, disapproving negative: *Leave me alone. I can take care of myself.* Irresolute, I remained rooted to the concrete walkway for one, far-too-long minute. Shamega gave me a straight, bristling look, then turned back to Tibby and continued to give him hell. The path to the parking lot skirted the library, and I set my leather sandals down one after the other as if I were an automaton. She wasn't my daughter. I had no responsibility for her. She was right: She could take care of herself.

Twenty-six

Helen Whitlow's coal-black eye peered at me through a heart-shaped keyhole. I woke with a gasp, the afterimage of that beady jet eye smoldering at me from the nightmare. In my dream Helen had served Jill and me tea sandwiches, small triangular slices of cream-colored paper spread delicately with brownish ink squiggles. The first bite was dry, and I gagged as I swallowed. Then I heard Jill choking as the gold locket she wore with her black crepe bikini tightened of its own volition around her slim white throat.

I sat straight up in bed and croaked, "Oh, my God!" *That's* why Helen had stared so intently at Jill the night we'd visited the Whitlow house: She, too, had recognized that locket! She'd known both Edith and Gerry; she would have seen the gold heart locket any number of times around Edith's neck. Maybe she'd even seen it in Gerry's possession—however it got there. The realization unaccountably set my heart pounding with fear for Jill. I was out of bed with my hand on the phone before I came to my senses. What was there to be afraid of?

Nothing. So an old woman had recognized an old locket? Big deal.

I was thirsty; the paper-and-ink sandwich had desiccated my mouth. Without bothering to turn on a light, I stumbled into the kitchen for water. Then I sat at the table with the cold glass between my hands until the sky outside the kitchen window choked itself with dawn.

Piotrowski removed the first packet of envelopes from the battered hatbox, and untied the string. A dozen small, cream-colored envelopes slid across the scarred table. They were addressed in Serena Northbury's rounded handwriting to Mrs. *Henry Linwood, Philadelphia, Pennsylvania*. The lieutenant and Sergeant Schultz had met me at BCI headquarters at nine A.M., and we'd proceeded immediately to the evidence room.

"I don't get it." Piotrowski shook his head. "How could this Northbury woman be in possession of a bunch of letters she sent to someone else?"

"It was a custom," I said, my eyes sliding past him toward the first envelope, trying to burn a hole through it with my gaze so I could begin to read the letter. "When somebody died, you sent any letters you'd received from them back to their family. As a kind of remembrance, I imagine. This—" I glanced at the envelope, "—this Mrs. Linwood—or her family—would have returned Mrs. Northbury's letters to her daughters when she heard about Northbury's death."

"Whatdaya know?" The big cop's expression turned from puzzled to sentimental. "That's kinda nice." He pondered the idea, then said, "But, Jeez, I don't know if I'd want my kids to get ahold of any letters I ever wrote."

"I didn't know you had kids, Lieutenant." For a moment my attention was diverted from the letters.

"Oh, yeah. Two boys—well, *men* now; they're both in their early twenties. Nice kids."

"Really?" I was so intrigued by the notion of the lieutenant as a family man—a father, sons—that I almost forgot why I was there. "Where do they—?"

"Humph." Sergeant Schultz interrupted our schmoozing with an irritated clearing of her throat. "The letters, Professor?"

Piotrowski placed both square hands flat on the table and pushed his chair back. "I'll leave you with the sergeant, Doctor. Just read through these letters; anything strikes you that could possibly relate to the homicides, let her know."

"It might take awhile." I gestured at the half dozen string-tied packets of letters. At the other end of the table, Schultz sighed.

"That's all right, Doctor," Piotrowski said, directing his comments to me but chastising his subordinate with a slit-eyed look. "I'm sure the sergeant's got plenty of reports to write."

"Humph." Schultz yanked a manila file folder from the canvas briefcase beside her chair, slapped it on the table in front of her, and proceeded ostentatiously to ignore my existence.

As the heavy door closed behind Piotrowski, I recalled that I'd intended to tell him about Wiggett's call to my editor. Too late now—he was gone. And I wasn't about to volunteer any information at all to this obnoxious little sergeant. I slipped the first letter out of its envelope. Earl Wiggett could wait.

The letter was dated *17 April 1856*, and had been mailed to Mrs. Linwood in Philadelphia from Serena Northbury's Fifth Avenue home. *My Dear Evelyn,* I read, *I did so rejoice to hear your joyful news. Another woman-child! And a Lucretia, to join sisters Elizabeth and Susan! I anticipate a new age of woman's rights to spring forth in Philadelphia—and all from under your roof! It is remarkable what a wondrous home can be built upon a clear envisioning of the right relationship of man and woman. Dear Henry! Would that I were equally blessed!*

Interesting, I thought. The supposedly conservative Mrs. Northbury was talking like an advocate of women's rights. I read on.

But, alas, as you know, I must keep my views hidden in order to maintain the calm and order of my own home, such a lack of sympathy here abides. But I dare say no more.

Aha! Maybe not so conservative, after all. Maybe in telling such conventional love stories—masterful heroes, submissive heroines—Serena Northbury had merely been prudent. I scribbled a note to that effect on my yellow pad.

"What?" Schultz raised her eyes from her report writing.

"Nothing," I replied. "Just an idea for my biography."

"You're not here to do research for your biography, Dr. Pelletier." The officer's gaze was stern under the straight reddish bangs.

I sighed. This woman was really too much. "Sergeant, I'm a professional researcher. It's my job to gather the information I need to reconstruct Serena Northbury's life. And I have a feeling this material is going to be tied up for a long, long time. I may not have a chance to look at these letters again for years—"

"Forget the book," Schultz snapped. "You're here to look for anything that might provide a motive for murder, and that's all. Got that?" Schultz's eyes goose-stepped back to her report. She mumbled, "Not that you're going to find anything. . . ."

"What was that, Sergeant?" Schultz really knew how to get on my nerves. "Did you say something, Sergeant?" I used the tired old teacher's ploy as if she were a sullen student. "I couldn't quite hear you."

She gave me a fish-eyed look. "You might as well admit it, Doctor: This boondoggle is nothing but a waste of time. God knows what the lieutenant has in mind; I sure don't. And I've got a heck of a lot better things I could be doing right now, instead of babysitting you. So I'd appreciate it if you'd just stop having *ideas for your biography* and get through this bunch of letters quick, so I can get lunch at a decent hour."

The thick paper felt stiff between my fingers as I glared at the truculent woman on the far end of the table. "You've got an attitude problem, Sergeant."

"Oh, yeah? Well, talk about *attitude*—"

I sighed. "Look, let's not get into this, okay?" I had neither the time nor the energy for a juvenile confrontation with this obnoxious cop. "We both want me to get through these letters, right? So we can *both* get out of here. Let's just leave it alone. Okay?"

Felicity Schultz pursed her lips with contempt, then turned back to the stack of forms she was filling in. Scribble. Scribble. Scribble. Busy. Busy.

I gave her my best professorial glower, but it was wasted; she didn't glance up once. I returned to Mrs. Northbury's letter.

Have you heard from our mutual friend? Does Canada East yet welcome the small band of intrepid travelers? Forgive me if I am importunate, but I have none else to ask. I fear I will lie awake each night until I receive word of a safe arrival. Of one brave heart in particular as you well know. Oh, dear friend, without your beneficent and large understanding, I should surely find myself driven to madness.

Canada East? Isn't that what Quebec Province was called prior to Canadian confederation? A special friend of Mrs. Northbury's was traveling to Quebec? Okay. But why the fear of "madness"? And why does she refer to Mrs. Linwood's "beneficent and large understanding"? This passage puzzled me. I read it over again. *Quebec?*

I must have said the word aloud, because Schultz demanded, "What about Quebec?"

"Oh, nothing," I replied, startled by her question. "It's just floating around in my head. Northbury mentions it in this letter, and I seem to link her in some other way with Quebec." I wiggled my fingers. "I just can't recall—"

"*Child of the North Star,* page four hundred thirty-two," Schultz recited.

"What?"

"One of the pages we found at the scene? Okay? The part where the little girl is dying? In the cottage? Mrs. Northbury talks about the mountains of old Quebec."

"So she does, Sergeant," I said, wonderingly. I was beginning to recall it now: something about *the green mountains of old Quebec.* "So she does." I stared at Schultz. "But how on earth did you come to remember that?"

"It's my *job* to remember things, Doctor Pelletier. I'm a professional investigator. You're not the *only* professional in the world, you know."

On campus, a voice-mail message from my Oxbridge editor awaited me. "Karen, Tess Holmes here. This Northbury manuscript thing just gets curiouser and curiouser. Do you know Sally Chenille? Call me."

I did. Immediately. "Sally Chenille?" I queried, incredulously. "What connection could La Chenille possibly have with Serena Northbury?"

"You tell me, Karen. All I know is, I got another call from that Wiggett guy. He said a 'big name' cultural theorist was 'chomping at the bit' to co-edit this mysterious novel he's got a line on. He wasn't going to let me know who that was, but I'm pretty foxy; I got it out of him."

"You're pretty foxy, and he's pretty dense." I aimed for *cool,* but my teeth were clamped together so tight I felt my ears pop: No wacked-out intellectual-trend-slave like Sally Chenille was going to get her hands on *my* Mrs. Northbury's manuscript. Not if I could help it. "So tell me, Tess, are you interested?"

"In working with the notorious Sally Chenille? Not on your life! Sally only looks out for number one, and if that means backing out on publishing contracts, no problem. She screwed us that way once already, and I understand Oxbridge isn't the only press she's left holding the bag." She paused, then continued, hesitantly, "I *would* be interested in seeing that novel manuscript, though. But that puts me in a kind of a bind, which is why I called you. You're one of our authors, and I don't know this Wiggett at all, but it seems to me that if anyone should be editing a Northbury novel, it should be you."

I unclenched my teeth. Breathed again. "Seems that way to me, too, Tess. Look, did Wiggett tell you he's actually *got* the novel?" I knew the state police had at least six pages of it, but the whereabouts of the rest was still a mystery.

"No. He was very hush-hush about it. Big secret. He's 'got a line on it,' that's as much as he'd say, and, oh yes, he said he knew Sally from grad school, and that she—now, I wrote this down word for word, so I know I've got it right—he said Sally was 'enticed by yet a further opportunity to violate the self-perpetuating power structure of the bourgeois academic literary establishment.' Does that make sense to you?"

"Hah!" I blurted out. "She's 'enticed' by yet a further opportunity to make a buck and get her skinny little tattooed butt in the limelight."

"Karen! Really!" Tess's mock horror was followed by a shared hearty laugh.

I hung up, determined to do whatever I had to in order to locate Serena Northbury's unpublished tale of interracial love and loss.

·   ·   ·

"Greg," I asked, between sips of chardonnay, "how would you feel about you and I having a little adventure?" Irena was visiting her parents in Greenwich for the week, and Greg was cozily settled with me at a corner table in the back room at Rudolph's as we awaited our orders of polenta and shrimp with cream sauce. Rudolph's had a new chef, and the menu was even more outrageous than ever.

"A little *adventure?*" Greg's face went pale. "But . . . but . . . what about Irena?"

I chortled. "Silly! That's not what I meant!" I slapped him on the hand.

"Only joking," he replied, with a small, embarrassed laugh.

Oh, yeah? I thought, but decided to let it go. "What I have in mind isn't anything quite so dangerous as what *you're* thinking."

A split second's hesitation was followed by a bawdy wink. "Too bad," he said.

Riiight! I thought. Greg was the most thoroughly *married* person I'd ever met. "Listen, here's the deal. I spent most of the day reading through a bunch of hundred-and-fifty-year-old letters. . . ." I went on to explain about the cache of Northbury epistles in the old blue hatbox now in police custody.

From reading those letters, I'd learned a great deal about Serena Northbury, her life, and her interests. She'd surprised me. In spite of the conventional men and women in her novels, this woman had been an early feminist. Comments to friends revealed her staunch belief in equal rights for women, and, further, a passionate interest in the abolition of slavery. The hatbox had held letters to and from women's rights leaders such as Elizabeth Cady Stanton and Lucretia Mott, and noted abolitionists such as Lydia Maria Child and Frederick Douglass. Evidently Mrs. Northbury contributed generously to both the women's rights movement and the abolitionist movement. But her contributions had been surreptitious. Because she did not wish, as she told Douglass, a former slave, "to incur the displeasure of the unhappy tyrant in my own home."

As the result of his "furious driving" on Broadway, Mrs. Northbury's husband Howard had been crippled in a carriage accident early in their marriage. *Aha!* I thought. *That explains why she had three children in the first five years, and then no more.* Left without income, the young wife had turned to writing novels to support her children and supply her invalid husband's needs. Reading between the lines of her letters, particularly those to her college friend Evelyn Linwood, I determined that Howard Northbury had soon become a soured, twisted domestic tyrant, playing on his wife's pity and guilt to create a repressive atmosphere in their Manhattan home. Meadowbrook seemed to have been her refuge from him, and she and her daughters had spent increasingly long periods at their country estate. *Poor Serena Northbury,* I thought, *from a sour father to a sour husband.* Despite her phenomenal success as a popular author, Northbury's life had been lonely and filled with recrimination.

I'd finished reading the last letter with a sigh, handed it over to Sergeant Schultz, and watched her bundle it with the others and slap the battered cover back on the blue hatbox. This brief immersion in Serena Northbury's life had only whetted my appetite. Then my editor's phone call had galvanized me into action. Before I'd pushed through the heavy English Department door, I'd made up my mind to scoot up to Eastbrook that very night. I had to try to get into Gerry Novak's ramshackle cottage with its treasure trove of old papers and magazines. After all, who would it hurt? And, besides, if I played by the rules, I could miss out on vital information that might help me locate the missing manuscript, and *that* would certainly help make this fascinating writer's story come alive for a whole new generation of readers.

Greg sat silent as I finished my tale, then nodded at

the waiter as he slid the outlandish concoction of sea-
food and cornmeal mush in front of us. I stared at my
plate and groaned. "Cholesterol city!" I exclaimed and
grabbed for my fork. Greg speared a hush puppy.

Halfway through the meal, Greg resurfaced. "This
guy . . . Novak," he mused, "wasn't he Jill Greenberg's . . . ah, you know . . . *inamorato?*"

"How'd you know that?" I laid my fork across the
still-laden plate. "She told me their relationship was a
secret."

Greg shrugged. "It may have started out as a secret,
but since Novak's death, everyone seems to know. Jill's
pregnancy makes it an especially juicy piece of gossip,
you know. Everyone's been trying to figure out who the
baby's father is. Let's see, Miles Jewell told me first. You
know what an old gossip he is. Then I heard it again
from Sally Chenille."

Sally Chenille! That woman's name kept popping
up! "Huh. Whatdaya know? Here I am, faithfully keeping confidence, and all Enfield is in on Jill's secret!"

"You know what it means, don't you, Karen?"

"What?"

"If Gerry Novak is the father of Jill's baby, then the
kid—excuse me—*Eloise,* inherits anything he owned."

I laughed. "So, you mean, I don't have to break into
the Novak cottage tonight. I can just wait until Eloise
turns twenty-one and gives me permission to go through
the moldering ruins? Let's see, that would be sometime
in the twenty-teens. . . ."

"Anyone ever tell you you've got a one-track
mind?"

"All the time. So," I laid my hand on his arm, "will
you come up to Meadowbrook with me?"

"Yeah. Sure." He laughed, and patted his stomach.
"If I can still move after this meal."

Pushing my plate away, I signaled to the waiter.
"Two coffees, please, *not* decaf."

"For dessert tonight we have New Orleans bread

pudding with bourbon sauce," the ponytailed young waiter announced. "And—"

"Stop right there," Greg responded. "Two orders of the bread pudding—and make my coffee a double espresso."

"Greg," I moaned, "what are you trying to do to me?" But somehow the waiter got away before I could cancel my share of the dessert.

"You seen Avery lately?" Greg asked, far too casually, running the sliver of lemon rind around the rim of his espresso cup.

"No." I gulped, and tried to pass it off as a reaction to the strong coffee. "Why do you ask?" Surely Greg wasn't about to badger me again about Avery Mitchell?

"Well, because a funny thing happened when I was in his office the other day. We were talking about the curriculum revision, when he got a phone call, went white as snow, then asked me if we could continue our conversation later. In other words, *get the hell out of here*. So I left, and when I tried to get back to him, he'd taken off for a few days, and Lonnie couldn't tell me when he'd return."

"Hmm," I said, recalling the voice-mail message Avery had left me saying he had to leave town unexpectedly.

"So—I wondered if you had any idea what's going on with Avery? He's usually so conscientious."

"Greg, what makes you think I would know anything at all about Avery Mitchell's private business?" I gave him a straight, dispassionate stare.

"No reason." He shrugged, hands spread wide. "Just wondered. That's all."

The Novak cottage was easy to access. The door was locked, but Greg trained my flashlight on it as I slid a thin supermarket savings card into the jamb. Life with

Tony had taught me a few useful skills: how to shoot a handgun, how to jimmy a window, how to pick a lock.

In the warm darkness of the late-June evening, Meadowbrook was deserted. Beyond the barn and the carriage house, the big house hulked silent in the near distance. "This is perfect," I whispered to my accomplice. "If I'd waited much longer, they'd have hired a new caretaker, and we wouldn't have been able to get in here."

"Why are you whispering?" Greg asked in a normal tone. "There's no one for miles around." He pushed the door. It opened with a loud creak, and he switched on his big lantern. An eerie glow illuminated the cluttered kitchen in front of us.

"No reason," I muttered. "I just think we've got to keep as quiet as possible. You never know. . . ."

"Do ghosts have ears?" Greg intoned in *Twilight Zone* cadences.

"Get serious." I elbowed him in the ribs. "Now, turn that lantern way down, give me the flashlight, and keep guard outside. I plan on going through this place room by room. Let me know if you hear anyone coming."

"What am I supposed to do? Hoot like an owl?"

"You'll think of something."

An hour and a half into the search, wheezing from decades of undisturbed dust, I'd reached a tiny unused bedroom on the second floor. Piles of *Saturday Evening Post*s from the 1940's and 50's were stacked three feet high on the bed, covering the faded pink chenille spread from top to bottom with the optimistic faces of Norman Rockwell's American working class. I'd already checked out the shoebox of household receipts from the Depression years that I'd found on the dresser, and the oatmeal sack of turn-of-the-century *Farmer's Almanac*s from under the bed. I sneezed. My eyes were itching from the dust, and I didn't know how much longer the flashlight batteries would hold out. This sortie was turning into a bust. Not only had I not uncovered anything relevant to Serena Northbury's life, I hadn't come across a hint of anything even remotely related to the midnineteenth-century years she'd lived at Meadowbrook. Evidently the pack-rat strain in the Novak family hadn't begun until the early twentieth century. I might as well give up. Greg had been faithfully standing guard for close to two hours, and it had been a good fifteen minutes since his last complaint; it was time to give him a break and get out of here.

Sweeping my light around the room one last time, I caught sight of an elaborately decorated candy box tucked into a niche between a china chamberpot and three chimneyless kerosene lamps perched on top of a foot-pedaled Singer sewing machine in the far corner. Climbing over an oak commode, I secured the candy box, untied the maroon ribbon that bound it, removed the cover, and shone my light down on the contents. A vaguely familiar face stared soberly up at me: an infant, swathed in Victorian ruffles, with Edith Hart's locket hung on a fine chain around her chubby neck. I gasped and dropped the box as if it were on fire. Stooping to recover the old photograph, I heard a heavy masculine step in the hallway. Just outside the window an owl hooted forlornly.

"Greg," I hissed, as I rose with my prize. "You'll never guess what I just found!" A dull thud behind me caused me to swivel sharply. The bright beam of my flashlight chose that precise second to dim, then fail, but not until it had swept across the stern face of the tall uniformed trooper who had just that second cracked his head on the low doorway of the room.

Twenty-seven

"Trespass. Breaking and entering." Sergeant Schultz gleefully ticked off my crimes on her stubby fingers. "Attempted burglary. Withholding evidence. Impeding a police investigation." Her short, reddish hair stuck straight out on one side, as if she'd rolled from bed right into her baggy gray sweats without bothering to look in a mirror. And she probably had; it was after midnight.

Schultz sat across from me at a square table in the Greenfield barracks interview room. She had left Greg in the reception area under the attentive gaze of the on-duty trooper. The sergeant didn't give a hoot about Greg; it was my blood she was after. Elbow on the table, rounded chin resting on her thumb, index finger straight up next to her small freckled nose, she mimicked a favorite pose of her lieutenant's. Then she favored me with a scaled-down version of his most intimidating slit-eyed look.

I sighed. "I want to talk to Piotrowski. Where is he?"

"Home in bed, where he belongs. *I'm* in charge now. You'll talk to *me,* and you'll talk good and fast."

The thought of having to deal with this hard-assed little martinette without Piotrowski's intervention chilled me. With a grim smile, Schultz noted my shudder. "Now, tell me again, Dr. Pelletier, what you were doing at the Novak house at eleven-thirty at night?"

"Research." Single words seemed like my best option. How much trouble can you get into with just one word?

"Research?"

"Research."

"A real dedicated scholar, huh?" When I didn't respond, she persisted. "And what did you say you found in this—er—research? A picture of a baby?" The sarcasm in her tone would have scoured the brown stains off the coffeemaker on its stand in the corner of the room.

I nodded. It was late; I was beat; I was stressed; I was even a little frightened. If Piotrowski had been present, he would have listened to reason. But this minimacho storm trooper had it in for me, and there was no telling what she was capable of. I'd probably end up spending the night in jail. I could envision the headline: COPS THROW BOOK AT ENGLISH PROF.

"So, Doctor, you do research into *babies?* Well, this one *is* cute." She lifted the top off the pasteboard candy box and peered inside, careful not to allow me a glance at the contents.

I sighed again. "I'm not talking to you anymore, Sergeant." I sat back and crossed my arms. "I'm not saying another word. I can't deal with your type. I taught a few like you when I was a grad assistant at BU, kids from Southie with chips on their shoulders the size of full-grown Douglas firs. And you—you're the worst kind: You've got a couple of stripes on *your* shoulder and a gun in your pocket, and you think that puts you in the big leagues. Like I said before, Sergeant, you've got a serious attitude problem."

Schultz went bone white; the freckles on her pug nose stood out, three-dimensional against her bloodless skin. Even her lips were pale. "Not all of us were born with a silver spoon in our mouth, Doc-tor Pell-lah-tee-AY." The French pronunciation sounded ludicrous given the flat Boston vowels.

I laughed. Even under the circumstances, it was amusing to be mistaken for a blue blood. "That's PELL-uh-teer, Sergeant, as you well know. And, face it, you don't know *shit* about my life."

As it turned out, Schultz had to let us go home at three A.M.; Edith Hart's estate, in the person of her lawyer/executor, sagely refused to press breaking and entering charges against a legatee of Edith's will. At noon the next day, just as I was sitting down with a tuna and red onion on rye and the CNN Headline News, a suspiciously conciliatory Lieutenant Piotrowski called. "So. Doctor. How *are* you?"

"What do you want, Lieutenant?" I stuck the phone between my ear and neck, settled back in the recliner and chomped down on my sandwich; it was lunchtime and I was ravenous. Not even the state police would come between me and food.

"You sound mad, Doctor."

"Mad? Mad? Damn right I'm mad. Dragged into police headquarters at midnight and snarled at like a common criminal by a woman who's got a grudge against me so deep you could plant potatoes in it—"

"I am sorry about that, Doctor. You know if I'd been on duty . . ." He let the statement die. If he'd been on duty he would have done the same thing, minus the snarling. Well, *maybe* minus the snarling.

"What do you want, Lieutenant?" I popped a corn

chip in my mouth. "Let's not play games for once. Just tell me what you want."

A pause. "This candy box? The one you found last night?"

"Yes?" I was instantly alert. "What about it?"

"Schultz says you said the picture of the baby in the box is the same as the one you found in that old book of Mrs. Northbury's?"

"Yes?"

"And I see here in my notes that you said there was a name written on the back of that photo—"

"Yes?"

"Was the name *Carrie?*"

"Yes!" Corn chips slid off my plate onto battered leather as I slammed the recliner into its upright position. "What did you find, Piotrowski? Your trooper wouldn't let me look at the picture. Did it have *Carrie* written on it?"

"No. No name." His voice was flat.

"Oh . . ."

"But we did find that name on a birth certificate—"

"A birth certificate!"

"Yep. Carrie Serena Johnson. Born the twenty-second of January, 1861, in Philly. Mother: Mrs. Serena Pinkworth Northbury. No father listed."

"Oh, my God! Piotrowski—by 1861, Serena Northbury and her husband were no longer . . . ah . . . no longer—"

"Enjoying marital relations?"

"Right. He'd been disabled for years, and their three daughters were well into their teens by then." I paused, considering the ramifications. "I don't know what to think."

"Well, I do." Piotrowski's words conveyed just a hint of laughter.

"Of course I *know* she must have taken a lover, Lieutenant! I just don't have any idea who it would have been."

"So. Doctor? . . . Can I . . . ah . . . entice you to come down here and look over the rest of this stuff—"

I slapped the half-eaten sandwich back on its plate. "I'm leaving right this second, Lieutenant."

The gloomy green evidence room was beginning to feel like home. Spread in a semicircle in front of me on the battered table were the contents of the candy box: the photograph, the birth certificate, a gold-clasped bracelet woven of intertwined strands of jet black and honey-blond hair, and a packet of letters tied together with a faded red ribbon. I reached immediately for the letters. There were six of them. The first was addressed to Serena Northbury at her Manhattan address.

> *Montreal*
> *4 May 1858*

> *Mrs. Northbury, My Friend,*
> *Another journey finished, and a few more souls of my alien race breathe free air at last in this country of the North Star. The annals of History may never note your goodness in harboring weary fugitives, but in the Heavenly tomes your name is surely etched in gold. I must lie low now a while, the hunters penetrate even here; we are not so far from the border that abduction is unheard of. But it is my prayer that I may be spared for yet another venture into the land of my Birth—if not of my Citizenry! That we may meet again is my fervent wish.*

> *Au Revoir,*
> *Joseph Monroe Johnson*

"Jesus," I breathed.

"What?" Piotrowski demanded. We were alone in the room. Sergeant Schultz, thank God, had made no appearance since my arrival at BCI. Maybe she'd gone home to bed; I'd given her a hard night.

"Shhh." I waved a hand at him. "Let me read." The second letter was again addressed to Mrs. Northbury, this time at Meadowbrook, in the same bold, blocky handwriting.

> *Montreal*
> *12 September 1858*

> *Mrs. Northbury—Serena,*
>   *I scarce know what to make of your last epistle! We have met but twice, my Friend, and, although thrown together under such circumstances, we cannot be said to know one another with heart-knowledge! But, yes, my Friend, I, too, am—*[Here a few words were heavily scored out.] *I, too, have felt the stirrings of which you speak, although I must be vague in this response, not knowing what eyes—Need I say more? Is it within your power to secure a safe postbox? Should you so inform me, I would write at further length.*

>   *Your Fugitive*

This letter was unsigned, but obviously had been composed by the author of the first. "Holy Mary, Mother of God," I exclaimed, reverting in my astonishment to a long-forgotten Catholic childhood. An absolutely astounding possibility was beginning to shape itself in the miasma of my incredulous brain.

"What!"

I waggled my fingers at Piotrowski again. "Shhh!" I

reached for the third letter; his strong hand clamped my wrist.

"Before you read any further, Doctor, you tell me what's going on." The lieutenant's words were slow and patient, as if he were speaking to someone who was mentally handicapped—or deeply disturbed. "I read them all, but couldn't make head nor tail of them. But you look like someone just walked over your grave!"

I shook my head to clear it and sank back in my chair. His gruff voice finally tore through my immersion in the long-ago and far away of these precious letters. Piotrowski was still holding my wrist, and I tugged away from his grip.

"Joseph. Monroe. Johnson." Each word was its own sentence. "Who would have *thought* it!" Glancing at the lieutenant for permission, I picked up the old birth certificate with its brown foxed marking, and read the name aloud: *Carrie Serena Johnson.* Then I studied the photograph closely: Yes, this child, although quite light-skinned, definitely had African-American ancestry; you could see it in the cloud of kinky blond hair, in the beautifully molded lips, in the round dark eyes. "Holy Mary—"

" 'Mother of God,' I know!" Impatiently, Piotrowski finished my exclamation. "Tell me what's going on!"

Glancing over at the third envelope, I noted that it too was addressed in the abolitionist's bold hand, but this time the letter was directed to *Mrs. Kate MacMahon, Meadowbrook Cottage, Eastbrook, Massachusetts.* According to Piotrowski, the MacMahons had been Mrs. Northbury's Meadowbrook staff. This had been sent to Serena Northbury's "safe" postbox!

"I'll tell you what I think happened in the 1860's, Lieutenant. But God knows *what* it has to do with murder in the 1990's!"

"Just tell me. I'll determine if it has any relevance to our investigation."

"Joseph Monroe Johnson was Serena Northbury's lover! This baby was their child!"

"Oh, really?" Piotrowski said. "And who was *he* when he was at home?" I hadn't heard that expression since my Canadian grandmother died.

"I'm sorry, Lieutenant. I always assume . . . Well, anyhow, Joseph Monroe Johnson is a major historical figure: a fugitive slave, a noted abolitionist, a hero of the Underground Railway."

"Hmm. A slave, huh? So he must have been . . . er . . ."

"African-American? Yes. Like so many slaves, Johnson was the child of an enslaved woman and her master. His father sold Joseph to a physician in Norfolk, Virginia, when he was twelve."

"Tut." Piotrowski's expression was appalled. "His own son! But, Doctor, how come if this Johnson was—what did you say? *a major historical figure?*—how come I never learned about him in History?"

"We're all only half educated about our nation's past, Lieutenant. The history we all learned in school? It's like . . . well, it's like . . ." How could I explain it to him without going into a long diatribe about racism and sexism? "It's like . . . well . . . a bungled investigation. You know, like that scene in *Casablanca*? The one where Claude Rains tells his men to 'round up the usual suspects'? Until lately history's been a bit like that—concentrating on white men, leaving out the white women and all the blacks and other minority ethnic groups. But as an abolitionist and as an African-American role model, Johnson made a great impact on the nation in his own day. Historians are finally beginning to realize that. But, as far as I know, no one suspected this relationship with Serena Northbury. This is big news! And a child! Wow!"

"Hmm. And don't forget that novel—*Child of the North Star?*—you said that was a biracial love story. She must've based it on her own life."

"Must have. My God, Lieutenant, I can't believe it!" I'd picked up the intricate bracelet from the pile of Northbury artifacts and was playing half-consciously with its gold clasp. "Think of the courage of those two, to live out that love in those dangerous times. From the letters it sounds as if Meadowbrook was a stop on the Underground Railroad, and Northbury and Johnson met during one of his expeditions back to the slave states. Then they must have met at least one more time, when—" I gestured at the photo with the bracelet in my hand "—when little Carrie was conceived."

"What's that you've got there, Doctor?"

"This?" I looked at the bracelet—*really* looked at it—for the first time. "This is a keepsake bracelet." I handed the gold-clasped band to the lieutenant, and he ran his finger over the glossy braid.

"Pretty. What's it made of?"

"Hair."

"Hair?" He stared at the trinket in amazement. "What kind of hair?"

"Northbury's and Johnson's hair, I assume."

"Ugh." He dropped the bracelet, staring at it as if he expected it to slither across the table. "That's sick!"

I laughed.

"What?" He glared at me, offended.

"Lieutenant, you look horrified. And after all the dead bodies you must have seen in your life!"

"Well—that's different. Nobody makes jewelry out of corpses."

The remaining four letters confirmed my speculations about a love affair between the abolitionist and the novelist. Serena Northbury had traveled at least once to Montreal, spending the summer of 1859 at a hotel on Sherbrooke Street, and Joseph Monroe Johnson had passed through Eastbrook on his final foray into the slave states, the one where he was shot to death in 1860, in an attempt to liberate his sister's family from a plantation deep in the Louisiana bayou country. I counted on my fingers. Johnson had died without ever seeing—maybe even without knowing about his child. Sad. The final letter was a brief note obviously dashed off in haste. I read it aloud to Piotrowski. Johnson informed Serena Northbury of his safe arrival in Philadelphia and of his impending departure with a "colored brother" for the deep South. *My Love,* he wrote, *whatever the consequence of this mad venture, think of me as one whose Spirit is forever kindred to Thine, e'en though the flesh may no more meet. Adieu. Your Fugitive.*

When I had slipped the final letter back into its envelope and looked up at the lieutenant, he was mopping at his eyes with a tissue from one of his ubiquitous packets. "Allergies," he mumbled, and blew his nose.

"Yeah," I replied. "A bad time of year. Lots of pollen." I allowed a tear to slide down my cheek unchecked. Doomed love. I seemed to be specializing in it.

The lieutenant bought me coffee and a fish sandwich at a Friendly's down the street from BCI headquarters. As I ate, he stared into his white ceramic mug, unresponsive to my attempts at conversation. I thought perhaps he was still saddened by the tragic love story we'd just uncovered. Cops are sentimental people—another thing I'd learned from my relationship with Tony. Scratch the most hardened officer of the law: You'll often find someone who can handle a three-day-old corpse without barfing, but who'll get all teary over the plight of an abandoned kitten. Well—maybe not Sergeant Felicity Schultz. Schultz was different. She was the hard-assed bastard macho cop from hell.

But, no, as it turned out, Lieutenant Piotrowski didn't have heartbreak on his mind. "I haven't been completely honest with you, Doctor," he announced when I'd finished the last succulent bite of my sandwich and was licking tartar sauce off my fingers.

"No?"

"No. There was one more item in that box. A document that maybe brings that sad story you just told me a little closer to our homicides at Meadowbrook. But I'm not sure how. . . ."

"What?" Damn this man. What did I have to do to prove to him that I could be trusted to handle evidence? That as a literary historian I did it all the time? "Show me."

"This." From a small manila envelope in his jacket pocket he took a sheet of ragged-edged cream-colored stationery. He slid it to me over the tabletop. It had been folded and unfolded over and over again, so many times that the paper was worn, and torn at its corners. The handwriting was Mrs. Northbury's now-familiar curlicue script. I glanced up at Piotrowski. "Read it," he said.

> *In lieu of a legal instrument of adoption, I hereby swear on all I hold most dear that I give my child Carrie, for whom the laws and customs of society and the circumstances of my own life leave me unable to care, to Gerard and Kate MacMahon to be treasured as their own dear child for as long as they shall live. I promise to provide support for her care and schooling and pray that these good people will allow me the right to watch over her from afar. Serena Pinkworth Northbury, 12 September 1861*

Speechless, I stared at the old document in my hands. Piotrowski's deep voice seemed to come from another era, through a long, narrow tunnel of years. "Serena Northbury gave her little girl to the MacMahons, who raised her as their own, Carrie MacMahon. According to Eastbrook town records, one of Carrie's descendants—a granddaughter named Carolyn—married Gerry Novak's father. Gerry Novak was—"

"Mrs. Northbury's great-great grandson," I breathed. "And the only living descendent of Joseph Monroe Johnson."

Twenty-eight

Felicity Schultz and I climbed Meadowbrook's steps in the gathering summer dusk. The porch light flashed on, and unexpectedly Willis Thorpe appeared in the front door. Schultz stopped short, and her hand dropped to her gun. I froze where I stood. It was eight o'clock that night, five hours after Lieutenant Piotrowski had dropped his bombshell about Gerry Novak's relationship to Serena Northbury, and nobody was supposed to be at the Meadowbrook estate but Sergeant Schultz and me.

"You realize the possible legal ramifications of this news, of course," Piotrowski had said, as we'd lingered over our coffee at Friendly's.

"What legal ramifications?" I clutched my half-empty mug so the waitress wouldn't whisk it away.

"Well, I'm not really up on inheritance law," he said, thoughtfully. "But if Novak really is descended from Mrs. Northbury, then he might have certain inheritance rights. . . ."

"But Novak's dead—"

"Yeah. And we don't have a motive, do we. Until—maybe—right this minute." He pulled a notebook from the pocket of his white shirt, and began writing.

"Money." I set my empty cup on the clean, damp table and sat back with a weary sigh. "You told me that at the beginning: *Money's always good,* you said."

"Yep." Looking troubled, he cut off his scribbling abruptly, slipped the book back in its pocket, pushed his bulk up and out of the booth, slapped a ten-dollar bill on the table, and said, "Novak's dead, all right. But Jill Greenberg is carrying his kid."

At his words, I stopped stone-still in my tracks; a curly-haired eight-year-old with a Rocky Road ice cream cone barreled into me as I swiveled, speechless, toward Piotrowski. The lieutenant took me firmly by the arm and steered me out the door. "Come on, Doctor. You and me, we got work to do."

It had taken Piotrowski the rest of the afternoon to obtain a warrant for Schultz and me to enter Meadowbrook, where I was supposed to search through the boxes of books in the storeroom off the kitchen.

"Karen," Will said, as he peered now from the dim hallway, startling Schultz and me, "what are you doing here?" Then, ever the gentleman, "Not that it isn't lovely to see you." The ruddy hue had returned to his complexion, and his shoulders were once again squared. For a man in his late seventies, he appeared amazingly resilient.

"What are *you* doing here?" Schultz barked. "That's what *I* want to know." The sergeant seemed to recognize Dr. Thorpe, but she didn't remove her hand from her gun.

Will acknowledged the officer. "Sergeant—ah—Schwartz, is it?" he ventured, seeming puzzled by her presence.

"Schultz," she muttered. Then louder, "Just answer my question, please."

"Well, Sergeant Schultz," Will gave me a quizzical glance, "this place is a second home to me; I've had a key for over fifty years, and I come up from the city whenever I can." Even in the half-light of dusk, I thought I could detect the pain in his eyes. "At least I used to. Call it an old man's folly, but I wanted to come here tonight and sit by the window in Edith's room one last time and look out over the mountains. I thought that at twilight I might feel especially close to her." As if to dislodge some too-persistent memories, he shook his head. Then he smiled, sadly. "Well, we can't bring back the dead, can we? Come in, Karen. Sergeant. Come on in."

Schultz held her ground, peering past the elderly physician into the shadowy hall, hand still on gun. "Anyone else here?"

"Ah . . . just Miss Greenberg—"

"Jill?" I broke in. "What the hell?" I remembered Piotrowski's words, and my heart began to race.

"Dr. Thorpe," Schultz said in a level, emotionless voice. "I want you to do two things for me. First turn on the hall light so I can see you, then step away from the door."

"Schultz!" I objected. "You can't treat Dr. Thorpe as if he were a criminal—"

"Mind your own business, Dr. Pelletier," Schultz snapped.

"It's all right, Karen." Will reached for the light switch. "Legally, I guess, I shouldn't be here. It's just that I'm so used to belonging in this house, I didn't even think about it. And I wanted to show Miss Greenberg—" The small Tiffany chandelier went on, illuminating the hallway, but not completely banishing the dark corners that had spooked Schultz. Halfway down the curving staircase, Jill Greenberg paused, blinking. She was dressed in something white and gauzy and, with her flyaway hair and startled eyes, resembled nothing more than some delicate Pre-Raphaelite specter.

"Jill!" I exclaimed, taking a step toward the staircase.

Schultz halted me with an abrupt motion of her hand. "You all right, Dr. Greenberg?" she asked.

"Yes—of course I am." Her pale brow furrowed with perplexity, Jill glanced over at Will. "What's going on here?"

Willis's sturdy shoulders rose, then fell. He spread his hands. The elderly doctor appeared to be the picture of innocent bafflement, but I was grateful for Schultz's presence—and her gun. Try as I might, I couldn't come up with a legitimate reason for Edith's old friend to be here alone in this godforsaken place at this godforsaken hour with the mother-to-be of the late Gerry Novak's child, a possible Northbury heir.

"Anyone else here with you?" Schultz asked again. They both shook their heads: *no*. "Then let's all sit down and have a little talk, okay? As I recall, the living room is in this direction." She gestured to the left, and then preceded Thorpe, Jill, and me into the front parlor, switching on the overhead light as she entered. Meadowbrook, unlit when Schultz and I had pulled into the driveway, was now half dark and half blazing with light, as evening turned into full night. I imagined how the big house would look from a distance if we were climbing the steep, deserted mountain road at this moment: riding the ebony hills like some ocean liner with a circuit outage, I thought. Like the *Titanic*, half submerged. I shuddered, as the gloom outside the windows began to invade my always too susceptible imagination. Jill's presence here, in her vulnerable state, made me uneasy; I had to resist an impulse to run through the house and turn on every lamp I could find. Someone was out to get Serena Northbury's fortune, and in my mind that someone was aligned with the forces of darkness. I shuddered again, and it took Schultz's slit-eyed look to bring me back to reality: I was in an elegantly appointed Victorian parlor with a pregnant girl, an aged man, and an armed police officer. What could happen?

"Willis has just told me the most amazing story." Jill gazed up at me from her perch on a needlepoint-covered ottoman. "And after I heard it I just had to come and see this place. Karen, you're not going to believe this, but my baby—Eloise—is a descendant of your Mrs. Northbury."

My mouth fell open with astonishment. Schultz and I turned simultaneously to Will Thorpe. I spoke first. "Will? You knew this all along?"

"Yes." His heavy eyebrows rose. "*You* know?"

"We just found out today. In some old papers. Who told *you?*"

"I've known forever." He sat back in Edith's bulky mission chair. "Such a romantic family story: How could Edith resist sharing such a tale with me? A dark stranger. A forbidden affair. A forsaken love child! Pure Northbury."

I recalled Edith's shocked reaction when I'd speculated that *Child of the North Star* was about a birth out of wedlock. "Edith knew about Gerry all along? That he was her relative? A Northbury descendent? And she never told him?"

"Well," Will countered, defensively, "she always took care of him. Saw that he got the best education—and any other opportunities he needed: writer's conferences, introductions to literary people in the city. It was just that she . . . Edith never really trusted Gerry—as a person. From childhood he was hostile to her, resentful of whatever Edie did for him. Always trying to take the easy way out. She honest-to-God believed that—given his character—money in the quantity he might inherit if his bloodline were known would be disastrous for him. She felt that he needed to keep working in order to keep himself . . . *grounded.*"

"So she let him remain a *grounds keeper?*"

Sarcasm dripped from my nasty pun. Will winced. "It wasn't that Edie didn't care. We argued about it endlessly. She was genuinely certain that she was doing what was best for Gerry—given who he was."

Patrician, I thought. What had—what's her name—Kendell Brown—said about Edith at the funeral? *A lady of the manor,* she'd said. *High-handed. Always thinking she knew best.*

"But you told Dr. Greenberg?" Schultz anticipated my question. "So you don't have the same qualms about Gerry Novak's child?"

Jill stared incredulously at Schultz. How could anyone in the world ever conceivably have qualms about little Eloise?

"I wanted to stop the lie," Will replied evenly. "Here and now. I don't even know if an inheritance suit would hold up in court. No one knew other than Edith and me, and as far as I can tell there's no documentation."

"Hmm," the sergeant said. "And, anyhow, if I remember correctly from my jurisprudence courses, the degree of relation is probably too distant for inheritance."

"That's right," Willis added, rubbing his eyes. Suddenly every year of his age showed in his weary face. "Or too many years may have elapsed—"

"In any case," Jill broke in, having followed our speculations with bemused attention, "I don't *want* the money. My child won't need it. My family and I . . ." She let the thought trail off; it should be understood that little Eloise would want for nothing. Then she jumped up from her footstool, and began roving around the room. "But the ancestry! That's a different thing. It thrills me that my child will have such forebears! Imagine! A heroic fugitive slave and a best-selling novelist! Eloise's great-great . . ." She glanced over at Will, who was smiling sadly.

"Great-great-great grandparents. And a fine ancestry indeed. I only wish Edith could have had a chance to know you. And Eloise. She would have felt so much better about—" He broke off abruptly. "She would have felt so much better," he concluded, somewhat brusquely. I assumed he was referring to the continuation of the Northbury family.

"Dr. Pelletier, I think it's time for us all to leave." Schultz had remained standing by the door. Her gun hand was now cradling her chin, and I thought the hard look had left her brown eyes. She had obviously decided to trust Will Thorpe. "It's too late to do anything here tonight; we'll come back in the morning. And these two aren't supposed to be here in the first place. I'm gonna check in with the lieutenant, and then we're all gonna vamoose. So, Doctor Thorpe," Schultz's lips curled in an indulgent smile, "if you want to make one last visit to Edith Hart's room, might as well do it now, while I'm on the phone. I can't see as that would hurt anything." I gaped at her.

"Thank you, Sergeant. Thank you very much. I think I will." He gave her his tired, melancholy smile, and headed for the stairs.

Schultz turned to me as Will Thorpe's steps, slow and heavy, mounted the steep staircase. "You know where there's a phone?"

"In the kitchen," I replied, gesturing toward the back of the house. "Sergeant Schultz," I said, as she turned to go. She swiveled toward me, macho-cop expression firmly back in place.

"Yeah?"

"That was a nice thing you just did. Who would have thought there was a soft spot under all that bluster?"

Deadpan, she stared at me. Then she turned and left the room.

Jill plopped herself down into Edith's armchair. "This whole situation is so unbelievable. Just think about it: A hundred years ago I would have been shunned in polite society—screwing around, getting myself knocked up. But what happens today? I end up with a kid who might be an heiress! Who says life ain't fair?" She flashed me her outrageous grin.

I grinned back. Will was right; Edith Hart would have loved Jill. In my wacky colleague she would have instantly recognized her own indomitable life force. I thought of Edith at my last visit, sitting squarely upright in the commodious chair with its bulky chintz cushions, her soft white hair framing her classic features, the gold locket on the fine chain at her throat. Nudged by the memory, I suddenly gasped, then jumped up from my perch on the love seat. "Jill," I blurted, "get up!" *Edith, I remembered. The chintz-covered armchair. The photograph of Carrie. Edith slipping the portrait between the cushion and the frame.*

"What?" Jill asked, but as I lunged toward her chair, she bounced out of it. On my knees, I slid my hand between the chair's cushion and its slatted side. Nothing. I wiggled my hand further back. Nothing. My fingers touched the chair's solid back. Nothing. Damn. Oops, not nothing! An edge of stiff paper protruded from behind the cushion. Aha! Pinching the corner between my thumb and forefinger, I carefully withdrew the stiff square. Yes! Just as I thought—an old photograph! Thinking how nice it would be for Jill to have little Carrie's portrait to show her own child, I glanced down at the picture.

"Karen? What did you find?" Jill's questions cut through my bewilderment; this was not the photograph we'd seen before.

"Jill," I breathed, "look at this. . . ."

The picture in my hand was almost twin to the ones I'd found in the Brontë book and the old candy box. The same size, same setting, same sepia tones. Even the same baby. But in this photograph, the beruffled, beribboned infant wasn't alone. She was cradled in the arms of a fair-haired woman dressed in severe black. Serena

Northbury. I recognized her from her portrait in the *Encyclopedia of American Women Authors:* the straight nose, the square chin, the delicate mouth. In this photograph, she gazed down at the beautiful child, and her look of loss and longing was enough to break your heart.

Heart! I stared at the picture. "Jill," I said again, still on my knees, "if there is ever any doubt that your child is descended from Serena Northbury, you only have to show this picture. Look, there are *two* lockets! Carrie is wearing one and so is her mother. The one you have was Carrie's. The one Edith wore belonged to—"

"What do you have there?"

The new voice caused my heart to leap and sent me scrambling to my feet. Jill spun around. Thibault Brewster stood in the wide doorway, gazing coolly at Jill and me. He wore his usual attire of navy blazer, white golf shirt, tan cotton slacks, and appeared very much at home in this elegant setting. "And what are you doing in Aunt Edith's house at this time of night, anyhow? I saw the cars when I pulled up, and couldn't imagine who on earth had any business here besides myself."

"Mr. Brewster," I managed. "You startled us." And indeed he had. Although there was nothing threatening about his pose, stocky frame now leaning casually against the door frame, hands loose at his sides, his presence made me nervous.

And, irrationally, I felt socially intimidated. This was Brewster's ancestral home, after all, and I had barged in without so much as a by-your-leave. A trespassing yahoo. Riffraff with a Ph.D. Then I shook my head briskly. Edith had made it clear in her will that she wanted me in this house. Her house. I had more right to be here than Brewster did.

"Perhaps I should ask you the same question, Mr. Brewster. Just what are *you* doing here? At this hour of the night?" I leaned against the quaint half-keyboard piano, slid my right hand, with the photograph, in the pocket of my denim jacket, and tried to emulate the Enfield manner of patrician aplomb. When you grow up in a factory town, you learn how to fight, but your weapons tend to be a little blunter than the cutting hauteur I was beginning to pick up in the Enfield College environs.

Brewster left his post at the door, and strode over to the piano to bang out a few jangling notes, causing me to jump three nervous steps back from the instrument. "I'm here to meet someone, *Pro-fess-or* Pelletier." He gave my title his usual sarcastic twist. "To conduct a little family business." Then, as he heard Will Thorpe's heavy step on the stairs, he started, and his hand jerked up. I froze. His gesture reminded me of Schultz's as we'd approached the house, when she'd gone for her gun. Will entered the room, exclaiming at Brewster's presence, and Brewster's hand, arrested at his waist for an interminable second, continued its rise, more smoothly now, to scratch at his graying sideburns.

"Tib!" If Will was concerned to find Brewster here, he showed no sign other than his initial surprise. I relaxed, but kept my eyes on Brewster's uneasy hand. Where *was* Schultz, anyhow? Will strolled across the room toward Edith's nephew. Jill, standing by Edith's chair, was silent, her bright hair ablaze above her pale face and snowdrift dress. I took two short steps toward her, then halted, baffled by the protective impulse. Really, Brewster might be obnoxious, but we were all civilized people here. No one was in any danger.

"Uncle Will?" Tib Brewster pulled at his earlobe, then rubbed the side of his long nose, before he allowed the hand to drop back to his side. His eyes narrowed, as if he were assessing this new wrinkle in the situation. "Well, well. This is looking like old home week. My dear aunt's longtime paramour; the lucky lady who managed to ingratiate herself into said aunt's good graces; and the unwed mother-to-be of a possible family heir." Brewster's tone maintained its assurance, but his right hand fidgeted, long fingers rubbing now against the thumb.

"How did you know that, Mr. Brewster?" I queried.

"Know what?" Brewster responded. "That Will was Edith's lover? I would have thought that was fairly obvious." He tapped his forefinger against his nose.

"No," I replied, suspicion rising. "How did you know Jill's baby might be a Northbury heir?"

Then Will spoke, his voice low and controlled. "Yes, Tib, how *did* you know? Edith never told anyone but me that Gerry was descended from Mrs. Northbury."

"No? Well, Aunt Edith must have had a change of heart at the last minute." Brewster's demeanor remained cool, but his hand slid from his nose to tug at his earlobe again. The hand fascinated—and unnerved—me; it seemed to have a life of its own, independent of Brewster's will. Three earlobe tugs, and it was back tapping at the nose again. Surely a self-assured man such as Thibault Brewster shouldn't fall prey to so many nervous tics. But his tone was cool as he continued. "She did tell Novak. And Novak simply couldn't resist blabbing to me."

"I see." Will and I spoke the words simultaneously. Our eyes met. We needed no words to communicate our appalled speculations. I took another involuntary step toward Jill. There was total silence in the room as we all, Brewster included, realized he'd just, to all intents and purposes, given himself a powerful motive for murder.

Where the *hell* was Felicity Schultz? I couldn't believe I was actually wishing for the presence of the annoying little police officer. And how long did it take to make a phone call to headquarters, anyhow?

"Hmm," Brewster said, thumb to chin, forefinger still tapping his nose. Then he broke the freighted silence with a nervous laugh. "What's the problem, Will? You look . . . stunned. Surely you don't think . . ."

Will did appear stunned. Even more than stunned, he suddenly looked startlingly ill, eyes dark and sunken, a gray tinge suffusing his usually ruddy complexion. This time I took a step toward *him*, then stopped at his abrupt gesture. "I'm okay, Karen," he said carefully. "I just need to speak with Tib for a few minutes. Alone. Why don't you and Jill go back to the kitchen, make us all a cup of tea?"

The kitchen. Schultz. Get Jill out of here. "Okay, I . . ." But as I shifted in my young friend's direction, Brewster's agitated hand jerked out to stop me.

"Oh, I don't think so, Professor Pelletier." Although the tone of his voice was as peremptory as ever, the man's air of smooth assurance had faltered. The patrician facade didn't crack altogether; its patina simply crazed a little, as if fine, glazed porcelain had shivered under stress. The forefinger jerked back to his nose, the right eye blinked twice. For an infinitesimal moment he looked profoundly pained. But not for long. His next words were, to all intents and purposes, a command. "Why don't you and Miss Greenberg stay right where you are until Uncle Will lets me know what it is he has on his mind?"

Will sank onto the piano bench, the only seat within reach. Jill rushed to his side. "Dr. Thorpe, what's wrong?" The elderly man had broken out in a sweat. His face was ashen. I stared at him, horrified. Will Thorpe had always been so hearty; I'd completely forgotten how advanced in age he was. Now I recalled his passing reference to heart trouble the night we'd had dinner at Rudolph's.

"Dr. Thorpe is ill," I said, turning to Brewster. "I've got to call for medical help."

"No." Brewster held up an imperious hand, as, with an effort, Will straightened up, leaning back against the wall.

"Karen," he said, weakly. "I'm all right. Really." The words were addressed to me, but he was looking at Brewster. "Tib, I don't know what you mean. I don't have anything in particular on my mind. While the young women make us some tea, we can have a chat, you and I." He paused, lips tight, then ran a quavering hand over his brow.

"Will, you're not well. I'm going to call—" My move toward the door was halted by the abrupt, spasmodic movement of Thibault Brewster's hand toward his waist. Did I detect a slight bulge in the otherwise immaculately cut blue blazer? Could Brewster be carrying a gun? I fastened my eyes on his restless hand, as if my fixed gaze might arrest any further motion.

"You know, don't you?" Brewster's appalled expression was directed at Will Thorpe, as if his aunt's longtime friend were the only other person in the room. "You *know*." He stammered both times on the word *know*.

"Tib . . ." A shudder ran through Will's body, whether of emotion or pain, I couldn't tell.

"All I wanted was what is rightfully mine," Brewster burst out, and stammered on *wanted* and *mine*. "That's all. My *inheritance*." His hand had wavered away from his waist, was now held halfway out to Will, open as if in supplication. Will sighed deeply, as if at the culmination of a lifetime of disappointment. Brewster hurried on, more confident now in his words. "And I was *patient*. But Edith lived on and on, and then . . . things got . . . got out of control. I had to have the money *now*." He seemed to be pleading for Will's understanding. "I *needed* it, Uncle Will." For a brief moment, he was a boy, caught out in some particularly nasty naughtiness.

Horrified, I blurted out, "You killed Dr. Hart!"

He pivoted toward me. His expression was sufficient affirmation.

"But she was your aunt!" A stupid thing to say, but I couldn't help it.

A lifetime of command is not so easily jettisoned, and Brewster's habitual control reasserted itself in face of a social inferior, his expression changing almost mechanically from tremulous to stony. "She was an old woman," said Edith Hart's nephew, "who didn't know when it was time to die."

Jill's eyes were wide. "Oh my God. Gerry. You killed Gerry."

He turned his eyes to her. "He had no right! No right to what was mine. I was supposed to get everything. I'd built a life on that! I don't understand how Edith could do what she did to me." Another fracture in the patrician facade. Brewster looked as if he might burst into tears at any moment: not tears of sorrow for Edith; not tears of repentance for his unspeakable deeds; but tears of hot disappointment for the thwarting of his life's monetary expectations.

The decades-long, arduous accumulation of wealth by Serena Northbury had not held tragedy at bay for the author or for her descendents. This was merely another chapter in the complex, passionate story that had begun with Mrs. Northbury's sour marriage, and continued with her impulsive following of her heart in a direction forbidden by a straitlaced and racist society. Around us the ornate chairs and sofas with which Mrs. Northbury had furnished this comfortable parlor stood mute testament to generations of family life, a life that seemed at once generous and courageous in the persons of Serena Northbury and Edith Hart, and stifling and destructive in the presence of the selfish, twisted man who stood here now, his right eye twitching as he poured out his bitter tale of frustration.

Will groaned, distracting Brewster for a moment. Jill, mopping the elderly physician's brow, stuttered, "Karen, do something. He's in pain." Eyeing Brewster carefully, I moved toward Will. All this while Brewster had made no overt threats to those of us in the hushed room. But it was difficult to imagine where he was going to go from here, after this admission of guilt, what he intended to do. I knelt by Will and scrutinized his pale face. Beneath half-lowered lids, the sick man's eyes were surprisingly alert. They flickered toward me, then toward the door. *Go.* He was right; I had to go, to get out—and take Jill with me. I rose, and reached for Jill's arm, as if reassuring her. Will groaned heavily, but Brewster noting my action, ignored him, pivoting quickly toward us, nervous hand rising to his waist. The well-cut blazer fell open, and suddenly Brewster's restless fingers were compulsively tapping the grip of a small revolver stuffed in the waistband of his Eddie Bauer casuals. Jill's mouth opened in a wordless *Oh.* Will sat up sharply on the piano bench. I tightened my grip on Jill's arm. What had we gotten ourselves into here? Just then—hallelujah—Sergeant Schultz spoke brusquely from the shadows of the darkened back parlor. "Police, Mr. Brewster. I'm going to ask you not to move." She stepped into the room, blue steel automatic extended steadily in both hands.

But Brewster had already jerked the gun from his belt. He froze for less than a second. Then, on the pretense of reaching out to drop the lethal-looking little weapon, he looped Jill around the neck in a cruel headlock, and thrust the gun into her side. Jill struggled briefly, then ceased, giving a strangled little cry as Brewster tightened his hold.

"*You* drop it, Officer." As Schultz stood paralyzed, indecision playing across her tight features, Brewster barked, "Drop the damn gun!" The situation had been decided for him. No more explanation. No more irresolution. His right eye blinked twice, then the New England Brahmin was firmly back in control.

Reluctantly, Schultz lowered her hand, let the automatic fall to the floor.

"Now kick it away."

"You watch a lot of television, don't you, Mr. Brewster?" Schultz asked. But she kicked the gun. It skidded across the polished hardwood—in my general direction. I know how to use a gun; Tony taught me to shoot on an automatic just like this one. All I needed was one chance . . .

But Brewster's grip on Jill was tight, and the gun he held on her was steady. He shook his head, in what seemed to be genuine regret, as he considered the gravity of the situation. "This is an unfortunate circumstance," he said. "I never intended . . . anything like this to happen. The piece of business I came here to conduct tonight would have compensated somewhat for the loss of my inheritance, and then this whole regrettable affair would have been over. No one else would have had to be . . . well . . . As it stands, I don't know—"

"Mr. Brewster," the sergeant's voice was flat, "the situation *is* regrettable. But I'm certain we can work something out."

"No!" he snapped, his eyes fixed on Schultz, as if at this moment she were the only impediment between him and his freedom. What threat were the rest of us, after all? A sick old man and two academic women? No threat at all. I sidled toward the sergeant's relinquished gun. "I'm not going to allow myself to be cheated again, Officer. Miss Greenberg is going to drive me out of here." Brewster laughed, nervously. "Perhaps that's ironically appropriate, since she's carrying a new Northbury heir."

"Please," Jill croaked, "the baby . . ."

"The *baby?*" He flicked her a glance of contempt, but his gaze returned immediately to Schultz. "Miss Greenberg is coming with me, Officer, and if I see anyone in pursuit, I won't hesitate to shoot her. Do you understand?"

"I understand, Mr. Brewster." Schultz's plain features were rigid. "But I wonder if you do. Wherever you go, we'll find you, you know. It would be better for you if you released Professor Greenberg now. It's not too late. Then we could talk about this. Just you and me. Don't make this any worse than it is."

He shook his head, as if in pity at her transparency. "Officer, do you really think I'm that stupid?"

"Think about *Joyce,* Tib," Will was attempting to

rise. His voice was weak, but steady. "You know how much she needs you right now. And *Tibby?* Don't let him down. Don't get yourself any more . . ."

Brewster paid little attention to Will; he was still fixated on Schultz. It was so hushed in the room as Thibault Brewster paused to contemplate Will's words, that a squeak, then a skitter from the hall startled me. I turned my eyes—not my head, just my eyes—in that direction, saw little but shadows, then identified the combination of sounds as heralding the passage of a mouse. Eyes front again, I took another baby step toward the gun.

Tib Brewster seemed to consider these words. When he spoke, he directed his words to Schultz. "It looks as if I'm already in it as deep as it gets. Doesn't it, Officer?" Then he glanced briefly in Will's direction. "But, don't worry, Will, I've made contingency plans, for Tibby—and for myself as well. Just in case." Then the gaze returned to Schultz. "All I've got to do is get myself out of here, and I'll be all set. That's all I ask. If everyone behaves themselves, Miss Greenberg won't even have to get hurt. That's reasonable, isn't it? I don't want to hurt anyone. I'm only asking for my just due."

A shadow moved abruptly in the hallway behind Brewster, then became a quiet black puddle among other pools of darkness. The mouse squeaked again. I blinked. The shadow had vanished. Had I actually seen a stealthy motion? Or had the almost phantasmagorical flutter in the darkness been nothing more than wishful thinking?

Then four things happened at once: Brewster turned to propel his terrified hostage into the hallway; I lunged for Schultz's gun; Schultz crouched and yanked a little revolver from her ankle holster; and Earl Wiggett, literary gumshoe, stepped inward from his dark niche behind the hall door and smashed Thibault Brewster senseless with his trusty little notebook computer.

Twenty-nine

The teakettle's whistle shrilled, and I poured boiling water over tea bags, then handed the steaming mugs to Piotrowski and Schultz. "There's no milk, of course," I told them, "since no one's living here, but I think you'll find sugar in that canister." It was long past midnight and the police activity at Meadowbrook was finally winding down. Schultz and I had just finished filling Piotrowski in on the evening's incidents. The lieutenant looked very tired, and his hair was mussed.

"I don't understand it, Doctor." He measured four teaspoons of sugar into the black tea. "You always end up at the point of a gun. How the heck does that always happen?"

I opened my mouth to protest, but Piotrowski held up a meaty hand and shook his head. "No. Let me finish." He took a loud slurp of his tea. "It's not that I don't appreciate your help. We coulda never unraveled this without you. But why . . ." Here he gave me one of his trademark slit-eyed looks. ". . . Why does it always have to come to gunplay? Huh, Doctor? Can you tell me that? A nice quiet teacher like yourself: Why do you always end up facing a gun? And, tonight, I understand you were all set to fire one."

"Uh, I—"

"She was real good, Lieutenant." Schultz's praise astounded me. Hot tea sloshed onto my hand as I plopped my cup down on the scrubbed pine of the tabletop. I sucked on a scalded finger and stared at the sergeant in amazement. "Real good. You shoulda seen her, boss. She knew right away why I kicked that forty-five where I did. And she moved fast; soon's Brewster turned his back for a second, she had that gun in her hand. Almost as fast as I got mine. Of course, by that time, we didn't need guns; the skinny guy, he'd already bonked Brew—er—rendered the perp unconscious."

The lieutenant emptied his cup and rose, still shaking his head at me. "You always look so—so—sort of ivory-towerish-like, Doctor, with those cool gray eyes and that I'm-better-than-you-are air. If I didn't know for a fact you were straight off the streets of Lowell—" Felicity Schultz shot me a startled look. I returned a cool gray stare. "—I'd think you were born—no—*conceived* and born—in the Harvard library. But you're a fighter all right."

"Well," I replied, "you can take the girl out of Lowell—"

"But you can't take Lowell out of the girl," Schultz finished sourly. " 'Kid from Southie,' huh?" She looked at me, slit-eyed like her boss. "Chip on my shoulder 'the size of a Douglas fir,' huh? Well, it takes one to know one."

I laughed.

So did Schultz.

Piotrowski gaped at us, baffled.

The despicable Earl Wiggett, of course, was the true hero of the day. Wiggett had been summoned to Enfield by

Thibault Brewster, who had represented himself as Edith Hart's rightful heir. Brewster had snatched the manuscript of *Child of the North Star* from his aunt's bedside, and, when he learned that he'd been left only peanuts in her will, he'd contacted Wiggett about the novel's potential for publication. The two men had arranged to meet at Meadowbrook that evening to search for the missing manuscript pages, the pages in the possession of the state police. But upon entering the Northbury mansion that night, the hapless Alcott editor had stumbled upon a scene as melodramatic as anything Louisa May—or Mrs. Northbury herself—had ever trusted to paper. Although Wiggett's personal habits may have left much to be desired, his hero's heart was true. At the sight of a damsel in distress, Wiggett knew precisely what an honorable gentleman should do: attack the villain with whatever weapon was close to hand. Earl Wiggett never went anywhere without his notebook computer, and the blow he gave Brewster with his little PowerMate stunned that villain long enough for Schultz to restrain him.

By the time Brewster had regained consciousness, Schultz had him handcuffed to a sofa leg. Then the backup she'd called in began to arrive. Jill and Dr. Thorpe were taken to the hospital for observation—Jill to be treated for shock and bruises, Will for a minor heart attack. Thibault Brewster was also in the hospital—with a concussion—*cyber-concussed,* the EMT had diagnosed, with a perfectly straight face, when she saw Earl Wiggett's dented computer. But Wiggett hadn't yet actually seen the manuscript, and Brewster wasn't talking. The manuscript of *Child of the North Star* remained among the missing.

"Professor Pelletier?" Shamega stood in my office door, a sagging Gap shopping bag seeming oddly heavy in her hand. It was three days after the confrontation with Thibault Brewster at Meadowbrook, and life was just beginning to return to normal. I'd come to campus to prepare my book orders for fall classes; the bookstore manager was calling me at least every other day to threaten me with bookless classes in September unless I got my orders in *now*. "Are you busy?" Shamega asked.

My eyes fell to the half-completed form in front of me. *Publisher?* it asked me. *ISBN? Edition?* I sighed. "Come on in, Shamega," I replied, and shifted a pile of textbooks from my green vinyl chair to the floor.

Shamega sat and placed the Gap bag carefully between her feet. She seemed to be wearing its original contents—overdyed, straight-legged jeans and a form-fitting short-sleeved orange sweater cropped to the waist. Her features appeared less tense than they had in months.

"So," she announced, "Tibby Brewster." She raised her slanted eyebrows at me.

"So," I replied, "what about him?"

"That bastard. I *got* him!" She sat back in the big chair.

An image of Rudolph's kitchen knives flittered through my mind. "Shamega, you haven't done any-thing—violent, have you?"

"Oh no," she said, her expression serious. "Worse than that. What I've done is perfectly legal—that's the joy of it." She paused, obviously uncertain. "At least I *think* it's legal." Her dark brows furrowed. "Well, maybe not. But if it isn't, I don't give a damn, because I've finally gotten back at that creep for all the things he did to me!"

"Shamega! For God's sake. What have you done?"

She sat up and clasped her slender dark fingers. "You know how gossip flies around here, Professor?"

"Oh yes."

"Well, I heard about Dr. Hart leaving her house and everything in it to the college for some kind of women's literature center. And that Tibby's father was Dr. Hart's nephew, which makes Tibby a great-nephew, right? And some kind of heir, right? And—I heard what his father did—that he killed that weird blond guy, the one that lived with Dr. Hart, because *he* turned out to be an heir. And . . . and—did he kill Dr. Hart, too?" Her dark eyes grew even more sober. "I liked her so much."

"The police still aren't certain about that, Shamega." And I knew they might never be. But Brewster *had* confessed to going out in the rowboat with Gerry Novak—ostensibly to fish for trout—then overturning the boat and struggling with Gerry until he drowned. Another claimant for the estate had proven to be too much for this spoiled little man to handle.

"I kept thinking about that manuscript," Shamega continued, "you know, that novel manuscript Amanda and I found? In the hatbox? The one that disappeared when Dr. Hart died?"

"Yes?" My breath snagged on the word.

"And it got me thinking. In the library, you and I looked for Northbury stuff in the Pinkworth archives, and there wasn't much there. And there was nothing at all under Mrs. Northbury's name. But last night, I started wondering if maybe there were letters and things filed under Dr. Hart's name, so I looked this morning. But—*nada*. Then at lunchtime, when I heard about Mr. Brewster, and that he was the one who'd taken the manuscript . . ."

"Shamega," I whispered, my eyes drawn inexorably to the oddly bulky Gap bag, "don't tell me—"

". . . I knew that someday Tibby might get his hands on it and maybe sell it for big bucks, and I couldn't stand the thought of him profiting from Mrs. Northbury's novel. So I went back to the library and . . . and maybe it *is* illegal for me to take things without permission, but I don't care. I just don't want Tibby Brewster ever to get this book. It doesn't really belong to his father, right? It belongs to the Northbury Center like everything else at Meadowbrook, right?"

"Right! At least, I think so. The lawyers—"

Shamega reached into the bag. I leaned forward, breathless. She paused, then sat back again, hands crossed loosely in her lap. "And I know I'm a real bitch, because Tibby's got it hard right now, what with his father . . ." Her voice faltered, as if she was just now realizing the appalling position Tibby Brewster was in. "But after all the things he did—"

"What's in the bag, Shamega!"

"Well, after I heard about Tibby's father, I decided to look in the archives under the *Brewster* name."

"Yes?" I was almost falling off my chair, I was leaning so far forward.

"And this is what I found . . ." She reached into the bag again and pulled out a string-tied bundle of ragged-edged pages: the manuscript copy of Serena Northbury's unpublished autobiographical sensation novel, *Child of the North Star*.

"And so it seems," I explained to Earl Wiggett two weeks later, as we sat at Rudolph's bar in the Friday evening crush and waited for our table, "that Tib Brewster filed the manuscript with his own family papers in the library's archives. Brewster was a trustee; he had access to everything. And his family was an old one; there were lots of Pinkworth/Northbury/Brewster records there. He must have slipped the manuscript in when the library was closed. On a weekend perhaps."

In my effusive gratitude that Wiggett had saved the damsel in distress from the dastardly villain, I'd invited him to dinner at Rudolph's. The moment the invitation was out of my mouth, I'd begun to regret it. But Wiggett was thrilled. And, as things had fallen out, in addition to dining with him, I was going to be coediting *Child of the North Star* with this "literary gumshoe." Once Wiggett realized that Edith Hart and I had talked about publishing *Child of the North Star* when we'd first found the manuscript, he'd backed out of his informal editorial

agreement with Sally Chenille. That turned out not to be
a problem. The words *interracial* and *love* had fused in
Sally's fevered intellect as *interracial sex;* as soon as
she'd understood just what kind of semi-sentimental tale
Northbury's novel actually was, she'd lost interest. The
manuscript was currently in probate with the rest of
Edith's estate. But when ownership was determined,
we'd have no trouble finding a publisher. We'd both
read a Xerox of the novel and agreed on that. Already,
two major university presses, including Oxbridge, were
making queries, but Wiggett was holding out for a commercial press. When it came to marketing sensational
literature, Earl Wiggett knew precisely what he was doing. And I wouldn't even try to snatch this prize from
him. Not after he'd saved Jill Greenberg and the baby.

Wiggett was drinking a brandy Alexander, while I
sipped on yet another margarita. He had made a major
sartorial effort for our dinner date. His denim-blue polyester leisure suit had snappy red stitching down the la-
pels and across the pocket. His raggy hair was plastered
flat across his shiny pate. Powerful waves of Aqua Velva
assaulted my olfactory senses. The new computer Wiggett's insurance company had paid for sat prominently
on the bar in front of him. I'd protested that he wouldn't
need it at dinner, but he'd insisted. "You and I are going
to be doing a great deal of brainstorming, Karen. You
never know when inspiration will strike. Better safe than
sorry." Cream from his foamy drink dripped down his
leisure suit and onto the computer's lid. He wiped the
computer with a pineapple-motif cocktail napkin.

"Professor Pelletier?" The ponytailed waiter had
been a student in my Survey course. "Your table's ready,
Professor." I left my empty margarita glass where it sat.
Wiggett stuffed his trusty computer under his arm,
plucked his brandy Alexander from the bar, and we followed the waiter. I glanced surreptitiously around the
cocktail lounge as I passed through with my new editorial partner. For once, nobody I knew seemed to be

around. Good. All I needed in this nosy little town was to kick off rumors linking me romantically with Wiggett.

Wiggett sat me at the table, fussing over which chair I should have, then over how comfortable I was once it was pushed into the table. Then he flapped my napkin open and handed it to me with a flourish. I suppressed a sigh, accepted the napkin with a show of gratitude, and ordered a double vodka martini, straight up. As Wiggett pored over the extensive menu, occasionally surfacing to ask me about such terms as *terrine* and *papillote,* I decided on filet mignon. It was always good at Rudolph's, if you ordered the béarnaise on the side so it didn't drown the meat. That decision made, I sat back and surveyed the room. My eye was immediately taken by an elegant woman with shoulder-length dark hair sitting alone at a table across from me, toying with a gin and tonic. She was strikingly beautiful, and mysteriously alone.

While Wiggett studied the menu as if it were the Rosetta stone, I studied the beautiful face at the table opposite us. I'd never seen such blue eyes on anyone—on anyone, that is, other than Avery Mitchell. To while away the time while I waited for Earl Wiggett to make his decision, I began to compose a romantic story about this mystery woman. *Alone, waiting for her lifelong love to reappear in the smoky cantina* . . . (Northbury's prose style was impacting even my fantasies.) . . . *the melancholy woman toyed with her exotic tropical libation. Suddenly, as she—* Suddenly, as she gazed at a point somewhere over my shoulder, the mystery woman's face lit up. Her dinner companion must be arriving. Anxious to see the man—it had to be a man—who could bring such an expression of pleasure to this lovely woman's face, I swiveled slightly in my chair—as if to see whether or not the waiter was coming with my martini—and gazed straight into the glorious blue eyes of Avery Mitchell.

"Karen," Avery said, and had the grace to look nonplussed. But not for long. Not this infinitely polished man. Pausing for a moment by my chair, he turned to the woman, who was smiling at me quizzically. "Liz, darling," he said, "I'd like to introduce you to Karen Pelletier." *Liz? Liz, darling? Ohmigod! His ex-wife!* "Karen is . . . ah . . . a member of our English faculty."

"So nice to meet you, Karen." Her manners were impeccable.

Before I could reply, my dinner companion emerged from behind the oversized menu, stringy hair flopping across his shiny forehead, brandy Alexander foam flecking the lapel of his polyester leisure suit. "Karen," Earl Wiggett brayed, "do you know the meaning of the word *flambé*?"

Epilogue

The truest love [Serena Northbury wrote in the
Epilogue to *Child of the North Star*] *will ne'er
submit to the tyranny of circumstance. Color,
caste, time, space, and nation are as nothing to
the hunger and thirst of the heart, which must
have what it must have, be all the world against
it.*

I sighed as I replaced the final page of the photocopied
manuscript, clicked off the bedside light, turned, and settled myself to attempt sleep. My head was still thick
from the second double martini. Closing my eyes, I
waited with suspended breath for the face that would
swim up out of the darkness.

Afterword

Neither Serena Northbury nor Joseph Monroe Johnson ever existed, except in my imagination and in the pages of this story. And the character of Serena Northbury owes much to the fascinating life of real-life novelist Emma Dorothy Eliza Nevitte Southworth (1819–1899). In addition, *The Duke's Daughter* was not written by Louisa May Alcott, but by her alter ego, Jo March, in Alcott's *Little Women*, where it serves to pay the March family's butcher bill. Alcott and other nineteenth-century literary figures mentioned in this novel actually lived and wrote, and their texts are currently taught in English departments nationwide.

About the Author

JOANNE DOBSON is Associate Professor of English at Fordham University. She is a former editor of *Legacy: A Journal of American Women Writers* and the author of *Dickinson and the Strategies of Reticence: The Woman Writer in Nineteenth-Century America.* Her first mystery, *Quieter Than Sleep,* was nominated for an Agatha Award. She lives in the New York City area, where she is at work on her third Karen Pelletier novel, *The Raven and the Nightingale.*

If you enjoyed Joanne Dobson's
The Northbury Papers,
you won't want to miss any of the
mysteries in this series. Look for
Quieter Than Sleep
in paperback from Bantam at your
favorite bookstore and for
*The Raven and the
Nightingale,*
coming in hardcover from Doubleday
in October 1999.